A TRAITOR'S FATE

Fen Fire buried the spearhead into his guts, as he uttered a choking cry of agony that shook the fortress.

"There are three sounds I like most in the world," she cried out as the warriors gathered below to gaze on the hated traitor, "the love cry of a woman, the babbling of a baby, and the gurgle of death in the throat of my enemy."

Taking a warrior's broadsword, she knelt down beside him. His eyes glared wide, and many who saw the sword sever his head thought they glimpsed his stricken spirit get sucked from his mangled body . . .

THE FIRE QUEEN

JACK HOLLAND

A ROC BOOK

ROC
Published by the Penguin Group
Penguin Books USA Inc., 375 Hudson Street,
New York, New York 10014, U.S.A.
Penguin Books Ltd, 27 Wrights Lane,
London W8 5TZ, England
Penguin Books Australia Ltd, Ringwood,
Victoria, Australia
Penguin Books Canada Ltd, 10 Alcorn Avenue,
Toronto, Ontario, Canada M4V 3B2
Penguin Books (N.Z.) Ltd, 182-190 Wairau Road,
Auckland 10, New Zealand

Penguin Books Ltd, Registered Offices:
Harmondsworth, Middlesex, England

First published by Roc,
an imprint of New American Library,
a division of Penguin Books USA Inc.

First Printing, June, 1992
10 9 8 7 6 5 4 3 2 1

Printed in the United States of America

For Ciaran,
and for Rosie and Gary.

“. . . after passing through those periods which probable reasoning can reach to and real history find a footing in, I might very well say of those that are farther off: ‘Beyond this there is nothing but prodigies and fictions, the only inhabitants are the poets and inventors of fables; there is no credit, or certainty any farther.’ ”

from Plutarch’s life of Theseus,
Lives of the Noble Greeks and Romans
translated by John Dryden
Modern Library, New York

PART
1

Chapter 1

The woods were full of the scent of flowering hawthorn and carpeted with the fairy flower, the primrose. On the surrounding hillsides the golden flowers of furze blazed their welcome to the summer season as the sun sank slowly into the western ocean. The May Day feast of Beltane was approaching. A stack of wood stood on every hillcrest ready to be lit. In the stocks and stables the cattle stirred and pushed against the gates and bars, eager to be out again after their long confinement to eat the fresh grass. The sheep in their pens could sniff the fresh young prickles on the furze-covered hills, juicy and ripe for nibbling. And everywhere men and women garlanded themselves in summer colors, making ready for the celebrations that would herald the new season and another turn of the endless cycle of birth and death.

A huge bristle-backed boar burst through the underbrush, shattering the stillness of the dappled woodland. Its charging hoofs trampled down the hawthorn and crushed the fairy flowers underfoot. It plunged headlong until it came to a riverbank, where it stopped and turned to face its pursuers. A pack of hounds followed, came panting to a halt, and crouched down, their teeth bared. Behind them Fen Fire came galloping, her mass of fiery red hair loosely braided back, her slim-shafted casting spear clasped in her fist. The huntress reined in her horse as the boar bent its head and turned its terrible flesh-tearing tusks towards her. She quickly but steadily took aim. The boar charged. She swung her horse round to avoid its attack, and let fly with the javelin, striking the boar in the side. The cast was a good one; the weapon sank deep into the boar's flesh. It slumped over, panting and gushing blood. She leapt off her horse and drew her ivory-handled dagger. Turning the wounded, dying animal over with a push of her foot, she knelt down beside it and slit its throat. A final gurgle of blood and the panting beast breathed no longer. The hounds gathered round the dead animal to lap its blood. The young woman placed one foot on the side of the boar and with her two hands pulled the spear free; only then did she recognize the place to which the boar had led her.

In the gathering dusk Fen Fire walked to the riverbank and looked across the rushing waters. In midstream the familiar flat rock was deserted. The waterfall tumbling over the rock shelter behind it now veiled no one from the eyes of the outside world. The little cave was empty where she had lain that long night in the arms of the unknown youth, her Beltane lover, whom she remembered simply as Sun Fragment. Unthinkingly, she plucked a branch of hawthorn; its female scent filled her nostrils, the white flowers glowed softly on the branch. Slowly she plucked the tiny flowers off one by one and flung them into the river. They spun and turned in the current, which carried them swiftly away around the river bend.

She watched them disappear. It would soon deliver them into the wide, endless reaches of the sea, but not before she had given her answer to Prasutagus, the King of the Iceni.

Caratacus, her kinsman, had brought the king's suit. With his brothers Togodumnus and Maglocunos, he ruled the kingdom of the Catuvellauni—a kingdom with only one to rival it on the island of Britain, that of the Iceni.

A long time before, the Catuvellauni had arrived in Britain from Gaul. Hard fighters they were, seasoned in wars on the fringes of the forests that separated the German tribes from those of Gaul. They subdued many peoples in Britain, but were themselves challenged by a power even greater than their own: that of Julius Caesar, founder of the line of Caesars that would rule Rome and its possessions for a hundred years to come.

Caesar came to Britain to break the power of the Catuvellauni, for he feared their influence among the Gauls. But after many battles, such was the ferocity of their resistance, he was forced to abandon any plans to crush the Britons as he had their kinsmen in Gaul. Thus when he departed, never to return, the reputation of the Catuvellauni stood even higher than it had before. (In these wars, Fen Fire's ancestor, Flame of the Field of Battle, performed such deeds as kept all of the bards of Britain supplied for years to come with material for their tales and verses.)

The Iceni were a match for the Catuvellauni in wealth and strength. But in one thing they claimed precedence over them, which no one did dispute: the age of their kingdom. The Iceni had resided in the land that stretched from the fens and uplands to the shore of the vast sea to the north for so long that only the memory of a bard or a druid could reach back to that age and pluck from its mists the deeds that were then performed. It was commonly said that the Iceni had lived there long enough to have seen an oak forest thrice up-rooted and thrice resown.

The wars the Iceni had fought were long ago, ages before the Catuvellauni set foot on the island of Britain, against monsters as well as men, for in those times, the bards relate, the fens were full of eels of enormous girth and length, large enough to capsize a boat and swallow a man whole.

Their wealth accumulated over the centuries, during which they lived secure within the vastness of the fenlands. They were the first to master the horse and chariot in Britain, and their skills were the envy of all. Their kingdom too was the site of the island of the goddess Andraste, deep within the marshes, that was sacred to women. From times immemorial they had made pilgrimages to the island to lay rich offerings in the temple of the goddess.

The Iceni and the Catuvellauni had lived in tranquility, each respecting the other. But as the power of the Catuvellauni grew, that tranquility was threatened.

The two kingdoms had come close to war but a year before, when the great king Cunobelinus, father of Caratacus, Togodumnus and Maglocunos still ruled. Through marriage with Prasutagus, Fen Fire, the foster daughter of Cunobelinus, could ensure peace between the two kingdoms.

Caratacus' merest glance was like the heat of the sun on morning dew: all faded before it. She did not want to remember his eyes on that day when she appeared to be refusing to entertain the king's offer; it was an experience she dreaded having to face again.

"Put policy aside," he had said, "and consider his majesty." Fen Fire was honing her swordblade to a fine edge, and looked up from her work.

"I do not need to be reminded of the majesty of the king. Clearly he is a man who is bathed in the afterglow of a life full of a warrior's fiery deeds," she answered firmly.

"You speak of him as if he were a setting sun! A man who already keeps five wives happy and fruitful is a man at the zenith of his powers, not one on the wane," Caratacus responded.

"I have no doubt but that he is the bull of the herd," she said. "What would it matter if he weren't—he is not the only bull in Britain."

She could be as brazen as she liked, even with Caratacus, who had impressed upon her as no other could—much less dare to—the importance of the match. "At any rate," she continued, "I am not so light-minded as to come to a decision of this importance through comparisons with cows and bulls. If I should go to his bed it will not be merely as another wife to be added to his herd. If I agree to the marriage, it will be to bind together our two kingdoms."

"His passion is not born of policy—do not discount the strength of his desire." Caratacus knew that the women from whom she was descended did not take to marriage easily, for they did not like the prattling of fools, the jealousies of weaklings, or the tremblings of cowards. They asked from a man what she asked: that he be as brave as they, and as generous and as free from jealousy. No mean-spirited man would ever win her, no matter what the cause.

"The King of the Iceni is renowned for his courage, his generosity and his open spirit," Caratacus said.

"His reputation is well-known to me. I have seen the man for myself, and upon that I must base my decision." Yes, she had met Prasutagus and looked into his eyes, where a man's spirit flickers into life. . . . He had been a spectator at the women's wrestling match at the games of the Feast of Lugus, which take place every year at the beginning of August. She had emerged victorious, and he had watched her every match. Even when the match was over, the king never took his attention from her. She remembered him from among all the others not only because of his handsome brow, his fine head of yellow hair, and his prowess with the chariot—which he had displayed to the marvel of all earlier on in the games. There was something about the way he looked at her which pleased her because of an easy familiarity she felt with him—though she had never spoken to him or seen him before that time. It was, in truth, only a passing feeling, which at the time she considered hardly more than a fancy, one she had not thought about until now, as she listened to Caratacus sing the king's praises.

As a priestess of Andraste she could not be compelled to accept Prasutagus' proposal, or any man's, however imperious and compelling his desires, however pressing the needs of policy. The unity of kingdoms, the clash of empires, the claims of destiny, all issued their summons to her. The enemy of the Britons was waiting like a carrion crow to feed off the corpses should the two great kingdoms of the Catuvellauni and Iceni come to blows. But in the scented twilight wood even that mighty summons resounded like the distant rattle of rusty chains or the banging of empty pots. The summer season was about to burst fresh upon the world; its very vitality gave her pause. It troubled her—this youthfulness, flowering and fruitful and laden with life. Its profligate abundance made her restive. In spite of her determination to do otherwise, like any young woman when she put age in the balance with youth, she found age wanting. Age inspires awe, but awe can make a pale, cold bed companion. Youth is cherished, even if its passion flows away like water between fingers, or burns like an all-consuming fire that leaves only ash. . . .

The waters grew dim, the cave where they had lain together became a dark, impenetratable place. Fen Fire had not told her brothers of that Beltane encounter or that her memory of it was enough to bring to its knees her proud desire to be the instrument of peace between the tribes. She turned away from the river. The rushing of its waters over the rocks had become tedious chatter. She dragged the slain boar to her horse, trussed it up and slung it securely behind her. She would go to give the king's envoy her answer as she was: in her shredded, close-fitting trousers of kid, her breastband of leather, and her white hands and arms and neck drenched in the gore and the mud of the hunt.

Fen Fire rode at a leisurely canter through the woods along a well-trodden pathway that she had used since childhood. She had not gone far when the sound of another horse approaching in the opposite direction made her halt. A skinny, bedraggled nag came out of the darkness with slow steps; its rider was caped and hooded. Two withered hands with long bony fingers held the reins. They were the hands of an old crone, whose haggard ancient face and gummy eyes peered at the young woman from under the tattered hood.

"May the night prosper with you," Fen Fire said in greeting.

"And with you," came the croaking voice in reply.

"It is a dark hour for one of such venerable years to be out and about in these woods," said Fen Fire.

"When you have reached my years, all hours seem dark. But it is kind and thoughtful of you to be concerned, nonetheless."

"My concern is born of respect for your years."

"Age can only earn respect, for it is too weak to compel it."

"Age brings wisdom which compels respect."

"Those are generous and thoughtful words, young woman."

"And where would you be going at such an hour?"

"To my own house, where else? This old nag is as weak as myself, and sometimes I think it would be kinder if I were to walk and carry it on my back than the other way around; so even if my heart desired to go somewhere else, my horse could not comply. Anyway, where else in the world am I fit for but my own hearth?''

"Then it can't be far,'' Fen Fire said.

"Not too far for an ant to carry its load without being winded or for a dove's feather to travel on the back of a summer breeze or for a beggar to limp with a begging bowl.''

Fen Fire was surprised. She thought she knew the woods around Camulodunum as well as anyone, and in all her time hunting and riding through them, she knew of no peasant's hut or settlement nearby.

"Would you have anything at all that might quench an old woman's thirst? For it is a long way I've come tonight.''

Fen Fire always carried a horn of ale to the hunt. She handed it to the old woman.

"You're welcome to all that remains, for I am near home myself and will find no further use for it.'' In a moment, the woman had drained the whole thing, and was smacking her lips in appreciation. The old crone laid a bony hand on her own, gently stroking it. Then, she touched her forearm.

"My skin was once as soft and white as this,'' she sighed. "And my bosom as full and firm. Now, I am as thin and dry as a withered branch in the dead of winter. I am an old sow. My summer season has ended, and yours has just begun.''

High up in the trees an owl hooted. "I hear you, I hear you,'' croaked the old woman. "I am coming.''

"If you would like me to escort you home . . .''

"Are you not anxious to get to your own, young woman?'' The crone's eyes seemed to gleam from under her hood. "There are many waiting for you at the old king's palace, are there not?''

"There are indeed, and I shall be off at once,'' Fen Fire answered her in surprise.

"Good—for you mustn't keep the king's envoy waiting. The king is most anxious for your answer.''

"How is it you know so much of my affairs?''

"The world holds few secrets from me.''

"Then we can hope to profit from your wisdom."

"Though my eyes see only dimly, they see deeply. Wisdom grows in the dark as well as in the light."

"And what do you see?"

"A young man as beautiful to be looking at as a tall tree in summer, a mighty warrior."

"Every woman's dream, no more!"

At this, the old crone cackled with dry and dusty laughter. "With you it is more than a dream. He is flesh. And that is why you linger by the riverbank and in the woods instead of going with proper haste to the king's envoy. Because of him I see a woman divided, a family sundered and a house torn. For it is from a wife that good or ill comes."

"A woman can heal divisions as well as cause them," Fen Fire declared, troubled by her words.

"You know what you must do, child."

The forest trembled in a cold wind. The old crone shivered. She clutched the reins of her horse and rode into the shadows. The owl called again from somewhere deeper among the trees, and the wind stiffened.

It was already dark by the time Fen Fire came in sight of Camulodunum, the capital of the Catuvellauni kingdom. The great palace of Cunobelinus, the late king of the Catuvellauni, stood at its center. It was ablaze with torches. Cunobelinus had spread the power of his tribe from the west of the isle of Britain to the east, where he had overthrown the Trinovantes and transformed Camulodunum from a small stronghold into a vast settlement, ringed with miles of dykes, ditches, towers and fortifications strong enough to throw back the greatest chariot armies in the world. It was her home, where her childhood and youth had been spent, and where the envoy of Prasutagus was now awaiting her answer.

Chapter 2

From the time when the first column of blue smoke from the burning leaves rose up into the sky at the beginning of the dark Samhain season, to the flowering of the yellow broom in spring, the vast round room of the palace of King Cunobelinus was dominated by the great blazing fire, which formed its hot hospitable heart. Fen Fire had grown up within the glow of its flames, under the watchful eye of the aging king.

The palace's hundred rooms, each large enough to hold three couples, were panneled with red yew; its great round thatched roof was supported by stout oak pillars decorated by the finest craftsmen in Britain and Gaul. Great serpents coiled around the posts, stags with branching antlers reared their massive heads on some, while the shapes of huge bristle-backed boars, heads bent, vicious curving tusks exposed, were carved on others; on still others were hunting scenes showing warriors with javelins poised. Each of the hundred rooms was hung with golden song birds, polished bronze shields inset with precious stones, high-crested helmets, swords with ivory and gold and silver hilts, and other treasures from the king's collection of arms and decorations. Each of the rooms was separated from the others by screens of copper into which were set silver birds.

In the center of the palace, above the hearth, hung the huge bronze cauldron, large enough to feed a hundred warriors so that each would stagger from it, his belly ready to burst his belt. The finest bronzeworkers had wrought it with skill, and delicate were the carvings of boars, birds and bulls with which they had embellished its bulging sides.

"Its bubbling to me is as pleasant as the babbling of little children," Cunobelinus used to say, "and I want to hear it always." So it was that the cauldron was never empty.

Cunobelinus always smelled of old leather mixed with the sweet scent of mead and the odor of roast boar meat and woodsmoke; his beard was vast and curly and grey like the ash left in the fireplace when the flames were spent; tufts of hair grew out of his nostrils and even from his ears. His hands were broad and strong, with creased palms full of callouses from clutching the hilt of his huge broadsword, which was large enough to split a tree, yet with a blade fine enough to slice a snowflake. It made a wonderful swoshing noise as he swung it through the air. To a little girl, it was a challenge.

"Can you touch the top of the hilt?" he used to say, planting it right in front of her.

"Yes! Watch. I can do it now!" she cried, stretching up, desperate to reach it. How many times did she try and fail? No triumph seemed greater than to reach that far.

Cunobelinus' skin was wrinkled and creased, full of folds and many scars of different shapes and sizes. One scar was made by an arrow, one by a javelin, and one by a broadsword as big as his own. In those three wounds could be read the story of how the king had made the Catuvellauni, over whom he and his ancestors had ruled for longer than anyone but the bards and druids could remember, into the most powerful people in Britain. The arrow wounded him during the great battle in which he overthrew the power of the Coritani to the north. The javelin struck him during the great fight at the ford, when he compelled the Dobunni in the west to pay him tribute. And the champion of the Trinovantes wielded the broadsword that wounded him during the battle in which the king brought that eastern tribe under Catuvellauni rule. It was after that victory that Cunobelinus moved the seat of his kingdom to Camulodunum and built his great palace. Such was the power and prestige of Cunobelinus that the emperor of the Romans, Augustus Caesar, sought a treaty of friendship with him, which the king was happy to give, for he had no desire to fight a war on that front when he was consolidating his power elsewhere.

In his private chamber, Cunobelinus kept a huge chest, stuffed with treasures and secrets, among which was the head of the Trinovantian champion. Nothing pleased Fen Fire more than when he fetched it out.

"He was as broad as a gate, as tall as a ship's mast, and the hairs on his head stood up like bristles on the back of a boar, and the clash of our swords was so loud that the birds in the trees for twenty miles around were scared from their nests, and for a year afterwards would not return to them," Cunobelinus told her. Truly, the head seemed massive, like that of a giant. It swung in his fist before her face so close that if it were alive she could have felt its breath. The skin was dark and shrunken, contracted around the sunken empty sockets where once there had been eyes.

"Where are his eyes?" she asked.

"When the soul leaves the body at death it is the eyes that waste away first," he told her, holding up the head as if it were a grim lantern, "because it is through the eyes that a man's spirit resides and looks out on the world."

"Where does the soul go?" she asked. He pointed up. Above the wide vent in the roof at night the stars shone, visible even when the smoke from the fire in the middle of the floor billowed through it. They were like sparks fixed in the black void of the sky, to burn forever.

"To some, the soul is like a fire," he said, "and when it leaves the body it aspires to rise up into the heavens to become a star."

She touched the head. It did not feel like skin but more like the leather of Cunobelinus' jerkin and trousers.

"We steeped it for a long time in water from a black bog until it was nice and tough," he told her.

"A black bog." The very mention of the words made her shiver. A black bog was full of bottomless holes brimming with murky black water, a place where no one dares set foot unless he knows what he is doing and where he is going, for if you were to miss your way in such a place, and darkness came, and the wind began to blow cold, you had to be very, very careful where you stepped. Or it's down into the hole you'd go—into the black water where no one would ever find you again.

Cunobelinus had four sons, Togodumnus, Caratacus, Maglocunos and Adminius. They too had wounds, but they were not as interesting to her as their father's.

Caratacus, who was the most daring, had a scar on his knee which he got from a fall from a rock that no one else ever dared to climb. Adminius, the most devious, had one on his hand where a dog bit him—though he lied to Fen Fire and told her he had been attacked by a bear (after that, she never believed him). Togodumnus, the most clumsy, had a tiny scar on his forehead because he once tripped over his javelin and fell on his face. The only mark on Maglocunos, the most beautiful, was a reddish spot on his left temple where, according to Cunobelinus, a princess from the Other World had kissed him when he was yet a baby lying in his cradle.

One night the old king sat by the fire watching her play. Tiring of her games, she asked the king to play with her.

"I shall teach you something about Mago, who was your ancestor and one of the great kings of the world," he said.

Cunobelinus retrieved his crane bag, in which he kept certain secrets, from the chest. He explained to her that this was the crane bag of Mago. From it he took out three straws and told her to lay them out carefully on the palm of her hand, side by side, then to hold her hand up in front of her mouth.

"You must blow away the middle straw without disturbing the other two," he said to the little girl. But no matter how she positioned herself, every time she blew, all three straws went flying away. She watched in growing frustration as time after time the straw spiraled down to the palace floor. She tried until she had lost all her breath and sat panting by the fire, her cheeks glowing red.

"I'll show you something," he said. Carefully Cunobelinus laid out the straws on his palm. He took a deep breath, sucking in his cheeks until his cheekbones stuck out like knobs. The old king bent two of his fingers over so that their tips held the two outside straws pressed securely against the palm. Then he blew so hard it was like a gust of wind sweeping through the palace. Only the middle straw went flurrying away.

"But you said you would teach me something about Mago," she reminded him, perplexed and annoyed at being so easily fooled.

"I have," Cunobelinus smiled, "for that was how Mago got first choice when the world was being divided into East and West. In those days, there were only two great kings in the world. Mago was one and Alexander was the name of the other. Mago knew that two kings as great as themselves could never live together in peace if they were near each other. So they got together to divide the world into two halves, East and West, but they couldn't decide on who would have first choice. Mago challenged Alexander to perform the trick. Whoever succeeded in blowing away the middle straw without disturbing the other two could have first choice. Alexander, though he was reputed to be the wisest as well as one of the greatest of kings, fared no better than yourself."

Mago took the western half because he had heard of the wonderful forests full of deer and boar, the wide rivers stocked with fish, and the bays replete with oysters that lay in that direction. So it was that her ancestors came to Gaul, where Mago took as his wife Dancing Flame—the first red-haired woman in the world. Maponos was their son, the founder of the race of the Britons.

From the earliest days, Fen Fire had heard the legends of Maponos and his descendents; indeed, she knew as much about them as she knew her own mother and father.

Since the days of her great-grandmother, Flame of the Field of Battle, who helped defend Britain against the legions of Julius Caesar, Fen Fire's family was fostered with that of the Catuvellaunian king. Fen Fire came to Cunobelinus at the age of five, and found herself thrown into the company of his four sons, all much older than she, who looked at the grey-eyed, red-haired little girl with a mixture of curiosity and disdain.

Togodumnus teased her on the playing field where he was master of the stick and ball game. He invited her to play, and then knocked three balls three times into the hole where she could not place one. Fen Fire was furious when he laughed at her efforts.

"All beginnings are weak," she told him, defying his scorn with indignant eyes. She practiced for days on the field alone. When they next met, she knocked three balls one after the other into the hole, then blocked three times three from Togodumnus. This pleased the king immensely, and made his sons tolerate her a little more. But they still treated her with condescension—until one day, when they were practicing with their javelins—before the king. When she asked to be allowed to join them, they scoffed and told her the shafts were too large and heavy for her to use.

Fen Fire left them and ran back into the palace, where she made her way to the king's private chamber. A few minutes later, one of the king's servants came running onto the playing field with a terrified look on his face, begging the king to come with him at once. "The little girl—I fear she'll hurt herself!" the man exclaimed.

Cunobelinus and his four sons ran to the chamber, where all stopped dead in their tracks. His chest of valuables lay wide open, and Fen Fire stood in the middle of it, her red hair dishevelled, holding above her head the Spear That Roars For Blood.

"Camulos the god of battle be my witness!" Cunobelinus exclaimed. "Until now no one has ever raised that weapon but myself." The spear had a short but thick shaft, and a broad head made not like that of an ordinary weapon but with twisted metal from which sprouted vicious sickle-shaped hooks.

"Since your ungracious sons will not let me have a throw of their javelins, I will use this," Fen Fire declared.

"That is a weapon not like the others," the king told her. "It was fashioned long ago by the hands of Maponos himself. It is the weapon which he took with him to hunt a boar the like of which was never seen before or since."

"How long ago was that?" asked she. The king replied with a question of his own.

"How old are the Grey Man and the Grey Woman?" These were the two upright stones that stood next to each other in the wide meadow in front of the palace. The Grey Man was straight with a bulbous head, and his consort, the Grey Woman, was holed and rounded. Fen Fire had fine sport around them with her friends, running between them and clambering over them. On May Eve, they built the great bonfires next to the stones to celebrate the feast of Beltane and the beginning of summer.

"I think they are even older than you," she said, after a moment's reflection, "because they are even more gnarled and wrinkled." Cunobelinus laughed.

"I'm speaking of a time almost as old as the Grey Man and the Grey Woman, but no one knows for sure. But so much time has passed between then and now that my own life is as brief as that of a may fly compared to it." The king took the spear from her and laid it down in the chest, promising he would one day tell her the story of the Boar Hunt of Maponos. The four boys, whose eyes had bulged from their sockets at the sight of Fen Fire with the spear in her hands, agreed to let her join them at their javelin practice. From then on, they treated her with more respect. All, that is, except Adminius, the youngest. Since he was closest to her in years, he resented her most; any triumph she enjoyed, however small, he thought lessened his status; any praise bestowed on her by his father, he acted as if it was stolen from his stock.

Early one fine summer's morning, the king went hunting the stag, accompanied by his sons and Fen Fire. She was on the verge of womanhood, as tall and straight as a reed by now, black eyebrows etched above wide grey eyes; a milk-white noble brow she had, and she carried herself with ease and grace. As she stood next to the old king in his light, fast chariot, built of spruce and wicker, people hailed her as she went by as if she were their queen. Notwithstanding her erect and regal manner, Fen

Fire was in no way haughty with the shepherds or cattle herders or pigkeepers that she met. On the contrary, she treated all with an open manner that was as warm as it was unforced. To Adminius, this was cause for even greater bitterness. Having, he brooded, thrust herself into what was his rightful place as the youngest in the family and won affection from his father that was his due, she was usurping his place in the hearts of the Catuvellauni.

For the whole day the yelping of the hounds and the bellowing of the stag echoed over the hills and valley. When they finally cornered the great beast, in a forest clearing near a grassy mound, it was a cast from Togodumnus which mortally wounded it. They set about preparing a feast on the spot, which was known as the Mound of Maponos. (There was not a corner of the kingdom of the Catuvellauni but did not have a ford, or a hill, or a ridge, or a mound named after the founder of the race.)

The grass on the mound was richer and more lush than any growing in the clearing. When Fen Fire mentioned this to her foster-father he replied:

"The grass that grows on a fairy mound is always greener and sweeter than that which grows on ordinary ground."

The flames roared up and the venison was soon roasting on one spit, while on another were a clutch of birds that Caratacus had brought down with his sling (he had the surest eye and the steadiest hand of any of the brothers). Twilight came and the flames cast their red glow onto the shadowy woods around them.

The fairies, or the Everlasting Ones as they are also called, live in the Other World, and the mounds are the entrances to their dwellings. When Maponos had come to Britain, arriving on Beltane Eve, he found it inhabited by small, swarthy people with thick, curly black hair; a magical, mischievous people given to music and dancing, and the making of potent spells.

They had a queen, a beautiful young woman with long black hair and blazing eyes. She could change shape, so that at one moment she was a huge writhing eel and at another an old hag with poisonous black, broken teeth, before suddenly changing back to her true form. Maponos and his warriors met her and her army at a place known as the Ford of Maponos (though which one it was of the many that now claim that distinction is not known for certain). During the great battle that the two armies fought, her shape-changing did not avail her. When she attacked him in the shape of a giant eel, Maponos struck her with his spear and gravely wounded her. When she returned to her true shape and her people beheld her dying, they gave up the fight. Maponos, seeing the beautiful young woman lying stricken in the stream, was overcome with desire for her.

"From desire springs life," he told her grieving people. He had a wonder-working cauldron in which he placed her. No sooner had its wound-healing life-giving liquid washed over her but she was whole again.

Maponos took her as his wife and reached this settlement with her people. They were to take the world under the earth, and Maponos would rule the world above it. Twice a year the mounds, through which the Other World was entered, would open to enable the queen to visit with her people and for them to visit her. On the eve of the Beltane Feast, she could journey back to spend some time with them, and on Samhain Eve, they were permitted to leave their world to visit ours to be with their queen. In this fashion, Maponos divided the world and the year into two different parts. Only on May Eve and the Eve of Samhain did they come together.

"I have listened with my ear to the ground of many a fairy mound and have heard no sound from within," she said to the king that night as they sat waiting for the venison to roast.

"Treasure of my heart—it's better not to hear," he replied. "Their life is happier than we can easily imagine. Birds are always in song, perched on trees with boughs of crystal, and it is mead that falls instead of rain. A day passed among the Everlasting Ones is the length of one of our years though, because they are so happy they do not notice its passing. Unfortunate are those mortals who have seen the world of the Everlasting Ones or heard its music. There is nothing more certain to make a man miserable for the rest of his days than for him to catch even a glimpse of perfect contentment, knowing it is unattainable.''

They divided up the meat and Togodumnus, because his spear felled the stag, took a portion of the thigh—the portion usually reserved for victorious warriors. Togodumnus was tearing away at it with great relish, when Adminius came up and sat next to him.

''Congratulations, brother, on being the first among us to win the hero's portion,'' he said. Togodumnus thanked him and continued eating. ''You are the first—but I will be the second to win it.'' The older youth looked at the younger.

''How?''

''Why, I will win it from you,'' Adminius said confidently. ''So it is only fair that you should control your appetite and leave me some meat on the bone.'' Togodumnus burst out laughing so loudly that he nearly choked. He was twice as strong as Adminius, and there was no feat in which he was not confident of beating him.

''Your audacity is very funny,'' he said, ''but let it go no further than words.''

''I cannot win it by words, brother; unless, of course, you have the courage to agree to a challenge of wits, and I'm certain you won't because you know I would be sure to triumph in that.''

Togodumnus put down his portion. He was always mocked by people for his clumsiness and lack of subtlety; nothing was more certain to rouse him.

''What do you propose?'' he demanded.

''I challenge you to a contest that will test our physical skills,'' he said.

''Name it,'' came the instant reply.

''Ear-wagging,'' Adminius said.

''Ear-wagging! That is not a test for a warrior who wishes to win the thigh portion, but for mere gleemen or clowns,'' said Togodumnus with contempt.

''It is a test you cannot win and are afraid to try,'' Adminius cried accusingly. ''If you cannot do it, you lose the hero's portion.''

''I am not afraid of such a challenge!'' Togodumunus

replied, accepting Adminius' challenge. At once he began to wag both his ears. "There, it's done. And the thigh portion remains with me." He smiled at Adminius.

"That's an easy one," Adminius said, doing the same. "But can you wag one ear without moving its fellow? That's a rare skill which only I have."

"I'll do it then, for I cannot tolerate the thought of you doing something that I cannot," Togodumnus said. But no matter had hard he tried, Togodumnus could not wag one ear without moving the other.

"It can't be done so," he announced in exasperation.

"I bet you the right to the hero's portion that I can do it with ease."

Togodumnus looked at his brother contemptuously. He could not be seen to back down from his challenge now, though he did not trust Adminius, and Caratacus advised he ignore him.

"I accept," he said, reluctantly putting the thigh meat on a flat stone in front of him. Adminius called the other two brothers to witness the challenge. Then he took his left ear between his fingers and held it fast while he wiggled his right ear vigorously.

"You cheated," Togodumnus cried in outrage at the trick. He was as furious at himself for falling for it as at his brother for deceiving him.

"I said nothing about how one ear might be prevented from wagging while you wagged the other," Adminius derided him. "But anyone with half a brain in their head would have spotted it immediately. Now, make him hand over the hero's portion." He turned to Caratacus and Maglocunos who, though they thought it was a silly trick, agreed that Togodumnus should pay the penalty.

Togodumnus stood up angrily, at which Adminius grabbed the hero's portion from the rock and was about to make off with it when the older brother caught him with a wallop to the side of the head. He went lunging sideways, clutching the precious joint and howling for help. Togodumnus caught him again, pummeling him until Cunobelinus intervened to stop it.

The king listened carefully to Caratacus. And no one could judge from the looks he cast at Togodumnus and

Adminius of whose conduct he more disapproved. To play tricks on the enemy was one thing, but to fool one's own family was despicable. But was it worse than to set upon a younger, weaker brother and beat him? However, it was Adminius who worried the king most. He was always the source of dispute between the other sons, setting one against the other, at times envious of all of them.

Cunobelinus walked up the sloping mound to think upon his judgment as to who should retain the portion. He sat down, and called Fen Fire to his side.

"My ash-eyed beauty," he smiled. "Does the color grey always bespeak great wisdom? For if it does, your eyes would suggest you are wiser than us all."

"They say that wisdom only comes after action," she replied, chewing thoughtfully on a blade of the sweet green mound grass, "and I have yet to act in the wide world beyond my own threshold. But I have ears and eyes in my head. And I have been thinking and ever thinking about that youngest son of yours."

"What have you thought?" the king asked, taking her on his knee.

"I know he is of your flesh and blood and you might take it ill for one like me, who is not, to say this, but say it I will: bad fortune will come from Adminius, for he is not to be trusted." Her words might have sprung from the king's own heart, for they expressed his own brooding anxieties.

"Is your advice then that he should give the meat back to his brother?"

"No, not at all. Adminius should take the hero's portion, though he does not deserve to win it."

"What justice is there in that?" the king asked, perplexed.

"Togodumnus deserves to lose it, and he might grow the wiser from the experience. For if a man pays not the penalty for being so easily fooled, he will be fooled again. It takes no druid to tell us that."

Cunobelinus saw the sense of what she said at once and awarded the thigh portion to Adminius.

Adminius took the portion, but the words of Fen Fire

deprived him of the pleasure of enjoying it. After a few bites he cast it to the hounds.

While the king's youngest son gave him increasing cause for concern as the years passed, Fen Fire proved a consolation. The blood of the women warriors from whom she was descended flowed with vigor in her veins. She had the powerful grip of Red Shaft, master of the hundred wrestling holds, which had enabled her to pin down and bind with willow thongs Scathach the Shadow Woman, when she was on her quest for the three-horned bull. And she had the agility of Flame of the Field of Battle, who fought against Julius Caesar in the ages gone by, and who could do the feat of the Salmon Leap from the platform of her chariot. Of her it was told that once, to avoid a hundred enemy javelins thrown at her at one and the same time, she leapt up so high that on her way down she caught a brace of geese for her supper.

Chapter 3

A huge oak tree of a man strode through the palace, driving a pack of hounds before him. He impatiently cried out: "Away with these brutes. The smell of their piss is not fit for the nostrils of a king's noble envoy!" Togodumnus fetched a laggardly dog a sharp kick in the backside. It whimpered and scampered behind one of the pillars. The clumsy youth of years before had grown into a big-sinewed giant of a warrior. His arms, decorated with golden bands, were as thick as the pillar behind which the disconsolate brute was skulking. His long, fair hair hung down over his massive shoulders. His temperament was impulsive, swinging between thunder and sunshine, storm and calm.

He glanced around him at the scattering pack of dogs; they ran this way and that. "Dogs! Dogs everywhere. Whingeing, barking, slabbering, yelping, howling, whining, whimpering, cringing, lolling, shitting, scratching, pissing—the palace is more like a kennel than a house!" He grabbed a passing servant by the neck and practically lifted him from the floor. "If I see another pack of dogs in here, I'll see to it you'll bark for your food and eat it from the floor on your hands and knees until you feel more like a brute than they do!" he bellowed. The trembling servant gasped that every dog would be chased outside at once.

The doors of the palace opened, and as the servant was driving out the dogs, two men weaved their way through them to enter. One was short and square-shouldered with dark curling hair that tumbled over his ears, reaching down to a powerful neck. He wore a close-fitting cape of royal red and a short tunic of old, well-tanned leather embossed with stones. His eyes were large, widely spaced and brilliant—a clear blue, limpid and pure. His smooth brow was broad and noble, his nose straight with flaring nostrils, denoting a nature passionate and proud and very high. Indeed, his manner—his swagger, his erect carriage, the firmness with which he gripped his ivory-hilted broadsword in its bronze scabbard that knocked against his thigh as he walked—all indicated a man of the noblest Catuvellaunian lineage. Only his skin, swarthy, almost brown, and his jet black curling locks which gave him a dark appearance, seemed to suggest that Caratacus, the brother next in age to Togodumnus, was anything other than a Catuvellaunian. Indeed, his brothers often joked with him teasingly that he must have been a product of some passing union between his father and the Everlasting Ones. The jest did not displease Caratacus in the slightest.

"Everyone knows," Caratacus replied, "that when the tribes first came to Britain and forced the people they found there into the hills and mounds, the Everlasting Ones got the better part of the settlement."

Next to Caratacus walked the Chief Druid Cunodunum. The long, white hairs and wrinkled brow bespoke a man of many years, but his age was not known for certain. His white beard was forked and well-trimmed and long—longer than an ordinary man's arm. He was tall and lean and spare. His skin, though wrinkled, seemed fresh and radiant with life: old yet ageless. But the most curious thing about Caratacus' companion was his eyes: one was green and the other a deep blue like a winter's night sky. His knowledge was as deep as a dark sky, his wisdom encompassed it: Cunodunum could name every star that could be seen, and even some that nobody could see but himself, he knew the riddles of the Double Spirals that unlock the mysteries of birth and death, he could read the secret alphabets that encode the mysteries of knowledge, and he oversaw the ancient rituals of sacrifice and prediction whose intricacies a lifetime would not be enough to unravel. And yet, he carried the great burden of this knowledge as easily as an ant carries a seed in its jaws. True knowledge, he told his pupils in the priestly colleges of the sacred Island of Mona, lifts a man up; it is only ignorance which weighs him down.

"And where is Fen Fire?" Togodumnus cried out in dismay when he saw she was not with them.

"Then she is not here?" Caratacus asked in return.

Togodumnus swept his arm through the air. "I am alone with my three hundred dogs, thirty-three children, one hundred servants and dozen wives. She has not graced our threshold or seen the inside of her chamber for I don't know how many days!" A barrel of ale was nearby. He lifted it up, opened the tap, and let the liquid gush down his throat. Then he threw it to his brother, who caught it as easily as if it were a ball of knitting wool. "We'll need this if she lets us down before the king's envoy. He will be with us before long. Indeed, when I heard you approach I thought it was he."

Caratacus followed his brother's example and took a gulp of the ale. He wiped his mouth and offered it to Cunodunum, who declined. "I last saw her galloping west on the track of a boar, crying to everyone that it was the biggest she'd seen near Camulodunum in many years. She invited me to follow. That was two days ago." When the druid heard this he groaned.

Caratacus looked at him in surprise. "You did not expect to find her sitting trembling in front of her mirror or combing her hair, I trust!"

"With Fen Fire do we ever know what we can expect?" the druid replied, creasing his brow. There was a loud barking from behind. They turned round thinking it might be her hounds, only to find that the pack of dogs Togodumnus had just kicked out were swarming back in through the doors. Togodumnus reached for a long-shafted javelin that was hanging nearby on the palace wall. Holding the spear by the head he charged at the dogs, walloping three at one stroke and sending the others howling among the pillars.

Cunodunum had a grave look on his face. "Gone hunting for two days! What if the boar were to run as far west as the Severn Valley—or decide to swim to Ireland—we might never see her again. I know better than to expect her to behave like a girl without a choice in these matters; however, Prasutagus might nourish such expectations."

But Caratacus' attention was being given to a carving around the base of a pillar. It was an old carving, lately reworked, of the Three-Horned Bull, the sacred beast of the goddess Andraste whose bulbous third horn had the potent power to cure any ill afflicting womankind. "Prasutagus will not be disappointed," he said, crouching down to examine the work. The huge pillar seemed to rest on the powerful shoulders of the bull. "Prasutagus is not fascinated by her because of her craft at spinning and needlework. The only time he saw the princess was when she was wrestling at the games of Lugus and had her opponent screaming for mercy." Satisfied, he stood up.

Togodumnus returned. "You may not be concerned, brother," he said, rehanging his spear. "You think you know Fen Fire's mind. But remember, the women of Andraste go their own way, do they not?"

"I know her loyalties well enough," Caratacus answered. Since she was a girl she had been as much a source of puzzlement to his oldest brother as she had been a source of delight to his father Cunobelinus.

A blast from the gatekeeper's horn ended their conversation. The doors were flung open and the arrival of the envoy of Prasutagus was announced.

He was a truly beautiful young man with hair the color of golden sunshine, and he seemed to glide over the floor towards them. The airiness of his appearance was enhanced by his silken garments wafting behind him. It was a marvel how they had withstood the long ride from Prasutagus' capital Stonea. It was a marvel how *he* survived, for he was reed-thin. Yet in spite of the journey along the dirty unpaved roads, neither he nor his silken attire carried one trace of the ordeal. Silks were rare among the Catuvellauni, but Latis, Prasutagus' first wife, had a fondness for them and liked to bedeck her more important servants in precious fabrics.

"Long life to your seed and breed!" Togodumnus cried in greeting, barely able to suppress a grimace at the inappropriateness of the salutation.

The envoy acknowledged the greeting and had his servants open the gifts from the king: a beautiful harness of gold trappings, a gold torc of wonderous workmanship and a bag of pearls. "This is a small measure, a bead of dew on a morning meadow, compared to the generosity my king would share with you." He looked around him at the magnificence of Cunobelinus' palace. But nowhere among the bustling activity or the splendor of the household could he catch a glimpse of the young woman whose answer he had come to learn. "I have furrowed a deep track to get here and . . ."

"Then you must be hungry and thirsty," Caratacus answered. "We have laid out refreshments for you." Before the envoy could respond, he was gently ushered through the palace to one of the side chambers (partitioned from the central hall with a tall screen of silver trellising inlaid with golden singing birds), where years before Cunobelinus would dine on those occasions he preferred to be alone or with only a few friends. Ignoring his protests that he was neither hungry nor thirsty but would rather speak with the young lady whose answer his master was so anxious to hear, they sat him down on the pillows stuffed with rushes and filled his cup with ale.

"Is there wine in the house?" he asked, wrinkling his nose at the frothing ale.

Togodumnus laughed. "Wine? There's enough to float the palace." He ordered a barrel of it.

"And the young lady in question?"

"She is readying herself and will be with us before long," Togodumnus told him.

The envoy smiled and was given a fresh cup for his wine. "The ladies are ever before their mirrors no matter what. Nothing is more urgent than their desire to make themselves beautiful. Well, it is only fitting." His dainty fingers raised the brimming cup to his lips, and he sipped with the delicacy of a housefly sucking up a spot of milk from the table.

A commotion outside arrested his hand, and he put the cup down. Thinking the princess was arriving, he was about to rise, when a tall, lean gentleman with a mass of unruly black hair peered unsteadily around the partition.

With a sort of lunge he entered the chamber. He was dressed in a tunic which was of a patchwork of six different colors—royal red, green, brown, black, white and yellow. In one hand he held a little craneskin sack and an alder cane, in the other he grasped a cup full of mead. When he swayed it tippled over the rim, sprinkling everything around him. When he seemed about to topple, he leaned on the alder cane. With surprising gravity, he looked down on the startled envoy and began in a rich sonorous voice:

"Born before the deluge, vast and huge,
Swifter than hawk or swallow, it flies through hill and
  hollow,
Without feathers or wings, voiceless yet it sings.
Swifter than horse or hare, it travels where none dare.
Without flesh, blood or bone, knows no pain, yet it
  moans.
Without head nor hand, and footless,
Higher than any tree yet rootless.
All I know when it has been, yet it never was seen.
Think, my friend, before you speak;
And tell me what it is I seek."

He balanced delicately with one hand on the cane, while with the other he took a long, slow drink of mead, his eyebrows raised, his face wearing the calm look of a man confident he had made a deep impression.

"The wind, of course," the envoy replied disdainfully, with hardly a moment's thought.

"I always begin with my simplest riddle first," said Bran, the unruffled bard of Caratacus, as casually as he could. "But if it's difficult riddles you're looking for, I have more of them than there are pebbles on a beach. Cunodunum the Chief Druid, who knows one or two himself, has often come to me scratching his head and asked 'Could you explain this one or that one?' " He paused, and unable to recall an example of this esoteric kind said, "Maybe it's a tune you'd prefer. I'm master of the three tunes that harpers know, the laughing tune, the weeping tune, and the sleeping tune." He dipped his hand into his sack and took out a small harp. His fingers were long and fine, and his palms broad. He put down his cup and swept his fingers over the harp. The envoy shook his head and looked around him. He was clearly in no mood to laugh, cry or sleep.

Bran put the harp on the table and took another drink. "In my time I have mastered three hundred and fifty histories, and three times as many verses cryptic and descriptive. I know the story of how every mound got its name from here to the western coast and beyond—for I've been to Ireland in my time and resided there with their kings and bards and priests. You cannot put your foot in a stream without me being able to tell you why it is called what it is called. Point to any mountain, meadow or mist-filled valley, I'll name it and tell you the origin of that name. For example, not far from here there is a ford called the Ford of Maponos. Do you know the one I mean, across the stream with the softest, sweetest water in the kingdom? Do you know how it got its name?"

The envoy sighed and shook his head. "I know, of course. Doesn't every Ford of Maponos derive its name from the same event—the great battle where he overthrew the power of the Everlasting Ones?"

"But only one of all that are so named is the true one. And I'm one of the few men in Britain who knows which it is. Would you not like to hear the story of it?"

"I am familiar with the legends of Maponos, and I now recognize the one you're referring to," came the weary answer.

"Now, the Great Boarhunt of Maponos, there's a wonderful story for you . . ."

"I know it, and I'm sure you don't have the time to do it justice."

There was a chilly silence which lasted a long moment. Then the poet said, "Riddle me this riddle: what is it that no house however large can contain?"

"Its own foundations, of course."

Bran nodded, wrinkling his brow. "I am master of one hundred and fifty secret alphabets and have the key to unlock them all," he said sententiously.

"Perhaps you have the key which will unlock Fen

Fire's chamber, for it seems to me she must be trapped, or why else would she delay so?"

"Why, I can make her appear before you right now!"

For the first time the envoy appeared vaguely interested; that is, until the poet picked up his harp again and intoned:

"Woman of the long white hands, and swan-white bosom,
Delicate as petals your fine fingers,
And small, smooth shoulders the color of fresh snow.
Woman of the long white hands, I would be a bird in the nest of your bosom . . ."

No sooner had he begun the parody of his own verses, than his fond memories of their subject made him pause. Sadness overtook him now that the prospect of losing her to another household loomed on the horizon. Caratacus had met Bran in the wild mountains beyond the Severn, where the bard had lived for many years with the tribe of the Silures—fierce warriors who were good at making war, making songs, and making love. Bran himself was not of that tribe—no one knew for certain what his true origins were. He himself liked to think he came from beyond the sea to the west—the son perhaps of a great Irish bard and princess of the Everlasting Ones, who was for some mysterious reason put into a corracle and set adrift only to be cast up on the shores of Britain. At least, that was the story he told Fen Fire, to her delight, when he first arrived in Camulodunum, after agreeing to go there with Caratacus as his bard. "The king will be a fortunate man if he gets Fen Fire as his wife. He was a very wise man to propose to her rather than one of her cousins who reside in the north," Bran mused. The envoy looked at him a little surprised.

"I did not know there was a northern branch of her family." The bard smiled and raised his raven black eyebrows. That was another story Fen Fire liked to hear.

"Indeed there is . . . the dark side of the descendents of Maponos."

The envoy pricked up his ears at this hint of scandal.

"When Maponos was an old man," Bran began, "much to his surprise his wife, the Queen of the Everlasting Ones, made him a father again. The queen informed him of the coming event shortly after her return from one of her May Eve sojourns in the Other World, where, as you know, she went to visit her people every year. In due time, the child was born: a girl, swarthy skinned, with a head of black hair shot through with streaks of red, and brooding black eyebrows. The same night she was born a horse foaled in the stable, bringing forth a glossy black little stallion. The child and the stallion grew side by side. The only person the horse would tolerate was the child, and the only thing that seemed to give the child pleasure was the horse.

"Maponos looked at the girl, whom he named Dark Flame, with deep suspicion. She was not like his other daughters. Old men are easily made jealous, and Maponos was no exception, especially since while he aged like a mortal, his wife seemed not to age at all but remained as beautiful as ever. He suspected that the yearly longing she had to return to the world of the Everlasting Ones concealed a passionate liaison with one of her own kind.

"He revenged himself on his daughter. When she was on the verge of womanhood he locked her away in a distant part of his kingdom—her raven-haired beauty, her long sloe-black eyelashes, had become a source of shame to him. She was hidden in a fortress, with only an old hag for company.

"The night she was taken, the stallion went wild, and many thought it would kick down the stables.

"Maponos thought he could now forget about his daughter. But he could not. Jealousy feeds on itself, so he was as preoccupied as ever with the conduct of his beautiful young wife. Indeed, as the months passed, he was convinced she was getting younger as he was growing older. Then, not long after Maponos sent Dark Flame away, strange stories reached him. Sturdy young men were disappearing as they tended their flocks and herds. Their mangled bodies, drained of blood, were later found in ditches. But no trace of the attacker, whether human or animal, was ever found around them.

"One day, the stablekeeper reported how when he came to feed the stallion in the morning, he often found it panting and sweating, as if it had spent the night being ridden hard across the countryside. Yet, the horse had remained locked up all night. Maponos' brooding and suspicious mind seized on these two strange occurrences and linked them. They were proof that Dark Flame was not the result of a human coupling. In spite of the pleas of his distraught wife, he set out with his warriors for the fortress where his daughter was held, intending her mischief.

"But when they reached that desolate spot, they found the fortress in flames. At the barred window of the cell in the tower in which his daughter had been held, they thought they saw a distraught figure, hair aflame, in desperation trying to free herself as the flames roared up on all sides.

" 'Let the flames consume the evil she brought into this world,' Maponos declared. He turned away from the inferno and was making his way back through the woods when he heard the sound of a horse galloping towards him. Then he heard a woman's laughter. And then—a dark-caped dark-haired figure flashed past along a distant pathway. 'Dark Flame!' he cried out. With his warriors he pursued the figure all that night. But the morning found him and his warriors, their mounts exhausted, lying in a disconsolate heap—they had been riding round in an ever-decreasing circle all night. To this wild delusion his jealousy had brought him.

"And when they straggled back like a broken army to his palace, he found the horse gone, and the stablekeeper trampled to death. Maponos agreed at once to go with the queen on her next visit to the world of the Everlasting Ones to see for himself that he had no cause for his gnawing jealousy. Of course, he did not return and has not been seen since. As for Dark Flame, she too vanished—whether in the flames of her fortress-prison, or to some other place, we do not know for certain. But I have it on good authority that her descendants live to this day among the women of the Brigantes in the north. In that harsh, wild country, her tormented spirit might well have found something to its liking. . . .''

A loud commotion made the envoy jump to his feet. The doors of the palace opened with a mighty crash, then came the loud clatter and the clip of horses' hooves. It thundered through the shadows of the darkening palace. The envoy looked at Bran.

''Fear not,'' said the bard, ''Fen Fire is from a different branch of the family—as I said.''

The envoy at once edged around the partition, leaving Bran, who had consumed his own mead, to drain what was left of the wine.

A powerful, proud-striding chestnut horse with a flowing mane and wide-flaring nostrils galloped towards him. Its hoofbeats resounded from the shields that hung from the palace walls until the vast round room shook. Fen Fire held the reins with dirt-encrusted hands, and her long bare arms were stained with the mud of the two days of hunting the boar that lay draped behind her. Her hair now hung loose, an orange veil down to her waist. Her white thighs seemed to have burst through the tatters that remained of the trousers she wore. Her stomach was streaked with red scratches, as were her throat and hands, showing the marks of the many thickets she had plunged through tracking her quarry. Behind her swarmed her hounds, and after them came the stray dogs. But this time Togodumnus paid no attention to them as he and Caratacus rushed to meet her.

The envoy stepped back in fear that he would be trampled under the hooves. Could Dark Flame have been any more fierce-looking than this? he wondered, trembling at what seemed like an apparition from the wild imagination of the bard by whom he had been (he had to admit) finally engrossed. But just before she reached him, she reined in. The horse slowed to a steady trot, then halted. The boar's blood dripped plop, plop, plop onto the floor. Dismounting, she drew out her dagger and turned, cutting her trophy loose. Then she gave it a tug. It slid from the steaming haunches of the horse and fell with a heavy wallop in front of the envoy's feet, the blood and mire splashing his legs before he could jump out of the way.

"This is for your king," she said. "We will have it at our wedding feast."

In his heart Caratacus never doubted what her answer would be. There was more at stake than peace between two powerful tribes. The treachery of his brother Adminius had seen to that.

Chapter 4

Age and sickness had taken their toll on Cunobelinus. For thirty years as ruler of the Catuvellauni his shoulders had borne that heavy responsibility. No king in Britain had endured so long, or fashioned a kingdom as powerful as his. And few men lived to such an age: the king was old enough to have known warriors who had fought against Julius Caesar when he had invaded Britain almost a hundred years before. Those warriors had seen the great power of Rome for themselves, and Cunobelinus as a youth had sat at their feet listening to what they told him. And he passed on to his sons what he had heard, endeavoring to impress them with the ever-present danger poised across the narrow channel separating Britain from Gaul. They listened respectfully, but it seemed like a distant threat. At the high tide of their young manhood, even the empire of the Caesars did not give them cause for much concern. Of the four sons, Adminius listened with the most interest to what Cunobelinus was saying. He was always first with questions about Rome, and the most curious about Romans. However, Cunobelinus' warnings about the power of Rome had a different effect on the youngest son from that which the father intended.

Towards the end of the king's life, a new Caesar was proclaimed. "I have outlived two—Augustus and Tiberius. But I will not outlive Caligula," Cunobelinus said—Caligula was younger than his own sons. By this time, the king was barely able to walk. A fall from his horse during a hunt had injured his leg. It had not healed well. "Once I could shrug off the blow of a broadsword," he laughed bitterly. "Now a little fall and I'm helpless as a baby!" He was forced to remain lying flat on his back.

The days of immobility turned into weeks. Rumors spread that the king had died. "Our enemies would like to think so!" he exclaimed. Subidasto, the war-like son of the Iceni king Prasutagus, was goading his father into challenging the might of the Catuvellauni on their northern border. News of other threats and disturbances made the king gather his four sons about him.

He lay in the vast bed propped up on pillows stuffed with rushes, which Fen Fire had arranged carefully, his great beard as white as the white lambskins which covered the bed's expanse, his broadsword with its glittering hilt and polished blade at his side, and his favorite trophies adorning stakes around the room. A servant refilled his mead cup from the huge oaken barrel which he always kept full in his bedroom. When Fen Fire was a child, the hairs just under the king's lower lip had fascinated her because they were stained red from the mead juice, which he told her was a better preservative of flesh than the blackest bog water. On that day, as his sons stood around his bed, and Fen Fire fussed to make sure he was comfortable, he reminded her of a childhood promise. "When I die," he said, drinking from the brimming cup, "you must see to it that my head is steeped in mead."

"You'll drink many another vintage before that day," she said.

"I think not," he declared. "But my death troubles me not—so long as our enemies do not get a chance to exploit it." He looked at his sons. "The curse that has kept our cousins in Gaul from resisting the power of Rome is division—tribe against tribe, wars born of envy, and petty hatreds. We too share that fault, being always ready to fight among ourselves even in the face of a threat greater and more dangerous than all the others put together: a new Caesar—youthful, eager to prove himself in war." The king sighed and shook his head. "But even now, we continue with the same foolishness as always. What do you know of Prasutagus' son Subidasto?"

"A hot head," Togodumnus declared.

"He has the reputation of a fine warrior," Caratacus said, "and it will be put to the test if he continues on his present course. But I fear there are others who would like to rival him in the race to challenge us. Boduocus in the west is blustering."

"And there is Verica to the south," said Maglocunos, the next to the youngest son. "He is boasting that the haughtiness of the Catuvellauni will be humbled before long." Maglocunos was now a slender young man, but wiry and strong. He had an easy manner, and his light blue eyes and handsome face deceived many into believing he was of an unwarlike disposition. But compared to the temper of Maglocunos, that of Togodumnus was as passing as a summer storm. And he despised Verica more than any man in Britain, calling him a sycophant, a collector of fine Roman vases, more proud of his wines than of his feats in war. "And look at this," Maglocunos said, producing a coin from his pouch. He passed it to his father. On one side was inscribed a vine leaf and on the other a profiled head, under which was written the word "Rex."

Nobody there could read it, but Maglocunos had been told by Cunodunum the druid what it meant. "It is the Roman word for king, which is as foreign to our tongue as the vine leaf is to our soil."

"Verica would doubtless like to see both take root here," said the king, handing the coin to the others. Each examined it in turn, none more carefully than Adminius.

"He is already sowing seeds of trouble for us," Maglocunos declared. "The 'rex' was bestowed on him by the new Caesar, Caligula, in recognition of his friendship." Cunobelinus rapped the hilt of his sword with his fingers.

"This is cause for worry, my sons," said the king. "Caligula has allowed our treaty with Rome to lapse, yet he favors Verica with titles. . . ."

"No one can crown a man king but the strength of his arm and the affection of his tribe," scoffed Togodumnus. "Let Verica amuse himself with worthless titles—mere trinkets."

"I think not," said Adminius. "To have the power of Rome behind you is not a mere trinket." He handed the coin back to Maglocunos.

"Adminius is right," said his father. "We cannot neglect this connection—much evil could come from it, unless we are equally alert to what Rome might or might not do.'' Cunobelinus turned to his youngest son. ''You would like to get to know Rome better, would you not?''

''If it will serve us,'' came the reply.

''It always serves to know your enemy well.''

Cunobelinus told Adminius that he would be sent to Rome as the ambassador of the Catuvellauni, to speak with the new Caesar and arrange for the treaty to be renewed on terms mutually acceptable. ''In these uneasy times,'' he told his sons and Fen Fire, ''with potential dangers on all sides, it is the best course.'' Already he appeared pale and weary, though he had not been talking for long. The old vigor was leaving him, and Fen Fire noticed that day how his cheeks sagged, his face was drawn, and his eyes had lost their lustre. He gave the others their tasks in a slow, measured voice. Togodumnus was to go north to deal with the problem of Subidasto—a show of force along that border should be enough, he thought. And Caratacus—he knew the western borderlands better than any man, having spent much time there and beyond, across the Hafren, so the king told him to answer the challenge of Boduocos, king of the Dobunni. To Maglocunos he gave the task of going south, to the land of Verica, to demonstrate that though the king was old and weak his kingdom remained strong and vigorous. Each had been given a congenial task, but no one was more delighted than Adminius was with his. For a long time, he had been a trouble to the king; his youth was spent in brooding, his wits wasted in devising wily schemes and foolish tricks to out-fox his brothers or make Fen Fire angry. When she had become a priestess of Andraste at the age of seventeen, Adminius had followed her to the sacred island of the goddess in a remote lake among the fens, on which no man is allowed to set foot. Under cover of fog, Adminius in a small boat with a few companions as rascally as himself, made their way around the island, searching for a place to come ashore, careless of the sacrilege, determined to spy upon the rites and rituals reserved for the goddess' devotees. Fortunately, they lost their way in the fog, circled the island three or four times, and caused such a splashing that the women were warned and drove them off. The profanity was not committed and, no thanks to themselves, they were spared a terrible punishment. But Adminius' disrespectfulness alarmed his father. "There is more backbone in the white of a watery egg," the king raged when he discovered his son's attempted insult. "To sneak and pry under cover of fog—that is not the act of a man!" Adminius, however, was contrite, while secretly mocking the old king's concerns for such taboos and traditions which he thought crusty and foolish. By sending him on a mission to Caligula, his father was giving him a chance to redeem himself and at the same time direct his scheming energies to more purpose. The king also hoped that the importance of the mission with which he was entrusted would enhance the young man's prestige, so that he would regard himself in a better light and be less prone to moody discontent and mockery.

As the sons were about to take leave of their father, having received their various missions, Fen Fire stood before him, her arms folded on her bosom. He knew what she wanted. She had no need to ask. "Ah, young woman like a flame," he sighed. "You are eager to leave me I see."

"Only so that through some deed I might add to your glory," she answered.

"My glory—I glory in your tender presence. That is enough for me. But I cannot deny you what you want: it is your heritage."

"Then I will go with Caratacus," she said, turning to the chief. "As your charioteer—I am as strong and skilled with the reins as any man."

"I do not doubt it," Caratacus answered. "I could have no finer companion at my side in battle."

"It is done so," she said with delight, giving the old king a hug; though she would be a warrior, she had not yet lost her girlish eagerness.

Next morning, around her wrists she twined the braided leather reins of Caratacus' war chariot, and pulled them taut against the tug of the quick-striding ponies. Cunobelinus was helped to the viewing stand in the meadow to see the battle hosts depart. When he saw Fen Fire ride out at Caratacus' side, he felt a chill take hold of him. Death had laid its hand on him, a brief touch, a hint of what was to come. But it was just as well—for he was an old man, and now he felt like a lonely one. . . .

Caratacus with Fen Fire at his side journeyed west and met the challenge of King Boduocos on the battlefield. And Fen Fire claimed her first trophy.

The fallen warrior lay on his face in the short grass, amid the buttercups and the poppies. He did not move. The only sound he made was a gurgle, a long rattle deep in the throat, and then there was silence. His arms were akimbo. In one hand, he still clutched the sword with which he would have split her in two when he charged at her aroused and bull-like in his battle fury. His broad, powerfully muscled back, his taut lean buttocks, his sinewy thighs lay naked under the sun; he'd gone to battle wearing only his shield and high-crested helmet that her blow had sundered. With a shove of her foot, she heaved him over onto his back. She stood astride him with her sword pointed at his throat—but he was dead, that was clear. His handsome well-groomed moustache was full of bits of grass, his eyes were coated in blood and splattered brain which had oozed from the deep wound she delivered. His lips were drawn back in a weird grimace of pain. On his chest, broad and shaved, was a scar, long and jagged, but no other mark. He was no longer the bull of the herd. A maiden, she had never felt a man's grip of desire; she had drawn blood before she saw her own flow, she had pierced before she herself was pierced, taken a man's life before any man had inflicted the wound that marked the death of her virgin self.

Boduocos, defeated in battle, submitted to Caratacus, and Fen Fire did what she promised the king she would do—bring greater glory to his household and his tribe. From the north, Togodumnus returned with the prospect that war between the Iceni and the Catuvellauni would be averted; Subidasto, the troublemaker, had been finally forced out by his father Prasutagus and his supporters brought to heel. To herald the new relationship, the Iceni king wanted the two peoples to join together for the games at the Feast of Lugus, and instead of spending their strength and spilling their blood in war, conserve it for the pleasures and challenges of the chariot-feats, the javelin contest, the wrestling match, the foot race. Cunobelinus agreed readily, though he knew he would not be there to witness the contests. Maglocunos came back from the kingdom of the Atrebates with word that Verica had agreed to pay tribute to Camoludunum as well as to Rome. Cunobelinus greeted all this with satisfaction.

"I can die in peace now," he told them, "without the specter of war to blight my last days, knowing that the crows have been scattered that would have fed off the kingdom as if it were a corpse, like I am soon to be." His chest heaved slowly, as he caught his breath. "We need but one to confirm that all is well." Of Adminius, however, there was no word.

As Cunobelinus lay ill and growing weaker, his youngest son was walking wide-eyed around the streets of the city of the Caesars, a crowd of curiosity-seekers following behind him.

In those, the early days of the rein of Caius Caesar, known to all as Caligula, a tremendous feeling of optimism filled the city. The young Caesar banished the gloom that had hung over the capital during the long reign of his great-uncle Tiberius, who loathed the city from afar and made its streets run red with the blood of all whom he suspected of harboring any resentment against him.

It was as if a lethal fog had suddenly lifted. The city was in a festive mood. Caligula's reign was no more than a year old, but already he had embellished the city's beauty to a far greater extent than Tiberius had done in twenty-three years. Among his first and most important acts, he completed the Temple of Augustus in honor of his ancestor, and finally brought to a finish the work on the magnificent Theater of Pompey—work that had lain neglected for many years. The citizens of the capital could be forgiven for seeing in these generous acts the portent of a reign that would be happy and free from the terrors that had stalked them during Tiberius' decline.

Thus they discounted the young Caesar's unprepossessing appearance as having no bearing on his true nature. He was already balding, with strange sunken eyes, a pallid complexion, and a body shape that was gangling and awkward. But, the people said, what matter if he is not as handsome as his father Germanicus—a man's nature is shown in his acts, not his appearance. Whatever was glimpsed of the emperor's true spirit, haunted as it was by forces more sinister than any that had tormented his predecessor, was for the time being easily ignored.

Caligula, after having received Cunobelinus' son royally, gave him a guide and an escort to conduct him on the tour usually afforded to visiting dignitaries. The first stop was the Theater of Pompey, which lay on the plain between the Capitol Hill and the River Tiber. As Adminius stood gawking at the massive front of the first stone-built theater ever constructed in Rome, the guide droned on while an interpreter followed him.

"This is the largest as well as the first stone theater in Rome . . . stage over three hundred feet long . . . auditorium nearly five hundred feet . . . room enough for fifteen thousand spectators to fit in comfortably . . . the main portico has one hundred columns and is decorated with some of the finest wall paintings in the world, recently renovated by the emperor at great cost." They soon found themselves in front of the marble statue of Pompey himself, which Adminius learned was eleven feet high. "It is at the foot of this statue that Julius Caesar fell after being stabbed twenty-three times by the conspirators who numbered sixty." Adminius examined the statue with some care, for it seemed to be sprinkled with blood. "People will tell you it is Caesar's blood still clinging there, because they say the marks of betrayal can never be erased or some such fanciful notion," the guide said with a skeptical smile. "Let me dispel that illusion. The red spots do not come from the blood of Caesar, as is commonly claimed by the ignorant and credulous, but from the iron pyrites which are common in all Greek marble excepting that of Paros."

Soon, Adminius' head was swimming from what he had seen, and from the numbers that came spilling from the guide's mouth measuring the height, width and breadth of what seemed like nearly every building in the city.

There followed banquets, circus games, and a trip to a lake near Rome where a mock naval battle was staged with great pomp and splendor—every ship had a different colored sail, and each was so vivid as to be almost blinding in the bright sunlight. The Romans destroyed more vessels for the sake of a show than existed in the entire fleet of a tribal king in Britain!

With such power, anything was possible. Wide-eyed though he was, Adminius realized that Caligula was being especially attentive to him. Clearly, given the might at Rome's disposal, it could not be because the new Caesar was anxious to ensure continued good relations with the Catuvellauni and see the treaty confirmed. Why go to such trouble when it was obvious that Cunobelinus needed the treaty more than Caesar did? There could only be one answer: Caesar was anxious to impress Adminius in order to win him for some purpose. Having discerned that, it merely remained to determine what the purpose was.

Caligula, who loved to shroud everything in mystery, was at first not forthcoming, preferring to hint and tease. But one evening, shortly before Adminius was expecting the treaty to be signed, his host turned their conversation in an interesting direction. "This treaty you have come to discuss is really an old agreement made by old men—a rather paltry piece of paper meant to help them sleep contentedly in their beds at night. Must we inherit their fears and anxieties along with everything else? Must their habits become our customs?"

"Truly, we are hedged in by many customs that were best left to die with those who devised them," Caesar's guest answered.

"Some die hard, over a long time. Alas—our lives are too short to endure their slow wasting away. Reason demands more determined action." Caligula paused a moment. "What will become of you when your father dies?" he asked.

"The king's inheritance will be divided among the sons. I will get a portion of the kingdom."

"A portion?" Caligula laughed. "I have heard of Caratacus and Togodumnus and Maglocunos—their reputations are well-known to me. Their ambitions have been noted—clearly they care not upon whom they trample. We have many friends in Britain who keep us closely informed of all developments. Pardon me for being frank with you, but your brothers are overbearing and greedy. We have cause to regard them as a threat to peace."

"I am aware of their faults."

"I suspect charity is not one of their virtues."

"I do not need their charity. I will claim my inheritance as a right."

"Your inheritance—that is, your portion." Caligula almost spat out the word as if it were a worm. "How does a man of true ambition define what his portion is?"

"It is that which he has the power to take," Adminius replied. Caligula nodded.

"Exactly. And what if he had the power to take all?"

"Then he would take it, of course."

Caligula smiled and rested his chin in his hand. "Did you know that my first name, Caius, was given to me because I am destined to follow in the footsteps of my ancestor, Caius Julius Caesar?"

"I have been told that there is a physical resemblance between you," Adminius replied. Caligula was flattered. "And I suspect that the resemblance goes beyond that." Adminius was probing, hoping Caligula would reveal himself. Caligula stirred his wine with his fingers, watching the eddies in the cup. "You are very alert. You have discerned it." He looked at the Briton. Adminius saw what Caesar was intending to do.

"Julius Caesar was the first Roman to set foot in Britain," Caligula said.

"And you are planning to follow him," Adminius added. The emperor smiled as if it was an already accomplished fact.

"And if you will agree to assist our efforts, you will soon be remembering talk of 'portions' as a bad dream from which real power has roused you. If all goes well, the kingship of the Catuvellauni might be yours."

Adminius drained his cupful of the strange-tasting

drink he had been slowly sipping, pretending to enjoy it. What could he lose? Even now his brothers might have begun dividing up the kingdom among themselves, and he knew he could expect no justice from them. He would be left like a beggar at their door. But with the power of Rome at his back . . .

"You would only be helping me to my rightful place," Adminius replied.

"I knew I had not misjudged you," Caesar told him, as the wine steward brought another flask of the emperor's favorite drink, one which he had concocted himself, made of pearls dissolved in wine. In a moment, a whole new vista opened up before Adminius' eyes—to be suddenly thrust in front of all others, no longer the despised youngest son, at the mercy of his brothers' whims. He would sit in judgment upon them—their fate would hang on his word. The spectacle of power which Caligula had presented to him was more intoxicating than any drink. However, Caligula's plans were only at an early stage. Indeed, they could hardly be called plans at all. They were based on the notion that the Britons themselves should call for his aid in resisting the tyranny of the Catuvellauni. Adminius was to recruit as many enemies of Cunobelinus as he could, with an unlimited supply of gold to fund him. When the time was ripe, he would inform Caligula. Caligula would march to Gaul and gather his fleet. Adminius would rise up, and send for his assistance. Caesar would sail, braving the whirlpools, sea monsters and other dangers the uncharted seas held, to come to the aid of the heroic fighters opposing the power of the Catuvellaunian king.

Though the plans were vague, the gold that Adminius brought back from Rome was real enough. But he found when he arrived on his native shore, the situation had changed, and the new circumstances did not sustain his earlier euphoria.

His father the king was dead. Togodumnus, Caratacus and Maglocunos had meanwhile dealt with all the threats to their security—the Dobunni were defeated, Prasutagus' son Subidasto had been forced to flee to exile at the court of Verica, who though cowed into paying tribute to the Catuvellauni had not yet given up hope of one day challenging them. It was at Calleva that Adminius secretly met Subidasto, and in Verica's company discussed their future resistance to his brothers and the role Rome would play. Adminius proudly displayed the Roman gold. Subidasto was impressed, never having seen such wealth.

Adminius' hopes revived somewhat after that meeting, and as he rode back to Camulodunum he began to entertain the kinds of dreams to which he had abandoned himself when in Rome.

It was high summer, and the Feast of Lugus was approaching. Plans were going ahead to arrange the games at which the Iceni king Prasutagus hoped to seal the new relationship with the Catuvellauni. The palace was a bustle. His three brothers practiced their chariot skills in the meadow, while Fen Fire raced and wrestled in preparation for the contest she would take part in against the women of the Iceni, as well as those from other tribes who would attend the feast and celebrations. Adminius had entered the javelin contest but was only halfhearted in his efforts to get ready for the match; he dreamed too much of what lay ahead, until one morning those dreams were disrupted suddenly and violently.

Just before dawn he was awakened rudely from his sleep by something sharp pressed against his neck. He opened his eyes. Around him stood his three brothers—each with a sword pointed at his throat. They told him to rise. Fen Fire was there also, supervising the warriors who were ransacking the chamber, opening his chests, pulling up the rugs, tearing down the draperies.

"She is looking for Roman gold," Caratacus said.

Adminius stared at them dumbfounded. "What gold?"

"His," said Togodumnus, pointing to a bust of Caligula that Adminius had brought back with him. With the flat of his sword Togodumnus smashed it to the ground.

"That was a gift from Caesar."

"Like the gold he gave you?" Maglocunos asked. Adminius' eyes followed Fen Fire anxiously. But she had searched the room with no result. She stood next to the mead barrel, uncertain where to look next.

"You dare accuse me of taking Roman gold," Adminius said, rousing himself.

"And much else," Togodumnus said. "You are plotting with Rome to bring Caesar to our shores."

Adminius laughed. "This is another fantasy."

"We do not think so," Maglocunos told him. Fen Fire ordered Adminius to get out of bed. He did so, urged at swordpoint. But the bedding was turned upside down to no avail. There was no trace of the gold. In frustration, she rapped her fist on the mead barrel. There was a hollow echo from inside. The barrel contained no mead.

"You have lost your thirst," she said as she picked it up and threw it to the ground, where it splintered, spilling out a stream of yellow gold across the floor.

"You have betrayed your family and your people," Togodumnus said.

"You fouled your father's name," asserted Caratacus.

"Death is too kind a fate," Maglocunos threatened.

"Let Cunodunum the Chief Druid determine that," said the oldest of the brothers.

Adminius' face showed no emotion. It was grey, and the eyes glassy. A kind of sneer played upon his lips. What could he say to them? He had seen the future. They had not. They knew only a way of life that was dying. He had embraced a new, living world that they did not even have the courage to recognize except as a threat.

A few days later they marched Adminius into the meadow before the palace to receive his punishment. A somber grey cloud drifted across the sky, passing in front of the sun, where it hung for a while like a stain upon the perfect disk. A great crowd had gathered, but their faces showed they took no pleasure in the spectacle they were there to watch. Adminius' crime brought shame upon the tribe. Their faces would wear the mask of shame until it was expiated.

Cunodunum waited on a bank of earth built in the middle of the meadow from where punishment would be pronounced upon the head of Adminius. Around him stood Cunobelinus' three other sons and Fen Fire. In one hand, the druid held an ash wand, and in the other, a cleft hazel stick, while Fen Fire clutched a broad-shafted javelin. A heavy, gloomy silence hung over everything, broken only by the wind stirring among the grass and the sound of marching feet as the guards brought Adminius to a spot directly below the platform. He hung his head and dared not look up to confront the gaze of the priest or his family, nor could he turn sideways, for the eyes of the people were upon him.

Cunodunum stepped forward and raised his ash wand high above his head. It quivered a little; the spirits of the gods were passing through it into the mind of the druid, who, his wisdom nourished on theirs, then saw with their eyes and spoke with their tongue. Then the druid spoke slowly, with great deliberation.

"You have raised your sword against your own blood, against your own people, and against the gods; the spirits of your ancestors, the voice of your dead father all cry out for vengeance. Their cry will not go unheard." He raised the forked hazel stick until it was directly over the head of Adminius. "You are expelled from your father's house for all time and will never again set foot across its threshold or that of any of his blood. More welcome a leper or a rabid dog than you! Should any of those who are the fruit of your father's seed defy this ban, they will be held as worthless as yourself and be driven out. You are expelled from this kingdom forever and from the soil of Britain. More welcome a viper or a plague than you! Should any who call themselves subjects or allies defy this ban, they will be held traitors like yourself and driven out. And should any who call themselves Britons aid you in any way, they will be declared enemies of the Catuvellauni and dealt with accordingly." The priest turned to Fen Fire. "Expel him!" he ordered.

She drove Adminius at the point of her spear across the meadow to the first gateway. A jeering crowd walked behind her, led by Cunodunum, their shame giving way quickly to anger, while Togodumnus, Caratacus and Maglocunos turned their backs on the banished one forever.

"None to give him food from the table, drink from the barrel or warmth from the hearth," they chanted. Others lined along the route threw mud and dirt at him while the women hissed and spat. They reached out to scratch and tear at him as he staggered past. Many averted their faces and could not bear to look on that of a traitor. He was driven through the gateway and onwards, stumbling and falling, until he came to the last gateway in the outermost wall where a horse was waiting for him. By this time, Adminius was coated in filth, bruised and cut, looking like a beggar of the most abject kind. Slowly, painfully, he mounted the horse. He turned to Fen Fire. A bitter smile broke through his grime-encrusted face.

"You poisoned my brothers against me. You usurped my place in my family. You drove me to do what I did. And now you drive me from my rightful home. But fear not—I go into the arms of true friends, more powerful than you or those plunderers who call themselves my brothers can imagine. And they will help me to return to claim what is mine!" Fen Fire did not grace his outburst with an answer—for her, he no longer existed. She struck the haunches of the horse with the shaft of her spear. It bolted away, carrying the outcast from their sight.

Adminius' departure did not dispel the gloom that hung over the palace. The death of the old king had already plunged the entire kingdom into mourning. The treachery of his youngest son added a sense of shame to that grief.

As the king lay dying, he had often spoken of Adminius, and wished that he were present. "When he returns," Cunobelinus said on the night he died, "tell him I do not think bitterly of him. He is my son. Take care to see he is treated fairly." His eyes only dimly saw the outlines of those he loved gathered around the vast bed, and the wavering blurs of the torch flames. The darkness was closing in. The king could not see their tears, but he felt each tear-stained face pressed against his own as one by one his family came and kissed him for the last time. And with his last breath he said: "Remember—stay together—abhor division. Keep your gentleness for women and the little children that creep about the floor; respect men of learning and the makers of poems. And do not take the devotion of the common people for granted."

A powerful draught blew through the palace, making

the flames in the central hearth roar upwards. Fen Fire ran to the fireplace and turned her face towards the stars. Sparks in clusters went spinning into the black sky. All but one was quenched. It rose far above the others until it seemed like a star.

All who were gathered there that night knew in their hearts they had witnessed more than the death of a man or a king. They had seen the turning of the great wheel, but as to whom it would raise up and whom grind down, they could not say.

PART 2

Chapter 5

The thickly wooded island cast a green shadow across the calm, clear waters around it. Gently, the waves lapped against the shady shoreline like caresses. It was an island of willows, which drooped their branches over the lake, an island of alders, which in turn stood as sentinels guarding the way to the sacred grove, and of huge oaks which formed a green canopied avenue leading to the very gates of the sanctuary ringed with earthen walls. Huge hares leapt and bounded from the underbrush; wild pigs went nosing through the grass; serpents coiled under stones, and enormous eels swam in swarms around its shores. The summer grass waved in the wind, and primroses, daisies and meadowsweet flowered everywhere in rich profusion.

A line of priestesses dressed in white linen tunics and bedecked with flowers and laurels was waiting to greet Fen Fire as she stepped off the little boat that brought her across the lake to the island. The expulsion of Adminius over a year before was still a vivid if gloomy memory; at that moment it was more so than ever. His brothers had spared Adminius' life only because their father, on his death bed, had made them swear to be merciful to his youngest son. He had fled to Rome where he continued to scheme against them. According to the reports they were able to receive, the only result of Adminius' continued vendetta had been a Roman expedition which ended in a spectacular and confused failure, with Caligula refusing at the very last moment to embark with his legions for Britain because of some childish fear. Yet, the continued danger from that quarter made it essential to establish a lasting peace with the Iceni to the north.

She had accepted the Iceni king's offer of marriage to ensure peace between his tribe and her own.

The rites of Andraste demanded that Fen Fire as a priestess spend the last days before her wedding on the sacred island. At the head of the line of priestesses waiting to welcome her stood a handsome woman, with hair as black as bog water hanging down her shoulders in a mass of thick curls. She was dressed in a hare's pelt wrapped around her waist; a necklace of small bones hung down to her naked breasts, and she wore little strings of bones around her wrists and ankles. Her skin was swarthy, her body taut and compact but well-rounded, with small, plump breasts and firm, lean thighs and arms. Nemain, the High Priestess who governed the most sacred sanctuary of Andraste, radiated with coiled strength. At the early summer games of Beltane and those of Lugus later in the season, no one could outrun her and she always took the first prize in the women's foot race.

"Woman like a flame," she said, her voice gentle and soothing, "the first milk from the ewe, the first bloom of spring, the first swan returning from the south in summer, is not more welcome to the goddess than your light step on the soil of her sanctuary." She took Fen Fire by the hand.

"I have come to the sanctuary as the goddess demands, bringing only myself. I am my only offering."

"Her claims precede all others, whether of kings or of princes," Nemain replied. "And no offering could be more sweet! Tonight, others take the same path as you. So, we will celebrate around the Cauldron of Inspiration. There will be dancing, old bonds will be strengthened, our hearts will open under the warmth of Her gaze like flowers with the coming of day. The heart is deeper than any well, yet it can hide nothing from Her eyes. Remember, before Her joy and sorrow are two streams flowing into the same river."

The priestesses formed a procession, which Nemain led, Fen Fire following immediately behind her, down through the stately avenue of oaks towards the sanctuary. The crows and ravens perched upon the boughs cawed and croaked their welcome to Fen Fire as she walked over the sacred ground between the oak trees, the dappled sunlight flitting across her face. Occasional sunbeams streamed through the over-arching canopy and struck the leafy ground forming pools of gold in the green shade. The voices of women in song welled up from behind the sanctuary walls, and filled her heart with joy.

The sanctuary was bustling with activity. A group of women were singing as they thatched the temple roof in the warm sunshine, just as they had been doing when Fen Fire had returned to the island for the first time since her birth. The dry reeds for the thatching had been stored since the previous Samhain season. All around the temple, outside the little huts that ringed it, women sat weaving the reeds into thick strands, which they then carried up to those on the temple roof, who laid them over the layers of tough sods. Then, when the thatch was in place, other women stretched ropes around the whole roof to hold it down firmly. They sang as they worked, the fresh summer breeze blowing through their hair and gently grazing and molding their limbs.

Bonfires will burn
To mark summer's return
As winter's old crone
Flees from her throne.
We shed no tears
As Beltane nears!
But reeds we take
From the reedy lake,
Our roof to make,
Our roof to make.
With reeds we weave
From dawn to eve,
As warm a cover
As any lover.
The wind a murmur
To welcome summer
Blows over the lake
Whose reeds we take
Our roof to make,
Our roof to make.
Where treads no man

Woman with woman
In furrows of pleasure
Unveiling our treasure,
Among us alone,
We sigh and we moan;
Then dusk dims the lake.
Sleep the duck and the drake
Until the daybreak,
Until the daybreak.

The dry reeds shone like gold in the sunlight, as its glow reflected on the women's thighs and breasts and faces. Like Nemain they wore pelts of rabbit or hare's skin, with ornaments of small white bones gracing their arms and ankles, or hanging around their necks. Occasionally, one would stop and with a long, wide-eyed thatching needle made of bone, mend a strand of reeds that had come loose.

Meanwhile, in the open spaces between the huts, other women were practicing for the Beltane games. Some were racing, others wrestling; in one corner a straw target had been erected for the javelin throwers to improve their skills. It was here that Fen Fire had been taught her hundred wrestling holds. It was here too that she learned the use of the broadsword and the javelin. For the priestesses knew every battle-skill—the use of the sling, the bow and arrow, as well as the making of many different poisons, potions and charms. They were also expert with the dagger, and with one cut could end a man's life.

The priestesses knew not only the secrets of death, but those of birth. In a special, secluded area of the sanctuary, there stood a ring of larger huts, from which could be heard the cries of women in labor. Many of the goddess' devotees wished their daughters to be born at the sanctuary and would travel great distances in order to give birth there. The goddess awarded strength, courage and beauty to those born near her temple, and her priestesses were expert at aiding mothers to ease their birth pangs. In return, the mothers dedicated their girl children to the service of the goddess, so that every three years they must make a journey to the island with a gift for

Her temple. It was a great honor to be chosen as a priestess to serve at Her shrine, and since only those girls born on the island could be so chosen, many women who were anxious for their daughters to serve there came from all over to have their babies in the shadow of the temple.

All males were forbidden to set foot on the island. If the child was a boy, he was not allowed to touch its sacred soil, and his mother had to vow to come herself every other year with a gift for the goddess. But the boys as well as the girls were favored with Her gifts. For the male with his destructive principles serves the goddess also, since She rules life's end as well as its beginning.

In one of the huts Fen Fire was born on a black and turbulent night when a storm was raging outside, and the wind lashed the lake against the shores so that it seemed at times as if the water would cover it. The cries of her mother were lost in the hollow howling of the wind; she had lived only long enough to see the fine crop of flaming red hair on her baby's head and to give her the name Fen Fire. In the hands of the priestesses the child was cared for, bathed and cleaned. And once more, before her wedding, into their hands Fen Fire must consign herself.

All work ceased when she entered the sanctuary. The women scrambled down the ladders from the temple roof and abandoned their games to swarm around her. All knew her as the descendent of Red Shaft, the High Priestess who had brought back the three-horned bull from the Shadow Land. She herself was famed among them for her prowess with the javelin, her mastery of the chariot, her feats on the wrestling pitch and on the battlefield where she had already taken her first trophy. The word of her coming marriage had spread quickly, and such a momentous joining of two great kingdoms was a cause of excited conversation among them.

They had prepared a great bronze cauldron of hot water for Fen Fire with every kind of scented soap. The women flocked around her, undressed her quickly, and plunged her into the water where they washed her, talking excitedly all the time about the coming wedding and the Beltane celebrations—its contests, and its games. And always there was the constant buzz of speculation around the topic of the lover they might find in the woods as May Day dawned. On that occasion every woman and every man took whom he or she pleased, without blame or shame; and if a child came from their coupling, it was recognized and reared in the woman's family, or if she was married, by her husband as one of his own. Like bees around a flower rich with nectar, they came back to the topic again and again.

"But this is not a matter that needs concern you this season," said Nemain, having returned to see if Fen Fire was ready to go to the temple. Fen Fire looked at her.

"True. This Beltane will be reserved for my husband."

"You are fortunate!" the other priestesses exclaimed with one voice. "For though it is fine to couple with some handsome youth if only for a night, to have a man like Prasutagus beside you night after night . . . !" One after another, they began to praise the king—his renown as a charioteer, his yellow hair (which was a mark of beauty among them), his generosity and his manly vigor which kept five wives satisfied and fruitful.

Fen Fire lay back in the bath, listening, smiling occasionally, as the mud and gore of the boar hunt, which had become caked over the days, was melted and scrubbed away from her white skin.

"You change as suddenly as the May Tree blossoms," said Nemain, when she saw the transformation. One spot of dirt remained on Fen Fire's breast. With one light stroke of the hand, Nemain swept it off, into the water. "Prasutagus is indeed among the most fortunate of men."

"And I of women," Fen Fire replied quietly.

The temple of Andraste stood in the center of the sanctuary, a round thatched building constructed of wood supported by nine pillars of alder. Massive doors of oak guarded the entrance; on either side of them little niches had been carved into the walls in which were piled the gleaming white skulls of men. The doors opened into a little chamber. Here the Cauldron of Inspiration was kept. Nine chalked white priestesses, as pale as lepers, attended it always and jealousy guarded its potent mixture of barley, acorns, honey, ivy, hellebore and laurel. On this evening, as Fen Fire prepared to go before the goddess, its fumes rose up, filling the chamber and the inner sanctuary of the temple beyond it.

There, the great statue of Andraste loomed above everything around it, in a crouching stance like a woman about to give birth; between her bent thighs there was a profusion of gold and silver offerings. Golden torcs, bejewelled cups, finely wrought bowls of silver, and every other imaginable object of value, seemed to stream from the gaping womb mouth which opened like a many-petalled flower, the very heart of tenderness and softness, all giving, just as the blank almond-shaped eyes of the goddess which stared into the darkness above were the very vision of doom, implacable and unforgiving. Two great black rooks were perched on either shoulder, croaking to each other as if in secret conversation. Occasionally, one or other of them would fly off, perhaps to perch on the skull of one of the three skewered skeletons which stood in a triangle around the statue. They hung where they were pinned, years before, the stakes thrust lengthwise through their bodies, the points exiting at the mouths—now only bony, broken jaws which hung open as if in a last but perpetual scream of pain. This was all that remained of the only men ever to violate the sacred ground of the island sanctuary. They were strangers who came from the empire of the Romans and whose ship had been blown off course by a tremendous storm. They were the only survivors when the ship sank in a bay a few days' journey from here. Somehow, they stumbled upon the island and then thought to plunder it of its treasures, the offerings left by untold generations of women. Instead, their crime of sacrilege was punished: no pain, no humiliation known to man was spared them, so that when death came it was the most welcome of gifts.

On this day, however, thoughts of doom were far from mind. The statue of the goddess was garlanded with flowers. A huge string of flowers hung around her neck; others were looped around her legs and arms. Flowers lay in heaps, strewn here and there over the floor of the inner sanctuary. They perfumed the air with their scent, which now mingled with the heady fumes wafting in from the first chamber where the cauldron's brew was being prepared.

Wrapped in a white linen mantle, Fen Fire came to the temple with a festive crowd of women linked arm in arm following behind her. Some threw flowers, others were singing, while little groups broke away to twirl and dance. As the declining sun sent its slanting shadows across the flower-strewn ground, she entered the temple escorted by priestesses, each one of whom carried an ash branch from the tree of birth, an acorn from the tree of life and a willow reed from the tree of death—for the goddess governs all three.

In the first chamber of the temple, where the cauldron bubbled, there was dug next to it a long but shallow pit in the ground full of white chalk dust. Nemain entered the pit first and lay down naked, while several priestesses gently dusted her body with the chalk. When they were finished, she left and made room for Fen Fire. The women stripped off her mantle and she lay down in the pit. First, they turned her on her belly and sprinkled the dust across her back, over her buttocks and down the backs of her thighs. Nemain knelt down beside them, helping them to tenderly spread the sprinkled dust over Fen Fire's white skin, making it leper-white, the color most pleasing to the goddess. Fen Fire rolled over, and the women began to dust her face, neck and shoulders, her breasts, her firm flat belly, and her thighs. She breathed deeply the sweet fumes that filled the little chamber, and her body felt buoyant. The women gently massaged the chalk dust into her skin with a touch that was tender but never shy or hesitant, for none holds any secret that their sisters do not share. They too breathed in the cauldron's heady fumes, slowly, rhythmically as they rubbed back and forth Fen Fire's breasts and thighs, crevice, belly and shoulders. With their every stroke, her body seemed to grow lighter, until she felt as if she was afloat. Completely whitened, she rose. Each of the priestesses who was to be wed, and who was to take part in the ritual with Nemain, was whitened in turn and then went to the cauldron, where the High Priestess handed her a cup full of the potent brew. As each raised the cup to her lips, Nemain sprinkled a fistful of poppy seeds into it, chanting:

Potent is the poppy flower
Whose seeds release their secret power
Long hidden in its petalled heart:
And now flows through our every part.

The cup was passed around again. Fen Fire took it from Nemain. She looked down. The cup seemed bottomless and the mash swirled giddily past her eyes, like a great whirlpool. She took one more sip and passed it to the other priestesses, each of whom sipped but once more also. The doors of the temple's inner sanctuary were opened, letting in a shaft of evening sunlight. The treasures between the thighs of the goddess glittered and sparkled, and the two great rooks flew excitedly into the dark spaces of the high-domed roof, flapping and croaking. The priestesses heard only the call of the goddess.

They laughed aloud, and cried, their bodies trembling and shaking. They ran into the inner chamber where on the floor had been laid soft cushions and pillows stuffed with fern and twigs from the topmost branches of the birch tree. A group of women with drums under their arms and pipes between their lips assembled at the entrance to the inner sanctuary and began to play a merry air, which none can resist without wanting to abandon themselves to the dance. All at once, the very temple seemed to pulsate as the music welled up as blithe and entrancing as fairy music from the mounds. Nemain took Fen Fire's hand, then she linked hands with the other brides until they formed a circle. Wild was the dance they did around the great statue, their chalk-white shapes like ghosts in the dim light of the temple, spinning and turning, each woman, hips swaying, lips parted, with Nemain leading them, tossing her dark hair back, her face lifted up towards the eyes of the goddess.

The dance has begun
O Swan-breasted One.

You sway and you turn
To make desire burn,
Woman like a flame
You dance in my name,
Naked and white,
Your step a delight.
And so you will tread
When you go to his bed
Who borrows my treasure,
A gift without measure.

Soon, exhausted, they fell on their knees or went tumbling on to the pillows and cushions. Now Fen Fire's limbs felt heavy like boughs overburdened with summer's fruits; they weighed her down with their delicious weight, and she sank softly, sobbing sometimes, sometimes laughing, into a pillow of ferns. The dim temple spun around her and the eyes of the goddess seemed to glow faintly. She breathed deeply, and drew in more of the cauldron's transforming fumes which hung in the air like a faint milky-colored mist. She rolled her head and arched her neck backwards. When she closed her eyes, she saw the whirlpools of the cauldron sweeping around, and at the center of the whirlpool a face: that of the youth she knew only as Sun Fragment. Nemain took the first priestess-bride by the hand and led her to a pillow in front of the great statue. Both women knelt down facing the goddess, Nemain behind the priestess; she put her hands over the other woman's eyes and pressed them gently shut. The others, including Fen Fire, gathered around them.

"Never was a woman wed, but had a secret sorrow. Look into the well which is your heart and tell us what you see—what you have concealed from all until now," Nemain said as she ran her fingers through the woman's hair and found the knot, which she began slowly to undo. As her hair fell down over her shoulders, the woman answered in a slow, hushed voice.

"I see Vedenos."

"What was he to you?"

"He was a warrior, a piercing javelin, but it was a

wound of pleasure he gave." The woman laughed and shook her head, letting her hair spread out. "He came to me awash in the blood of a slain stag. In the woods at twilight he took me, and so my virgin's blood was mixed with that of the stag; our blood flowed as one."

The temple's walls vanished. She was in the woods again. Vedenos was beside her, his hands running over her shoulders, stroking her breasts. "Then death had not claimed you from me," she sighed, as he enfolded her again. She sank under his desire, and felt the cool leaves of the forest floor against her back.

Nemain took another of her priestesses by the hand and led her to the center of the circle of women. She knelt down in front of the goddess, with Nemain behind her. When the High Priestess had closed the woman's eyes, like the first she told the secret of her heart, sobbing all the while.

"Only a lurking shadow at first, he was my Beltane companion," she said, "a companion of one night only." He stood before her again, powerful, of coarse aspect. She shrank back, her face a mixture of fear and desire. But he reached through the darkness and with his strong grip took her by the arm. "Tonight," he said to her, "care not for your honor. You will mix shame with ecstasy." Her cries of pleasure were mixed with tears of sorrow and pain. And when she ceased, and lay shaking on the temple floor, Nemain was with another woman kneeling before her ready to reveal what was hidden in her heart.

". . . He was a man of wisdom . . . He knew me as a fisherman knows the lake where he fishes, all its deeps and mysteries, moods and movements, in storm and calm. Yet, he married another . . ."

". . . He was a bard, dark and bearded and tender with women as he was with words. Fame stole him away from me . . ."

". . . None could guide the chariot like him, but he went from me into the arms of death . . ."

And what each woman saw appeared before the eyes of the others. Seasons came and went, yet when the last of them spoke it seemed as if all had been told with the brevity of one breath. Then there were no more voices. The women's eyes were fixed on Fen Fire. Nemain took her by the hand and led her to the same place in the center of the circle of women from where the others had seen their visions and told what they saw. Fen Fire knelt on the pillow and faced the goddess as the High Priestess slowly undid her hair. It fell in a tumult of red over her chalk-white shoulders; Nemain let it flow through her long fingers as if she were sifting flour. Then, gently she placed her hands on Fen Fire's eyes, closing them.

"You do not need eyes to see into your heart," she said. "Look into that well and tell me what you see." Nemain's fingers pressed softly on Fen Fire's eyelids. Fen Fire felt dizzy, her head spun slowly around, and she began to rock back and forth.

"A vision of happiness that has now become a cause of sorrow," she moaned.

"Fear not, but speak."

Was it Nemain's voice she heard? It was far away, more like an echo from a distant valley than a voice. And when she herself spoke, it was as if she was sitting at the feet of someone else listening to a story that only she knew. . . .

She stood within a ring of low hills. The crest of each hill was a stack of dry sticks and wood ready for the bonfires which would soon be ablaze. It was the Feast of Beltane, almost exactly one year before. In the meadow behind her she could hear the cheers as the women's races came to an end. From another part of the meadow rang the shouts of the javelin-throwers. Young warriors rode by and saluted her; others sported with young women near the edge of the meadow where there was a fringe of trees, the beginning of the wood beyond which flowed a gushing stream with rock pools and waterfalls; some were hoping to impress the partner they had set their eyes on for the coupling which would follow the feast, while others as yet unsure of what the night might bring tried to cut a fine figure in front of all the women there. . . .

And on the crest of a hill a strange creature appeared, with a birdlike mask and arms stretched out and covered with foliage, twigs, and branches to look like wings. Yet, his nakedness showed him to be more man than bird. Soon, other men joined him, masked and similarly attired, standing between the unlit bonfires. "The firebird race is about to begin!" someone cried. All eyes turned to the crest of the hill. When all the birdmen were in place with their arms outstretched, stewards with blazing torches stepped up to each of them and simultaneously set fire to their wings. As the wings began to blaze, the birdmen sprang down the hillslope racing for the standing stone close to where Fen Fire was watching.

Their wings were streaming smoke, then crackling, as the flames spread through all the twigs and branches. As the birdmen ran, they streamed fire and smoke behind them. Like huge blazing firebirds they swooped down. Burning foliage scattered in their path, falling in flames to the ground, setting fire to the grass and leaving a trail of smoke and ashes. One threw himself to the grass and rolled over and over to put out the fire which was burning so quickly through his wings that it was scorching his skin. Men with buckets of water doused him until the fires were out. The others streamed onwards to the foot of the hill. By now one had raced away in front of the others. On lean but powerful thighs he ran towards the standing stones, arms outstretched, crackling and burning and billowing smoke. The spectators cried, unable to restrain themselves, as another fell, howling in pain, begging for the flames to be quenched. The leader ran towards her and in the direction of the stone, his arms like twin bonfires whose blazing flames almost blinded her. Through his bird mask he darted a glance at her suddenly, then he was gone, leaving only a plume of smoke swirling around her in his wake and a few flaming leaves and twigs that dropped to the grass. And within seconds he had reached his goal between the standing stones. The crowd cheered. Fen Fire cheered and shouted with them. As the crowd surged round him, he threw himself on the ground and began rolling over and over in the grass. Like a ball of fire he came tumbling towards her, as men ran behind him hurling water over the flames. By the time he came to rest at her feet he was a mass of black, smouldering twigs, leaves and sticks. He lay panting as black sooty streaks streamed from under his mask and down his cheeks. A few strands of his light brown hair, which she could see sticking out, were singed black. Through the mask his eyes twitched, red and sore from the smoke and ringed with black soot. He lay smouldering and smiling up at her—practically unscathed.

"A fragment of the sun has fallen from the sky," she said.

"To lie at your feet," he replied, staring up at her. His blue eyes were clear and bright as they shone out through the strange discoloring fumes that still streamed down his hidden face, over his lips and chin. His arms and legs were also black with soot and ash. He sprang to his feet just as the crowd came swarming around them. Before she could speak, they hoisted him on their shoulders and swept him away in a triumphal procession. As they carried him off, he turned to her, still smiling under his bird mask, and tore off a burnt stick from a charred wing.

"A feather from a fire bird, a fragment from a fragment," he cried out, throwing it to her as he disappeared with the crowd into the twilight. The twig landed at her feet, just where he himself had come to rest. She picked it up. She regarded the blackened thing curiously for a while, turning it over and over in her hand until it had left a track of ash on her palm.

That night, at the Beltane Eve Feast, she looked from table to table, each crowded with warriors and women, hoping she could see someone who resembled Sun Fragment; but it was a useless, frustrating task. What had she seen of him but his eyes, his soot-stained limbs, a few strands of his brown hair? Warriors called to her from across the hall, begging her attention; others staggered to her table where she sat with Togodumnus, Caratacus and Maglocunos, to brag of their triumphs. She scrutinized them all, and none had his clear piercing yet laughing gaze. Caratacus noticed she was restless.

"Your thoughts are on some young warrior." He smiled.

"A figment of my fancy, or a falling star, for he is nowhere to be seen," she answered sadly. Since it was considered bad luck for a woman to tell anyone of the man she desired as her lover for the Beltane revels, Fen Fire fell dumb and could say no more of where she had seen him or of what he had done. Doubtless, if she had, Caratacus would have been able to find him—or at least identify him.

"Do not fret. It is Beltane Eve, the gateway to the Other World lies open, and the heart's desires can take on flesh and bone," he replied. "Look around you. My finest warriors are here—men who speak with their swords on their thighs. He must be among them—for you would not choose a man of lesser stature."

She cast her eyes once more over the chaos of the Beltane feast. Caratacus spoke the truth. Among the assembled host, there were many men whom any woman would have been pleased to take on Beltane Eve. But that night, none of them pleased Fen Fire. She would join in the race to the woods, when the warriors took their women—none, however, would be able to match her for speed and agility and she would easily evade them. . . .

She raced across the meadow under a huge full moon whose beams turned the grass to silver and brightened the cloudless sky. All around her women were scampering in every direction, laughing and crying out as warriors on horseback swept around them. Many stumbled and fell, rolling in the grass, shaking with mirth and excitement mixed with a little fear. Others glanced anxiously behind them hoping that the warrior of their choice was in close pursuit. Fen Fire darted this way and that, sending the would-be suitors crashing into each other. Soon, she outstripped them all and reached the woods. Only for an instant did she pause to glance back across the meadow at the Beltane mayhem. But there was no sight of anyone resembling the youth on whom she'd set her heart. Though she had not seen his face, apart from his eyes, she felt she would recognize him again at once—if ever she were to see him. She bit her lower lip, wondering why he had abandoned the feast and celebrations so suddenly and so soon.

Even the woods at the meadow's edge, usually dark and forbidding at night, were no longer a black barrier:

the light of the moon was like a silver sword cutting a pathway through their shadows. She raced on, into the woods, along a well-trampled path. From behind her came the sound of charging hoofs; she looked round, but that brief bloom of hope faded at once. She saw nothing but the woodlands lit by the moon—a beauty that was lost to her because she could not share it. Then a woman laughed aloud. Within moments, the woods were throbbing with the laughter and cries of men and women mating. She ran on with a powerful compulsion, deeper and deeper into the woods that she knew so well since her childhood. Her feet crunched the dead leaves and carried her effortlessly forward, as if she were running along a trail of moonbeams. She sped past the trees and bushes, scattering unseen night animals in every direction. Soon, she had left behind the Beltane couples; their last faint cries faded away in the distance among the gulfs of shadow that lay around and beyond the moonlit path. From in front of her came the sound of the river rushing over the rocks. What a sound it made in the dead stillness of the night—like a great wind soughing through the woods!

What drove her to the water's edge she could not say: the urge was wordless. But only when she reached the riverbank did she feel a calm come over her. The compulsion to run left her. The river rushed beneath the bank, full of silver ripples and moonlit eddies. Further up, the water tumbling over the rocks caused it to froth and foam. There was a little overhanging cliff, down which the river plummeted, and in under the cliff edge, a cave or grotto that she knew. She pulled off her white tunic and plunged into the moonlit river. With a strong, steady stroke Fen Fire swam upstream until she reached the waterfall. The water poured down on her face and back as she swam under it and began to haul herself up the rock to the cave below the cliff. Inside, it was large enough for her to stand upright. The walls of the cave were of grey rock with white quartz crystals glistening here and there; patches of green moss clung to them, soft and furry and damp. She had made it a place secret to herself, which she occasionally shared with a girl friend who was especially close to her. Over time, she collected little piles of dried moss which she made into soft seats and pillows. She sat down on a seat of moss facing the waterfall, through which she could dimly see the bank where her white tunic lay crumpled in the moonlight.

Where water falls the world of dreams begins. The sound of water cascading is a sound that puts you deeply into thought, and sometimes deeper than thought can go. Had not Caratacus' bard Bran told her that when he needed inspiration for his verses he would come to the river's edge and sit for a while? And sometimes a thought would climb out of the water, and sometimes no thought at all—which was better; for a poet to write well it was often necessary for him to stop thinking, so that his mind would be filled with nothing but sounds and visions. He had spoken to her of the power of water, how the sound of the sea running up the estuary can foretell the death of kings, and how there was a well far away in the west owned by the moon in which lived the salmon of wisdom, and whoever drank from that well would be wise and possess the gift of foretelling. It was guarded by three old hags, who were jealous of its properties and would not share them with anyone. Once, when Bran was a little boy, he was out hunting and his hounds chased a deer near the well. The old hags came running out in a bad temper, their faces almost black with rage, screaming at him. One held an old cup, which she flung at Bran's head, hoping to scare him off. In the cup was a bit of well water, which splashed over his face. Several drops fell into his mouth. Thus, he told her, he grew wise enough to be a poet.

Often she came to this river to swim or fish or sport with her companions, and always the sounds of the waterfall lured her away from them to sit and think in the solitude of the little cave hidden behind the veil of falling water. No, it was not thinking, but dreaming—all the time seemed to stretch behind her and before her just as the river flowed towards her and away from her at one and the same time. She closed her eyes. How long had the water been falling thus? There was no sound so ageless. It had sounded so when she was a young girl, and the old king Cunobelinus told her that it had sounded so when the ancient kings who first came to the island of Britain settled this countryside and erected their settlements beyond these woods. And before them, when the Mound People lived upon the earth, it was here they would sport, for they loved water in all its forms—rivers and wells and ponds and lakes and seas. Surely, in those far-off times some fairy child had sat on this same rock and thought these thoughts, wondering under the waterfall at the great immensity of time? Deep in the woods, somewhere among the silver-topped trees, an owl hooted and then took wing; something had disturbed it. The heavy beat of its wings could be heard above the sound of the waterfall. She opened her eyes. The eyes of wolves glow in the dark like those of cats, and they howl at the moon when it is full. She looked and listened, but through the veil of water she could see no sign of any wolf on the riverbank. The bushes rustled again. Something was stirring that was not the wind. She went closer to the waterfall and peered through it in the hope of catching a glimpse of a boar or stag come to drink at the stream.

A man stepped from out of the shadows of the trees into the full light of the moon. He led a grey pony by the reins. He wore a bird mask on his face and his tall, lean form was covered by a loose, light cape thrown over his shoulders. It was he. He came to the edge of the river and stooped, picking up her discarded tunic. He crouched down and looked around him, while the pony drank its fill of water from the river. Perhaps he thought she had already been taken by another. When he stood up again it seemed as if he was going to turn and retreat back into the woods, perhaps unwilling to disturb a Beltane tryst. She was about to cry out to him when he turned and looked towards the waterfall. No words came from her mouth. The moon shone down upon the cave where Fen Fire stood, her figure a dim shape behind the watery veil. She knew he was looking directly at her, and yet she did not move or make any attempt to reveal herself more fully. What if he turned away, not knowing it was she? But she knew in her heart that he would recognize her though he could not see her plainly, just as she would recognize him behind any mask.

There was a splash. He was no longer on the river-bank. She stood still listening to the sound of the strong strokes that were bringing him closer to her.

First, she saw his hands gripping the rocks at the cave mouth—then the strange mask emerged through the water which cascaded down upon it. Fen Fire remained motionless as he hauled himself up into the cave. He stood erect in front of her, his clear blue eyes shining through the mask, the only thing that revealed the humanity of the hidden face.

His body was as hard and smooth as a well-polished tusk. Water ran down it forming little beads around his broad chest, beads that seemed to capture and carry off little drops of the silver moonlight. The water streamed down over his belly and his thighs, and her eyes followed its course to where his sickle-shaped shaft reared up. Fen Fire reached out as if about to take the bird mask from his face. Then she hesitated.

"Are you afraid?" he asked.

"Of what?"

"That you will be disappointed when you see my face, or that you will find that I am not the one whom you supposed me to be." Fen Fire smiled, and put her hands on his round, hard shoulders.

"I will show you how sure I am," she said. She planted her lips on his breast, and with her tongue caught a silver bead of water that hung there. Only then, when she had made it clear she would be his, did she reach up and pull the mask from his face.

His brown hair, singed black in places, flopped wet and sleek like an otter's around a face she had never seen before. The blue eyes were widely spaced beneath a high, rather austere brow; the nose was long and straight, the lips thin, surprisingly delicate; the chin firm and strong. Hungrily her eyes roved over every detail of the stranger's face, while her hands with equal eagerness relished the touch of his wet, glistening skin.

"Sun Fragment," she said, "you have partaken of two

elements in one day. You were fire and now you are water."

"And I will partake of three—for you are earth."

"The water has not quenched your fire."

"Only the earth can quench it."

"Must we make do with knowing each other only as earth and sun?"

"Is it not enough?" Who knows the earth better than the sun?"

"And if I have your child, what will I tell him of his father?"

"Why, that the sun begot him," the stranger replied.

They sank down on the layers of dry moss, which made a soft bed for her back where the moonlight quivered on the cave-floor. She looked through the cascading water at the shimmering pale globe peering in. And somewhere deep in the woods, a wolf was howling at the moon. . . .

For a long time Fen Fire lay at his side, looking at him as he slept. How complete he seemed! No trace of yearning in his soul as he lay there contented and fulfilled. This stranger had taken her at once, with hardly a word, with no inclination afterwards to do anything other than rest—even though he had filled her with such pleasure as she had never known before, creating a yearning which she now cherished.

She'd only ever been this close to a man before on the battlefield, brought together by the intimacy of violence and death. Now it seemed she had taken life from a man again—but through desire, not death. And what peace she brought to him—almost the peace of death indeed! She wondered at him so quiet, while she stirred restlessly by his side, perplexed, curious, anxious to know whether on waking he would want her again. She could contain herself no longer; gently she stroked him. He opened his eyes and sat up.

"How long have I slept?" he asked, somewhat abruptly.

"Into the beginning of another summer."

He sprang to his feet. "I must go."

"Go where?" she asked. She could not conceal her disappointment.

"The sun will soon rise, and I have a long journey ahead of me."

"And what is so important about this journey that you must leave at once? The Beltane games resume today—and the feasting is not yet—" She paused. Perhaps Beltane Eve was a passing dream after all, and all its passions as elusive as a half-remembered dream. Her manner became more aloof. In the dim cave, seeing her red hair cascading around her grave face and grave grey eyes, he could not move. The call of the world beyond the waterfall grew faint until it could be heard not at all. He turned and fell on his knees beside her.

"I do not wish to break this spell," he said, stroking her hair, kissing her neck.

Her eyes gleamed. Never before had she felt such a yearning. When the young women talked about desire, sometimes learnedly—quoting the bards and the priests—sometimes wonderingly, in a kind of daydream shared with the others, they talked about it as if it were a form of hunger that must be satisfied. But they were wrong—for what kind of hunger was it that grew worse with feeding? It was not like a hunger at all, but like a fire that when fed with fuel grows hotter and more fierce. Her aloofness was no defense against such feelings, no more than a late spring frost can resist the rising sun. She threw her arms around his neck. She bit and licked him, kissed and caressed him—to taste, to touch, to smell him, until there was not a finger's width of his body that she did not know. The coolness of the mossy floor pressed against her breasts and her cheek; he had turned her on her belly, and was gently stroking her white haunches, which were stained green with moss; at once, she felt the earth's coolness and the sun's heat! Heat and coolness, passion and restraint, abandon and control—what a wonderful configuration desire makes of them all.

The sun had reached the treetops on the distant hills, and the whole wood was alive with birds; the first beams of day streamed through the waterfall and lay in wavy lines along the floor of the cave where the once-neat layers of moss were now strewn this way and that. The world seemed to take a deep breath of fresh summer air, finding itself free from the confining fogs and dark mornings and cold nights of the winter season.

"I give my word," he said, pausing at the cascade that had hid them through the dim hours of night and dawn. "I will return." Fen Fire lay, chewing a piece of moss, wishing that Beltane Eve had lasted a whole season and not just one night.

"I do not know where you came from, and I do not know where you are going," she said quietly. "How do I know that I will ever see you again?"

"I will show you," he replied. "Come." Taking her hand, he brought her to the little ridge at the entrance to the cave where the water splashed. "I propose a contest. A swimming race to the bank." She looked at him, her brows wrinkled slightly with perplexity.

"That will only guarantee that I will leave you behind even sooner than I had intended," she replied, "for I am a strong swimmer." He shook his head.

"Whoever wins will have the right to spend a night with the other whenever he or she demands it, and the loser cannot refuse. When you are the prize I will not be beaten, and you can be certain I will come back to claim it. No warrior if he values his honor can do otherwise."

"Prepare to feel the kick of a woman's heels," she told him.

They plunged through the waterfall and into the river. At first, her pride carried her ahead of him and she struck out with a strong stroke. But had she not won enough contests in wrestling, in running, in javelin throwing? And this was a contest different from the others—only a man was fit to win this race, for it was he who had to demonstrate determination and desire, without which all his affirmations and all her hopes would come to nothing. Her victory would be a hollow one indeed if it allowed him to escape the responsibility which by nature was his, not hers. As she was worrying this matter, he swam by her and before long all she could see was his heels. Immediately, she surged after him—forgetting her debate. But her legs would not cooperate. They still suffered from the effects of the Beltane contests, particularly the wrestling match, during which her opponent had stretched and twisted them before Fen Fire rallied to force her submission. This time, however, her rally came too late. He was on the riverbank waiting for her. He reached out his hand to help her up.

She sat on the bank rubbing her legs. He bent down and began massaging them slowly, sensuously.

"You had an ally in that woman I fought yesterday." She lay back as his fingers soothed away the ache. "She was a fierce one—but I managed to break her grip."

"Had it been me, you would not have slipped from my hands so easily," he said.

"The grip of desire is stronger than any. No woman willingly relinquishes it. It is the only grip to which I will yield. For a woman to surrender to desire is no defeat. It has brought a victory sweeter than any I have ever enjoyed."

"But for now I must surrender you," he said. "Only to reclaim you as soon as my task permits." But what the task was he would not say; that he kept a mystery.

He mounted the grey pony that was grazing quietly nearby. She turned away suddenly and faced the river. She did not want to look as he rode off; still, she could hear the beat of the hooves on the woodland floor's carpet of dead leaves. The summer faded and dwindled. The dark season came and the woods were bare. The river ran cold and chill over the bare rocks. The cave lay empty and cold. The north wind brought its black frost. And she did not see his bright face again. . . .

"He knew me like no other, yet I know him not; that is my grief," said Fen Fire. How many cycles of the moon had passed since then? Not many, perhaps, by most measures. But it was the distance between her girlhood and her womanhood. Now, she was to be a wife, and she would bring with her this memory at once a source of joy and grief to her. She looked up at the blank eyes of the goddess set above the vast imperturbable face. The rooks croaked in the darkness of their domed realm. Moments later, a drumbeat began to throb through the temple. A pale figure appeared before Fen Fire's eyes, as if coming forth from out of the womb-mouth of the goddess; she carried something raised aloft and covered in a cape made of black feathers which glistened in the dim torchlight. It was Nemain.

"He Who Nourishes, the Hooded One," the priestesses chanted together. The High Priestess set it down and, taking each other by the hand, the women began to circle slowly around it.

"He sows in the furrow," said Nemain.

"He has banished barrenness from our wombs," replied a priestess.

"He has brought the fruitfulness of summer," said another.

"He is the seed of life," a third intoned.

"He is the healer of every wound," said Fen Fire.

Nemain pulled off the feathered cape. The third horn of the sacred bull, covered in softest stitched deer's skin, stood before them. A woman entered with a branch of hawthorn, another came with a bunch of berries from the rowan tree, to lay them at the base of the Hooded One. And once more, the air rippled with the sound of pipes; from the sanctuary outside came the smell of oak wood burning in the bonfires all around and the sounds of women singing and dancing together. The season of light was approaching. They had shared their sorrows with the goddess. A grief shared is a burden made lighter. Now it was time to celebrate the joyous unions to come. Fen Fire's spirit soared upwards. She breathed in the sweet fumes of the burning wood, the still-lingering smells from the cauldron's brew; the Hooded One would heal all and remove the last remaining ache. They worshipped him. Their joy was consummated. The void was filled.

Around the temple, the other women danced with the glow of the bonfire's flames on their faces and limbs. Above them, the sky was sown rich with stars—seeds of brightness—scattered by the hand of a planter profligate with light.

Chapter 6

A gull wheeled over the white chalk cliffs, swerving, lifting and dipping in the powerful wind that blew off the sea. The waves crashed against the cliff base, rattling the smooth, round pebbles, sending spray high up to be caught by the wind and swept inland. So strong were the gusts that the spray was sent splattering against the thatch of the round huts huddled together behind a flimsy stockade in a narrow valley not far from where the high cliffs overlooked the turbulent and dangerous channel separating Britain and Gaul.

The wings of the swerving gull caught the last gleams of the setting sun as it plunged behind the distant, rolling hills to the west. As night came on, the doors of the peasants' huts were shut fast against the dark. On the coast not far away, beneath the village, a fishing boat entered the shelter of a quiet cove, and quickly dropped anchor. A caped and hooded figure clambered over the side and splashed into the shallow water to begin wading the short distance to the shore. Then, swiftly, like one who knew his route by heart, he found a pathway, narrow and stony, but well-trodden by shepherds and returning fishermen alike. It wound up from the shore, threading its way between white projecting rocks to the grassy hinterland, and thence to the outskirts of the huddle of huts—an obscure village in a lonely corner of the Kingdom of the Atrebates, ruled by Verica, on whom the Romans had bestowed the title "Rex" in recognition of his friendship towards them.

A solitary hut stood on the very edge of the village, separate from the others. The sea-borne figure made his way there, and without knocking, pushed open its door and vanished inside. The newcomer found himself in a small round room with a dying fire glowing in a hole in the middle of the floor. A crudely made wooden table was on one side, a seat of dried grass and a barrel of ale beside it, while hanging nearby from one of the poles that supported the thatched roof were a few pieces of dried salted fish and some cured pork. He found a few pieces of stick and some chaff with which to get the fire going again. But the chaff made the fire smoke badly. He groaned at the poverty of the surroundings in which he found himself. Adminius was accustomed to better. The wind blew more strongly, unusually cold for the season, which was approaching Beltane, the beginning of summer. It sent the smoke from the holes in the roofs of the huts trailing away, or sometimes forced it back down into the rooms themselves where the poor were gathered about their fires, weary after a long day's herding or hunting or tending their few crops, watching their cauldrons boiling with the scarce scraps of meat mixed with vegetables which comprised their repast, before slumber overcame them.

Even in the sheltered cove where the fishing boat lay waiting, the wind caused the waves to rise, lifting the vessel with them. The captain peered gloomily at the sky and paced about the deck impatiently, hoping he would not have to wait too long. He feared the strong wind would catch the high tide, still some hours away, and do with his frail craft what it had done so easily to the more sturdy warships of Julius Caesar a century before, when it had hurled them against the rocks and smashed them like twigs.

Not long after Adminius had closed himself safely inside the hut, the ground trembled with the beat of a troop of galloping horsemen. They came from the direction of the setting sun, caped and hooded, the urgency of their errand obvious from the sweat that streamed down the sides of their mounts. The first rest the horses had from the time they left Calleva, the Atrebatian capital, was when they came to a halt near the hut on the far side of the village. The riders drew their swords and formed a circle around it. One man dismounted and went to the door while others broke away from the group to patrol the village. Any peasant who dared stick his head out to see what the disturbance was, was promptly ordered to mind his own business or face being hung by the heels and beheaded. The rider who now stood before the door of the hut wore a heavy grey, hooded cape pulled closely around him so that there was nothing to distinguish him except his size; he stood a head and shoulders higher than his fellows. From within Adminius' familiar voice answered his knock, asking gruffly, "Who is it?"

"One who glories in the title 'Rex'," came King Verica's reply. The door was opened at once and the hooded king disappeared inside. There was no light in the hut except that given off by the fire, but Verica could see Adminius clearly standing against the wattled wall. He was dressed in rather tattered trousers, a thick but torn tunic of coarse wool, with a heavy cape around him made of similarly unrefined stuff. But while the clothes looked like those of a peasant, the manner, the finesse of the Catuvellaunian's features, the set of his jaw, and the firm strong white teeth, showed that he, like his visitor, came from a high family. Verica noticed that Adminius had grown a little fatter since they last met.

"In spite of your poor clothes you seem to prosper," the king said.

"The Romans are generous with those who remain loyal to them," he replied. "And one soon forgets the disadvantages of living outside their ordered world. It is good to be reminded of them—at least occasionally." Adminius coughed and rubbed his smarting eyes. The gusting wind combined with the chaff used to get the fire started were making it smoke badly.

The Atrebatian king threw back his hood and revealed a mass of long fair hair, well-combed and groomed. It fell around a fine, keen-eyed face, narrow and long. He walked nearer to the fire, where his face came into full light. Verica was not an unhandsome man. But the eyes, though alert, were closely set together under black eyebrows that suggested a nature ill-humored and abrupt. And there was around the mouth, the lower lip of which was slack, a certain softness which showed a character too prone to pleasure. Had he removed fully his cape, that opinion would have been further enhanced by the thickness of his waist and the heavy, soft bulge over his belt.

"Things are moving rapidly," said Verica. "Your brothers have proved more cunning than you thought. They have further strengthened their alliance with the Iceni."

"How was it done?" Adminius asked, disappointed that the threat of hostilities between the tribes had come to nothing.

"In brief: Fen Fire," Verica said.

"Fen Fire?"

"She is to wed Prasutagus. I am surprised she did not send a messenger to invite you to the festivities."

"Fen Fire with Prasutagus!" Adminius sat down on a stool and leant back against the wall. "That female demon will test his kingly powers of rule, poor man!"

"You may contemplate the union from the safety of Gaul or Rome," Verica continued bitterly. "I will be the one to bear the consequences."

"You are not jealous, are you?" Adminius joked. "Perhaps *you* should have taken her as a wife."

"Since your brothers are better to have as allies than as enemies, I would sleep more safely in my bed if I had."

"I think not: she would cut your throat if you failed to please her."

"But at the moment it is your brothers who intend to cut my throat, now they have secured their northern border against the troublemakers among the Iceni who followed Subidasto; and that to me is no laughing matter." Verica leaned across the crude wooden table. "It is time for me to present myself before Caesar in person—as an ally in need of his aid, whose life and kingdom are under threat. That way, I am certain, I could convince him to do more than send mere affirmations of his support."

Adminius tensed a little. A frown spread across his face.

"No—this is not the moment. I have just come from an empire recently shaken by the bloody assassination of

Caligula, its emperor, the massacre of his family and the near rebellion of its nobles against the whole family of Caesar,'' Adminius replied. ''In spite of all the other problems to be confronted by Claudius, I have pressed your case with unrelenting urgency.'' He paused, twisting the straw in his hand. ''Be assured, the new Caesar is aware of your position as he is of the ambitions of my brothers! The fact that I am here is proof of that.'' He looked around him in disgust at the squalid hut. ''There is no point in your coming to Rome now—it might be interpreted as a sign of weakness, a sign that Rome's allies have no faith in her strength.''

''Is he aware that his ally is being humiliated? That your brothers exact tribute when they will, ignoring Rome's treaties, vaunting their power with unchecked arrogance?''

''I have made sure that Rome knows full well the truth about them. Exile provides a soil deep enough and rich enough to nourish my hatred of them and my desire for revenge. Both are hardy plants with strong roots that grow more vigorous with every year that sees me barred from my rightful place!''

''But does Rome's desire to honor its pledges grow with them, or does it wilt like Caligula's long-promised invasion?'' Verica asked with a mixture of weariness and contempt. ''How long did we listen to Caligula's messages and promises, detailing his planned conquest of Britain? While his enemies plotted his assassination, he was plotting our salvation. And I believed it—and why should I not have? What a fine display he put on for the world to see! Julius Caesar himself would have been proud of the army he assembled. No one can deny it made a wonderful spectacle on its march from Germany right to the shores of Gaul, where his fleet was bobbing up and down on the waves, everything ready to embark for Britain. No doubt those rousing speeches he made will be remembered, even if the enterprise itself will not—except as a notable farce, the product of his fickle and demented brain.'' Verica thought for a moment, then with a grim smile added: ''Yes, but unfortunately, the island was inhabited by ghosts—as everyone knows—so the emperor changed his mind and all your influence upon him could not convince him otherwise, is that not so? Can we expect better of his successor who they say cannot even make a speech without stammering like a fool?''

Adminius was galled by the mention of the debacle of the invasion, in which he had invested so much hope. Caligula had appointed him his ''adviser'' on Britain. When the projected invasion collapsed, Adminius was left to be mocked and derided by everyone as the puppet of a madman's whims.

He stood up and tore a piece of cured pork from the post where it hung nearby. ''I have not risked this journey here to be reminded of past failures but to discuss future plans—and coming triumphs,'' he snapped, taking a bite of the meat. His face was twisted into a look of disgust as he spat the unchewed meat into the fire. It tasted like pure brine. It sizzled and hissed in the flames. ''I have spoken with Narcissus . . .''

''Narcissus?'' came the question.

''He is an adviser to the new Caesar. Without Narcissus, Claudius does nothing.''

Verica nodded skeptically. ''You once enthused about your influence with Caligula's closest adviser, who turned out to be a ballet dancer, more concerned with curling his hair than waging war in a distant and dangerous place.''

''Narcissus is a learned Greek who knows as much as any man in Rome,'' Adminius went on with some irritation. ''He is not subject to foolish whims, believe me. It was Narcissus who asked me to undertake this journey.''

''I do not doubt but that your learned Greek friend knows all there is to know about Britain,'' the grey-cloaked king said dryly. ''But I am not interested in what he knows. I want to hear what he is advising Claudius Caesar to do.''

''Bridle your impatience and I will tell you,'' Adminius told him firmly. He was determined to show Verica that his confidence was not shaken. ''Claudius is fresh to the mantle of the Caesars; many regard his shoulders as too weak to wear it. Narcissus tells him that he needs a military victory which will rank with those of the greatest of his predecessors—Julius Caesar himself . . ."

"Yes—as the ballet dancer advised Caligula."

Adminius ignored his goading and continued. "War is the surest way for a king to show he is fit to rule. And what more convincing proof of prowess could there be than to conduct a successful invasion of Britain? That way, he would go beyond even Julius Caesar, who tried and failed at the enterprise. That is the message I bring from Narcissus to you." Adminius leaned closer to the other. "Your plight is well-known in Rome and their concern runs deep," he said. "You are highly thought of. Your reputation is unblemished there as a loyal ally; indeed, it is enhanced with every insult my brothers cast upon it."

"Why then does Rome continue to permit me to suffer insult from them? Surely Caesar and his learned adviser see what everyone else can see clearly: that the longer they allow their allies' rights to be trampled upon, the lower Rome's reputation falls and the more bold become her enemies—of whom there are none more fierce than Caratacus and his brothers."

"It will not have to be endured much longer," Adminius told him.

"How long?" Verica pressed him. The wind shook the thatched roof. The poles supporting it creaked plaintively, and the smoke from the fire swirled everywhere except where it was supposed to go, through the hole and into the night.

"Right now, Narcissus cannot give an exact date," Adminius said, reaching over and untapping a small keg of ale. He filled one cup and gave it to Verica, then took one himself. "There is much to be done. An undertaking of such importance needs the most careful planning, involving as it will many thousands of men." As Adminius spoke he sipped at the ale, but he found it almost as distasteful as the briny pork he had just spat out. He threw it aside with a look of disgust on his face. "Wine is a far superior beverage," he said. "I will always be grateful to you for introducing me to it. Especially since I have recently had the chance to taste some old vintages at a dinner party given by Narcissus at which Caesar and his young wife Messalina were in attendance. And a great beauty she is, too.''

Verica listened, but the hut sapped his spirits. Its dingy squalor was too concrete, and the talk of Roman dinner parties, the plans of Narcissus, of Claudius Caesar and his generals that Adminius uttered with such confidence, were too distant and too vague in comparison. Adminius, he decided, might have grown more confident during his stay in Rome, but he was no less impressionable than he had been before. By now, Verica's eyes were smarting from the smoke and he had still heard nothing more than yet another promise of commitment from Caesar to undertake the defense of his allies. ''I have risked your brothers' wrath in coming here to meet with you—as if the situation wasn't already perilous enough for me. Am I to be told yet again that I must be patient? It would be better, and safer, if I were in Rome to make the case myself . . .'' he said, angry that the danger he was incurring in meeting with the exiled prince had produced nothing solid.

Adminius rose and got ready to leave. He bundled his cloak around himself and went to open the door. ''Don't be so hasty. Have no fear, Claudius must act in order to be taken seriously as emperor. And I remain in Gaul, at Lugdunum,'' he said reassuringly. ''Narcissus is in constant touch with me, as I will be with you.'' He took Verica by the arm and squeezed it with a confident grip. ''Soon I will return to Camulodunum to step across the threshold from which I was eternally barred—and you will reign secure, more prosperous than you now think possible. I know, I have seen the power of Rome and its wealth, and I share the confidence and intimacy of the men who wield them.''

Outside, the wind had gathered force and was howling around the frail huts where the village lay dark and quiet.

''So Prasutagus prefers to take a young wife than to keep his son's respect!'' Adminius said with a smile. ''What has become of his rebel son?''

''Subidasto remains with me, and is well-concealed in Calleva. He is in touch with his supporters among the

Iceni, still hoping to outflank his father and revive his campaign against your brothers."

"Might he be of use to us? I know how much he opposes the ambitions of my brothers. If he can gather enough support among his own people . . ."

Verica shook his head. "Yes—Subidasto is as determined as ever to check the Catuvellauni's hopes to dominate the whole island and wants nothing more than to confront them. But he hates Rome more than he hates Togodumnus."

"Perhaps if we just leave them alone they will tear each other to shreds," Adminius mused.

"That might suit you, safe as you are. But I have no wish to be found among the bloody rubble that they leave behind. Remember, I do not have the forces to challenge your brothers if they decide the time is right to get rid of me. That is why Caesar must act soon. Impress that upon your Narcissus."

"I will, have no fear," Adminius answered, and started up the path that led to the cove and his vessel. He walked quickly as the powerful, now gusting wind blew at his back. It had been a long, uncomfortable journey, but a necessary one. He had, he thought, successfully reassured Verica of Rome's intentions. It was unfortunate that he had to mislead him—somewhat. Yet, there was no other way. Before Adminius left Rome, Narcissus had made that clear.

"Verica's chief value as an ally," the Greek had told him, "is that one day he will provide the excuse we need to intervene. But he must be kept there until that day arrives."

"And when will that day arrive?" Adminius had asked.

"When he is overthrown and crushed by the ambition of your brothers. What better cause could there be to launch the conquest of Britain?" The Greek paused and put his finger to his lips. "That, of course, is our secret, for in the meantime you must convince him to remain at his post."

Verica, his cape again wrapped closely about him, watched Adminius vanish into the darkness. Only when his ally was out of sight did he mount his own horse and lead his troops in the opposite direction out of the poor village, their hoods drawn down over their faces. They had passed the stockade when through the darkness a peasant came towards them carrying in his arms a bleating lamb. The peasant stopped in his tracks when he saw the horsemen approach. They were riding at a slow canter. As the king passed him a sudden gust, more powerful than before, caught his hood and flung it backwards from his head, revealing his face. The peasant looked into the eyes of the tall, fair-haired horseman. He almost dropped the animal, so startled was he to see the king, whom he recognized, in such a place at such a time. Verica halted, swung his mount around, and trotted back to where the peasant stood staring and amazed. "You know me, man?" he asked. The peasant fell on his knees and bent his head. Verica looked down carefully at the bent neck as the peasant said in a hushed voice, "My king, Verica!"

The fair-haired horseman drew his broadsword swiftly, noiselessly, and with a powerful, sudden stroke, struck the kneeling peasant on his bent neck. The peasant's head bounced to the ground, spiraling drops of blood as it went. The headless body slumped forward twitching into the waving grass. The bloodstained lamb went bleating and kicking into the night. Verica leaned over and rubbed the bloody blade through the grass until it was clean; such lowly blood would only corrode his noble metal. He goaded his horse into a gallop, his grey-cloaked troop behind him, passing the stricken head whose eyes were still fixed in solemn amazement that so humble a soul should have had the extraordinary fortune of coming so close to a king.

Chapter 7

"Aaaye!" Latis, the king's first wife, cried out as Fen Eel, one of the four others, poured a bucket of ice-cold water into her bath. Before Fen Eel could step aside, Latis scooped up a handful of water and hurled it at the younger woman, splashing her. "First you would boil me to death and now you try to freeze me!" Latis glared at Fen Eel, whose soaked hair drooped over her face, then at the other three wives who were getting Latis ready for the coming festivities to mark their husband's marriage to his sixth. Mournful Mound was lathering her legs and body with scented soap. Barrel was polishing her bronze and silver ornaments which she intended to wear. And Screech-Owl was scrubbing her back. "I sometimes wonder why the king can be bothered with another one," Latis exclaimed. "He has not had much luck with women, with one exception, of course." She nudged Screech-Owl with her elbow. "Please, more gently. It's skin, not hide! And delicate skin too!"

"Fen Fire is very, very beautiful," said Fen Eel archly as she wiped the water from her face and trundled away with her bucket to a safe distance.

"Beautiful?" Latis exclaimed, following Fen Eel with her eyes, which had a sour look in them. "With that red hair of hers that looks like the rags of elder tree leaves in autumn?"

"It is red like flames," said Barrel, looking up from her polishing. Latis shook her own golden yellow locks about her ivory-smooth shoulders.

"You've drunk so much you can no longer see properly," Latis retorted poisonously. "The king cares not for her hair. He marries her for her allegiance—no more!

Only politics would make a man take on another one of you!" Latis had a tongue that could be as bitter as her look when she wanted. But in her heart she knew that it was not only mere political expediency and the desire for peaceful coexistence with the Catuvellauni that dictated Prasutagus' decision to marry Fen Fire. Of all his wives, Latis had been married to him the longest. Latis came from one of the most noble families of the kingdom of Cantii, in the southernmost part of Britain, nearest to the Gauls and the empire of Rome. She had been married to the king since she was twenty—fifteen years almost. A flaxen-haired beauty, she stood straight and regal in her manner, with high cheekbones and a haughty look in her blue eyes with their thin, delicate eyebrows. Many were the chiefs and kings of the Britons who had been suitors at her door, from all corners of the island. She married first at the age of fifteen to a chief of her own tribe, and bore him a son. Her first husband was the handsomest man in the kingdom, and the boy had all his advantages. But the boy died in a hunting accident, and afterwards she could not bear to look at the father—for she blamed his carelessness for the death of her son. She did not renew the marriage contract, and stayed aloof from men until she met Prasutagus, who was then some fifteen years her senior. She was overwhelmed when she saw him display his chariot skills at the games—he had a calm yet commanding presence, the very essence of kingship, she thought. And his hair—such fine yellow strands gathered about his powerful shoulders. She accepted his offer of a seven-year contract—to be renewed, if both so wished it. That was the only long-term marriage the king had entered into, and he was not to do so again until he met and desired Fen Fire.

She went to the Iceni with some misgivings, knowing them to be more rustic compared to her own people. She had been brought up with trinkets from the finest craftsmen in Gaul and Italy; her household was used to drinking the best Italian wines; they were in constant touch with merchants who visited their coast regularly from Gaul. And with the trade back and forth came news and gossip of all sorts, so that Latis felt she could be living the life of one of the ladies of the Gallic nobility, with their fine villas paved with colored marble. She loved nothing better than to chat with her friends about the latest intrigues at the court of Caesar in Rome. She spoke as if it had come fresh from some noble Roman lady's salon, when in fact most of the tales she heard were third and fourth hand, and long out of date by the time they reached her ears. She realized that going to the kingdom of the Iceni would mean leaving that life behind. But her admiration and desire for Prasutagus was such that she readily abandoned those advantages for a place at the king's side in the remoter, wilder regions of the fenlands.

She understood that in spite of his reputation for being a steady and judicious ruler, concerned with assuring the prosperity of his people, he cherished the world of his warrior youth, and a fine and brave warrior he had been. No one cut a finer figure than he on the battlefield. But those days were gone, and his passion for Fen Fire would not bring them back. Yet, it could cause mischief enough to both the household and the kingdom, if what was a passionate indulgence became exploited by his new wife's mettlesome family.

She had given all the other wives nicknames and refused to call them by any other: Barrel was round and plump, but the real reason for her nickname was her capacity for drink. Mournful Mound was possessed of a large bosom and a pair of ever-doleful eyes which gazed down upon it as if it were the worst affliction in the world. Fen Eel was as slippery as an eel whenever anyone tried to lay hold of her to do some work, and Screech-Owl earned her name because when the king mounted her she emitted such squeals and squawks and cries that she kept all the other wives (and half the palace) awake at night. Latis believed that this was why, of all the wives, she was the only one not to have given the king a child: her noise froze the king's seed, making it sluggish with fear so that it was unable to proceed, or alternatively, expelling it altogether because of her shaking and thrashing about.

Latis knew they were looking forward to Fen Fire's coming to live with them, hoping she would be a check on her. Being first wife, she had rule over them, which she relished exercising. But Fen Fire would have to buckle under like the others, and would—whatever they hoped to the contrary. Indeed, Latis was looking forward to the new challenge. Fen Fire's reputation was fiery like her hair. But that would soon be quenched! She ordered Screech-Owl to stop scrubbing and go mix her ochres and paints. "I will remind them of what beautiful really looks like," she said to herself.

Latis stood up and had Mournful Mound dry her vigorously. She stepped from the bath and, wrapped in a light linen robe, went for her mirror, which was made from the finest polished bronze, its back embellished with delicately etched interlacing spirals and its handle inlaid with enamel. It would have graced any Roman lady's chamber. Screech-Owl had mixed the preparations and began dusting dry chalk on Latis' cheeks, making them moon pale and emphasizing the deep blue of her eyes. Latis followed her work carefully in the mirror. "A touch more of the juice of the alder bark," she said, wishing the spot of red on each white cheek to burn more vividly. Fen Fire had youth, of course, and regardless of what she said to the other wives, Latis knew she was exceptionally beautiful. But then Latis had given the king a son, now seven years of age and fostered out to one of the richest royal families in the south of Britain. She had hopes for him, even though the king had another boy, Subidasto, much older than her own. Subidasto's mother had been the king's first wife, who died while giving birth to him. It would have been better for the king had she died before, Latis thought, for she brought nothing but trouble into the world. Latis gazed at her face as it was being transformed through the vivid contrasts of white and red and black.

No woman can be blamed for what her womb brings forth. Subidasto was fostered out to a fine, noble, wealthy family but disgraced his father by running away from them. He stirred up trouble against the Catuvellauni, almost bringing the two kingdoms to war. Subidasto had looked on the growing power of Cunobelinus with anxiety, believing that the Iceni would suffer in the end unless his father showed he was prepared to face the Catuvellauni in war before they dared impinge upon Iceni borders. Indeed, the wild, impetuous boy would have welcomed a conflict between the two great kingdoms. And many of the young warriors listened to him, for never was there such a powerful and convincing advocate of battle. But his father the king denounced his zeal as that of a raw, impatient youth, heedless of the true state of the world, and blocked him at every turn. She prayed to the goddess Brigit that some day they would hear that his head was now part of some warrior's collection of trophies. Her own son was springing up strong and fine and reliable; in only a few more years he would be ready to take his place at the side of Prasutagus. And then . . . She turned her face to one side, then the other, pleased with the effect.

"Screech-Owl," she said suddenly, "you would not hide anything from me, would you?"

"You know we have no secrets from each other," came the reply.

"When the king is in your arms, does he ever whisper in your ear words concerning my son?"

"He spoke of him only once," she asserted.

"And what did he say?" Latis asked.

Screech-Owl shrugged. "Nothing very much, except to say that he reminded him of you."

"In that case then, I need have no fears for his prospects. He did not speak of him in comparison with his other son?"

"Perhaps, but I don't remember—it was some years ago, just after I became his wife . . ."

"The third, I believe?"

"The fourth."

"You must excuse me, my dear, my husband has made so many of these arrangements that I cannot be blamed for not remembering all the little details." She stood up and looked disdainfully at the other wives. "Now, you may fetch your mirrors and do the best you can with yourselves while I finish my preparations."

When she had done, Latis put on her finest silken robe, only to find that it was damp. She had warned Prasutagus about this place, which he called the Palace of the Mists; that it was not comfortable until high summer. Usually they would come here to enjoy the Feast of Lugus and not until then. It stood on a little rise surrounded by fenwater, and though a fine and splendid building—it was made of pine and had fifty rooms, each with a handsome copper partition—it was often fog-bound and damp. But the king loved it most of all his palaces, and insisted that the three days of feasting before the wedding on Beltane should begin there.

There was a roar from the guests gathered outside on the parade ground to take part in the games celebrating the coming marriage and the Feast of Beltane. Latis pushed open one of the fifty windows and looked out. Two pure white steeds, broad-chested and narrow-haunched, pulled the light frame of the king's chariot swiftly across the level ground. Prasutagus, his hair tied behind him, stood erect, the reins wrapped around his sinewy wrist. He was steering the chariot towards an incline built of smooth sods. It rose up to a sheer drop. Directly opposite it was the sheer side of another incline which sloped down to the parade ground again. The gap between the two was as wide as two chariots side by side. Only the most skilled of charioteers could perform the feat of Leaping the Gap. Prasutagus had performed it many times; in his youth he was famed for his skill in this feat. But it had been many years since he last attempted it. Now, to prepare for the wedding games, where he must excel if he were to win the admiration of his young bride, and to impress his guests with his still-youthful vigor, he was set to try again. His chariot thundered towards the incline then up it, the steel-rimmed wheels making it shudder. Latis closed her eyes. During the games of Lugus the year before, she saw a chariot shattered and its driver hurled to his death while attempting to cross a gap of the same width. She heard the thud of wheels and hooves as the chariot landed on the other incline, and then the roar of the spectators. She opened her eyes. Prasutagus was doing a triumphal circuit of the parade ground, his eyes glowing wide with pride. She ran out of the palace to greet him. He swept her up into the chariot and made another circuit. "Your skill grows sharper with the years," she said, throwing her arm around his waist, which in spite of the fine figure he presented, was growing plump and heavy.

"My skill increases with my desire," he answered. "Never has it been more keen and demanding than now. I have never been more dissatisfied with my achievements." He was panting slightly. "A width of two chariots to leap is nothing. I will do three on Beltane Eve!"

"I'm sure the princess will be impressed enough with two," Latis suggested quietly. Because of the roaring and cheering the king could not hear her. She could only hope he would think better of it when the time came. Whatever remained of his skills and strengths (and that was considerable), Latis believed that the king had reached the age when he should be content to listen to his bard sing about his triumphs rather than attempt to reenact them.

The games lasted until twilight when the warriors and their women began drinking and eating. The feast went on until midnight, ending earlier than usual because the following morning the king and his retinue would depart for Camulodunum and the wedding. Prasutagus rose from his table and summoned his wives. Only Latis excused herself, saying there was something which she had to take care of before going to his chamber.

She left the palace and climbed the steps to the rampart, then went along the walkway, glancing occasionally around her and out over the dark, misty fenlands. She stopped when she came to a small watchtower outside of which a guard stood to attention at her approach. She glanced past him into the tower's interior. A large cage sat near the wall. Latis gave another quick glance around and, making sure no one was abroad, stepped into the tower. The guard saluted Latis and she returned his salute with a smile.

"Is the swan ready for his journey tomorrow?" she asked.

"Yes, he is well rested," the man answered.

Latis came close to him. She had chosen him specially for the task of watching her swan, which would perform an important role at the marriage celebrations on Beltane. "And he has not been fed, as is the custom," she said, her face almost touching the guard's long, fine-combed moustache of which he was so proud.

"Of course not, Lady, I followed the instructions of the

priests most carefully, as ordered.'' The guard was standing rigidly to attention, his fist grasping the javelin. Latis put her delicate fingers on the shaft of the weapon, curled them around it, allowed her hand to slide down to his.

''Are you prepared to follow my instructions with equal care?'' she whispered. The soft white fingers of the king's first wife were now stroking the back of his hand.

He nodded nervously. ''I shall obey you as you command, Lady.''

''Good. I knew that you were a reliable man, and that I could depend on you. Why else would I have picked you from all the others for the task?'' She was so close to him now that he could feel her breasts brushing against him. She leaned over and kissed his neck. ''My thighs will be yours. You have my word. Go, now. Leave me to do what must be done,'' she said.

His eyes narrowed, a momentary flash of fear and doubt swept over his face.

''Is the word of the king's wife not enough?'' she demanded.

The guard turned pale. ''Of course, Lady.'' Without more ado he turned and walked into the darkness.

Latis crouched down beside the cage and the great bird became restless. ''There, there, my pet—my poor, starved pet,'' she whispered, her lips at the bars. It struggled upright on its great webbed feet and stuck its neck out towards her, its beak knocking against the cage. ''Look how thin you've grown, poor dear. And all because of her! Well, we'll see.'' Latis took a little bag from under her cape. Quickly she opened it. Grain began to tipple out. The swan stirred restlessly and stuck its head through the bars trying to reach the spilled grain. Latis closed her eyes for a moment. ''Oh, Triple Goddess, Protector of Women and the Virtue of Wives, Guardian of Rivers and Springs, forgive this little transgression of your rule! I swear by all I possess that I will give you more than ample compensation. And I have faith that you, being a woman, will not look too harshly upon me. You know well the dangers we wives confront with aging husbands and their changing needs.'' Then, in a whisper Latis listed the donations she would make at the spring of the goddess: a gold bucket, two silver drinking cups, a handful of newly minted coins, a torc from the finest workshop in the kingdom (and the Iceni were renowned throughout the land for the beauty of their torcs), a cauldron of bronze, and the blood from a young bull. When she finished this litany she poured a copious palmful of seed into her hand and held it near the bars of the cage. The swan, who had not been fed in days, pecked frantically, then she poured another palmful. The swan gobbled it down its long slender throat. Soon the bag sagged. Empty. Latis stroked the bird's head as it finished the last few grains.

A shadow fell over the white form of the swan. The guard stood behind her in the doorway of the watchtower. "Is it done?" he enquired. Then he saw the swan peck the last grain of seed from the lady's palm.

Latis stood up and turned to him. She thrust out her empty palm. "There, you see how hungrily he ate! Proof of what a virtuous wife I am!" she laughed provocatively.

The guard stepped into the tower and gripped her narrow wrist. He brought her hand to his fleshy mouth. Her palm was still sprinkled with the dust from the seed bag. He licked it clean.

She pulled her hand free. "You must see to it that the cage is kept scrupulously clean," she told him firmly. "There must be no droppings, no sign that the bird has been fed. You know the penalty for those who violate the wedding rituals of the goddess."

The guard shook his head slowly, a sly grin appearing on his ruddy-cheeked face. "Is the goddess Brigit as stern a guardian of the virtue of wives?" he asked, moving closer to Latis. She stepped back against the cage where the swan now lay sleeping, well-fed and contented. "Do not fret, you will get your reward in due time," she replied. "When all has been accomplished."

Latis had no fear of Brigit's strictures. She knew when the time came the goddess would avert her eyes, choosing perhaps to contemplate the many trinkets she had been promised. In that, as in so much else, Latis was confident of the goddess' understanding; after all, she was a woman very like herself.

Chapter 8

The bonfires burst into flame. The flames leapt up at the sky as if they would lick the sinking sun back to life, restoring its waning vigor and so doubling the day's length. On hillcrest and in meadow the fires blazed, acknowledging that Beltane Eve had come, and with it the wedding that would unite the Iceni and the Catuvellauni.

At the heart of Camulodunum the palace of Cunobelinus radiated light like a huge wheel of fire. His greatness could have asked for no finer monument. And at the heart of the palace the great cauldron still hung, a monument to his generosity. After his death his three faithful sons, Caratacus, Togodumnus and Maglocunos saw to it that the cauldron was never empty as the king had wished. Next to the cauldron were long spits for roasting the milk-fed hogs and the oxen reared only on milk and grass and corn. Barrels of ale and mead and wine were placed in every room; no guest wanted for a drink under that roof.

There was always a commotion in the palace, but this Beltane Eve it was redoubled. The swarms of children that raced around with the packs of dogs playing between the pillars got in the way of the servants rushing this way and that to make sure everything was in place. Workmen hurried to finish the last touches to some mould or carving, wary of the gleemen next to them trying out some new juggling trick that threatened to brain them. Cooks attending the spits where the hogs, boars and oxen turned and hissed, used their forks to fight off the hounds, and women making a final effort to clean out the refuse found that their brooms swept away some enraptured poet rehearsing a new story. But the palace of Cunobelinus, however capacious, was not expected to be able to hold all the illustrious guests who were coming from every part of the kingdom and beyond it. So alongside it the brothers had erected a long, rectangular feast hall especially for the celebration. The roof beams were so massive that six of the strongest men in the kingdom were needed to lift them, and the corner pillars were three times as heavy as that. The feast hall had its own cauldron which required three oxen to drag into place, and its own spits, each of which could roast six hogs, nine boars or one ox. And if the barrels that were placed by each table were all to burst at once the flood of drink would be enough to float a fair-sized sailing ship.

Outside in the wavy grass of the wide meadow which lay before the palace, workmen completed the wedding platform built of sods and earth. It stood between the two tall, grey, weathered stones that had been there since the beginning of time, the Grey Man and his consort, the Grey Woman. On either side of the stones, hordes of children piled sticks and branches and larger pieces, anything that they could carry or haul from the woods to make into big stacks. These piles would be the biggest bonfires of all, and they were always the last to be lit on Beltane Eve, so it was a special honor to build them and the children worked feverishly. They were full of high spirits, knowing the night would be a long one filled with music, games and feasting. If they could stay awake they would be permitted to watch the dawn come up on May first, when the royal marriage would be contracted. But these bonfires were never built without a fight. Those stacking the wood on one side of the platform began looking enviously at their friends' efforts on the other. Soon one side had accused the other of stealing wood. The battle began, and was only brought to a halt by the thunder of approaching horsemen and chariots.

Fen Fire heard them too, as she was being fussed over and readied by her women companions. She was still in a pensive state from her sojourn on the island sanctuary. She'd been paying little attention to the chatter around her. But the sounds of the arriving guests roused her. Her friends left the chamber and hurried to the sun room that Cunobelinus had built especially for the women and which overlooked the central hall of the palace, as well as affording a view out over the meadow and beyond. She followed her companions and arrived in time to see the glimmering chariot of Prasutagus emerge from the cloud of dust. On either side of it hung two man-length shields, purple at the center and rimmed with gold. On his high, broad forehead shone the yellow circle of the Master Charioteer. Over his shoulders he wore a cape of royal red, fringed and fine. On his hip he carried an ivory-hilted broadsword in a scabbard of bronze embossed with precious stones. His long yellow hair, now greying, hung loosely down his back, and his beard was forked and finely trimmed. His retinue came to a halt behind him. Some wore purple cloaks embroidered with gold thread, some grey cloaks with red-embroidered hoods, and some had cloaks speckled with gold and silver. Each warrior wore a massive gold torc about his neck. Some carried short stabbing spears with gold collars around the head of the spear. Others had broadswords on their sides encased in scabbards of bronze richly and profusely inlaid with shapes of stag and horse and boar and deer and bull. Each man carried a long shield, some round in shape, others rectangular, some embossed with yellow gold, others with hard bronze, some scalloped-edged and others rimmed with bronze.

Their women came behind them in long carriages, the king's five wives dismounting first, led by Latis. They wore fine fringed capes of different colors and tunics of softest silk. On their feet were sandals with leather soles and bronze clasps. Latis, stately and straight-backed, stepped up to the king and took his arm to go meet Togodumnus and Caratacus who had come to greet them at the door of the palace. Barrel was already slightly unsteady and had to be helped by Fen Eel, who took her arm. She rested her head on her companion's shoulder. "Why is it," she sighed, "that weddings always make me sad, and wakes make me glad?"

"That's because it's always *your* husband getting married!" Latis shot back.

The colorful procession filed in under the eyes of Fen Fire and her friends and attendants.

"I have a fine husband and five fine wives to go with him!" Fen Fire observed, looking with interest at those with whom she would share her new household.

"In truth," a companion asserted, "his bed is never cold."

"I do not like the look of that stiff-backed one," said Fen Fire.

"Certainly she has a sharp snout on her like a rat," another one of her attendants replied.

"No doubt but the king is a fine specimen and wears his age well. A wrinkle or two here and there never hurt any man," Fen Fire observed. "I like a man with powerful wrists."

"Aye, if he controls his wives as well as he controls his chariot ponies you'll all be in for a good ride." One of the women laughed. There was a stream of handsome warriors and beautiful women flowing into and around the palace, arriving for the festivities. Each woman viewed the guests with thoughts of the night to come. After the games and the eating and drinking were finished, just before the dawn of May first the merrymaking would move to the woods, every woman with her May Day mate.

Each man had the bearing of a king, and each woman the grace of a queen. There were wild, sturdy men with hair dyed yellow with bracken juice. A band of woad-painted near-naked warriors arrived carrying slings and slim-shafted spears. They were swarthy skinned with hair as black as night. The array seemed endless, and soon the eye grew weary of the panoply of color and the flash of polished metal. Fen Fire and her companions were about to leave the sun room, thinking the parade of guests had come to an end at last, when another arrived.

Two powerful glossy black steeds with flowing manes harnessed to a silver-plated chariot pulled up at the palace door panting, with steam streaming up from their sides and out of their delicate nostrils. The leather reins were wrapped about the wrists of a tall slender woman, with hair black and flowing freely behind her. She wore a delicately fringed green cape over her shoulders, clasped at her breast by a silver brooch in the shape of the crescent moon. Under her cape, which billowed in the wind, was a short green silken tunic. And around her white and slender thighs supple thongs of willow were tied in five-fold criss-cross fashion. Behind her on furious broadchested mounts three huge warriors came galloping, with savage countenances, beards bristling like thorn bushes, and foreheads wrinkled and scowling. The people forgot the other sights and swarmed around her. Her eyes were as green as a twilight wood, with long black eyelashes curled and delicate as a spider's legs.

"Is she a creature of this world or of the Other?" one of Fen Fire's companions asked. The others shared her amazement at the dark beauty of the late arriving guest and pressed closer to the window to get a better look.

"She is Cartimandua, a princess of the Brigantes," Fen Fire told them.

"Indeed, she deserves her name—for she is a sleek pony," her friend agreed.

"She rarely stirs from the desolate kingdom she rules," said Fen Fire. "She is an unexpected arrival."

"And an unexpected rival—though she brings her own three fellows, from the look of her she'd be able to take all of ours as well," the women lamented.

"But come!" said Fen Fire. "It is May Eve—give your hopes a more summery aspect. The doors of the Everlasting Ones fly open. We need not set limits to our hopes or restraints to our desires. The warrior you desire will pleasure you till dawn. And afterwards? Why, the day will gather him up and he will vanish in its bright light more completely than if he had stepped into night's deepest shadow . . ."

A trumpet blast announced the beginning of the games. The charioteers were ready to test their skills.

At the crack of the whip the horses surged forward and the iron-rimmed wheels threw up slivers of grass. The dozen light-framed chariots bounded swiftly across the meadow like boats blown by a strong wind over the waves. There was room enough in each for a warrior and all his weapons; but on this occasion the warriors needed nothing more than three casting spears and all the skill that they commanded.

They bounded towards the first obstacle—a row of steeply rising inclines built of sods. The inclines ended in a sheer drop, then there was a gap the width of three chariots side by side before the next incline began, sloping away in the other direction. Prasutagus and Caratacus were the first to hear the wheels of their chariots strike the rising slopes, but others followed close behind them. They rolled up the slope and then seemed to take wing as horses, vehicles and drivers flew through the air to come down with a thud and a shudder on the far slope. Both men, leading the pack, glanced over their shoulders to see the fate of their fellows. A chariot raced behind them riderless, the warrior having been flung over its front. Another chariot's horses struggled to haul it up from where its wheels had struck the edge of the incline. A third shattered upon landing on the far side of the gap and its horses pulled a one-wheeled wreck through the grass.

Prasutagus reached the course of the posts first. Without slackening their furious pace, his horses responded to his every movement. He wove the chariot around the posts with the ease of a woman stitching a cape. Here too Caratacus was his equal; neither man touched any post and both emerged from the other end of the course with all in place.

The king took the first javelin in one hand while holding the reins with the other. A straw warrior swung back and forth as it hung from an old tree that stood alone in the meadow. The target was the warrior's heart—a red spot fixed on its breast. The king's first throw struck the straw man in the shoulder. He swung round and threw the second, which missed the object completely. But on the third throw the javelin sank into the dummy's heart. The crowd roared their approval.

Caratacus reached the straw warrior which was still swinging from the force of the javelin blows. He gripped the reins with one hand and took aim with the other. His hand was as steady as if he were standing on a rock, not bounding over the meadow with such speed that the wheels seemed hardly to touch the ground. The first javelin struck the target in the center of the red spot. The second landed within an inch of the first. With his final run past the target he cast the last javelin with such force that it passed between the first two and carried the dummy away with it, pinning it against the tree.

"There is no finer sight in the world than a chariot leaping the gap," Togodumnus affirmed as the charioteers brought their vehicles to a halt and began to dismount, the game of feats having finished. Prasutagus and Caratacus, the two victors, were congratulating each other on their fine display of skills.

"I would rather watch the women at their games," Bran replied. Togodumnus and the bard were standing surveying the activities around the meadow.

"Chariot feats are the finest feats of all. Beyond all others in beauty and excitement."

"Away with you and your chariot feats. To see two fine naked women grappling, or a woman racing as swift as the wind on a spring day—there's far more beauty and excitement in that than in all the chariot feats in the world."

"What about the feat of straight steering we just saw, without a post knocked down? No skill is greater than that. You yourself have said so in your poems. Don't deny it."

"You're a foolish man if you think a poet must believe everything he says in his poems."

Leading his sweating horses, Caratacus overheard the talk.

"What say you?" the poet asked him.

"I say the chariot is a fine vehicle for showing off, but its day on the battlefield is coming to an end."

Togodumnus looked at Caratacus in amazement.

"There, what did I tell you," Bran said to the older brother. "That's one thing which will never be said about women."

But Togodumnus howled with laughter. "My right arm will fall off first before I see the day dawn when the chariot won't be the platform from which memorable deeds are done."

"I do not deny that, brother," Caratacus replied. "But in the wars to come courage will find other challenges.

Brave men will never find it difficult to discover ways to fight their enemies."

"The old ways will serve us well enough as they have served our father, and his father before that," Togodumnus asserted without a doubt in his mind.

"Yes, the old ways for the old wars. But war changes, like everything else."

"War is always war: splitting of skulls, breaking of bone, slicing of flesh, hacking of necks, yesterday, today and tomorrow."

"But the horse races have begun and we are in their track," cried Bran. They dove to one side in time to feel the wind in the wake of the riders as they surged past. A black steed, with a flowing mane and wide flaring nostrils, was already a head's length in front of the others. The white hand of Cartimandua lashed the stallion's side, and her thighs pressed its glossy black hide urging it on with every ounce of her strength. The track ran around the meadow, with one dangerous bend at the foot of a slope. Cartimandua's stallion turned the curve without slowing, and pounded forward with such ground-covering strides that all her opponents could see of it was its fine bushy tail, its hooves and its rider's stream of black hair pulled taut behind her. It was well on its way into the second lap before the others completed the first. By the time they completed the second, the princess of the Brigantians was claiming her prize at the finishing line. Caratacus had followed her course without once taking his eyes off her. He burst into applause with the crowd.

"In my opinion, you're wasting your time applauding that creature, for the day of the horse is well and truly over. Surely it is doomed to go the way of the chariot," said Togodumnus, with a most philosophical demeanor.

"I applaud the rider more than the horse," Caratacus retorted.

"At this moment, I would be happy to go the way of *her* horse," said Bran, who likewise had not been able to take his attention from the Brigantian princess.

"Then she would still be standing at the starting line," Caratacus told his bard. "I think your words will serve you better than your hooves when the race is for the lady's heart.''

Meanwhile, Cartimandua had brought another horse onto the field. With one of her warriors holding the two steeds side by side, she leapt on to their backs, striding them. Gripping the reins of both horses with one hand, she lashed them forward with the other. In the middle of the field was a wall built of turf as high as a man. The broad-chested steeds galloped together, one in perfect time with the other, until they reached the obstacle. The crowd gasped to see both horses leap over it as if they were one, the princess astride them, steady and well-balanced on their powerful backs.

Cartimandua took a slow victory trot around the field, followed by her three huge companions. A tall fair-haired warrior put himself in her path, offering her a cup of mead.

''Stallion Princess,'' he said, eyeing her white breasts over her tunic as she bent down to accept his gift, ''tonight let me press my lips upon those peaks.'' She took the cup in both hands and drained it in one swallow. She looked at the warrior, then wiped her hand across her mouth.

''I would drain you like I did this cup. But first, they would make your blood flow red as mead.'' The three huge warriors attending her thrust themselves in front of the gift-giver and he stepped back. She rode on until another warrior, powerful and dark, stepped in front of her. He held up a joint of roast boar.

''Stallion Princess,'' he said, seeing her white thighs bound in willow, ''tonight let me plough in that sweet country.'' She stripped the meat off the bone with her snow-white teeth.

''Bare as this bone I'd leave you before an hour was through. But before I would know such ecstasy they would pulverize your bones to dust.'' Again, her three companions confronted the gift-giver, and he shrank away from them.

She threw the bone aside and rode on. Warrior after warrior thrust offerings at her only to be overawed by her protectors. Only he who could overcome them would be able to take her that night. Finally, having rejected them all with disdain, her eyes came to rest on Caratacus. She had watched him with great attention performing his feats of straight-steering, leaping the gap and striking the heart of the target. Now, he stood blocking her path, his hands on his hips.

"What has the wind-swift charioteer to offer me?" she asked. If her eyes were as dark a shade of green as a wood at twilight, his were as clear and sharp as the eyes of a hawk on the topmost branch of a tree in that wood.

"Only a hard man in a pass," he replied, folding his arms across his chest. The three huge guards glared at him. But their mistress cast a look which lingered with pleasure on the stocky powerful form of the Catuvellaunian chief.

"You offer me only defiance?" asked Cartimandua. Gently she stroked her stallion's robust glossy neck.

"There is no desire without defiance," Caratacus responded.

"There are desires which defy satisfaction," she answered.

"Satisfaction comes when you find strength equal to desire, for nothing can defy that," Caratacus told her. She laughed. Her three protectors were about to block him, but a glance from her kept them at bay. Caratacus put one hand on her thigh, running it over the sinewy willow thongs which were wrapped around her white flesh as high as the top of her thigh, where his fingers came to rest. To touch their mistress so provocatively was too much for her three companions to bear. All at once they rushed for the chief, their thick arms outstretched to take him. One took him by the left arm, one grabbed his right, and the third gripped his neck. They dragged him back a little ways. But Caratacus wrenched his arms forward with a sudden powerful movement that brought the two who held them crashing against each other, head to head, knocking the wits out of them both; they staggered and fell to the ground roaring, clutching their skulls. Caratacus took the third by the wrists and broke his grip. Then hoisting him onto his shoulders, he threw him on top of his fellows, still stretched out on the grass. He turned to Cartimandua.

"Tonight, I will claim you, and let none dare challenge me," he announced.

With a sudden leap from the horse's back, she landed on Caratacus' chest, grabbing him by the ears. The two tumbled in the grass.

"But have you the strength equal to my desire?" she cried. "Compared to that challenge, the overthrow of those three is a boy's game." Her hands with their long, black-painted fingernails were as powerful as the talons of an eagle, clutching him. But Caratacus quickly turned head over heels, carrying Cartimandua with him. She found herself pinned beneath his thighs.

"It is desire that gives me strength," he replied. The droplets of mead on her breasts were like beads of blood on snow. One by one, he licked them off. She shuddered and heaved under the gentle but rough stroke of his tongue.

"Beware," she said, rolling her hips with voluptuous ease, "to tame a wild horse you must do more than mount her."

Her three guards staggered to their feet, furious at their humiliation. They came pounding towards them. With a sudden backward thrust of his elbows Caratacus caught the first two (whose heads carried nasty red bumps) with sharp, bitter, man-sickening blows to their groins. They fell to their knees gasping and groaning. One end of them was now as sore as the other. The third went to grab him from behind by the throat only to find his wrists taken in a bone-crushing grip, as Caratacus flung him over his head to a heavy rump-bruising collision with the earth. The Catuvellaunian sprang to his feet, ready to receive their next attack. But they lay, too stunned to do anything other than struggle up as far as their hands and knees.

"You clumsy fools," Cartimandua cried out, looking at their dazed, stupefied faces, "leave off your blundering and assist me to my feet." With difficulty, one leaning on the other, they staggered to their feet, then helped her up. Caratacus laughed at them, and turned back to where he had left Togodumnus and Bran holding the reins of his two chariot ponies.

"There, my beauties," he said taking the reins. Gently, he patted the ponies' snouts, then began to lead them to the stables.

"Sleek Pony has the kick of a wild horse," said Bran.

"She will know the weight of my bridle soon enough," Caratacus replied.

"But beware," the bard reminded his chief, "they say the blood of Dark Flame flows in her veins."

"And they say that Maponos was a jealous man. And where there is jealousy, there is no judgment," Caratacus answered. "The only men with cause to fear women are those who disappoint them."

Darkness was falling, the women's foot race—the last of the Beltane contests—was finishing, and the odor of roast boar was wafting across the meadow to remind them that the feast would soon begin.

"You should have allowed us to grind him into dust. He has treated you with nothing but arrogance," one of her guards said as the other growled in agreement.

"Are you blind as well as dumb?" she hissed back. "Can you not see that the man with the hawk-keen eyes pleases me? What he wins he takes. But no one, not even he, can take from me what I do not want to give."

The games concluded, the guests left the meadow and made their way to the palace or the feast hall for the night's revelries.

Prasutagus was seated at the central table in the palace with Caratacus and Togodumnus on one side of him and Cunodunum the Chief Druid and Bran the bard on the other. Prasutagus' wives sat with their hosts' wives at a separate table, with Latis the first wife occupying the most prominent position. The games had given both men and women a great thirst, and an appetite to match it. The oxen, the boars and the pigs were hissing away on the spits, and the great bulging cauldron was simmering. But the knife would not go into the meat until Fen Fire herself appeared. Latis wasn't slow to complain that they were being made to wait too long. "Perhaps she's gone hunting again and forgotten us," she said. The envoy had told her all about Fen Fire's late arrival and the state of her when she finally returned to accept the king's suit. "Who can tell? She might well show up in her shredded trousers, or perhaps she has been wrestling tonight and will come to her wedding covered in goat's fat."

"That would be perfume to the king's nose," replied Mournful Mound. "The first time he set eyes on her she was wrestling. For one whole night he spoke to me of nothing else. He went to sleep, his head resting on my bosom, muttering her name."

Latis flashed a poisonous look at her companion. "Since when has the king been in the habit of confiding in you?"

"When he seeks the sympathy of a woman not prone to jealousy."

Had it been another occasion Latis would have taken a swipe or made a grab at Mournful Mound, and a fine fight it would have been. But what a spectacle it would have made of the king's household—with people asking themselves if the man had lost his senses taking on another wife when he was not able to control those he already had. So she thought better of it and contented herself with a whispered threat. "When I'm through with you he won't bear to be able to look at you, never mind seek your sympathy!"

The women's squabble was cut short by a loud bellow that startled every guest in the palace. The doors were flung open. Into their midst rode Fen Fire, her white thighs astride the massive shoulders of the sacred bull of Andraste, her long, pale ring-sparkling fingers gripping its third bulbous horn which sprouted at mid-point from the beast's majestic head: white without blemish on profoundest black, a swan's white feather resting in a crevice of a lightning-blasted oak! A chain of gold was around its huge neck by which Maglocunos led it into the palace as the guests stared in wide-eyed wonder. Behind the bull came the priestesses of Andraste dressed in their cloaks of raven's feathers, with Nemain leading them. Each carried a brightly burning torch.

Fen Fire herself was dressed in a flaming red silk robe and a light speckled cape fastened with a gold brooch.

Her serpent-shaped torc of gold was on her slender throat. Its eyes of precious stones twinkled in the torchlight. Her hair was woven into a mass of tresses, each with a golden band at the tip. Over each breast was a brooch of red gold, while on her feet she wore silver-clasped sandals made of soft red leather. Her eyebrows glistened black over their fine ash-grey eyes. Her rowanberry lips etched a rich border against skin as white as the brief blossom of the rowan tree. She was garlanded in flowers—a crown of primroses on her head and little bands of meadowsweet around her arms, wrists and ankles.

While the eyes of the men lingered on Fen Fire, those of the women were fixed on Maglocunos, the Herder of Andraste's bull. Well was he known as the Bright Beautiful One. His soft brown hair was fine and curled, tumbling copiously from under his three-horned helmet of gold and silver. His eyes were bright and blue like those of his brother Caratacus, but his face was broad, more like that of Togodumnus, with a haughty forehead and well-ridged eyebrows. In form he was more slender than either of his brothers. To matrons and maidens alike, no man was more pleasing. But it was the sight of the bull that intrigued Cartimandua. It was as black as if it had been dipped in bog water. The sinewy muscles of its massive neck rippled as it moved ponderously through the palace. The vast head of the beast moved in a slow, kingly manner from side to side, regarding all disdainfully. The power that coursed through the sloping back along the beast's neck culminated in the central horn, thick and swollen at the top, not curved like the others, but straight: the Hooded One, He Who Nourishes, beloved of Andraste and her priestesses, whose strength was worshipped by all women. Never had she beheld such concentrated potency as when its haunches heaved.

"Force has become flesh," she gasped. Cartimandua possessed many fine and powerful bulls for the great herds that she grazed on her northern pastures. But compared to this they were poor, piddling, paltry creatures.

As Maglocunos brought the bull nearer—and it followed him like a lamb—the crowd fell back in awe. But as long as he was there such fears were groundless. The bull obeyed him in every way, for he had been chosen by the goddess to be its keeper. (She chose the Herder in this manner: when the three-horned bull had sired for the last time and was close to death, its throat was slit open for a cupful of its blood. The High Priestess mixed it into a potion and drank it. This powerful concoction induced a deep sleep. The man that would be the Herder for the young bull would come to her in a dream. When Nemain had performed this ritual, she dreamt of Maglocunos, and he had been the Herder ever since.) The procession proceeded through the palace doors slowly and majestically. Some of the priestesses beat a gentle rhythm on drums which hung on their hips; others played sweet melodies upon their pipes, while others went before Fen Fire and the bull to strew flowers around the room, until the whole palace was full of the scent of the woodlands. They made their way through the gaping crowd into the heart of the palace.

The first time Prasutagus had set eyes on Fen Fire she was hardly recognizable as a woman. He arrived at the wrestling match in time to see her lift her opponent high above her head and bring her down with a crash face-first to the ground, then leap on her back to wrench her head back until, her neck almost broken, she cried her submission. Covered in goat's fat, painted with blue dye, and begrimed with dirt, only their naked breasts and buttocks revealed them to be females of the human species—or indeed members of the human species at all. They had more of the appearance of demons sprung from the bowels of the earth. It was her ferocity and strength that pleased him in the beginning. All knew of her origins and the legends concerning her ancestors, among whom ranked some of the fiercest women warriors in the world, and of all time. He thought of the fine sons and daughters he could father with her. His own brood by the other wives was a disappointing one. Subidasto, his eldest boy, liked nothing better than to defy his father, and Latis' son was even less promising: a sickly malevolent stripling who was as spiteful as he was weak. The others gave him girls. Yet even if Fen Fire were to give birth to nothing but girls, the king would be well off if they were anything like their ancestors, or their mother. No one could want for braver or stronger warriors.

The king had watched Fen Fire fight another opponent stronger and more powerful-looking than the first. With both hands they locked fingers, as one strained to force the other to her knees. But with concentrated will, Fen Fire brought the woman slowly down inch by inch until her knees touched the ground. Letting go of one hand, Fen Fire quickly stepped behind her opponent, gripped her around the neck and wrenched her other hand up her back. Struggle as she did, she could not free herself from Fen Fire's powerful hold, and soon cried out her submission. And after the contest was finished, and the prizes awarded, the victor insisted on sharing her triumph with her beaten opponents.

Fascinated, Prasutagus had followed Fen Fire back to where her women companions had prepared a bath for her. They undid her hair, which fell down her back a crackling fiery red. With soap they then scrubbed clean her neck and shoulders, revealing their fine bones and swan-like curves; her back, having been stripped of its muddy veil, appeared graceful as it tapered to a narrow waist with high white haunches between broad hips. The goat's fat and blue dye, the dirt from the grappling on the ground, was washed away from her breasts, so that they now were revealed as white as the foam of a wave breaking on the beach, with nipples red like the berries of the quicken tree. The fierce warrior melted away before his eyes, and in her place, as if conjured out of the muddy water, stood a radiant young woman. "She has strength and yet seems full of tenderness, beauty yet shows no trace of vanity, and a spirit that triumphs but yet is not lacking in generosity," he had thought as he watched her that evening. At once, it occurred to him how this new friendship with the Catuvellauni might be formalized. To marry Fen Fire became his obsession. And finally, this May Eve, it was close to consumation.

"May this day prosper with you, Woman of the Flowers," Prasutagus greeted her as she stopped at the central table where he was seated.

"And with you, Yokemaster," came her reply.

The king rose, held her by the waist, and lifted her from the great beast's shoulders. She took her place at his side. By the sizzling spits, the chief carver sank his knife into a milk-fed hog. A loud cheer rang through the rafters. The gush of mead and ale and wine that began flowing into the cups was like the sound of a flooding river that has burst its banks. And many a guest was carried away on that torrent of drink like a log on a flooding stream. The food was as plentiful as the drink. There were pigs, boars, cows and oxen (the pigs had been reared on nothing but gruel and fresh milk, the cows and oxen on fresh herbs and the juiciest of twigs and sweetest of grasses), as well as salmon baked in honey and other kinds of fish baked in salt, vinegar and cumin, along with the plumpest wild geese brought down that very day, and many other different sorts of bird.

But the prize of the feast was the great boar slain by Fen Fire. She herself rose to slice it. The first portion she cut was the hero's portion—the thighs, each of which she gave to Prasutagus and to Caratacus in recognition of their triumphs at the chariot games. Latis watched her like a hawk. One of her companion wives, Barrel, nudged her in the ribs.

"The hero always wins the thighs. And before long Prasutagus will be adding hers to ours." She chuckled and took another gulp of mead. Latis gave her a whack on the back of the head. Barrel's nose went into the cup, making her splutter and sniff.

"I'm surprised that you can't breathe in drink like a fish in water by now!" Latis chortled. But she was none too pleased with the other women's signs of rebelliousness—before Fen Fire even moved into their household, she was the cause of trouble.

Amid general feasting Bran staggered to the front and was groping in his bag for his harp. He shook the Great Chain of Silence that hung nearby. But the clamor of the warriors and women was undiminished. He shook it again. He was to sing the praises of Fen Fire, exalt her ancestors, extol their triumphs and the triumphs of the tribe: their military prowess, unflinching courage, godlike strength. The palace seemed to turn like a great wheel around him. Before him stretched a tumult of mead-stained beards, ale-soured tongues, huge fists gripping bones, meat-stripping teeth, mouths full of the mush of food and drink. To send forth words into that crowd would be no wiser than jumping off a cliff. Yet he was not a bard if he did not believe his words could fly and carry him on their wings. He drank.

Fen Fire called up to him, "Tell us the story of Maponos and the Hunting of the Great Boar."

He looked at her, bleary-eyed. "None finer! I have sailed to one hundred and fifty islands, and on one of them I lay with as many women," he announced, and his voice trailed away like the cry of one plummeting down. He smiled and took another swig. "And they gave me and my crew everything men might ask for—a palace to live in, all we wanted to eat and drink. In truth I would still be there now if it were not for homesickness, and indeed I would go back if I could remember where it was. But that is nothing compared to the story I'm about to tell you now. On another island there were ants as big as dogs with great pinching jaws that ground rocks down to the size of sandgrains. We gave that one a miss. But that is nothing compared to the story I'm about . . ." He paused and mustered his strength. "I saw on another island not far from that one a monster sitting on the beach, and you know, it had the body of a cow, the legs of a pig, and the head of a horse; and it sang as sweetly as a little bird. But that is nothing compared . . ." He sighed.

Mago and Maponos, the Division of the World, the Hunting of the Great Boar, Dancing Flame and Red Shaft who brought back the Great Bull from the Underworld in springtime, and Dark Flame who vanished in the dark season. They all swirled before his eyes in a dim blur. All he had to do was strike his harp and the gates of the Other World swung open. In a shaft of light they poured forth, trampling the intervening centuries to dust to throng again amongst them and grip the minds of those in whose veins their blood still pounds. . . .

Mago the Great King of the Western World had settled down in Gaul and had taken as his wife Dancing Flame, the first red-haired woman in the world, and Maponos was their son—so the story of the Hunting of the Great Boar invariably began. Maponos was an unusual boy: he sprang from his mother's womb three months before he was due, with a mop of fiery red hair just like hers. Though he came early, his hair already reached down to the nape of his neck. He was already walking by the time he was due to have been born. He was learning to ride a horse by the time he should only have been learning to walk, and by the time he should have been starting to talk, he was composing the most complicated, mind-puzzling verses ever heard. By the age of seven there was no chariot feat or hero's feat he could not perform.

At that time, the kingdom of Mago was afflicted by a terrible plague. It came in the form of the most terrifying, ferocious boar that anyone had ever laid eyes upon. It was huge as a hillside. The bristles on its back were so thick, sharp and long that one of them could skewer a whole treefull of apples. Its tusks were so large and powerful that they dug trenches in the earth too deep for two men standing one on the shoulders of the other to reach from the floor of the furrow to the ridge. The brute went about the kingdom, trampling on people, uprooting their crops, killing their hounds, leaving any village it went through looking like an army of plunderers had just visited it. The people appealed to Mago for help. But where was the hunter, the horse and the hound that could pursue such a monster? A few brave men who got close enough to the brute to use their javelins reported that the boar's hide was so thick that they might as well have tried to stick straws in it: it shattered their weapons harmlessly.

"It is clear to me," Maponos announced to his father one day, "that it is time I took the matter in hand myself." Mago sighed with relief. He had been wondering when Maponos would come forward.

"See what you can come up with, my red-haired beauty," Mago replied. A few days later his son came back to him.

"I am ready to hunt the boar," he said.

Mago looked down at the little fellow, who was all of ten years old. "Have you a surprise for it?"

"I have that."

Mago nodded. "I could tell by the glint in your eye."

Maponos unveiled the Spear That Roars For Blood. Mago examined it carefully and quickly gave his approval. Never had he seen a spear with such a terrible, flesh-rending, bone-breaking, gut-goring head. Moreover, it had a special trick to it. "If only I'd had the like of it when I was starting out on my adventures." Mago sighed. "But the young have all the advantages these days!"

Maponos set out at once to find the boar. That wasn't difficult. It left a trail of devastation very easy to follow, and it stretched all the way to the vast German forests on the fringe of the kingdom. Maponos' companions told him that now that the beast had gone into the forest it would be pointless as well as impossible to continue tracking him. The forest had never been visited by anyone other than the Germans themselves. No one knew how far it went or where it ended, or what was in it at all.

Maponos would not hear such talk, nor would he listen to their pleas to turn back and not risk the dangers ahead. "I won't rest till I've brought that brute back ready for roasting. After the destruction he has visited upon us, it would be wrong to let him go." So he bade farewell to everyone and plunged into the trackless gloom, where because the huge towering trees formed a thick impenetrable canopy of leaves it was almost as dark as night. But when in doubt as to which way he should go, Maponos simply held out his spear, and the shaft quivered until the head pointed in the direction the giant boar had taken.

Finally after three days and three nights he tracked the boar to a cave under a cliff. When the boar saw the boy it gave a scoffing howl of laughter. "Boy," the brute said, showing its huge tusks, and glaring at him through fierce, scowling red eyes. "You would be ill advised to advance any further. For though it means nothing for me to trample a whelp like you into the dust, I fear that will be your fate. And that is not a pleasant prospect for one who should still be at home with his toys."

"Indeed, you are right: no one, boy or man, would welcome such an end," Maponos answered with a steady voice that showed no fear. "But had I been concerned about that, I would hardly have spent the last three days of hard riding through this dark and pathless forest full of wolves and other beasts every bit as fearsome as yourself, to follow you to this lonely place. Nor did I come here to discuss the good of my health or yours. On the contrary, my intentions are very different, for I plan to put an end to you. Then you will learn not to make derisive remarks about my age."

He raised his javelin. The boar charged furiously. Maponos' horse jumped over the beast, which turned round to charge again. But before it could, the Spear That Roars For Blood gave a quiver, then went hurtling from Maponos' hand. The spear struck the boar with such force that it transfixed it through the neck to a nearby oak tree.

As the beast lay dying in a pool of dark blood, Maponos addressed it again. He said: "You see the sort of toy I play with now, and how well I wield it. That will teach you to be so cheeky."

"I regret it now," the boar answered with its dying breath, "and I see that you are made for greater things than hunting poor brutes like myself. If you must hunt, your skills would be better tested in Britain, where the boars are three times as big, three times as fierce and three times as fast as I am—and, as you can see, I am no mouse. Truly, it is a land where a brave lad like yourself might be happy." At which, with a gurgle of blood, the boar died.

The young lad mulled over the boar's words while he set about making ready to return with his prize. This was the first time he'd heard of the Island of the Mighty (as Britain was called then) and he was intrigued. However, his musings were interrupted by a bellowing sound vaguely resembling a human voice. "What is this?" came the roar. "Someone's mother has been very neglectful!" The boy looked around to find that he had company—in a manner of speaking. For what he saw were the foulest, hairiest, biggest, smelliest, ugliest, dirtiest men he had ever seen. Their bellies were bloated out of shape; their legs were crooked; their necks were so squat that their heads seemed stuck to their shoulders which though broad and powerful were bony and misshapen. And their feet were the hugest and the flattest imaginable, and were pointed inwards as well. They carried the crudest axes ever made, being simply heavy lumps of stone stuck on the ends of sticks. For shields they had hides which were in tatters and for horses brutes as ugly as themselves: scraggy, dirty creatures with matted filthy hair and bent, crooked legs. And when they opened their thick-lipped mouths to speak, each man revealed a row of broken crooked pegs. From what he had heard, Maponos recognized them at once as Germans. Throughout the world, the Germans had a terrifying reputation for ferocity.

"Sirs," Maponos replied calmly, "if any mother has been neglectful it is your own, for only a neglectful mother would have let you out of the house in such a state."

The Germans fell silent and did not answer for a while, but gaped stupidly at each other and then at the lad as if their eyes and their ears were at odds, for how could it be that this defiant speech could come from someone so small? Then their chief, who was the biggest and ugliest one of all, came down off his old nag and approached the boy. "Who do you think you are talking to?" he bellowed. So foul was the stench of his breath that Maponos was almost knocked over.

"I cannot say, since you did not have the courtesy to introduce yourselves," the boy answered, looking him straight in the eye.

"Introduce ourselves!" their chief exclaimed, spitting and spluttering over everything. "Introduce ourselves to a scamp like you? If you knew who we were, whelp, you would know that we have no need to introduce ourselves!"

"That is beyond dispute," Maponos replied directly, "for if I knew who you were, then what need would I have to be introduced to you, for no one has to be introduced to someone he knows."

The chief glared down at him and his dull eyes blinked. He grinned and grabbed the boy with his great, grimy paw.

"Clever with words as well as cheeky, are we, heh? Well, Wordmaster, see if you can explain how a mere stripling like yourself comes to be standing over one of our boars, and by all appearances, making ready to steal it from us right here in our forest where no man, however brave, dares tread without our permission?'' He pulled Maponos right up against him so close that the boy could count the crumbs in his beard and make an intelligent guess as to what he had been eating for dinner for the last six months.

''You are gravely mistaken. I cannot steal something which belongs to me. You see, this boar is mine.'' This made all the Germans roar with laughter and beat the sides of their tattered shields with their dingy, rusty broadswords. The chief laughed so loud he shook a torrent of crumbs from his beard that formed a layer so deep it covered the boy's feet up to his ankles.

''It seems this lad has a head well-stocked with fancies as well as a tongue over-ready to make them known,'' the chief said with a great grin. His row of broken teeth, mere black stumps, looked like a forest after a fire has ravaged it. ''Now if you would have the courtesy,'' replied the chief in mockery, ''would you be so kind as to tell me how it comes to be yours?''

''Gladly. The truth is I killed it, and so it is mine.''

But this brought forth greater gusts of mirth from the Germans, who shook their great bellies laughing. It took some time before the chief could collect himself to ask the next question. ''And tell me—if you would have the courtesy—how did you kill this great beast I see pinned to the oak tree? Did you perhaps trip it up with your dainty little foot as it walked by?''

Maponos did not laugh, but quietly and with dignity said: ''I killed it with a cast of my javelin, which you see is stuck through the neck of the brute and has fixed it to the tree.''

''And I say to you, little one, that the javelin you point to is not your own, but a German's; for a snip like you could no more handle that weapon than that boar there could talk to us,'' the chief bellowed.

At this the boar promptly opened its mouth and said to the chief clearly and loudly, ''I could talk as well as you before this boy ended my life with a throw of his javelin. And a bitter, hard, warrior-fierce throw it was too!'' Though the boar was dead (nothing could have withstood that spear and that thrust) his spirit had not yet left his body. The face of the chief was drained of blood. Letting go of Maponos, he jumped back as white as a mushroom, while his companions' horses reared up and threw them off. The whole gang of them fell with as clamorous a clatter as ever was heard in the world—what with the banging of their rusty armor, dingy helmets and old bent broadswords.

''Don't be afraid,'' Maponos announced. ''The beast cannot harm you, thanks to the strength of my arm and the sturdiness of my javelin.''

The chief recovered his composure but was angrier than ever. Drawing his sword he cried out, ''There is trickery around us! The little scamp thinks himself a wizard as well as a hunter.'' He came forward cautiously and poked the boar with his sword. When he was sure it was quite dead he put his sword down, spat on his hands, and rubbed them together. Then he grasped the shaft of the javelin with one hand. ''When we've freed our boar from this tree, we'll deal with you,'' he said. His companions who had stumbled to their feet, grunted in agreement.

''Let's cook the brat in a pot!'' they growled.

With one hand the chief gave the javelin a powerful tug, but pull as he liked, it would not budge. He took the weapon with both hands and pulled with all his might. Still the javelin remained fixed in the tree. Cursing, he asked one of his companions to help him. The two Germans then grabbed the shaft and exerting every ounce of their strength they strained and pulled and tugged, digging their heels into the ground and then placing their big, fat misshapen feet against the tree itself so that they looked as if they were trying to walk up it. Seeing it was to no avail, the others then lined up behind the chief, one holding the waist of the man in front of him, and together they made one almighty effort. Grunting, groaning, sweating so profusely that they were standing in puddles, tugging, pulling, wrenching, teeth clenched, grim, fierce looks in their eyes, their huge muscles bulging and breaking through their raggedy shirts, the chief and his men expended all their strength and energy, until their heels were dug deep into the forest floor and the hands of the chief were smoking hot as his palms rubbed against the wood.

Meanwhile, Maponos watched quietly and kept his counsel.

All at once the whole gang collapsed in a heap on the ground. They lay there moaning with no more power in their limbs than a gaggle of old women. The boy looked at them and shook his head. Regardless of the spiteful things they said to him and their silly threats, he felt sorry for them. Putting one foot on the tree trunk and gripping the shaft with one hand, Maponos gave the javelin a sudden twist, pulling it at the same time. Out it came as easily as if it had been a dagger embedded in the soft white breast of a woodpigeon.

For the Germans this was the final blow. With one voice they gasped in disbelief, then rolled over on their big bellies, their faces buried for shame in the leaves of the forest floor. They began to beat it with their fists. Maponos went over to them with his spear in his hand. He tapped the chief on the shoulder. The chief glanced round, his eyes dripping tears.

"Go ahead," he groaned, "put an end to all of us; we deserve no better. We, grown men, most feared warriors, humiliated by a boy!"

Maponos had no mind to see them humbled any further—there was something in their simple and unbridled ferocity which he admired. "Strength is a necessary thing in a man," he said, "but sometimes it is not enough by itself." Then he pointed to the head of the javelin and showed them how he had made its peculiar twisted shape so that a man must turn it before it came loose.

The Germans sat up, full of childlike wonder. Their contempt for Maponos changed to undying admiration, especially when he told them he had made the spear himself. The chief begged his forgiveness for the way they had treated him.

"It is our custom to terrify anyone who dares come into our forest," the chief explained, "because we do not welcome the attentions of outsiders. We are used to living our lives in the way our forefathers did. Thus we believe we can best preserve those things which made us fierce and feared and strong. We have witnessed what has happened to a race of warriors such as the Gauls when they allow themselves to come under outside influence which brings with it so many fine, soft luxuries. A love of luxury soon becomes a habit, and habits like that make men weak. Our brains may not be the quickest, but we know enough to realize that if a race of warriors is to remain strong then it must never acquire such habits. Those who need luxuries will not remain free."

"What you say contains great wisdom," Maponos replied, impressed by their simple and forthright vision. "When a people grow dependent on luxuries they soon lose the willingness to face hardships. Without that willingness freedom cannot be defended and men become enslaved."

Maponos went on his way with the slain boar, his new-found friends acting as guides through the forest. He regretted saying farewell to them in the end. Often, he would think about what they had said. As the years passed, he noticed all around him that the people were falling into easy habits, neglecting the old ways. They were growing rich and fat and complacent. Often too he would look up at where the head of the great boar hung from the palace wall, and remember what it had told him about the island of Britain. . . .

"So in the end he came here," said Bran, "for what he saw among the Gauls was not pleasing to his eyes. Too many were eager to extend the hand of welcome to Caesar, who came as a 'friend,' promising protection, enrichment to a few, while using them to betray the rest." The bard paused to refill his cup. "Maponos knew the cost of such friendship was slavery. He knew what some in Britain have by now forgotten: Rome will not rest until she has enslaved the world, and those whom she embraces today, tommorrow will wake to find themselves in chains."

Bran would say no more. He was already speaking of the world the feasting warriors knew and of the time they lived in—topics too sobering for a night like this.

Chapter 9

The predawn wind rustled the leaves in the surrounding woods, swept back gently the meadow grass, and stirred softly the feathers of the sleeping swan. The steps of the wedding platform creaked and the long neck of the bird uncoiled. The first day of summer glimmered just below the horizon as the procession climbed up. Cunodunum, the Chief Druid, and Nemain, the High Priestess, walked before Prasutagus and Fen Fire. Behind them came Togodumnus and Caratacus, and then Latis and her companion wives. The other guests came crowding into the meadow, a riotous torrent that broke the stillness of the sunrise and startled the swan where it lay in its wooden cage on the wedding platform. They halted beside it. Cunodunum looked at Latis. "The rite has been observed?"

"It has. The bird has not been fed in three days."

The swan shook itself. Latis' eyes glanced towards the floor of the cage for a moment. The crackling torches around her revealed the cage was clean. She let her eyes rest on the glow of dawn. The druid took a small pouch from his cloak and gave it to Fen Fire. She undid it and poured a stream of grain into her palm.

"Are you worthy of holding the hand of a king?" Cunodunum asked.

"I am."

"Then the swan will feed from your hand," the king answered in turn.

Fen Fire crouched down in front of the cage, the seed clutched in her fist. She gently put her hand through the bars. The swan arched its head a little. As Fen Fire's fist unfolded like a blossoming white-petalled flower, Latis turned her head slowly away from the dawn towards her. Suddenly the swan swelled up and its great white bosom puffed out menacingly. Fen Fire urged her palmful of seeds. The bird hissed fiercely and began to unfold its immense wings. Its neck curled like a thick white lash getting ready to strike out. Fen Fire raised her palm up a little. Her hand was steady and her attention fixed on the black encircled eyes of the bird. Its great beak hovered above her palm. It hissed again viciously and brought its two huge wings crashing against the sides of its prison. Latis now preferred to scrutinize the face of her husband as the Chief Druid put his hand on Fen Fire's shoulder. The face of the king was ashen, his eyes rivetted in disbelief on the angry, defiant swan.

"Fen Fire, the bird will not eat from your palm," the priest said.

Another thud of the wings made him step back in fear as the whole cage trembled.

Caratacus scrutinized Latis. "You are certain the rites were strictly observed?" he asked, appalled at the humiliating prospect of the marriage being abandoned.

"It is not my virtue that is being tested, but hers!" she shot back. She found it hard to suppress a look of triumph.

"Her virtue will never be in doubt!" he answered with fierce and unwavering faith, yet worried that the alliance of the tribes which he so keenly sought against the threat from Rome would be sacrificed because of a bad-tempered bird.

The swan beat its wings; they were powerful, swishing blows. The cage shook again, but the bars held, though it seemed at any moment they would collapse. Everyone stepped back towards the stairs except Fen Fire and Caratacus.

"Beware!" Prasutagus called out to her, "the bird can break your back with a single blow."

Fen Fire stood up and took a step backward as if heeding the warning, the uneaten grain still in her hand. The bird puffed up, spread out its wings, and regarded her fiercely. The glow of dawn shone pink on its feathers; it swung its head toward the rising sun.

"I know what ails this bird," she said, and fetched the side of the cage a powerful kick. The cage shuddered. She kicked again. And again. Inside, the swan smashed its wings against the bars more furiously than ever.

"The woman has gone mad!" Latis cried out, edging slowly down the platform steps. The side of the cage caved in as its bars were smashed into sticks. Fen Fire then struck the front. Within moments the front broke into splinters of wood which went spinning up into the morning air. The swan finally thrust its wings out their full length and burst from the tangle of shattered wood. The guests cried out. Caratacus reached for his sword. But the princess put her hand on his.

"There will be no need of that, the bird means no harm," she said. And once more she extended her palm full of seeds.

The swan came towards her, its wings still outstretched, only to nestle down beside her, taking the seed from her palm quietly and gently, as if it were feeding peacefully on a lake.

"He was not protesting my lack of virtue," she said, "but his own lack of freedom." The bird finished the seeds and began to flap its wings.

"Clear a path for him," the princess cried.

"It will fly away!" Prasutagus' first wife shouted, not anxious to lose her pet. Even as she spoke the bird rose up off the edge of the platform and flew away towards the breaking dawn. Fen Fire watched the white bird soar into the reddening sky.

"My greatest virtue is my love of liberty. And it was his also," said Fen Fire as the bird became a speck.

"There is no greater virtue," Prasutagus answered. The king and the others had come back to resume the ceremony. Latis kicked the step with her heel. Liberty indeed! A pious word for the antics of a troublemaker! Her bird had been perfectly contented in her cage until now, just as the king's other wives seemed happy with their lot until they learned of Fen Fire's coming. The king will realize before too long that it is easy for a woman to rouse up what she cannot restrain . . .

Fen Fire walked to one side of the Grey Woman stone,

the king to the other. Cunodunum watched the brightening horizon while beneath some boys stood near the stacks of wood at either side of the platform holding blazing torches in their hands. A hush fell over the meadow. The first rays of Beltane, the dawn of summer, were about to fall upon the waiting earth. Slowly the princess extended her arm until her hand was in the hole of the ancient grey stone. From the other side the king did the same. As the sun's bright rim broke over the horizon they clasped hands. The young summer poured its bright warmth through the stone, its golden light gilding the flesh of man and woman, making them one.

The priest raised his arms to the east. "Sun and earth, man and woman, fruitful unions both."

On a little table nearby was a small heap of toasted oaten cakes. The king took one and gave it to Fen Fire. She took a bite and gave it back to him.

"I welcome you to my household," he said.

"Be sure that it will prosper with me. May your table never be bare, your pot never empty and your bed never cold," she told him.

The boys lit the great bonfires on either side of them. Maglocunos led the sacred bull towards them. Behind came the cattle herd, behind that a flock of sheep and behind the sheep a herd of pigs. The bull thundered first between the fires, the red flames glowing on his powerful sides and shoulders and haunches; his herd came crowding after him, followed by the sheep, and the pigs. The heat from Beltane fires would thus ensure the fertility of the animals for the coming year.

Fen Fire stripped off her speckled cape and leapt into the meadow grass, summoning the young women to follow her. They ran sunwise between the bonfires and around the stones three times, while the warriors mounted their horses to pursue them with switches made from May-tree branches. After completing the third turn, Fen Fire let her tunic fall and bared her panting bosom. The king rode towards her, and bending down, tenderly drew the branch across her heaving breasts. With a bound, she leapt away from him and made for the fringe of trees. He urged his horse after her.

The other women quickly followed her lead and hoisted up their tunics or hauled them down, exposing their breasts or thighs or buttocks, eager to receive a blow from the branch that brought fertility, wielded by some warrior they desired. When struck, they turned and ran across the field, the warriors racing after them. One by one, the young men snatched them up easily and, laying them across their mounts, rode off towards the still-dark woods. But Fen Fire, swifter of foot than any, was almost into the woods before Prasutagus swooped down on her. With a cry of triumph, he caught her securely around the waist and scooped her off her feet. They vanished into the shadowy woods. She lay across the horse's neck, her heart beating as hard as the hooves pounding beneath her. Heady with mead, she swooned; the wood seemed to breathe and its breath was perfumed with the dew-drenched scent of flowers. The king slowly drew up her tunic; his hand stroked her, resting under her buttocks, against the backs of her thighs. Already the birds on every branch were bursting full-throated into song to greet the approaching dawn. The woods rang out with laughter; it was alive with the love cries of women. She felt the whole world trembling with ecstasy on the verge of the new day, which would see the summer season fresh and fruitful begin to unfold. Exhilarated, Fen Fire suddenly dropped from the king's grasp and ran ahead of him as he reined in his horse.

"You must prove yourself to be a hunter before I take you as a husband," she cried out, darting into the shadows among the trees. Her smooth white haunches flashed through the deep dark green and vanished. Keeping his head low, he urged the steed forward. It leapt over the bushes and undergrowth easily, as the king circled round searching for her. The woods concealed her well. It was a while before he could find a trace of her: a strand of red hair dangling from a low-hanging branch. He halted and bent down to pick it up. Panting with excitement, she watched him. The fear of being caught was as pleasurable as the pleasure of successfully eluding him was fearful. She dashed from behind a nearby tree. Prasutagus bounded after her, and before she could vanish, his hand had grasped her by the wrist. He dove and pulled her to the ground, pinning her securely under him.

"The hunter claims you with a single thrust, but deeper and more pleasurable than any," he said.

The king was as firm as well-seasoned wood. His wrists and arms were as sinewy as mature vines, his thighs as supple as willow branches, and his belly, which pressed down on hers, seemed as taut as a fine-grained plank. Above her in a hawthorn bush was a delicate round spider web hung with beads of morning dew and beyond that, soaring up towards the gradually brightening sky, the huge forms of the dark trees. Her panting made the web tremble, shaking its little drops on to her eyelids. Her back still pressed against the dew-wet grass, he hoisted up her legs and draped them over his shoulders.

"Oak-master," she cried out. He sank his fingers into her thighs, pulling her towards him.

"Oak is the wood of kings," he answered.

She shuddered and reached out to grip a branch hanging nearby, thrusting her hand through the web, tearing it. Silken and damp, it clung to her hand, as close to her as a second skin. With her other hand she clutched at the grass growing around her, ripping it up by the roots. The king was oak hard. And soon, the creamy white juice of the mistletoe was hers.

Caratacus reined in his horse and found himself unexpectedly in a wide field—a pasture ground on the edge of the woods where cattle grazed peacefully in the dawn light. The black stallion of Cartimandua stood riderless at the foot of a little hillock at the far side of the field, near another patch of woodland. Slowly, he rode across the field, through the cattle. The powerful black steed pawed the ground, its sides steaming, its mouth a little frothy. As the ceremonies were ending Caratacus had caught sight of her leaving the meadow. He went after her, losing her in the woods. But another glimpse of the dark-haired princess, fleeing before him, made him ride harder and before he realized it, she had led him to this place familiar to him since the time of his childhood. The hillock rose up, its top higher than the surrounding trees. The cattle turned their slow gaze towards Caratacus as he quietly passed. A rustling that was not the wind told him someone was near. In the dim light he thought he glimpsed her flitting behind the hillock. He slid from his panting horse and followed. A laugh, enticing and playful, rippled through the twilight. "Come to me," she said to Caratacus, "or do you believe those stories that say I am descended from Dark Flame?" Her voice came from the shadowed fringe of the clearing where the rags of night still clung and the slope of the hill merged into the wood. Cartimandua had appeared from nowhere, presenting herself to him. "I await you under the willow tree." A crescent moon glistened in the shadows. It was her brooch, and it held her finely fringed green cape to her moon-pale breast.

Cartimandua stood with her back against the bark of the tree. In her fingers she entwined the willow thongs, slowly loosening them from her thighs, while under her long, finely curled lashes that cast a shadow over her cheeks, her green eyes never wavered from those of the Catuvellaunian chief. Caratacus came towards her. "The willow is my tree," she said.

"It is the tree of witches," he replied.

She laughed. "It is owned by the moon that governs the waters of the earth in their rise and in their fall. It is the tree that loves what is moist and wet. And its thongs . . . they are the only things that can bind a witch."

Caratacus grabbed the loosening thongs around her thighs. He knelt down, took them in his teeth; he tugged them off, he licked her thighs with his tongue; his mouth ravened her, his teeth furrowed into the soft welts left by the willow thongs.

"Bind me," she begged hoarsely.

Her cries roused the surrounding woods, startling them into motion. All around, there was a tumult of flapping wings as the birds of the forest flew up from the boughs of the trees, flocking into the air, the sparrow with the hawk. The deer and boar scampered together with the wolf, the rabbit with the fox, all bounded from their concealment to run pell mell towards the clearing. As before a raging forest fire, all ancient enmities were forgotten.

Chapter 10

A solitary horseman rode slowly from the west towards the remains of the bonfires smouldering by the twin grey stones. A coarse brown woollen cloak was thrown over his shoulders, and its hood was a dark cave in which his features could not be discerned. A broadsword in a bronze scabbard engraved with boars and horses hung from his hip. His well-tanned leather trousers were splattered with dirt after a long journey. He halted by the dying fires and gazed up at the stones and the deserted wedding platform, covered in fragments from the shattered swan's cage. All around the bonfires the flames had scorched the grass brown. The grass in the gap between the fires was trampled flat by the hooves of the cattle and sheep, herded through the flames to ensure their fertility, the same gap through which Fen Fire had lately led the young women in their race before they disappeared with their warriors into the woods. But now the field was deserted, though it was not silent. The birds sang in the woods, and bursts of laughter and shouts rang out from among the trees where the warriors and their women-of-a-night still enjoyed their May Day trysts.

He dismounted, and after leading his horse to a fresh patch of grass to graze, slowly climbed the steps to the platform. A few swan's feathers tumbled away, white puffs in the gentle morning breeze, the first breath of summer. Some scattered seed lay near the broken cage. No doubt the new wife had proven her virtue to the satisfaction of all. Nearby, he found a stack of oat scones—the wedding cakes, the first bread broken between man and wife, and by their families. They lay in a pile, some half-eaten, others untouched. They were cold, unappetizing. But he was hungry. In his haste to reach Camulodunum he had not thought of food, until now. Perhaps the peaceful champing of his horse had whetted his appetite. He picked up the scones. They were still edible to a man who had journeyed long without enjoying the pleasures of the feast hall. He walked between the stones munching on scones, inspecting curiously the busted cage, then he bent down to peer through the holed stone. Through a ring of stone he could see the woods on the meadow's edge. Occasionally, he caught a glimpse of a vague figure in the dawn light, among the trees. But he was too far away to see a face clearly or make out more than the long loose hair of a woman, her naked skin flashing ghostly pale against the dark green before disappearing among the trees. He finished the scones, left the platform and led his horse slowly across the meadow to the palace. Having reached his goal, he felt tired and weary.

The gatekeeper lay slumped at his post, snoring contentedly. A huge piece of uneaten roast pork was on the floor beside him, next to a cup which had been knocked on its side; a little puddle of spilt ale was seeping into the ground. The gates were wide open. He would not bother disturbing the man. He would find Caratacus himself.

The palace doors were also thrown ajar. From its dark interior came the smell of sour ale, mingled with that of wine and mead; the fumes of roast boar and pig and oxen still hung in the air. His long brown cloak trailed through the mess of spilt drink and trampled food that lay strewn about the floor of the palace; his boots crunched on bones. He threw back his hood. His brown hair was tangled and unkempt, his face youthful and wind-tanned, with eager blue eyes. He walked slowly, smiling a little at the chaos left by the Beltane wedding feast. A dim column of light came down through the hole in the roof above the embers of the great fireplace. From the surrounding darkness came the occasional grunt or snore. It was as if the world was steeped in an eternal stupefaction from which it would never wake. But awake it must, and soon.

A dog lay curled on the lap of a warrior who slept propped up against a pillar. Quietly, he stepped over the outstretched legs and turned towards the passageway that gave access to the palace's private chambers. Its torches extinguished, it was profoundly dark, except for the faint gleams of light from the main hall reflected on the polished engravings that decorated the partitions separating the chambers from the passageway. He was wondering which way to turn, when a sound made him look round.

"A late arriving guest," a voice said from behind him. "But I fear you have missed the feast." He swung round. The huge figure of Togodumnus loomed up out of the darkness, his arms folded like a titan surveying the chaos from which one day the order of the world would spring. He came closer to the newcomer.

"I do not believe it!" Togodumnus cried in surprise. "That Subidasto would deign to visit us without his sword raised!"

"It will be raised soon enough," Subidasto answered. "But not against you."

"So your father's wisdom has finally brought you to your senses."

"I have my own reasons for coming here, regardless of what my father does or does not do," Subidasto replied scornfully.

"So clearly you did not come to bring your father his wedding gift! Then what reasons could bring you here, and at such an hour?" Togodumnus asked.

"I will speak with Caratacus."

"You will speak with Caratacus! And what makes you think Caratacus will speak with you?"

"Because what I have to say to him he knows to be of vital importance," the young man responded calmly and confidently. It would have been better not to make such an assertion, implying as it did an important matter shared with Caratacus from which Togodumnus was excluded, but his pride took precedence over prudent diplomacy.

"Then you can tell me. I am his brother—what is vital to him must be vital to me also," Togodumnus replied, rankled by that very suggestion. He glowered down at Subidasto. "Speak," he ordered.

"I have sworn to speak only to Caratacus."

"My brother would not keep from me any matter of import only to share it with his enemy."

"I am not your enemy," Subidasto replied. "We have a more powerful foe to confront now."

Caratacus strode into the palace, his jerkin torn, his breeches ripped so that his thighs were bare, and his neck scored and scratched, as if the mounds had let loose a demon that he had somehow subjugated. But his victory, if such it was, had exhilarated him.

"Subidasto! You have news for us?" he asked, embracing him as Togodumnus looked on in growing surprise.

"Adminius has returned. Verica met with him secretly a few days ago in a little fishing village on the coast. He was sent back from Rome with a message from Caesar. All the signs speak of an early invasion. It can only be a matter of time before their armies land."

Togodumnus could hold his tongue no longer. "What? Oblige me with an explanation, brother."

Caratacus was succinct. Subidasto had gone to Verica at first as a refugee, hoping to continue his vendetta against the Catuvellauni. But he was not long there before he had discovered that Verica was in league with Adminius, and both were endeavoring to bring Caesar's legions to Britain. Subidasto realized that whatever threatening ambitions he attributed to the Catuvellauni, they were nothing as compared to those of the exiled Adminius and the Atrebatian king: they were planning to help Rome achieve the complete subjugation of the Britons. "It was then he decided to come to me with what he knew," Caratacus explained. "Their plans still being at an early stage, I told him to return to Calleva, Verica's capital, and remain in the king's favor as long as he could gather useful information about their schemes." The most secure secret being that which is known to the fewest, Caratacus decided that only he and Subidasto should know of the youth's double life.

"But he has forsworn his old enmity for us and found a new cause for unity."

"It is not for nothing you are called a fox, brother," said Togodumnus. He smiled at Subidasto now that he saw him in a new light. "And it is a wise choice you have made, lad. Verica will soon be in need of refuge himself. It is a wonder that my flesh did not crawl when Adminius set foot on this island again, and so alert me of his return. He will not be allowed to do so again! We must move against Verica at once. Come, it is day already. Though the summer season has barely begun, there is a crop of traitors ripe for cutting!" Togodumnus threw his arm around the young man's shoulders. "This reconciliation is very timely. It will be yet another cause for your father to celebrate."

"Yes—he will want to renew the feast when he finds you here as a friend and not as a foe," said Caratacus.

"It is a long while since we have shared a cup," Subidasto answered. "But the time is past when we can afford such disputes." The quarrel with his father had been a bitter one, but he was determined to set it aside. In any case, it was now irrelevant.

The palace was beginning to stir again. The three went in search of the king, but got no further than the palace doors when they met the returning revellers. Men and women came wandering in bleary-eyed. Dishevelled, their cloaks and tunics awry, with blades of grass clinging to them, they yawned in slothful contentment, while the women called for mirrors to fix their hair. The other wives of Prasutagus were among them, but there was no sign of the king in the throng. Arm in arm the couples swayed into the room, kissing and fondling, most of them reluctant to relinquish each other and return to the world of everyday responsibilities. But Master Order was slowly reasserting his rule over Mistress Chaos, reassigning his subjects to their usual places, until a woman's fondly plucking of a grassblade from a warrior's cape was the only indication of the predawn, carefree intimacy that had prevailed in the world.

Meanwhile, the servants filled great basins with cold water, and left the guests to douse themselves. There is nothing like a splash of cold fresh water to bring back a man's appetites. And before long, they were calling for more food and drink.

Subidasto saw his father come riding across the meadow, easily recognized even from afar because of his long yellow hair. A pair of white arms were flung around his waist as he cantered toward them on his even-gaited steed. The head of his young wife rested sleepily on his shoulder, her face snuggled against his neck.

It was as if Prasutagus saw a spectre. The king reined in his horse abruptly. His son stood before him, the two men who were formerly his sworn enemies on either side of him.

"There is another cause for joy," Caratacus said, hailing him.

"Indeed, if my eyes do not deceive me!" exclaimed Prasutagus. His son stepped forward and extended his arm. Subidasto noticed for the first time Fen Fire's long red hair.

The sound of voices awoke her. The king was talking excitedly. Within moments, he had dismounted and was hoisting her off the horse and into the embrace of his newly returned son. Her haunches were stained green from the juice of freshly crushed grass. He hugged both son and wife until they were almost touching—almost as close as they had been once before when they lay together under the waterfall and each took what pleasure they wanted from the other through one long night, until the grey unwelcome dawn parted them.

"May every good thing you wish for come to you," said Sun Fragment to the woman who was now his father's wife.

"And to you also," she replied. She turned away abruptly, sure that her eyes were betraying the surge of shock and confusion which threatened to overwhelm her. Recovering her calm demeanor, she pretended weariness and asked to be taken to her chamber and allowed to sleep.

Her heart was bounding in her breast like a startled deer.

The blast of the horn made Fen Fire glance back from where she was sitting in the rear of the king's huge carriage. The host was riding out of the gates of Camulodunum, a blaze of flashing bronze at the height of the day, on their way to settle with Verica, ally of Rome, and co-conspirator with the hated Adminius.

The intervening days had been a blur to her. Having excused herself that first morning when she discovered the truth about Sun Fragment, she'd lain awake plucking the petals from the flowers on the bracelet she still wore until there were no more left to pluck. She had spent the whole day feigning tiredness, trying to avoid the company of her husband and his son, her lover of Beltane a year ago. Thankfully, the following day was easier. Subidasto was absent for much of the time with Caratacus, Togodumnus and Maglocunos planning the coming raid on the Atrebates—a raid which his father opposed vociferously. Often, their voices had been raised in dispute, the king arguing that to attack Rome's ally was to invite the intervention that they were seeking to prevent.

"Caesar intends to attack anyway," Subidasto had replied. "It is better that we oppose him with no traitors like Verica in our midst, ready to welcome him. Since on his account and that of Adminius they plot against us already, it cannot be said that we provoke them." But when he spoke, Fen Fire was too distracted to pay heed to the issues or the reasons behind what he was saying; his voice was so like that of his father's, that in the arguments that took place during those days it was sometimes impossible for her to tell who was who.

Somewhere among the profusion of well-armed men with their high-crested helmets and flowing cloaks was Subidasto. But she did not linger long enough to pick out his fair face and well-fashioned shape. She turned her face away and looked at Prasutagus comfortably cushioned in the center of the carriage among his wives. Far from bringing her relief, it only increased her anguish: for to look at the face of the father was to see the face of the son.

"You seem pale," said the king.

"I am merely tired," said she.

The king reached out his hand. "Then come—sit with us where it is more comfortable. You will make your eyes sore sitting at the back with all the dirt and dust that the wheels throw up. Indeed, I see you have already made them red with rubbing." Fen Fire glanced back quickly. The great host had streamed out of the gate and turned west. It was an indistinct shimmering blur of colors. She took his hand and sat next to him on a comfortable cushion stuffed with ferns that he had arranged by making Latis move back a little. His new wife settled down between him and Barrel, who was looking remarkably pleased with herself, just as Latis seemed more grumpy than usual. Fen Fire was too preoccupied at that moment to do more than notice the ill humor of the king's chief wife, which she attributed to what seemed the most obvious cause: rivalry with herself for their husband's attentions. Unknown to Fen Fire, this was but one of the annoyances Latis endured with such obvious irritation—and at that moment it was far from being the most important one.

"I think you regret not accompanying Caratacus and his brothers to war," Prasutagus said as they bumped along. He put his arm around her. Fen Fire shifted a little, pretending to adjust her cushion more to her liking; but it was his touch that made her feel ill at ease. Such a short time before it had been familiar and comforting. But now her husband's touch was strange to her because it had become familiar in a different and unsettling way—it reminded her of how his son held her, caressed her, desired her.

"You will soon be happier with the carriage as a means of conveyance when you grow used to its comforts," he went on, "though I know you are accustomed to the chariot—but here you are safe from the gusts of the wind and the pelting of rain."

She smiled, but said nothing.

The king's carriage rumbled heavily down the track, creaking and swaying, its massive wheels grinding through the ruts for which they seemed so well-fitted—a far different motion from that of the wind-swift light-framed war chariot as it bounded over the battlefield; it was the heavy lumbering rattle of domestic life Fen Fire felt now, full of ponderous jolts and bumps, as they rolled slowly along towards the Palace of the Mists, which was to be their summer home, behind the thick-haunched plodding oxen.

Truly, her domestic life had begun with a jarring start.

PART 3

Chapter 11

The waves rose up like hillsides and broke across the boat, soaking the fugitive king and adding to the woeful state of flight and exile the discomfort of a cold drenching. When Verica's boat plunged into the troughs between the waves and there was no sight of land on any side of him, he hung over the side and heaved. Britain had disappeared from view; he despaired of ever seeing it again. Only desperation had forced him to entrust his fate to the sea. He had been right all along. If they had let him plead his case at Rome when he had requested it, Caratacus and his brothers would never have dared set foot across his borders for fear of retribution. Adminius and his delays and promises! They had brought him to this. Abandoned by his chiefs, scorned by his people, he was fortunate to snatch a few valuables, some clothes, and escape from Calleva to the coast before the Catuvellauni host descended to plunder and destroy the wealth he had taken years to create. But he was too quick for them. He deprived them of the prize they wanted more than anything—his head. No thanks to Adminius and his powerful friends in Rome. If he had followed their advice, his head would be adorning a stake and the rest of him would be a crow feast. He consoled himself by thinking of what he would say to Adminius if he reached the safety of Gaul. And he worked himself up into an even greater fury imagining his fellow exile lounging in the comfort of some Roman dining room, chattering with his new friends and savoring their wines. Wine! When Adminius first met him he knew nothing about wine—no more than a pig-keeper.

The threatening seas finally grew calm. The coast of

Gaul came into sight—the very coast from which a century or more before, Commius had fled in hatred of Rome. The great Commius, his own ancestor, who had left Gaul for Britain vowing never to come into the presence of another Roman again. After his former friends had tried to assassinate him, Commius turned his back on Romans forever, coming to Britain where he built Calleva and founded the kingdom of the Atrebates. The bitter irony was not lost on Verica as he was compelled to entrust his life to the very people his great-grandfather had anathematized forever for their treachery. Now, for the first time in many generations, a warrior of his bloodline was about to set foot in Gaul as an ally of the Caesars.

Just after dawn, his vessel was intercepted by a Roman naval patrol and Verica, wet and shivering, was taken aboard. The king, apart from explaining as best he could who he was and what had happened, remained sullen and silent.

When they reached port, the governor of Gaul was notified at once of Verica's unexpected arrival. Orders came back that he should be brought under escort to Lugdunum, the capital. The fact that the governor himself had not deigned to meet him confirmed Verica's gloomy fears that he had been cast aside in favor of a continuation of the old policy of accommodation to the ambitions of the Catuvellauni. The cold formality of the officers in charge of the escort enhanced that view. In fact, Verica had good reason to feel the cold hand of indifference keeping him at bay. As he made his unhappy journey to Lugdunum, Rome's agents were busy trying to establish the truth of what had precipitated their ally's flight. The authorities were well aware of his eagerness to throw himself on Rome's mercy at the first opportunity and thus deprive them of a legitimate reason to mount an invasion. But by the time Verica reached the capital of Gaul, they had established that the king had given them an honest account of the events that had led to his flight and was not merely exaggerating to excuse his cowardly behaviour: there had indeed been a serious incursion into his territory by a large army led by Togodumnus and his brothers.

A delegation of leading citizens was waiting to greet the exiled ally. Among them stood Adminius looking provocatively prosperous. They swarmed around Verica, enquiring after his health, expressing their concern for his cruel fate, offering him all the city had to give to make him comfortable and secure. The king, still shaken and confused, glared at his fellow Briton.

"See what your policy has achieved! It seems only fit for turning allies into exiles," said Verica to Adminius. "I warned you this would happen—the very last time we met . . ."

"It will be remedied," Adminius replied, taking him by the arm. "See the sympathy your case has already created."

"Welcoming committees will not intimidate the Catuvellauni," Verica scoffed.

"Great powers are slow to rouse, but once roused they are unstoppable."

"What does it need to rouse Rome? For Caratacus to land in Gaul?" the king asked.

"Rome is already roused. The folly of my brothers, their attack upon you has seen to that."

"Roused? How?"

"The governor of Gaul has already sent word to Rome explaining in detail what has happened. We can expect word from Narcissus at any time."

"Word—I have heard enough words from Narcissus," Verica retorted; when he contemplated his position, an exile, now cast upon the kindness and dependent on the good will of strangers, he grew sick with despair. "Wars are not won with words!"

Gradually, however, the king's despair began to lift. The governor arrived from another part of the province and held a long conference with him. Verica's confidence grew as the days passed and he had a chance to look around the capital, always accompanied by Adminius who proved to be an eager guide. Adminius remembered his own first experience of Rome and how that had made him realize the possibilities that such power might bring. Of course, Lugdunum was far from being as impressive as the seat of the empire. But nonetheless, to a man like Verica used only to the hilltop settlements of his native land, its comparative splendor could not fail to impress.

Lugdunum was built as a military colony on the site of a former tribal hillfort in a bend of the river Soane, near its confluence with the Rhone; but it had expanded far beyond its original boundaries. The Soane-side quays bustled with ships from every corner of the empire that were being loaded and unloaded with every kind of produce. The quays were lined with huge warehouses, larger than a king's palace, and bursting with oil, wine and wheat. As they strolled past one warehouse, an enormous bag crammed with neatly shorn locks of blond hair was dragged out towards the gangplank of a waiting ship and opened. Immediately a group of passersby gathered to admire them.

"It is from Germany, where the women sell their hair to Roman merchants," Adminius explained to his wide-eyed guest. "And it is destined for Rome, to be made into wigs for the ladies to adorn themselves. To be blond is the height of fashion since Caesar's wife Messalina began wearing a wig of blond hair." Adminius only paused in his constant commentary on what they saw to gaze around admiringly.

One day, soon after Verica's arrival they found their way to a street paved with stones which Adminius proclaimed to be the widest in the whole of Gaul, being over thirty-six feet from one side to the other. He seemed as proud of it as if he had himself built it. The street was lined with silversmith shops, bookshops, goldsmith shops, metal-workers, and money-lenders.

"Until recently, Lugdunum used to mint all the coinage of the empire. It is still the greatest city in Gaul. To think that only two generations ago this was no more than a rude hillfort, whose facilities consisted of a few pens and stables for sheep and cattle!" Verica's guide exclaimed. "It will not take long before the hillforts of Britain will be transformed as Lugdunum has been. Indeed, Narcissus is of the opinion that we Britons are quicker than the Gauls, so he expects our development to be more rapid." But mentioning Britain again only filled Verica with gloom, reminding him of his own precarious position against which all these prospects of change seemed uncertain indeed.

Adminius, however, was not put off and decided to

show his friend his newly acquired skill at reading. They made their way into a nearby bookstore. Casually, Adminius picked up a book and studied the title. It was, fortuitously enough, a small collection of the speeches of Claudius Caesar on the nature of empire. Adminius was delighted when he could make out the name of Caesar, which he read proudly to Verica. But he understood almost nothing else.

The next morning, a splendid galley came to the quayside, carrying a troop of Caesar's personal guard, the Praetorians. They were instructed to escort Verica and Adminius to Rome, where Claudius was anxious to meet with the Atrebatian king, his outraged ally. Verica's mood swung back again, and he began to think that perhaps Adminius wasn't being overenthusiastic about the prospects for a return to his homeland after all.

They sailed down the river and into the tranquil blue waters of the great inland sea across which the commercial and trading sinews of the empire stretched, linking province with province and all with the city itself. The sky was a clear, washed blue all the way across, without a grey storm to threaten them, or mountainous seas to swallow them; instead, a gentle western wind carried them swiftly to their destination. Verica's anxieties were further soothed.

Finally they arrived at the Roman port of Ostia, a few miles to the west of the city itself. Claudius had begun reconstruction of the old harbor, and great engines were at work such as Verica had never dreamt of, with innumerable men laboring away on every side of them. It made him giddy to gaze on such activity. But it was as nothing compared to Rome upon which the astonished gaze of Verica fell a short time later.

Huge buildings that gleamed with marble of many colors stretched away in every direction. Smaller edifices of dusky red brick reared up in the little valleys between the hills on which the grander structures stood. The city seemed to spring out of a never-ceasing, ever swirling whirlpool of humankind, which flowed in different colored currents between, around and through the buildings. It was as if the city had drawn all of mankind from all the corners of its empire to its center, as a whirlpool draws in everything around it. Only with difficulty did the guard cleave a path through the waves of people. Even a sudden shower of rain did not discourage the curious—who had heard that a foreign king from unknown lands was coming among them—from swarming after the newcomers as far as the Forum. There Narcissus himself was waiting with a delegation from the Senate.

Verica was helped out of the sumptuous Imperial carriage which had brought him from Ostia. He stood for a moment dazed in the brilliant sunlight of late morning, hesitant before the pressing multitudes whose faces gawked at him from every side. The people, whose chief occupation was exercising their curiosity, had grown used to the sight of exotic foreigners. But those who came from Britain were rare enough to still be thought of as a novelty. They gaped at the king's long hair, swept back like the mane of a lion and stiffened with lime—a sight they would have been used to in the days when Gaul was still a free country, but one that was never seen now that Roman fashions had spread as far as the channel, obliterating those of the tribes—and at his all-enveloping multicolored cape which was fastened at his breast by a splendid golden brooch that glittered in the sunlight. His impressive figure was enhanced in the eyes of the idlers by its association with the island of Britain, where, they believed, only demons, witches, and wicked bloodthirsty priests held sway in the fog-bound forests. They looked at the king as if expecting him to turn into vapor in an instant, or to spin around himself a veil of fog which would transport him beyond their ken or transform himself into some hideous and foul beast of myth. Instead, stepping forward to return the greeting of the Senate, he slipped on the wet pavement and fell. The recent shower had made the Sacred Way a treacherous place for those who, like Verica, were unaccustomed to the dangers brought about by progress; he glared up at Adminius: in all his praise of the greatness and convenience of paved streets he had never once thought to mention how dangerous they could be when wet.

Narcissus remained stonily aloof from the outburst of

popular mirth all around him. There was almost nothing that could make the line of his thin, fastidious lips bend in any direction other than slightly downwards in faintly discernible contempt; but such a downward turn of hardly a hair's breadth could mark a truly precipitous fall in the fortunes of the one who had provoked it. Verica's misadventure at once made him very popular with the Roman citizens, who ever afterwards followed him around the city in gangs hoping for a repeat performance, but it was so far beneath the notice of Narcissus that it seemed as if he had not seen it at all.

Verica was more perplexed by this man, almost expressionless and eerily distant, who occupied the powerful post of Caesar's general secretary, than by anything he had seen or heard so far since leaving Britain. The feeling of oddness was heightened by his touch, brought about through the formalities of greeting. Narcissus' skin was strangely soft and limp—though he was far from fat. It felt puffy, rather like a baby's. Later, when Verica was discussing his impressions with Adminius, he alluded to this.

"Narcissus is not a man," Adminius told him.

"How is that?" Verica asked, for he looked like a man—at least, what might pass for one among the Romans. "He does not look like a woman."

"He is between the two—a eunuch. That is a man who has been emasculated." Adminius liked to stun his friend with displays of his newly acquired and esoteric knowledge.

"A man who has been emasculated can have a name, other than that of corpse?"

Adminius assured him it was so.

"He who travels has many tales to tell," Verica concluded, more perplexed than ever.

Narcissus was very insistent about one thing, which he repeated again and again prior to Verica's first meeting with Claudius. The druids—emphasize the druids, he told him. Claudius was concerned with the tribal priesthood, and had lately passed a law making it an offense punishable by death for any Roman citizen to belong to it.

Caesar seemed glassy-eyed and extremely tired on the morning of their first meeting. A tall, angular gentleman, with hair worn longer than the normal Roman taste would seem to permit, and a high, forbidding forehead, was deep in conversation with him when Verica was announced. On hearing the king's name, the angular gentleman broke off his conversation with Claudius and fixed his gaze on Verica. All through the formalities, during which there were many expressions of anguish and woe at the cruel fate of a faithful Roman ally forced into exile, and so forth, this gentleman, later introduced as Seneca, never wavered in his concentration on the king; sometimes he screwed up his eyes as if to gaze upon him more intently. And always, his imposing brow was a tangle of thoughts.

Seneca turned out to be as strange a creature as Narcissus. He was a philosopher, and Claudius had invited him to attend at this particular occasion because of his great knowledge of the druids.

On completion of the formalities, Verica gave a description of the events that led to his exile. To conclude his account, he began to talk about the druids, as instructed by Narcissus.

''Forgive me for interrupting,'' said Seneca, all of a sudden, ''but can you tell us if there is a connection between the druid's secret finger code and the Greek alphabet as used by the ancient Etruscans?'' Clearly Verica did not know what he was talking about; nevertheless, Seneca began describing at length his theory of how many years ago the Trojans, after leaving Troy when it fell to the Greeks, migrated first to Italy, and then by stages found their way through Africa, Spain and Gaul, reaching—he asserted—as far as Britain and Ireland.

''The proof of this,'' he concluded at last, ''is the Greek alphabet found on some old vases in Caere, the Etruscan religious capital north of Rome, taught to the Etruscans by the Trojans, and bearing a striking resemblance to what Posidonius has said of the druids' secret cypher alphabet by which means they communicate with each other using their fingers.'' Whereupon he opened both his raised hands and began to flex and straighten his fingers and thumbs with frantic speed in front of Verica.

''I have just named the thirteen sacred trees of the druids,'' he crowed triumphantly. During this performance the emperor was heard to emit the occasional low groan. "It is a code as secret and cunning as anything devised by the Jews," said the philosopher. Caesar took notice at this, straightened himself up, and announced: "That is precisely what we have come here to discuss!"

"The Jews?" Seneca responded with puzzlement. "I was sadly misled into thinking otherwise."

"No, not to discuss the Jews as such," Claudius snapped, "but to draw out the resemblances between the fanatic priesthoods which both they and the Britons have spawned—priesthoods dedicated to the destruction of anything and everything Roman. The Atrebatian King, our ally, lately a victim of the druids, is not here to pronounce about their lexigraphical or linguistic connections to the Trojans—however well-founded and profound your theory—but to report on their viciousness, cruelty, and their determination to export their revolutionary anti-Roman zeal throughout the empire. Now," he said, turning to Verica, "please continue." Verica did so, and with conviction.

As for Seneca, a short while after this interview, Messalina accused him of committing misdemeanors with the sister of the previous Caesar, Caligula, and demanded he be banished. It seemed her husband was all too happy to comply, remarking that Seneca was fortunate that he was not charged with assassination for having almost bored the emperor to death.

So impressive was Verica's diatribe against the druids that Claudius got the Senate to invite him to address them on the subject. It was in the midst of the second of his addresses to that august body that word came from Britain about the slaughter of the Roman merchants in Calleva. The Senate and Caesar needed no further excuse to decide upon what course they had to take. Soon, Verica was bent over a map of the southern coastline of Britain, marking the spots where a Roman army might best be landed.

When the Catuvellaunian host had come to a halt in the wide plain, they were as numberless as the white-crested waves of a storm-tossed sea, and as angry, eager for battle. Beyond them lay the earthworks of Calleva, the capital of the kingdom of Verica. But instead of an army to confront them, the north gate suddenly opened and a crowd poured through it, obviously not intent upon war. It was a confused mob, shouting and screaming; they were pushing a group of men in front of them against whom they howled abuse, with frequents blows from fists and feet. At first, Caratacus and his brothers thought they were bringing Verica to them. They were soon disappointed to see that it was not the king the crowd was driving before them.

"The city is yours!" they shouted with one voice and hailed the Catuvellauni as their liberators, inviting them to enter at once. "And so are these." They pushed the gang of prisoners forward; a few stumbled and fell on their knees. It did not take the Catuvellauni long to realize they were not Britons or Gauls—but Romans. However, they were small recompense for the fact that Verica was no longer in his capital.

The king had eluded them, fleeing in the night like a criminal, and abandoning most of his retinue to the anger of those among the Atrebates who had opposed and hated his slavish policies towards Rome. Verica's supporters were easily overpowered and slaughtered, and the city gates were thrown open.

That night, the citizens held a great feast to celebrate the overthrow of the king they said they had grown to despise. Loot from Verica's palace provided the drink as well as the food for the feast. The people were astonished at the quantity and variety of the wine he had stored away. At first, they pored over the strange marks denoting the places of origin of the different amphorae. But they soon grew weary of trying to decipher these puzzles, broke the vessels open and consumed every drop, indifferent to age or source, and before long, indifferent to taste as well, mixing Verica's rawest vintage with his finest.

Meanwhile Togodumnus and Subidasto explored the palace, with Subidasto acting as a guide. Subidasto found his way to the king's private chamber, which he had never been permitted to enter. It was soon apparent why. Everywhere they looked there were Roman busts, four of which were kept in a little sanctuary in one corner of the chamber. They were the Roman emperors Augustus, Tiberius, Caligula and Claudius. But Togodumnus recognized only one.

"My brother Adminius possessed the same one—a gift from his masters," he told Subidasto, and picked up a bust of the murdered emperor Caligula. "How proud he was to own it!" He dashed it to the floor, and ground the broken fragments under his foot. Both men gazed in amazement at the other statues and the figurines showing naked bodies round and full, in every detail like they are in life.

"Is it magic that gives them the power to turn human beings into stone?" Subidasto asked, for the tribal workmen, no matter how skilled they were at carving, never made their statues into such eerie likenesses of real, living men and women.

"Stone made to look like flesh is not pleasing to the eye, no more than flesh turned to stone is pleasing to the touch," Togodumnus answered. A crowd of people came into the chamber and began to tear down the statues and haul away everything they could lay their hands on.

They built a great bonfire in front of the palace and fed the flames with those artifacts of Verica's for which they found no use. It was soon roaring higher than the palace roof. In the midst of its flames the once white marble of the broken statues was scorched black. The people, merry with drink, proclaimed it the finest bonfire they had ever built.

"It's only a pity Verica himself is not in the middle of it," Togodumnus lamented.

"But we have his favorite benefactors here with us!" someone shouted from the crowd.

"Yes," a woman hissed, "they would have bought and sold our daughters into slavery!"

"After abusing them first!" another shouted. In the general mirth that followed the arrival of the Catuvellaunians, the Romans had been forgotten. But now they were dragged in front of the crowd gathered around the bonfire. Many of the Catuvellaunians had never set eyes upon Romans before, and clustered around the frightened men to take a closer look, poking at them with great curiosity. They were generally confounded at how such hairless, flabby creatures could belong to a race of empire builders. The women particularly made sport of their bulging fat paunches, contrasting them contemptuously with their own men, who were summarily fined if they allowed their bodies to grow so distorted and ugly.

"How they used to strut about the place as if they owned it when Verica was here! Now see how pale they are with dread!" a woman exclaimed.

"They acted as if they own the city!" came a cry from the crowd.

"They would have made slaves of us all," Togodumnus said, glaring down at them as he picked his teeth with a bone. He was still angry at Verica's escape. He had longed to savor the taste of revenge upon the man who dared to conspire with Adminius, and he had been deprived of it.

"We came only to trade as we are permitted to do by treaty," the oldest of the prisoners replied. Togodumnus noticed that each wore a small box tied with string around his neck. He drew a dagger and thrust its bright blade under the merchant's throat.

"I have a friend who says he never saw you among the other traders in Calleva before," Togodumnus replied. With a sudden downward stroke, he sliced the string that held the little box. The box fell to the ground and broke open. Togodumnus jumped back, and the crowd moved out of the way. From of the box crawled a large grey house spider. It was a charm against misfortune. Everyone knew that it was bad luck to kill a spider. The crowd carefully moved aside to let it pass. An old woman pushed her way to the front and began howling abuse at one of the Romans, accusing him of mistreating her daughter.

"You used her like a slave!" she screamed, and began punching and kicking him.

"Anything I have taken I have paid for," he replied, looking at her with a mixture of disgust and fear.

She grabbed a younger woman by the hand and pulled her out from the crowd.

"This is my daughter!" she said. She gave the pretty, brown-haired girl a nudge. "Well, tell us what you told me." The daughter hung her head low at first, as if afraid to confront anyone. "Is this the man who abused you?"

the mother asked. The girl muttered something. "Speak up!" she was ordered.

"Yes," came her reply, half-choked with emotion.

"Tell the people—tell those who have rescued us from what it is we have been saved!"

"Verica the king gave me to him! And told him . . ." She put her hands to her face and began to sob. "Whatever pleasure he wanted he was to take from me. That he knew Romans liked boys, but I was almost as good as any boy!"

"She lies," the merchant retorted, trembling. He took his young accuser by the chin and forced her to look up at him. He recognized her and smiled bitterly. "I treated you well—gave you gifts!"

"See—how he touches her again!" the mother cried out; with a blow of her fist, she struck him in the face. Instinctively, the merchant swung round and fetched her a slap which sent her staggering backwards. All at once, the crowd rushed forward at the prisoners and dragged them to the ground. Togodumnus turned away from the melee to get himself another cup of mead, contenting himself with a warning to the crowd about not trampling on the spiders.

Caratacus, unlike his brother, tried to intervene when he found out what was happening. He believed that the Romans might prove useful prisoners. But by the time he fought his way through the crowd, it was too late. The prisoners were no longer men. Overwhelmed with pity for the wretches, he agreed they should be put out of their misery.

The people of Calleva arranged the heads of the slaughtered men on a row of stakes which they erected before Verica's ransacked palace. On the stakes they tied the boxes which had held the spiders. They now contained not the good-luck charms but the trophies the women had taken when they emasculated their victims. All the spiders had been carefully and tenderly removed before their owners were tortured and killed. The people had obeyed meticulously Togodumnus' injunction not to hurt the little creatures.

Chapter 12

In the main bedchamber of the Palace of the Mists, the king lay sleeping with his wives. Prasutagus and his court had gone to the Palace of the Mists, as was his custom, for the summer months. But it did not feel like summer. Outside, during the day, the sun did not disappoint them, the skies were usually clear, and the air was wholesome. And at night, the breeze was refreshing and pleasant—weatherwise, almost perfect was the season. But inside, gloom prevailed and the mood of the season could do nothing to lift it.

The main bedchamber was large enough to hold six couples comfortably between its oak paneled walls, so there was ample room for all the wives. Their bedding was of the softest material—a great white linen mattress stuffed with tender green rushes and birch twigs taken from the highest branches of the tree. It was so large it took up half of the chamber. Covering them were skins of softest lamb's wool, which because of the turning and tossing of the wives during the night, lay in disorder here and there like drifts of fresh snow. If all the women were to move at once, there was such a rustling that it seemed like a wind blowing through a leafy wood. But none of them tossed and shifted about so much as Prasutagus himself. Though many would look at him with envy, as he lay there surrounded by six women, each of whom had her own particular charm, and one of whom was beautiful beyond compare, the king was not a contented man. How could he be, when the one he desired the most, his new wife Fen Fire, had grown so strange to his touch?

The trouble had begun the very night they arrived. The

servants had been busy in the palace—decorating it with every kind of flower, hanging hawthorn around the bedchamber, sprinkling fine, fresh scents everywhere, making ready the great baths with scented soaps, and preparing a feast that would especially delight the young woman coming new to the household and show her what fine food she could expect. And they knew Fen Fire, having lived with Cunobelinus, was accustomed to a generous table stocked with the best of meat and fish and fowl and supplied with drinks to match. Prasutagus had impressed this upon them, and they were at pains to meet his every wish and anticipate hers.

That evening, however, the young woman sat before the great table which groaned under the weight of the feast and ate with little enthusiasm.

"You eat like a sparrow," said Prasutagus. "Or is there something in the meat or in the sauces that displeases you?" He scowled at the servants, who trembled with fear, their eyes fixed on Fen Fire's face trying to discern what was the matter.

"Everything is a delight. It is merely that I am tired, that is all," answered his young wife.

"Then you should rest," the king told her. She rose. He put his hands on her breasts and gave them a gentle squeeze. Fen Fire smiled and kissed him on the cheek.

"Tired!" exclaimed Latis to her husband. "After so short a journey!" As Fen Fire was leaving to go to the bedchamber, Latis watched her like a hawk. "Dear husband," she said when Fen Fire had gone, "I hope she is not so easily wearied that you must rush your food and abandon the feast to catch her before she falls asleep insensible!"

"Easily wearied!" laughed Prasutagus, as his eyes followed Fen Fire with relish. "You will see soon enough who is wearied first!" Prasutagus did not linger long at the table. He wolfed down what remained of his fish, drained his cup of ale, and rose. Even Barrel, who rarely left the feast if there was a cup to be emptied, stood up at once and went with the other wives after him into the bedchamber. The king had talked so much about Fen Fire, rhapsodised about her beauty, and how he desired her, that they were anxious to experience for themselves the excitement.

They were disappointed to find on entering the bed-chamber that the new wife seemed to be asleep. Latis looked at them, from one to the other, a knowing smile on her lips. Fen Fire had not even taken the time to undo her hair. The king concealed his disappointment and lay down beside her, gently stroking her cheek while the others combed out their hair before their mirrors, glancing back occasionally at the two of them. Fen Fire stirred and opened her eyes a little, reluctant to look upon her husband's face. Why had she never noticed the resemblance between father and son until now, she wondered. There was the same high, proud brow, long fine nose, strong chin, thin lips on which disdain sat so easily—the same clear blue eyes so expressive of every passing whim, that had looked into hers as they lay together in the little cave behind the waterfall. But now the face was older, wrinkled, and bearded, with a graver look. A wild fancy came into her mind that she and Subidasto had somehow leapt across the years, forgetting everything of their life together between youth and age; so she found herself in his aging arms after she had just begun to enjoy his youthful vigor.

She closed her eyes when the king touched her breasts and thighs, caressing, kissing every part of her with lips that lingered reluctant to relinquish her white skin. But not being able to see her husband brought no relief from the disturbing memories he provoked. When he caressed her, stroked her, fondled her she fancied she felt the same confident touch with which his son had induced her to abandon herself for the first time a year ago on Beltane Eve. It brought her to the verge of that joy again. She opened her eyes. It was a cruel deception to find the father, not the son, beside her. Incest was the most accursed of crimes, and she had unknowingly been guilty of it. Frantically, she pushed and struggled. The other wives were amazed to see her suddenly and violently free herself from Prasutagus' hold, sending the king rolling on his back. She sprang from the bedding, clutching a lambskin around her. The king regarded her with amazement and consternation as she stood at the far side of the chamber near the partition, a distraught, anxious look in her eyes.

While the other wives went to Fen Fire to see if they could help, Latis raced to her husband's side to assist him to his feet. He disregarded her plaintive offer, and clambered from the bedding. Pushing the other wives aside, he confronted Fen Fire.

"I ask the gods to tell me why . . ." he began.

"I am sorry," said she, anxious and distressed, "but I meant you no insult."

"No insult when you repel your husband as if he were a vile thing! You shame me before my other women!"

"Forgive me, kind king, I have not been well this past while. I cannot say why. But there are many things that cause me sorrow. Your care for me is . . ." She could hardly look at him as she spoke. ". . . is a comfort, I assure you."

"What things? A husband should know such things if they distress his wife!"

"Things of a nature more political than personal," she replied. In truth, Fen Fire had not been happy with the king when he refused to join in the expedition against Verica. Caratacus had advocated strongly that he join them; Subidasto too had pleaded that the presence of the Iceni would demonstrate to all the unity of the tribes, and thus deter those beyond the shores of Britain who might contemplate an attack. The king had dismissed their arguments as foolish and their actions as certain to lead to greater troubles. But it was an issue on which Fen Fire at the time felt confident she could persuade him eventually to agree. At that moment, however, in her desperation she could think of nothing else to tell him. It now assumed a prominence it did not warrant.

Prasutagus sighed and put his arms around her. "This is no time to debate these matters. The bedchamber is a place for peace and pleasure, where the loud alarms of wars must not penetrate. I leave your brothers to their own counsels. My son I leave to his, for he is of an age when he is able to take responsibility for his own foolhardiness. And I leave you free to counsel me whatever way you see fit, but I ask only that your wifely duties take precedence over your warrior's instincts.'' In his embrace she felt stiff and ungiving. He relinquished her.

''I have no wish to make them clash,'' she said quietly, ''but you must be patient—the ways of a warrior are familiar to me, those of a wife yet new.''

The king smiled. ''Rest,'' he said to her. ''Tomorrow, these upsets will seem foolish.''

That night, the king slept with Latis in his arms. Fen Fire slept next to Barrel, who hoped that in the privacy of the darkness when the others slept she might exchange some intimacies with the new wife. When the chamber was silent, she plucked at Fen Fire's sleeve.

''Beware of Latis,'' she whispered. Though Fen Fire was wide awake she did not respond. ''She is the cause of this upset, I'm convinced.'' Fen Fire lay looking up into the darkness, Barrel's breath on her cheek. ''What did you eat tonight?''

''The same as everyone else, of course, but I ate little, for I had no appetite,'' Fen Fire replied at last, somewhat impatiently.

''You did not detect something strange in your food?''

''No. Now, I must rest,'' said Fen Fire.

But Barrel was persistent. ''She is clever. She has put a charm on you to make you see the king as hideous and repulsive. Such is her jealousy . . .'' She paused, thinking that she heard someone awakening. ''I have a notion of what she is capable of in order to preserve her sway over the king, and us,'' she whispered. She thought better of saying any more at that moment, and after reassuring the king's new wife that the other wives desired only her happiness, she turned on her side and went to sleep. Fen Fire did not dwell on Barrel's whispered intimations of Latis' malice. The first wife's jealousy she already strongly sensed, and did not give it much thought, assuming with time it would fade. But Fen Fire had now too many of her own worries, which were more real to her and more terrible than anything mere jealousy might arouse. She spent the long night in contemplating how she could be a wife to a man whose son she desired more than anyone she had ever known.

The day did not dispel the night's troubles as the king had predicted. Fen Fire rose before the others, and the dawn found her with her javelins, before the target in the parade ground beyond the palace. Many of the guards gathered to watch as javelin after javelin found its mark. Soon, word of her exercises spread, and people began coming from all over to witness her skills with their own eyes. The king found her there, surrounded by admirers. When he arrived, they poured out their congratulations for his having chosen Fen Fire as his wife; her beauty dazzled them, her skills amazed them. The people's joy brought him little satisfaction, however. When he was in her company, it was clear to Prasutagus that her feelings of the previous night had not changed—she seemed aloof, and wary of him. He left her to the praises of the people and nursed his wounded pride in private.

So it was as the summer days went by. Fen Fire, still desperate to conceal the truth about her discontent, used another source of discontent to hide it. Knowing full well how he had opposed the action, she celebrated the news from Caratacus about the overthrow of Verica, and told her husband that he should celebrate too.

"A traitor has been driven from the shores!" she proclaimed. "Every true Briton should rejoice."

"Innocent merchants have been slaughtered," he replied sharply. "And soon, all Britons will pay the consequences." She scoffed at his concern, calling the merchants killed by the mob spies and collaborators, who had been preparing to enslave everyone.

"It is strange to find a woman so anxious about the state of the world and so disregarding of the matters that immediately concern her," he said bitterly.

"Perhaps we should have paid more attention to the swan," said Latis. "Did not the bird refuse to eat from her hand until she broke open his cage and permitted his escape? That was an omen warning us of the troubles to come!" A sad expression stole over the king's face. That same thought had haunted him, but he was still too enamoured of the young woman to express it.

Fen Fire was ashamed of provoking him by deliberately and loudly advocating courses that she knew would upset him. It pained her to dispute with Prasutagus and though she did so only to avoid causing him a greater pain, it still made her gradually more miserable. Prasutagus left her alone. Since she had rejected him so humiliatingly that first night they spent together in the Palace of the Mists, the king was determined not to compel her to his side by insisting on his rights as a husband. He let her go to sleep at the far side of the bedding without protest, supposing that her former warmth for him would return. Each night, the pattern was the same. She would withdraw early from the feast, protesting her weariness. The king and his wives would enter the bedchamber later. For a while he would stand looking at her longingly as she lay curled up near the edge of the vast bed. His brow was wrinkled with puzzlement as to why she had turned so cold to him and remained so distant.

"It is clear as day," Latis told him one night, "she has been put up to it by Caratacus in the hope that you will be so desperate for her affections you will eventually have to agree to commit your warriors to serve with those of the Catuvellauni. Only then will she condescend to give you the wifely attentions which are your right as her husband."

Fen Fire opened her eyes. "You have a tongue in your head as poisonous as the skin of a toad," said she, sitting up and glaring at Latis. "I do not bargain with my affections."

"Then tell me the true reason why they have been withdrawn," the king replied. The other wives watched tensely. Prasutagus sat down next to her. He touched her fondly on the cheek. She turned to him with grey, grave eyes. She could not tell him the truth, yet it tortured her to continue with the other pretense. She sat stubbornly, dumbly refusing to admit to any deeper cause for her rejection of her husband than that which Latis was so delighted to twist and distort.

"She can no longer deny you. Claim your rights as a husband! I will gladly relinquish to her my cherished place by your side if it will bring you happiness. Insist she lie next to you tonight," Latis urged the king. Now that she was sure of Fen Fire's aversion for Prasutagus,

Latis thought it might be amusing to witness the young woman being compelled to have to mate with him. But the king rejected her suggestion with indignation.

"To take that course is alien to my character," he replied. "I would derive no pleasure from such a joyless union! She must come to me willingly because she desires to, not because she has regard only for my rights as a husband. She must be with me as she was before, on Beltane Eve—or was that a dream of happiness conjured up by the Everlasting Ones to make a mockery of our mortal hopes?"

"It was not a dream," Fen Fire responded.

"Then this must be a nightmare!" said he. The king stood up. Without thinking, Fen Fire, overcome with sympathy for him, reached out and clutched his robe. He turned to her. Then, realizing what she had done, she abruptly let go of it. He nodded with resignation, and without saying anything further, left her.

"I am made yet more wretched," Fen Fire thought that night as she lay in the darkness. "He bears the injuries I inflict on him with such dignity that I grow fonder of him than ever before." His nature was proud, disdainful, solitary. But to contemplate this only brought its own, even worse distress; it only served to remind her of Subidasto. Did not the son have those same virtues as the father? A character so high and sure that it would not stoop to take advantage but must earn every victory, in war through courage and in love through mutual desire. And any way in which the father reminded her of the son only widened the gulf that now lay between her and her husband's arms.

The whole household was steeped in gloom. Among themselves, out of reach of Latis, Barrel and the other wives avidly discussed the unexpected crisis. And soon they became more and more convinced that Barrel was right: Latis had indeed put a spell on the new wife. How else could Fen Fire's inexplicable behavior be accounted for? Barrel longed to tell them of what else she knew, but she was fearful of Latis and kept silent.

The king grew more remote as the days passed, irascible and impatient with all his wives. The only one who had cause to celebrate was Latis. Each night, he found some comfort in her arms. And she used the opportunity to whisper maledictions against not only Fen Fire but the other wives. After all, they had sympathized with her rival—they had hoped and planned that she would oust her from control of her own household. She grew more imperious towards them with every passing day, and at night she poisoned his opinion of them by alleging that Fen Fire denigrated him in their eyes, and that all but she were turning against him. So the king began to disdain the others and slept only in the arms of Latis. And with every chance Latis got, she sought to especially humiliate Barrel, who had shown the most sympathy for Fen Fire. She loaded extra chores on her, goading her with the most senseless tasks, never leaving her a moment's peace. Barrel knew, however, that it was not her friendship alone with Fen Fire that caused Latis' wrath against her. Each had a secret about the other which neither wanted made known to the king.

The summer had reached its mid-point, and the Feast of Lugus was only a few days hence. The unhappy bedfellows lay in the casual intimacy of the main bedchamber, asleep. Or so it seemed. Latis lay in her place beside the king, twitching now and again because his long yellow beard tickled her. Her persecutions had failed to detach Barrel from her fondness for Fen Fire, and the two women lay side by side. It was a pleasant summer's night, with a fresh breeze coming in across the fens from the sea; blowing under the bronze partition, it stirred the hairs of the lambskin coverings. Barrel slowly, carefully, pushed herself up and rested for a moment on her elbows, waiting until her eyes had grown accustomed to the darkness. When she had made sure that the others were still sleeping, she cautiously edged towards the end of the huge mass of bedding; fortunately, she was closer to it than any, and the rustling she made was drowned out by the noises caused by the others as they shifted about in their sleep. Confident that she was undetected, she threw a cape over her shoulders and slipped behind the partition and left the bedchamber to make her way towards the back of the palace. She found her way through the rear entrance into the stables. Just beyond the stables, across an open patch of grass was a stairway to a secluded part of the rampart which encircled the grounds of the palace. She walked quickly to the stairway and halted in the shadow of the ramparts.

"Esup," she whispered. A figure beckoned her to come in under the stairway.

"We must be brief tonight," he replied as he embraced her. "I am due to go on duty at the main gate until dawn."

"But you told me tonight was free!" Barrel answered. She looked up into his handsome face, clean shaven except for a long, elegant and well-combed moustache that hung down as far as his breast. She pouted with disappointment.

"They're overloading me with duties," he complained.

"Just as that witch Latis tortures me!" she replied.

"I sometimes think the king suspects ours was more than a Beltane tryst." He kissed her.

"The king will soon have more than mere suspicions!" a voice said from behind Barrel. Latis stormed across from under the shadow of the stables and grabbed the other woman by the hair, dragging her from the arms of the startled, frightened guard. With fists and feet Latis battered and kicked Barrel, while the guard stood stiff with dread. Latis glared at him. "And you!" she hissed. "I hope your tongue has not proved to be as loose as your other appendage, or I will have difficulty deciding which to cut off first!" He did not reply, but scurried away into the darkness under the rampart.

Fen Fire had not been enjoying a sound sleep. She was awake when Barrel slipped out of the bedchamber. Her departure at so strange an hour did not surprise Fen Fire. Once before, when she herself had risen to take an early morning walk along the ramparts to watch the sun rise, she was looking out over the flat fen landscape in the glimmering light, listening to a moorhen cry greeting the day, when she heard something stirring underneath the wooden boards of the walkway. She glanced down and caught a glimpse of Barrel's caped figure dashing from under the stairway near the stables. She had smiled to herself, and hoped that her affectionate friend would be careful enough not to get caught. But on this occasion, after Barrel had left and just as Fen Fire was about to close her eyes, Latis also sneaked away. Fen Fire concluded that Barrel had been found out. Frightened for her friend, Fen Fire stole out after them, which left only half the king's wives still sleeping where they should be.

Latis had by now dragged her other rival as far as the stables, where she continued to rain blows on her. She wrenched a fistful of hair from Barrel's head. The horses in the stables began to fret at the noisy fray, and shifted about restlessly. When the victim tried to protect herself by sinking her teeth into her attacker's hand, Latis fetched her a vicious slap across the face with her other hand, knocking Barrel into the straw. Barrel screamed. The horses banged and thumped against the stable bars, threatening to wake the household.

"I'll give you what you deserve, you little whore!" Latis tried to kick her victim again, but she rolled out of the way.

"Dare touch me once more and I'll tell the king about your tricks," Barrel shouted back.

"Prasutagus would not believe you, and Esup obeys me," Latis laughed.

"I know he obeys you, and I know how far he was prepared to go, even to commit sacrilege to please you—lay another finger on me and I'll tell the king why the swan wouldn't eat from Fen Fire's hand."

Latis' expression changed instantly. Her smile vanished. She strode across her fallen foe and picked up a nearby pitchfork.

"Not if I let the air out of you with a thrust of this!" She raised it up threateningly. Barrel gave a fearful screech which made all the horses rear up, almost breaking down their stalls.

"If it is an interesting tale she has to tell, let us hear it," Fen Fire said. She had been standing behind them for long enough to have heard everything. Latis lunged at her threateningly with the pitchfork. But Fen Fire easily avoided her clumsy attack and took hold of her wrist.

A wrenching twist forced Latis to drop the weapon and brought her to her knees. Then, Fen Fire hoisted Barrel's tormenter above her head, and spun her around squealing in the air. One easy heave concluded the conflict, sending the king's first wife flying into the nearest stall where she landed amid a mess of horse piss and dung.

By now the screeching, the neighing and banging of the horses had brought the guards rushing to the scene. The disturbance had also reached as far as the king's bedchamber. When he found that three of his wives were missing, he rose at once to follow the sounds of consternation. Prasutagus and his other wives came rushing into the stables just in time to see Fen Fire, having leapt after Latis into the horse's stall, take her by the throat and demand that she tell the truth or have the life throttled out of her. Latis, her hair full of straw and horse dung, soaking with horse piss, spluttered out the story of her attempt to pervert the marriage ritual, miserably picking bits of filth from herself as she spoke. But she was quick to point the accusing finger at Barrel, whose own infatuation with the guard was now exposed.

"Why don't you admit while you're at it how you have bewitched Fen Fire. You put a spell on her, didn't you, that made the king seem repugnant to her eyes?" Barrel shouted at her when she finished her account of feeding the swan. Latis shook her head, denying it. But Fen Fire tightened her grip; after all, would it not be to everyone's advantage if the king were to believe she had been the victim of a charm? In a real sense she had, though it was not due to the magic of Latis. Latis gasped as Fen Fire seemed about to wring her neck.

"Yes—I was driven by jealousy . . . to make the king . . . and his new wife . . . unhappy," she choked out. When she seemed about to faint, Fen Fire relinquished her hold. Prasutagus looked down at his first wife, slumped in the mess of the stable, bedraggled like a beggar.

"It was a wicked, foolish and dishonorable thing that you did," he said. "A dreadful violation of sacred ritual and of the sacred laws of hospitality which protect anyone taken into my household regardless of rank or status.

And Fen Fire has the right to demand that you be punished severely and that Esup, your accomplice, also suffer the consequences of his sacrilege." Barrel's look of triumph vanished when she heard Esup's name coupled in castigation with that of Latis. The king turned to Fen Fire. "You have been injured by this woman, so it is your right to fix the punishment. You can demand that she be cast out of my house forever, and her accomplice be driven like a dog into the wilds, exiled until death."

Fen Fire could see clearly the look of terror on Barrel's face, dreading the loss of her lover. She had no wish to revenge herself on Latis other than to enjoy the satisfaction of seeing her schemes exposed, and she felt no anger at all towards the guard who did what he did, not through malice towards her but in order to please Latis. Without hesitating she told her husband what her demands were.

"I ask only that Latis treat the other women as her equals instead of her servants," she said, "and that she refrain from conspiring against me with whatever spells and charms she has tried to exercise." Latis agreed at once, promising never again to interfere. "As for Esup," Fen Fire continued, "I ask that he be spared the king's wrath for I spare him mine."

Prasutagus was pleased to exercise mercy, and in the shadow of the serious crimes committed by Latis the behavior of Barrel was given no more than a moment's notice. "Indeed," he said, "it is my fault. I have been guilty of neglecting my other wives so it is no wonder that they looked elsewhere for satisfaction. It is a bad thing when a good woman goes in want of a man."

"No worse surely than when a good man goes in want of the woman he desires," said Barrel, looking at Fen Fire. The other wives gathered around her, whispering into her ear and urging her into her husband's arms.

"Until he has you he will have none of the rest of us!" they said. "So, for our sakes be a wife to him or we'll all be without a husband."

They were right, and Fen Fire knew it. The king would waste away and they all would pay the price for her fastidiousness. Which was the greater crime: to refuse a noble and generous man the pleasures which were his right and reward, or to transgress the ban preventing her from mating with both the son and the father? In the meantime, she would be spending sleepless nights regretting something over which she had no control. And all the while she would be depriving herself of the pleasure of pleasing the king, her husband—a pleasure that was a woman's special privilege to give, so that to refuse to give it seemed more of a rebellion against nature than would coupling with a father and a whole tribe of his sons, if he had them.

"The spell had been broken," she said, going over to him, her arms open. "I have returned to my senses."

The king needed no more proof than the warmth of her embrace. He held her for a long moment, savoring her tenderness from which for so long he had been exiled. His eyes glistened with tears. "Come, we will fetch our fishing poles and spend the day in the fens. And we will return with such a catch that tonight's feast will be like no other since the beginning of the world."

The women, indeed the whole household, were delighted to see the two of them going off into the fens together in the little corracle, the king rowing, and his young wife humming a snatch of an old tune she knew from childhood. All day they drifted about in the summer sunshine among the tall reed banks, hardly stirring the tranquil waters except when the king would haul out his catch. In the middle of that reedy wilderness with the flat fens stretching away endlessly on every side of them, the sky above seemed huge. It bestowed a kind of peace on her that she had not felt since Beltane—floating under such a vast dome, how could her concerns not appear but as passing and insignificant? Near noon, they disturbed a solitary crane from its nest among the reeds.

"It is well that the sun is already high in the sky," said the king, "for it is bad luck to see a crane in the early morning, as it is to hear its screeching in the dead of night." That was a sound that had become all too familiar to Fen Fire as she lay awake in the bedchamber during the troubled nights of her sojourn at the Palace of the Mists.

"The crane accompanies Camulos the god of battle of

the Catuvellauni,'' said Fen Fire, ''to feed off the flesh of the slain. But if a Catuvellaunian warrior sees three cranes on his way to battle, he must return home at once,'' she told the king, ''for that is a sign that the day means ill. So it is forbidden among us to eat the flesh of the crane.'' The king told her that the Iceni had that same taboo imposed upon them. And he listened attentively while Fen Fire told him of the stories she knew about these birds—how the egret is especially beloved of the goddess because it builds its nests in willows and perches on the backs of bulls where it kills and eats all the parasites that trouble the beast, and of how the bag in which her ancestor Maponos carried all his secrets was made from the skin of a crane.

''Among the Iceni, the crane is a most malevolent or ill-portending bird,'' said Prasutagus, dipping his fishing pole into the water. ''For the crane is always a woman in a different form. Either a wicked woman who has brought about her husband's death, or sometimes a mean woman, greedy and unpleasant, who because she kept a cold and unwelcoming house was transformed thus. Or, saddest of all, she is a beautiful young woman changed into a bird by the magic of her jealous rival.''

''Jealousy has power only to harm,'' said Fen Fire. ''It is as ignoble as greed or meanness or cowardice; yet it is worse than any of these and more destructive. A mean and greedy person must eventually die and leave behind what he or she has accumulated—so it is beyond his power to prevent his wealth going to benefit others in the end. And a person's cowardice, though it imperils his friends, will always benefit his enemy. But jealousy benefits no one—neither the person who feels it nor the person who inspires it, for unless it is checked it destroys what it desires.''

''Aye,'' replied the king, pensively, ''a jealous person is blind to the great diversity of the world with all its people. Our nature craves diversity. To try to frustrate that craving is as cruel as it is mean. Must we always eat porridge? Why not pluck a berry from the bush now and again, and instead of milk have mead?'' He smiled as a fish gave a tug on his line.

Prasutagus spoke at length of the other marsh birds—the heron, the egret, the stork and the bittern—their habits and the stories associated with them. He could name every passing sea bird and wading bird. He knew every stream that entered the marshes, every place where there was a quiet pool or little lake and what kinds of fish might be found in them. By early evening they had collected a fine sack of fish, and were making their way back. They came to a bank of mud on which, from a distance, Fen Fire could see something silver gleaming. As they drew closer, they saw nine little fish laid out in the shape of a circle.

"Some fisherman has been here before us," she said.

"Only the heron about the selfsame business as us—fishing for to feed herself and her dear ones," said he in reply. "It is the heron's custom to leave her catch in the shape of a wheel." Fen Fire leant over and was about to pick up one of the little fish when the king took her by the wrist, restraining her. "They must not be touched—for to remove one would break the wheel, and that brings bad luck, particularly to a king. It is said that the life of a king is wheel-shaped, like that of the world, ever turning and returning."

"And what of death?"

"Death is but one interruption in a long, long life. What the wheel carries down it raises up again." They left the fish where they found them, glimmering in the dusk, and rowed back towards the palace, ensuring that was the wheel unbroken.

Chapter 13

The king and his court feasted on fish through the warm summer nights. Music from the harps rippled through the flower-scented air. The palace was transformed—its former gloom banished.

It was on one such occasion, later in the season, that Fen Fire's newly found contentment was even further enhanced with the announcement of the arrival of an unexpected guest.

The lumbering gatekeeper interrupted their revels by proclaiming that a "gangling, mop-headed gentleman, a dispenser of riddles" was begging admittance.

"Bran!" Fen Fire exclaimed. "Admit him!" The king nodded his consent, and within moments the bard himself appeared before her.

As he walked towards them his boots squelched. His multi-colored cape was spattered with mud, as was his crane-bag hanging by his side. He paused, resting on his alder cane, and smiled at Fen Fire.

"Riddle me this riddle," he began, bending forwards, and regarding each of the wives in turn with his bright eyes. "What beast," he said:

"Is hunted above but not below
None on foot can faster go
And yet it moves at such a rate
It needs a night to rise and set;
Not ashamed to show its love
Mates like the Pict or turtle-dove
Where all can see—thinks nothing fitter!
Beloved of Her for its triple litter . . ."

"The Hare," said Prasutagus. "Because it is a beast whose flesh is taboo among us, we cannot hunt it. Yet, in its starry form it is pursued by the Great Hunter across the winter sky; though fast of foot, its constellation rises and sets slowly. It mates openly and gives birth to three offspring at a time, hence it is seen as a favorite of the Triple One." He paused, while Bran screwed up his eyes, wrinkling his forehead, trying to come up with another, more difficult riddle.

Before he could, Fen Fire leapt up and raced to his side. "Don't trouble your wits—you're tired and in need of some refreshment," she said, looking with honest concern at his sodden condition.

"Ah yes," he nodded. "As evening fell, and I followed the stars, wanting to make sure I did not take a wrong path. I fear I took a false step and fell into the marsh. So easy it is for those who exalt their gaze to miss the obvious that is before them! So while finding my way I almost lost myself."

It did not take long for Prasutagus' servants to provide Bran with a new, dry suit of clothes, into which he gladly changed, keeping only his cape of three colors, each of which derived from the alder tree: red from its bark, green from its flowers and brown from its twigs. Then he settled down, near to Fen Fire, with a cup of mead in one hand and a good portion of pork in the other.

"News, my dear bard—news of the world beyond!" she exclaimed, clasping her hands with delight and leaning fondly towards him. She longed to hear of what was happening elsewhere; it seemed to her at times that the fens amidst which they lived formed an impenetrable barrier against the rest of the world—one she wanted to breach. Bran sipped his drink and looked thoughtfully into his cup.

"Two new serpents have been seen on the streets of Rome," he said. "In their jaws they were carrying maps of the coastline of Britain. One is called Adminius and the other, more lately arrived, is a certain Verica."

"They plot with Caesar!" Fen Fire glowered.

"Of course they plot with Caesar!" the king put in with some impatience. "With the ousting of Verica, Caesar has been given the excuse he seeks to intervene in our affairs. Didn't I warn Caratacus of what would befall us?'' Prasutagus sighed, and called for more drink. He did not want to be reminded of such matters, fearing they would disturb his young wife just when she seemed to be growing contented.

''Caratacus—what of Caratacus?'' she asked.

''He has gone west,'' Bran told her. ''On a mission to the tribe of the Silures. But he will return before the winter.''

''Enough talk of politics,'' Prasutagus declared. ''You haven't come all this way to worry us about such mundane matters—a story is what the women would like to hear to wile away the long evening.'' Fen Fire and Bran exchanged glances. She gently touched his arm as if to say, we will talk later. The bard nodded in acknowledgement.

''Yes, Bran,'' she said, leaning back with a smile, ''a tale!''

''Something not too frightening,'' pleaded Screech Owl. ''This palace has so many drafts that when I hear a story of monsters and ghosts . . .'' She clutched Fen Fire's hand.

''A tale of handsome warriors,'' Barrel suggested. ''Let us hear of the deeds of the past, of the fine heroes and their women!''

''Nothing would please us more,'' Prasutagus agreed, looking down with a proud smile at his young wife as she sat surrounded by the other women, who gazed at her admiringly. But Fen Fire shook her head.

''Rather a tale of bards, and of that bard most beloved of women—yourself, Bran. That's what I'm in the mood for,'' said she. The others concurred at once, for every woman there was curious about Bran's origins.

Bran smiled. And Fen Fire was reminded of the first time she laid eyes on him. Then too they had discoursed on the Hunter and the Hare. . . .

She had been just a child when Caratacus brought Bran back from the west to the court of King Cunobelinus. His face had puzzled her.

"Are you young or old?" she had asked him.

"I am my age," he replied. But she could not tell if his face was a young face or an old face. Sometimes it seemed one or the other and sometimes both. "Anyway, young and old—what does that mean?" he continued, looking up at the wintery sky, richly sown with stars. He pointed to the constellations of the Hunter and the Hare. "How long has the Hunter pursued the Hare across the sky?" he asked her. And she had replied with childish confidence:

"He hunts the hare from the beginning of the winter season at Samhain until Beltane and the arrival of summer." She had often perused the skies and noticed the rising of the Hunter and Hare in winter and saw how they set earlier with the approach of summer.

"You have been chatting with some druid, or a shepherd perhaps."

"I often used to speak with the druid, but I pestered him with too many questions he could not answer."

"Only the poet can answer the really difficult questions, such as those asked by a child," Bran had assured her. "Particularly questions concerning age. Now, since winter and summer eternally return, the Hunter has pursued the Hare for all eternity. And when we gaze upon that which is eternal, youth and age lose all significance. To say which is which is like—well, like trying to find two drops of water in a stream and identify one from the other."

Fen Fire thought about this for a while, giving the bard an occasional sideways glance.

"If it is all the same, youth and age, why are birthdays so important?" she then asked, determined to make him give her a straight answer.

"Birthdays?"

"Yes—you wouldn't like it if no one remembered yours, would you?"

Bran laughed. "I will tell you a story," he said, "about young and old, and birthdays. It is the story of how I came into the world."

Fen Fire knew that this would be the story he would tell again tonight, even as he took the harp from the crane-bag at his side. Slowly he drained his cup, and waited until it was refilled. Then he struck the harp's airy chords. The palace was filled with sounds as clear as the wind.

"I will tell you a story about how I came into the world," he began. Once more she was a child at his feet, listening breathlessly.

"My father was a bard at the court of the High King of the island of Ireland, far to the west, on the edge of the world. That is the land of the giant wolfhound, a dog the size of a small horse, and of the giant elk which is twice the size of a horse. That is also the land where Maponos left his magic cauldron; whatever you put into it comes out whole and healed, and some old lady has it in her care to this day.

"One night when the wind was blowing from the west, making the fires of the palace crackle, the king gathered his court around him to listen to my father's words. They were intent upon some story that he was telling when the gatekeeper announced that there was an old woman at the door, seeking bed and shelter. The king, being as hospitable as a king should be, bid him let her enter. He did so, and in came the ugliest, most repulsive old hag that any of them had ever seen.

"She had two black stumps for teeth and there was a competition between her mouth and her nose to see which could dribble the fastest. Her skin sagged with wrinkles and her old withered breasts were simply two wrinkles that were slightly larger than the rest. Her hair was coarse and ragged and looked like the tails of rats who'd been drowned in a black bog.

"Nonetheless, the king accommodated her, putting her next to the fire, and ordering his servants to feed her whatever she wanted. Throughout the night she sat there munching her food, sniffing and coughing continuously, and every now and again rubbing her hooked nose on her sleeve. When the time came for the warriors to retire, the king told her she could sleep by the fire.

" 'I have a request to make,' she replied.

" 'What is that?' he asked civilly.

" 'Would you let me sleep with you in your royal bed

tonight?' she queried, squinting up, a watery bead hanging from the tip of her snout. The king shuddered. That was going beyond the bounds of even his hospitality, for which he was renowned. When he refused her, she went from one warrior to the next, begging to be allowed to sleep with them. Each refused, turning her away in disgust. And each time they did so, she mourned her fate, lamenting: 'I was once a beautiful young woman, and you would have shed blood to have me in your arms at night. But now you push me away as if I were a leper. Truly there is no worse disease than old age!' Then, she hobbled across to my father.

" 'Can I sleep with you tonight?' she asked, her bleary eyes gummed up. But he saw there was a bit of a twinkle in them.

" 'Why not,' he answered without hesitation. She clapped her bony hands together in glee.

"There was a great stride in her legs as she went to his chamber. When my father came in behind her, she had already begun to undress. He was about to quench the torchlight when the first of her ragged garments fell from her shoulders. He stared in disbelief. The wrinkles of her skin melted away, leaving it smooth and white without a mole or an unseemly spot. The ragged filthy mop of rats' tails that had been her hair instead became a cascade of gold. Then her skirt slipped down around her ankles. Where he had expected to see shrunken, withered haunches he beheld instead broad hips, and round white mounds of perfect shape, gentle hillocks of snow at the arching base of a delicate fine-boned back.

"She turned to him, her swan-white bosom bare, with the red glow of the torch-flames on it. Never had he seen such nipples of succulent red!

"Her rowan-berry lips curved in a smile. She reached out her arms to him.

" 'I knew you would accept me, because you are a poet,' she said. 'And it is only poets who understand women. Who else can see through our disguises? Who else fears us not?'

"She took him in her arms and at once, because of the delicacy of her skin and the green color of her eyes, he recognized her as a princess of the Everlasting Ones. That night they spent together, I was conceived.'' Bran paused and took a sip of mead. ''The next morning, they both had vanished. They say she'd been charmed by the beauty of his harp-playing and had come out of the mound with the intention of bringing him back with her, which is plainly what she did, for not a hair of my father was ever seen again.''

''So you were raised among the Mound People!'' Fen Eel exclaimed. Bran looked doleful and shook his head.

''Alas—when I was born, I amazed and surprised my mother by crying, so she got rid of me.''

''Got rid of you? Sure, anyone knows you can't have a baby without crying,'' Barrel interjected with astonishment.

''The Mound People are different creatures from ourselves,'' Bran explained. ''The women especially. To my mother I was an undreamt of discomfort which gave birth to a nuisance. Though they like children well enough, the women of the Everlasting Ones, they don't like to have them. They prefer instead to steal human children—but only those whose parents praise them continually. That's why the Irish, being wiser in these matters than most, never praise a child but instead have never a good word to say about it, especially if it is beautiful and well-behaved—a fairy could be listening nearby and decide to run off with it.''

Mournful Mound looked sadly upon the mop-headed poet.

''Poor little thing to be cast out into the world!'' she said softly, her bosom heaving with a sigh. Such was the effect that Bran had on the women.

''I will tell you how it was done,'' Bran said. ''I was put into a basket made of alder and entrusted to the care of Lir the sea god; alder is the wood that resists water the most, so I arrived without a scratch on the west shore of Britain, having traversed the whole of the sea between Ireland and there riding on the backs of the steeds of Lir. My mother left me a whistle in the basket, and when I was washed ashore by the waves, I blew it with all my might until I had attracted the attention of a shepherd of the Silures tribe.

" 'Faith,' said the man when he looked into the basket, 'that baby has a pair of lungs that could fill a sail!' He brought me to the queen of the tribe, and she reared me. And there I lived until Caratacus came on a mission looking for a bard, since the old bard of King Cunobelinus had died. And that's how I came to court at Camulodunum."

"What of your adventures in the basket, riding the waves?" enthused Screech Owl. "The sea-beasts and monsters you must have met!"

"In truth, I met enough of those to fill a hundred tales and more," Bran said, drinking. The magic of his words had put them in a mind for more, and he did not disappoint them.

And so they listened, and drank, and ate, until the king judged it was time to go to bed.

Fen Fire, however, lingered behind.

"I would talk a little longer with Bran about the days of my childhood," she said to her husband. "His presence brings them alive again." Prasutagus, not being a jealous man, bid her come to his chamber when she'd had her fill of the bard's words, and so left them together and retired to his bedroom with his other wives.

As soon as they were alone, Bran took her by the hand.

"Caratacus sent you," she said, her grey eyes grave. He nodded yes.

"He has heard nothing from you since the wedding feast," Bran said.

"There have been unforeseen problems," she told him, looking away from his sharp, piercing eyes. "Latis the first wife has conspired against me. I am not accustomed to intrigues."

"That is because you are not accustomed to marriage," the bard suggested.

"Mine has contained more surprises than I could have expected," answered she. Bran regarded her curiously. She shook her head. "No, dear bard, of them I cannot speak, not even to you." She paused and glanced around her. "But it is not my own thoughts I want to hear but of what Caratacus thinks and plans."

"He is with Queen Du Lliant of the Silures, she whose kingdom looks towards Ireland and whose mother raised me after I was plucked from the grip of the sea. The Silures are hard fighters and have never known defeat. Luxuries they disdain—they wear no gold, nor cherish it. Caratacus believes they will make dependable allies when the time comes that we must face Rome."

"He is convinced it is so?"

"As spring follows winter. Verica and Adminius . . ."

"I curse the day I did not bury my spear in his guts!" she exclaimed, grinding her fist into the palm of her hand. Bran nodded.

"Indeed, it would have been better—he would not be enjoying the fruits of his betrayal as he does even now at the court of Claudius in Rome." There was a pause before he asked: "And the king's allegiance?"

She sighed. "It is not the right moment for me to speak with him about such matters. My life here has been consumed with other things. The scheming of Latis . . ." She halted and lifted her gaze up to the smoke-hole in the palace roof, through which she could see a few summer stars. "The affairs of Camulodunum and Rome have been swept from my mind." She turned to Bran again. "I never knew that women could be so treacherous—as treacherous indeed as fate." Then a smile banished the looks of perplexity and exasperation from her face. "No matter—tell the chief my heart is with him; and where my heart is, so is my strength. When Prasutagus has gotten used to me as a wife, I will be a more forceful political adviser. Though the king is stubborn . . ."

"Caratacus has confidence in you, as I have," Bran interjected. Seeing her smile had made him forget the problems of allegiances. "Since before I departed from the kingdom of the Silures, those many years ago," Bran told her, "I knew the tales of your ancestors—of Movran the Battle Raven, and Red Shaft who brought the three-horned bull from the north, the savior of the women of Britain, and Flame of the Field of Battle, who confronted the mightiest Caesar of them all. When I look at you, I see their spirit—the spirit of old—that has been brought back. Life is bound to the wheel of the eternal return."

"Sometimes I wonder for what purpose."

"To fulfill itself, to live out its destiny," the bard said.

"You speak of destiny as if it were a thing," she said.

"It is not a thing but a force, a force that at times seems almost separate from the person in which it is manifest, but yet without that person it could not exist."

From the bedroom of the king came the sighs of desire. Soon they were followed by the love-cry of one of the wives. Fen Fire stood up.

"Could I exist without my destiny?" she asked. Bran shook his head.

"You would not be you," he told her. "You could as well try to imagine a swan that would fly south in the winter without its young, or a lapwing that would betray her nest to a thief." He paused, and added: "Or a tale that would make a poet blush."

Bran could remain at the king's court for only a few days, during which time Fen Fire relived all the times of her childhood and youth so that it was as if she had never left the great Palace of Cunobelinus. When it came time for the bard to depart, she accompanied him a little way along the path through the fens. She was silent for most of the journey, half-listening as he recited some old verses that were beloved by Cunobelinus. As they reached the end of the path, where it left the reedy marshes, he turned to her.

"I leave you saddened and unsure," he said.

"The future is not decipherable," she answered.

"Indeed, it is not like cracking eggs," he agreed. "You are preoccupied."

"With a riddle," she told him.

"I am good at riddles."

"Then riddle me this riddle:

> A triangle such as n'er was found
> My own heart has bound.
> Same flesh, same blood
> Gives cause to brood
> When in one woman both contend

All laws of blood to offend.
This only I have cause to dread:
An act that blessed a marriage bed.''

''This is the riddle at the heart of your marriage,'' he said.

She turned her gaze back towards the fens where a gentle wind was rippling through the reeds.

''That is the truth. You may have the wit to solve it, but I cannot.''

''Wit is too weak a light to reveal the secrets of a woman's heart. Or of a kindgom's.'' His eyes gleamed. He leant over and kissed her farewell. ''You will hear further from Caratacus,'' he said, suddenly spurring his horse forward.

She watched him disappear, knowing that however much he had discerned, he would not betray it to anyone.

''I was interested in what I have heard you say about the native women,'' said the Emperor Claudius, folding up the maps of Britain's coastline that were spread over the table. He retired to a couch making room for Adminius beside him and ordered a flask of wine. ''Of how they count themselves as equal to the men in deciding matters of state, which frequently seems to be the case among less civilized peoples where women exercise undue authority.'' Then in a lower tone the emperor continued, ''There are even stories—probably legends—that they customarily copulate in the open . . .''

''In the more barbarous west, where my brother Caratacus has not surprisingly gone in search of supporters, and in the far north, they do so without shame or blame,'' Adminius affirmed. For a moment Claudius turned over in his mind the idea of public coitus. It amused him to think that mating in the privacy of one's own bedroom might fill a people who practiced public coitus with the same fierce sense of moral outrage as sober people feel about public displays of indecency.

''So it is not some legend or . . .''

''It is one of the barbarous defects of our people, which only the progress of law will correct,'' Adminius replied, flattered by the easy familiarity with which Caesar accommodated him. Spoken like a veritable Roman, Claudius thought. There was a fetching, childlike quality to these Britons when they rushed to embrace the manners and habits of Roman life in unquestioning confidence of their all-pervading virtues.

"Our government is steady because it is undisturbed by the fickle counsels of females, as our beds are by their overweening demands. We hold sway in both spheres," Claudius said firmly.

"Of course, as is right," Adminius went on with growing fervor. "I know too well the consequences when they have too much freedom to do as they please, take mate after mate, ignore their husbands, pursue their own lusts, and demand of men that they serve their every desire. They want control and savagely oppose any man who resists them. They are both insatiable in lust and implacable in war."

"There is something about all women that is intractable, unpredictable, something that like a force of nature—a sudden storm, an earthquake, an eruption—remains beyond our understanding and our control," Caesar mused. "Consequently, is it not the height of folly to allow ourselves to be ruled by what we do not understand, or cannot contain, whether it be in our private lives through submission to an inordinate passion, amorous or otherwise, or in our conduct of public affairs, by elevating those individuals undisciplined by philosophy as are the great majority of females?"

"In Britain, they know nothing of reason, much less philosophy. They abrogate to themselves every right and privilege and make fools of the kings! They are the source of dissension wherever they hold sway. Their powers of inheritance, their rights of rule, must be curtailed if civilization is to flourish," Adminius said with great animation. For a moment he was transported from Rome. Fen Fire was standing before him, her spear pointed at his throat. He relived the horror of his humiliation at her hands.

"And there is one woman of the Britons—the foster-daughter of Cunobelinus,'' he continued, ''in whose form each of these vices has found embodiment.''

''Your knowledge is derived from experience then,'' Claudius said. He had heard something of the story of Fen Fire, and was now curious to learn more.

''Yes—unhappily,'' Adminius answered. ''She is most arrogant, the most ambitious and the most cruel of them all.'' He paused, seeing that he had stimulated Caesar's attention more than ever. ''And she is the most beautiful.''

Claudis was enthralled. His preference for dominant women was well known; indeed, it was a scandal. In the eyes of his fellow citizens it was worse than lusting after boys. ''A woman and a warrior?'' he mused.

''Yes—and she collects trophies,'' Adminius told him. Claudius shuddered a little at the thought.

''She would make a interesting hostage,'' Claudius smiled. ''One we could have some sport with—in the arena. Of course, it might be wise to bring her here in a cage.''

''Just grant me the right to be her keeper,'' Adminius said, his eyes aflame with the fire of revenge.

Chapter 14

"Do these men look like ghouls?" General Aulus Plautius cried out, his face red with frustration and anger. He pointed to Verica and Adminius, who were standing next to him on a dais surrounded by gangs of men from the four legions chosen to invade Britain. The two Britons were dressed more or less like Romans, and to the unprejudiced eye might well have seemed indistinguishable from them, with their clipped hair, knee-length tunics and hairless faces. But to the eyes of the restless, troubled legionaries gathered around the dais at the Gallic port of Gesoriacum, they might as well have had two heads each. The men of the Second, Ninth, Fourteenth and Twentieth Legions were refusing to embark for Britain. That they were expected to at all, they blamed mainly on Adminius and Verica. To the exasperated general's question, they replied with one voice:

"Away with them!" And immediately afterwards, the soldiers began to chant: "We won't be led to the Land of the Dead, we won't be led to the Land of the Dead." For this was the name the Romans, following the Greeks, used for Britain, basing it on an old story that after death the souls of the dead migrated there. Plautius could not be heard above the racket. He looked at the chief centurions standing directly beneath him, his eyes full of desperation. But their faces were covered in shame. They had tried everything from threats to bribes, from flattery to insult, without success: the men refused to budge from what they knew—the safe and solid land of Gaul—to a place that was as insubstantial as mist and as dangerous as a snake pit. The general's appeal to the evidence of the obvious humanity of the two Britons beside him meant little compared to the stories told around the legionaries' campfires at night. As the chanting continued, Verica and Adminius began to fear for their safety. Plautius ordered the centurions to form a guard to escort them back to their quarters in Gesoriacum. Then he himself retreated with dignity. The whole episode had been painful and humiliating—a man of his rank and status, whose family had been close to that of the Caesar's for over a generation, having to plead with such disrespectful rowdies. He at once dictated a plea for help to Claudius.

"To Tiberius Claudius Nero Germanicus, Greatest and Best of Men, greetings.

"I trust that you and the Senate and the People of Rome are well.

"There is no sense in not coming to the point at once. The men are in mutiny. They will not set foot on the transport ships and are refusing to go to Britain. All attempts by the centurions and other officers have failed to move them. I myself directly appealed to them and endeavored to quell their fears about Britain by exhibiting on the dais alongside myself the two most notable specimens of British manhood we had, our advisers Verica and Adminius, as proof that the Britons are after all as human as ourselves. However, my efforts were greeted with derision.

"The miasma of superstition that clouded the hopes of your predecessor when he set out to conquer Britain has to my regret settled on the expeditionary force. And through it the men perceive only the shapes of their own preposterous fears. To trace the orgins of this disorder was a necessary, if demeaning task, but I have done it.

"I have discovered that an old soldier, one Gnaeus Saturninus who once served as a procurer of horses with your illustrious brother Germanicus in Germany, and who is now settled in Gesoriacum, is the immediate cause of the current disturbance. I have been able to ascertain that a chance encounter with some of the men of the Fourteenth at a wine bar led to the usual drunken soldierly reminiscing, during which the veteran poured forth tales of horror concerning the fate of several of his comrades when they were returning from Germany. As I have no need to remind you, Germanicus embarked several of his legions on ships for the return journey, which were separated and blown off course during a fierce storm. One was lost near the British coast. The tales Saturninus told to the men, and later was delighted to repeat to me, concerned the alleged fate of those shipwrecked in Britain. Please bear with me while I report what he has been saying, if only as an example of how, in the superstitious mind, the most fallacious of tales can take on the aspect of an unshakable truth.

"The tales were full of the usual ghosts and druidic demons. But what impressed the men most was the story Saturninus told of the tribe of powerful, dagger-wielding female witches who, he claims, inhabit the island's swamplands and are semi-naked, being dressed only in animal pelts—all the year round! Apart from being thus immune to this wretched northern climate, among their many other powers is that of shape-changing—they can turn themselves into huge crows, and various other birds with evil associations. Their predilection is to hunt well-endowed men whom they take back to their groves where they castrate them (after being serviced first, of course), which groves are therefore decorated with the 'trophies' they collect from them.

"With great flair and vigor he described these Amazons performing other unmentionable acts on the unfortunate castaways who somehow—he could not remember these finer points with any clarity—fell into their hands (or should it be talons?). Apparently, they are also rather wealthy witches, since Saturninus spoke of a treasure trove of enormous proportions being in their possession. Clearly, though they could easily afford to live in a somewhat more comfortable style, they choose not to—which to my mind is final proof of the utter absurdity of the rumor.

"As proof of the story's authenticity, however, Saturninus claims that his tales are based on an account told to him at first hand by one of the men who apparently survived this shipwreck and escaped from the clutches of the crow-women. He only remembered his first name, Lucius. When I upbraided him for believing and spreading such ridiculous stuff, he confidently replied that if I didn't believe him I could go and talk with Lucius himself. I agreed, thinking that if I fetched the originator of the rumors and made him recant them in front of the men it would persuade them to come to their senses. However, when I asked him where this Lucius was, he replied 'Rome.' I asked him where in Rome. He shrugged and said he didn't know. I patiently pointed out that the city has a population of a million or more, and asked him to guess how many would have the first name Lucius. In any case, he asserts that Lucius had gone to Rome many years ago where he settled, no doubt in one of the warrens of slums in which it would be, I suppose, an impossible, and probably in the end, worthless task to try and locate him.

"I am certain, Greatest and Best of Men, that you will devise a more expeditious solution to this crisis. I do not need to impress you with the urgency of my request. We are well into the spring, and if we delay our sailing much longer it will, as you are well aware, deprive us of much essential campaigning time so that a postponement until the following year might be forced upon us. This would be an intolerable humiliation from which the honor of Rome, that you hold dearer than your own, would only with difficulty recover. As I am certain that you realize the extreme importance of quelling this rebellion among the expeditionary forces, I do not hesitate to suggest that you yourself might directly appeal to the men. Your august and honored presence would surely be enough to return them to their sense of duty as soldiers of Rome, its Senate and its People."

Plautius read it over quickly, and at once dispatched it to Rome.

Having been safely escorted from the legionary camp, which was on the outskirts of Gesoriacum itself, Adminius and Verica, doleful and glum-faced, made their way through the town gates. Verica cast a sour look up at the lighthouse that Caligula had built on a hill just to the north overlooking the port. It was over 100 feet high, and dominated everything in the vicinity. He had erected it just before abandoning his invasion of Britain.

The wharfside bar that Adminius had suggested they go to was crowded, but they elbowed their way through to the counter and ordered themselves a flask of wine. Adminius, in spite of what had happened, was still confident—at least he spoke as if he was. The army would come round. The leaders of the mutiny would be exposed. No Roman army had ever mutinied—that was a fact, he asserted, for he had read the history books or so he liked to boast. Claudius would intervene. The project was too prestigious for him to allow it to be abandoned. Verica said nothing. He had said nothing for hours. After the hostilities and tensions in the camp, the noise and confusion of the bar only aggravated him even more. But he was happy to have a cup of wine. Just as he was about to put it to his lips, someone nudged him. He looked round. Though he did not know him, he recognized him as a soldier from the camp.

"You are one of them Britons, aren't you," the soldier said drunkenly. "You'd like to see us dumped in some foggy swamp, wouldn't you! Well, we've gotten too smart for that—no demon-invested fog-bound wilderness is going to claim me! And no witch is going to get her hands on this pride and joy." He flipped out his penis and waved it from side to side. "Unless I want to give it to her, and then I don't intend to let her take it home with her, of course!" There was a roar of laughter from the crowded bar. Though the soldier was smaller than he, and Verica could easily have crushed him with one blow, he thought better of it—the bar was swarming with legionaries and sailors. They began to grumble menacingly at the two Britons. Without touching his wine, Verica put the cup down on the counter and left, Adminius following behind him. The customers laughed and hooted derisively. "I hope you know how to swim," one cried out, "for that's the only way you'll get back to Britain!"

"Well," Verica said, glaring at his companion, "have you any more wonderful ideas? I am eager to hear them."

The news of the mutiny threw Claudius into a panic. The suggestion that he go to Gaul and appeal to the troops made him perspire nervously.

"Of course, I w . . . will go if there's no other way.

B . . . But my position would never survive a rejection," he said to Narcissus, whom he had brought at once to his private chamber for consultations. "It would inspire every general with an eye to my throne to challenge me. For if you c . . . cannot control your troops, and get them to obey you, you cannot be Caesar. It is as . . . as simple as that."

Narcissus did not seem to be listening, but was scanning the message from Aulus Plautius, and thinking to himself how these Romans of the senatorial class could no longer command the respect of their own men. He handed the message back to the emperor.

"Well, what do you, uh, what do you think?" Claudius was stammering more than usual—a certain sign that he was frightened. The Greek pictured him shambling about on the dais, stammering and spluttering. He smiled. An amusing sight, but one that might well precipitate a disaster for the rule of law and order—maybe even a civil war of succession.

"It is an interesting specimen of the old Amazon myth," Narcissus replied. "Why does it keep recurring?" Why do men—I mean normal men—seem to harbor this inordinate fear of warrior women? Perhaps it's because they dread the prospect of women who already possess the secret of sex, from which stems their power, possessing also the power to compel, which derives from greater physical strength thought to be the proper province of the male."

"Narcissus!" Claudius exclaimed, nervously twisting the message in his hands until it was almost torn in two. "I am s . . . sure your thoughts are very, are very profound. B . . . But we have a very important problem at hand. P . . . P . . . Please devote some t . . . time to it."

"I have already solved it," the Greek replied, calmly and matter-of-factly.

"You do n . . . not agree with P . . . P . . . Plautius I hope."

Narcissus shook his head. "I will go to Gaul myself." Claudius appeared relieved and shocked at the same time. The idea that he would not have to confront the mutineers pleased him, but the thought of sending a eunuch and former slave to do the job of quelling an army uprising was a novel admission of imperial impotence. And it took some moments before Claudius, among whose titles was that of "Glorious Father of Our Country," would agree to it.

Dawn broke over the ramparts of the fortress and found Caratacus seated opposite Bran, locked in a game of chess. The fortress commanded a view south, where the grassy headlands met the incoming waves of the channel separating Britain from Gaul. It was one of the posts from which the Catuvellaunian army kept watch upon the shores, awaiting the arrival of Caesar's legions. Togodumnus commanded a position further east, and Maglocunos another to the west. No matter where the Romans might land within a stretch of coastline many miles in length, the Catuvellaunian forces could concentrate and strike at them quickly. Subidasto, meanwhile, was approaching from the north with forces raised among the various allies, as well as from his own tribe, the Iceni. His bid for his father's support had failed. However, though the king had forbidden it, many young warriors ignored his commands and chose instead to follow the son.

"My wits are scattered like a flock of sparrows before a hawk, sheep before a wolf, or little fish before the preying eel," yawned the bard, rubbing his eyes as Caratacus took one of his men and placed his king in jeopardy. Bran's eyes were bloodshot, and his face was peaked.

"They lie dissolved at the bottom of a cup, or spent between the thighs of a woman," the chief said, clutching the fallen piece in his fist. He looked up towards the rampart. "A horseman approaches," he said, though from where they were sitting it was not possible to see the plains beyond the fortress walls. And though Bran listened intently, he could hear nothing.

"If an ant moved a grain of wheat across a field a mile away, could you hear it?" he asked Caratacus.

"Surely, and I could tell you if it had a limp. Now move." But the bard was distracted by the thought that a messenger might be coming with news of the Roman fleet's approach. And he became even more distracted when, after some minutes had passed, he could at last hear the hoofbeats with his own ears. So when he moved it was a foolish blundering move, exposing his king. Caratacus saw the opportunity at once and the poet, his king trapped, was forced to surrender.

"In any battle, whether of blades and spears, or of pieces of wood, he who loses possession of himself loses everything," Caratacus said, as the guard announced the arrival of a messenger from the coast to the north. "He cannot concentrate on the task in front of him. Without self-possession, he falls into the possession of others."

"Bards are exempt from your prescriptions. It does not require self-possession to compose verses about battles, though it does to fight them," Bran replied, glancing around him as the dirt-bespattered messenger came panting into their presence.

"They refuse to embark!" exclaimed the messenger. "They will not be persuaded by beatings, bribes or the begging of their officers to board their ships for Britain."

"Have they abandoned their camp?" asked Caratacus. The messenger shook his head.

"Not yet—but their officers have abandoned any attempt to persuade them to do their duty." He quickly explained what he had learned from spies in Gesoriacum who had passed word across the channel about the mutiny. Caratacus at once called his two brothers together for a council meeting to decide what course they should take.

The warriors, who had been in a state of battle preparation for many days, were restless; the news of the mutiny immediately caused elation and calls for a huge celebration to mark this, their second bloodless victory over the forces of the empire.

"Who waits on a coward to come to fight waits in vain," Togodumnus announced, as if he was not at all surprised by the turn of events.

"They have gone the way of the madman Caligula. His fears still haunt them," Maglocunos said.

"But Claudius himself is not there. Until they refuse

his orders, they have not reached a final decision,'' Caratacus suggested. In spite of their conviction that it was aimless to continue their vigil, Caratacus persuaded them not to abandon their positions but to wait longer, arguing that if Caesar himself intervened the legionaries might be shamed or frightened into obeying their superiors. But then on the heels of the first messenger, a second came with word that Claudius had refused to leave Rome and instead a former slave was being dispatched.

''There is proof our victory is won,'' said Togodumnus. ''Only a man despairing of all hope of success would stoop to sending a former slave—and one who is not even a man—to do his begging for him.''

''No warrior will take orders from a slave,'' Maglocunos said.

By now, the Catuvellaunian host had grown too restless to hold together; the word of the Roman mutiny quickly spread through the whole army and Caratacus knew it was futile to try. Though along with his own picked warriors he decided to maintain patrols along the most vulnerable stretch of coastline, he agreed that the others should be free to disperse if that was their wish.

The army was preparing to break up, and Togodumnus and Maglocunos were saying farewell to Caratacus when Subidasto returned with the men who had followed him against his father's wishes. Subidasto looked haggard and somber, and even the news of their bloodless victory did not seem to move him.

''It would have been better had you been king,'' said Togodumnus when he learned of Prasutagus' refusal to join them in opposing the enemy.

''And more worthy of the hand of Fen Fire,'' Maglocunos added bitterly. ''As it is, we have lost more than gained through that marriage.''

''I pray you will not lose all. Fen Fire is with child, and weakens,'' Subidasto told them. ''She had not the strength to stand when I saw her last.''

''Fen Fire weak?'' Caratacus said. His bright eyes were suddenly dimmed. ''I can more easily believe that the empire of Rome totters at its base.''

''I myself caught her in my arms,'' the king's son affirmed, "where she lay limp, like a wounded deer." He hesitated, his voice dry and strained. He could not confess how he would have abandoned even the defense of his homeland to be with her, in spite of his bitterness at her marriage to his father. The news at once convinced Caratacus to leave for the Iceni king's Palace of the Red Yew, where Fen Fire lay stricken. His brothers said they would accompany him. Caratacus turned to Subidasto.

"On you I place the responsibility of maintaining the coastal watch, day and night . . ."

"But if there is no need, and she is ill . . ."

"I will let her know of your concern, have no doubt," Caratacus told him and firmly reiterated his command. The thought of waiting and watching for something that would not take place while Fen Fire lay ill made Subidasto desperate to return again to his father's palace. He had to restrain himself from leaving at once, regardless of all other considerations.

"Have no fear," Caratacus added before he left, "Fen Fire does not succumb easily."

Taking their strongest, fastest steeds, the three men rode hard and within a day had reached the valley of the river Medway, which they crossed and turned north towards the Thames. They crossed the marshes near its mouth, and carried on, until they came to Camulodunum. Before continuing their northward journey, they rested for a day. Though one could hardly call it rest—for all three men were distracted by anxiety that Fen Fire would worsen and even die before they reached her.

Meanwhile, from the wild, windy headland Subidasto looked down upon the deserted beaches that stretched for miles in either direction. The seething of the surf on the pebbles seemed like a sigh—a sad sigh born of solitude. With dawn, thousands of sea birds launched themselves from their perilous nests lodged in the cliffside below his post, and with evening returned again: gulls and puffins, petrels and sea ravens flocked around him, cried and squawked to each other all day long. A pair of seals came in under the headland and flopped over the rocks below. The two of them would call to each other through the twilight. And their call was like a moan. In the evenings, it sounded like two old women keening, and put him in mind of the story that seals were people transformed through the power of magic.

On the morning after the brothers' departure, a mist obscured the shore, and the sea was dead calm. Subidasto heard a cry from nearby. Drawing his sword, he rode down towards a hollow, where he found a young shepherd boy in a state of distress.

"I have lost a lamb," the boy cried. "I fear he has fallen over the side of the cliff and plunged to those rocks. But in this mist, I fear for my own life if I try to go down to search for him." Subidasto told him to be at his ease.

"I have patroled this desolate place long enough to know every path and every foothold. I will find your lamb," he said. On foot, he edged his way down, listening to the sea below as it dashed against the shore, without seeing more than the mist in front of him. Ferns grew from the stony slope, and he scattered sea birds that he came upon; they flew off screeching, surprised to meet a mortal man in a place they thought belonged only to themselves.

Subidasto reached the shore, and quickly scrambled over the rocks. After a short time, he heard the bleating of the lamb up ahead of him, though as yet he could not see it. It was a plaintive, sorrowful cry. Quietly, he crept along until he caught a glimpse of the lamb wandering lost and frightened along the beach. He moved towards it very slowly, hoping not to scare it off. As he drew near, the lamb looked at him, uncertain what to do—whether to run this way or that. It gave another distressful bleat, and turned towards Subidasto. The lamb, startled by a loud splashing noise coming in from the sea, started to run over to him and was almost within reach when it stopped suddenly, shuddered, and fell forward, an arrow sticking from its side. Its blood gushed over its white fleece and onto the sand. Subidasto fell on his knees beside it and gripped the quivering arrow. He looked out to sea. A huge galley was ploughing through the mist, a host of Roman archers perched on its prow, which split the tranquil waters and churned them into a white foam. Arrows thudded into the sand around him, sending the grains spurting up into the air. Huge banks of oars rose and fell from the galley's sides, the water cascading in streams along their length. Subidasto threw himself to the sand, and began rolling towards the rocky foot of the headland down which he had just descended. Galley after galley loomed through the mist, creaking and groaning like monstrous animals about to give birth; the sea was split apart by the massive prows until the ships came to a grinding, crunching halt on the sand. Subidasto reached the foot of the headland's steep and rocky slopes, and turned to look. Armored legionaries poured over the bulging sides of the boats. The silence of the beach was shattered by the clatter of metal and the shouts of command. He froze, crouching, staring in fascinated horror at the spectacle, half convinced he was witnessing some mist-inspired nightmare. A unit of legionaries, the first three men off their ship, came racing towards him, shouting. When he stood up, two of them, shields on their arms, raised their javelins. The third carried a long pole crowned with a shape like that of an eagle, which he thrust into the sand. Subidasto could not understand what they were shouting at him. But when he drew his sword, they hurled their javelins, which clattered harmlessly on the rocky slopes behind him. Before they could draw their swords, Subidasto sprang at them, decapitating the first with one sweep of his weapon, and shattering the other's shield with his second blow, which landed with such force that the Roman was flung on his back. Thousands were swarming towards him and the mist seemed to be vomiting spears. Grabbing the severed head by the crest of its helmet, he turned and raced up the rocky slope until he found the narrow pathway by which he descended. Behind him he could hear the shouts of the invaders, and the crunching sound made by their tread as they hurried across the sand was like that of the millstones of giants grinding grain. It anguished him to have to turn his back on the enemy, but he did so with the satisfaction of knowing that he had collected his first trophy and at least one thirsty patch of sand was soaking up Roman blood.

Subidasto was quickly lost in the mists. Leaving his

pursuers far behind, he scrambled to the top of the headland and warned the shepherd boy of the danger at hand.

"Go," he cried as the young lad gaped pale with terror at the severed Roman head, "tell the people that the armies of Caesar have landed!" The boy needed no other incentive. He took off at once. Then, mounting his horse, Subidasto set out with all speed for his own encampment. The scattered forces of the tribes would have to be gathered together without delay or the Romans would think that having left their shores defenseless the Britons were now prepared to surrender the whole land without resistance.

Caratacus and his brothers were about to set out from Camulodunum for the Palace of the Red Yew when word reached them of the landing. They received it in grim silence. Each man thought the same thought: that their children and their children's children would remember them as the men who left their land defenseless allowing the enemy to set foot on it without a fight. There was but one means of removing that disgrace. "Roman blood will wipe it clean!" Togodumnus exclaimed. Word went out for the warriors of the Catuvellauni and their allies to march south to oppose the Roman advance. They had to abandon their journey to Fen Fire's side. "Now, I have no doubt but she will mend," said Caratacus, "if only so that she can join us in opposing Caesar."

No one knew for certain what had happened to convince Caesar's legions to embark for Britain. Togodumnus for one concluded that the story of the mutiny had been a trick to make them abandon their positions on the coast, thus affording the Romans an unopposed landing. He simply could not believe that an army of men would obey a eunuch.

Indeed, when Narcissus had first arrived in the army camp outside Gesoriacum, no one believed he would be obeyed. He was greeted with so much derision by the mutinous soldiers that his task seemed doomed to ignominious failure.

"They send a man without balls to deal with the stiffest cocks in creation!" someone howled at him as he came into the camp in his gorgeous coach.

"A real woman would have been better—she would at least have had something to offer us. Or a real man—we would have listened to him—at least for a few minutes! But not this creature—neither man nor woman, neither flesh, fish nor fowl," they shouted in jest. But it was a bitter jest that Aulus Plautius knew could take an ugly turn—the legionaries were offended that Caesar refused to come himself and had instead dispatched a former slave, and one who was not even a man—or not in any sense that soldiers could appreciate. Hence, when the general in command of the expedition greeted Narcissus, he could not conceal his anxiety and frustration.

"This is badly done," he said through clenched teeth as the Greek was quickly escorted past the hissing, laughing, booing crowd (for it no longer resembled an army except in the manner of dress) into general headquarters. Narcissus said nothing until they were inside the general's private quarters.

"Instruct your officers to assemble the men as soon as possible. I intend to address them at once," the Greek said in precise, clipped tones. Plautius went pale.

"No, it is not possible," he exclaimed. "It is bad enough as it is—they are in no mood to listen to a . . ."

"A eunuch? A Greek? A former slave? Which of my afflictions offends them the most?" Narcissus shot back. His small, close-set eyes had a stony, detached look that made the aging commander feel distinctly uncomfortable. Gazing out of them Aulus Plautius saw a soul without illusions, a thing as shocking to behold as any deformity of nature. What he also saw, but did not recognize, was merely a kind of honesty that was often mistaken for cruelty.

"They are aware of the trust in which you are held by Caesar," the general responded, "but it is a matter of . . . tradition. Soldiers will only listen to and obey those put in command above them—their superiors." Narcissus handed Plautius a letter bearing Caesar's stamp.

"Caesar has instructed you to allow me complete freedom to deal with this disturbance in whatever way I see fit, as you will read for yourself. I am here not to undermine but to reinforce the authority of their 'superiors' which is, from what I saw when I arrived, clearly one tradition that is already no longer respected in this camp. All superiority is provisional. One man is recognized as superior by his fellow man only as long as he is seen to earn that recognition; once he ceases to earn it, his destruction is only a matter of time. For the inferior are not content to reduce their superiors merely to their own level—they need to extirpate them utterly, partly because the inferior always resents the superior for simple reasons such as envy, and partly because the inferior have as many illusions about their superiors as their superiors have about themselves, and are inflamed by having those illusions shattered. A general whose troops refuse to obey him is therefore a man very close to destruction. So, instruct your officers immediately.'' Plautius read Caesar's message and obeyed, though with undisguised reluctance.

''Remember,'' he said as Narcissus walked out to the dais, ''such philosophizing will bore them.'' Narcissus did not reply, but mounted the steps without looking one way or another, ignoring the hoots from the assembled men. Plautius came behind him, and when he reached the platform called out to the soldiers to be quiet.

''Why didn't Caesar send his wife, Messalina?'' a soldier at the front cried out. ''At least she's a dishy little number!''

''Yeah, and then every man would have a chance to make a little Caesar for himself!'' someone roared from the back. The whole crowd erupted with laughter and floods of ribald remarks poured forth.

''First a pair of Britons, now a man without a pair of balls!'' someone shouted up. ''What next? A lady with a beard?''

''He speaks with Caesar's voice!'' Plautius shouted, trying to be heard above the noise.

''S . . . s . . . silence!'' Narcissus cried out, twitching a little as he spoke. As he began to limp about the dais, the soldiers looked up at him in puzzlement. Their first reaction was one of shock—was the eunuch, the former slave, daring to make fun of his master, Caesar? This effectively silenced them long enough for Narcissus to continue.

Narcissus' head shook with nervous little jerks; he began to dribble at the mouth. His eyes rolled around in their sockets in a grotesque parody of Claudius Caesar's stammer which afflicted him when nervous and tense. And when he opened his mouth no words came. Instead a discordant series of fractured syllables poured forth, intermingled with sucking, gasping sounds as if he were suffocating and struggling for breath. Sometimes he froze suspended, his hand raised, his mouth open, ready to make a fine point or deliver a stinging rebuke but instead nothing came and he appeared to be more like a statue of a speaker than a living being.

"Be . . . be . . . hold the very form of Caesar himself," he said, finally, hobbling about the stage exhausted. He had engaged in a ludicrous wrestling match with words, wrenching them from the air, being thrown by their elusive syllables, pinned and battered by their intimidating vowels, dragged around by their long consonants.

The men stared silently at first. But before long shock gave way to mirth, and soon the whole army was clutching its sides laughing. Even Plautius had begun to smile.

"We declare another Saturnalia!" a soldier called out; the feast on which servants and slaves are allowed to dress up as their masters was already over, of course, but it seemed like Narcissus had decided to declare it anew. This was received with a loud cheer. The soldiers' bitter-edged, rather menacing humor was transformed through mockery, and the spirit of rebelliousness and mutiny was suddenly lifted. Narcissus sensed this immediately.

"As I am to Caesar," he continued, "your fears are to the truth: an absurd distortion of the world." A hush came over the soldiers. All eyes were fixed on Narcissus. He had resumed his dignified manner. He looked down at them, going from face to face with his scrutinizing gaze. He said no more. He had no need to. The men shifted about uneasily, as if they had just been caught in a shameful act. Each man hung his head. They had refused to obey orders. They had jeered their general. They had jeopardized a vital expedition and threatened to stain the honor of Rome. Then they had joined in a mockery of Caesar, the Father of their Country, to whose service they had dedicated their lives. Yet, by some strange alchemy it was this very act, defiant parody that it was, which had purged them of everything else, so that after it was over, and Narcissus faced them again as Narcissus, the eunuch, the former slave, the despised Greek, the soldiers felt cleansed, restored to themselves, ready to accept their duty. It enabled them to feel their guilt yet rid themselves of it at the same time. The miasma of fear, disrespect, superstition and mutiny was blown away by a joke.

"By restoring to them their sense of humor, I restored them to their sense of duty: with a jest I launched a thousand ships," Narcissus wrote to Claudius later that night in the rather cryptic manner that his master had come to expect. But of course, he did not spell out exactly what kind of jest it was. That was his secret, one which he shared with some 40,000 men who were soon on their way to Britain.

"When they leave their camp to search for fodder, strike then. When they send their patrols to scout the pathways, that is the time to attack. Burn the crops, slaughter the animals, so that they advance into a wasteland." Caratacus paused. "We are too weak to meet them in battle until our allies from the west and north can join us. Our only course is a war of little bites." Even Togodumnus, who usually opposed his brother in all things strategical, and who preferred an open battle on which all was staked, saw the sense of this. At once bands of Catuvellaunian warriors set out, posting themselves in hidden places. They struck at isolated columns, ambushing fodder gatherers, vanishing afterwards into the woods. Aulus Plautius was angry and frustrated, declaring that he could find no enemy to fight. At last, he struck on a plan. He ordered Adminius to accompany a patrol and use his knowledge of the Britons to find them and bring them to battle. Adminius was none too pleased with this, dreading to fall into the hands of his brothers. Plautius allayed his fears by telling him to disguise himself as a Roman centurion. He had no choice other than to obey. The first attempt brought no results, and Adminius returned empty-handed. The Britons were cunning enough to avoid attacking such a powerful force so close to the main camp. Plautius told him to be more daring, and venture further afield. Before long, what the general hoped would happen, happened.

A spy in the Roman camp brought word to Togodumnus that Adminius in disguise was leading a column. His eyes lit up. At once, he ordered every man he had to prepare for battle. At the time, Caratacus and Maglocunos were operating nearby, and Togodumnus was asked by one of his warriors if he should go and warn them so that they might join the attack.

"No," the chief answered, "I am the oldest of Cunobelinus' sons. It is fitting that the honor of bringing in his head will be mine alone. And it is even more fitting that when I do, it will be wearing a Roman helmet."

Aulus Plautius was stationed not far behind Adminius' column when the warriors of Togodumnus swept out of the surrounding woods.

"Brotherly hatred is always more dependable than brotherly love," he said, ordering his men to advance in close battle order. It was a perfect place to engage—a flat wide meadow on which the legionaries had plenty of space to maneuver. The Britons were caught between Adminius' column and the forces of Plautius. The Catuvellaunian chariots became wedged together and useless.

"Ever since he was a boy and he played his ear-wagging trick on me, he has been able to deceive me," Togodumnus lamented when he realized that once again he had been fooled. His men, crowded together, were being cut down on all sides. His every limb had a wound. The ranks of the Romans bristled on every side like a thick thorn bush. "I regret that I tried so selfishly to reserve the honor of cutting off Adminius' head to myself, for if the truth were told, I could do with some assistance at this moment."

Camulos, the war god, must have heard his heartfelt words, for no sooner had he uttered them than his ears were pricked up by the blast of another Catuvellaunian battle trumpet. It was that of his brother Caratacus who, accompanied by Maglocunos and Subidasto, appeared on the scene with a band of their warriors. They too had heard of Adminius' presence. Though greatly outnumbered, they caused enough confusion and panic among the Romans—who thought it was an entire army of Britons—to enable Togodumnus to fight his way to safety.

"Well," said Togodumnus to his brothers after they had put a good distance between them and the enemy, "though I tried to deprive you of the honor of killing Adminius, I have given you the honor of saving Togodumnus."

Caratacus was not amused. He feared their defeat, though minor, would have serious consequences. They soon learned his fears were justified. When they had reached the river Medway and halted there, word came to them that the king of the Dobunni, Boduocus, who as their subject was expected to send warriors to aid them, had instead sent his pledge of submission to Plautius. Hard on the heels of this came news that the Coritani, a northern ally, had done likewise. These developments provoked divisions among the Catuvellauni. A war council of all the most powerful men of the tribe was called to decide what their next step should be. Subidasto was permitted to attend and speak if he wished, in recognition of the services he had rendered the tribe, though he had no power to vote.

"We have no choice now but to fight it out here," Togodumnus said at the meeting.

"If we try to avoid battle and retreat any further inland, it will be seen as a sign of weakness," Subidasto argued in support of Togodumnus. He told them it would provoke more defections from among their allies. But Caratacus was convinced otherwise.

"Until the western tribes are ready to stand beside us, we must fight with our wits—as we did before, wearing the invader down, straining his resources, forcing him to spread his army over as wide an area as possible—then we can confront him when we are ready, on the ground of our choosing, with more confidence of success," he told the war council. "This is a war of the fox, not the bear."

"We fought with cunning—with ambush and trap—only to find that we were ourselves tricked," Togodumnus replied vehemently. "And it will happen again. For the enemy has an inexhaustible supply of cunning, especially with Adminius at his side, who is more of a fox than any of us. We must instead use our own inexhaustible resources—the courage that is in our hearts and the strength that is in our arms."

Though Maglocunos sided with Caratacus, when the vote of the other Catuvellaunian chieftains was taken, the majority were in favor of following the course advocated by Togodumnus. They would stand and fight on the north bank of the river Medway. Caratacus and Maglocunos could, if they wished, take their own warriors away and conduct the war as they chose—but both knew that to do so would hopelessly weaken the Catuvellaunian resistance. They remained to fight at the side of the others.

Watching the army of Caesar approach was like seeing some huge insect with thousands of legs moving in unison. The tramp of their feet was a regular and monotonous beat, pounding the ground. Wave after wave of anonymous men, they came to a halt at the river. Their first attempts to cross proved disastrous. The strong current made them unsteady; they were unable to maintain their footing and became easy targets for the slingshots and javelins of the Britons. The river began to redden with their blood. The Romans withdrew, abandoning any attempts to cross en masse. But towards late afternoon, when the Britons were getting ready to camp for the night, Plautius sent over a detachment of his army made up of warriors from the island of Batavia, at the mouth of the river Rhine. They were strong swimmers, and were able to cross the Medway with a full kit of armor. They landed further down, where the warriors had stabled their chariot horses. The Batavians attacked the horses, slaughtering them. By the time the Catuvellaunians had driven the attackers off, it was too late: all but a few of their horses were slain.

The following day, the battle was renewed. But it was a different kind of battle—one that was new to the Britons. The warriors were alerted by the sound of creaking and groaning, and beheld emerging from the Roman ranks huge contraptions of wood with ropes and skeins of leather attached to them. These machines the Romans loaded with great rocks, some larger than a full-length shield. Suddenly, the sky was grey as the rocks rained down upon the Britons, crushing skulls, spattering brains on the ground, mangling limbs, reducing men to a tangle of blood and bone. No shield, however stout, could stop the storm of doom which broke upon them. The Catuvellauni were forced up the bank away from the river. At the same time, the Batavians began to cross the river once more, and Plautius led a general advance down the bank, ready to brave the current now that the Britons had been forced back too far to strike at them with their javelins and slingshots. Soon, the enemy was swarming up the north bank of the river. The Catuvellauni, without their chariot horses and forced to fight on foot, made a final, desperate charge to throw them back. Many slipped on the bloody slopes of the riverbank. Warriors sank to their beds of blood, others were swept away head to toe with their enemy down the blood-red course of the river. The Batavians pressed them on one side, the legionaries advanced relentlessly on the other. The Catuvellaunian host, in danger of being completely overwhelmed, was driven back.

Caratacus found Togodumnus with a crop of freshly harvested heads tied to his belt and around his horse's neck. He stood upright, his both hands gripping the hilt of his bloodstained broadsword which was thrust into the ground. Togodumnus' face was spattered with blood. It was pale and drawn. Though he was obviously seriously injured, he grinned broadly when he saw Caratacus, whose own shoulder was badly cut from a gash made by a fragment of a rock from a catapult that shattered near him.

"It was no hailstone did that," Togodumnus said.

"Nor was it anything inflicted by a man—it is a different world when machines make war, and battles are not won by courage and strength," Caratacus replied.

"Aye," said the other, "fighting is no longer the manner of it."

A warrior came staggering past them, blood pouring

from his stomach; he fell forward on his face. Another lay near Togodumnus' horse, his eyes bulging wide open, staring up at the clouds scudding across the sky, a javelin thrust through his back. One crawled on his hands and knees like a wounded animal vomiting blood, his bowels hanging around his ankles. Another had lost his arm beneath the elbow and spouted fountains of blood. Yet another dragged his stone-crushed legs behind him, their broken bones poking through the torn skin. One poor man, his face smashed by a rock hurled from a Roman catapult, groped blindly, stumbling over the heaps of the dead.

"This is not like catching birds," Togodumnus said. He breathed in short, harsh snatches. There was not an inch of his white skin but it was covered in wounds.

"Subidasto and Maglocunos are already taking their forces north towards the Thames," Caratacus told him, "and it is time for us to do the same. We will regroup and gather our strength. There will be better fields than this on which to fight."

"Truly, the day meant ill," his brother answered, with a groan which he could not stifle. He clutched his side. "A curse upon it—for a little nick like that to cause such trouble!" Caratacus could see it was far from a mere nick that pained his brother, but a long, raw, red, angry wound. "Still, it is not in my nature to show my back to the enemy. Somewhere not far from here Adminius is skulking!" He swayed forward unsteadily. Caratacus put his arms around him.

"Conserve your strength. Before you can inflict another wound you must heal your own." The sound of Roman voices made Caratacus glance over his shoulder. Through the dust and confusion of fleeing men he could see the unbroken ranks of the legions advancing towards them, their officers shouting orders. They had sent a fresh detachment onto the field without a mark on them. They were pausing only to slash the throats of those wounded lying in their path. Caratacus leapt onto his horse. With the help of another warrior, he managed to lift his brother up behind him. He strapped his belt around the two of them, holding Togodumnus firmly upright, then urged the steed forward from the field of slaughter.

"It is a shame that you should see me like this," the wounded man muttered into his ear as they rode away. "I was a hawk among sparrows, a wolf among sheep."

"And so you will be remembered," Caratacus replied. He felt his brother's head fall on his shoulder, and a trickle of something warm on his neck. It was blood, oozing from Togodumnus' mouth. The years of their youth flashed before his eyes, when Togodumnus' grip was strong and could not be broken; now the arms that once could hoist a man over his head with ease hung slackly at his sides. His brother's breathing became harsh, his great chest heaved.

"Remember the day you taught me the trick of leaping the gap?" Caratacus asked, glancing round. "And the day with Fen Fire, when she threw her javelin and proved a better shot than us all?" There was no response. He talked on—as memory after memory came flooding back down the dark river of the past. Perhaps by reliving those moments he could somehow revive the man who had shared them with him in all their warmth and vigor. But Caratacus spoke through his tears. Togodumnus, who had so often lifted him from his feet and carried him on his shoulders, was dying on his back. Soon, he was beyond the reach of words. His brother breathed no more. He grew cold. Caratacus rode blinded by tears, his brother's dead body tied to him. A Roman axe had felled the Oak of the Britons.

"But we will not be oaks standing there for them to hack at as they please," Caratacus swore. His brother's death only confirmed his belief as to what kind of war the Britons must fight if they were to survive.

The flames of the funeral fire were still blazing on the banks of the Thames when Caratacus told the weary, defeated remnants of the Catuvellaunian host of his decision.

"The walls and dikes of Camulodunum will be no obstacle to Caesar," he said. The fire crackled around his brother's body, enveloping it. Such futile heroism had cost them too much already. "Our only hope is in the west. If we can draw them west, we can fight the kind of war we need to fight—wearing them down slowly, and only striking with concentrated force when we are strong enough and they are weak. Among the far western tribes on the Severn and beyond are men who have never known defeat. In the north, too, we have potential allies powerful enough to destroy even Caesar's might.'' He outlined his plan. From the west he would fight a war of hit and run. Meanwhile, with the support of the northern tribes such as the Brigantes, they must prepare to launch a large-scale, coordinated attack from the west and north, isolating Caesar's soldiers from their bases, annihilating them before they had a chance to concentrate against them. Maglocunos agreed to go as their ambassador to the princess Cartimandua. At the Beltane Feast she had promised him the sweetest pastures in her kingdom to graze the sacred bull—sweet pastures and wide domains, where the beast could roam freely and now be safe from the grasp of the invaders.

''It is a sweet task I have given you,'' Caratacus said. ''One that only the need to build our forces in the west prevents me from undertaking myself.''

''It is better that I am going, brother, for she has had you under her spell once before and might distract you from all thoughts of war,'' Maglocunos smiled.

''Don't take lightly the power of her charm—keep to your purpose—win her to our allegiance quickly.''

''I am not so easily bewitched,'' he assured Caratacus. He would set out at once for the north.

But the majority would not hear of the plan. They wanted to fight as soon as they could reorganize their forces in the only way they knew how—with massed chariots, army against army, on a battlefield where glory could be won, even in defeat. The chiefs proclaimed they would not retreat beyond the north bank of the Thames. The idea of abandoning their land to go to a distant, unknown place like the western mountains beyond the Severn appalled them. Only Maglocunos and Subidasto could grasp what Caratacus had in mind and agreed with him.

When the funeral flames died down, the wind carried the ashes across the wide river. The two brothers said farewell to the land of their fathers. They knew that unless their mission succeeded, they could never return to it.

It was agreed that Subidasto would not yet go west

with Caratacus. The chief had given him a task to perform first: to journey to his father's kingdom to speak with the king and Fen Fire. Even if Prasutagus still denied them his support, his wife would not.

The feast of Lugus came. The fields to the west of the palace where the soil was fertile were full of golden grain sprinkled with the late-summer purple of poppies and the sunny yellow of buttercups. Then the scythes of harvest swept through them, leaving only stubble and gleanings for the crows and seagulls to peck until the field was bare. Mists gathered over the fens in the morning, and the days grew colder and shorter. The season of light was giving way before the approach of the dark season of Samhain. Blue smoke from burning piles of dead leaves spiralled up into the sky, the swan flew south with her young and the rags of leaves on the elder trees turned blood red.

One morning Prasutagus woke to find a bitter wind rustling through the reed beds. The king decreed that it was time to leave the Palace of the Mists for the Palace of the Red Yew which because it was farther inland and protected from the winds was where he liked to spend the winter.

The Palace of the Red Yew took its name from the fact that its inside walls were panelled with red yew. It was smaller than the summer palace, and better prepared for the winter storms. Each of its thirty chambers had windows with shutters of copper fitted snugly to keep out the strongest of winds and the slyest of draughts. Prasutagus and his court arrived there just before the feast of Samhain.

The next morning, Fen Fire woke early, pulled on her breeches of kidskin, threw a heavy woolen cape over her shoulders, and took a handful of her javelins and went out to the parade ground in front of the palace. The short grass was white with frost, the ground stiff and cold. In the gray dawn she raised her javelin. She took aim. Her hand began to shake. She tried to steady it, but the target began to sway and blur before her eyes. A feeling of nausea gripped her belly and she was sick. She made her way back to the bedchamber and lay down. Two days later, on the feast of Samhain, she felt the clutch of life in her womb.

Her husband's joy was boundless.

"The New Year brings with it the promise of new life!" he said, stroking her still-flat belly gently. He sent for the Chief Druid, Cunodunum, who came at once. The druid asked Fen Fire to lie down and raise up her tunic. When she obeyed, he put his right hand on her belly and put the little finger of the other hand in his left ear. It was always through the little finger that the secrets of life were revealed. Then he closed his eyes and listened to what the spirit of the child told him. The druid sat motionless in a trance for a while. Had a bull charged through the bedchamber, he would not have heard it. Everyone gathered around, waiting; the king paced up and down stopping now and then to anxiously scrutinize the priest's face. But Cunodunum's face was like a mask. For the druids can control their facial expressions to ensure that they are as hard to decipher as the alphabets in which they encode their most precious secrets. Fen Fire lay motionless listening to the crackle of the bonfires burning outside the palace and the cold wind whistling through the thatch. The druid's hand lay so lightly on her skin that it seemed hardly to touch her at all. Finally, the priest opened his eyes.

"There is no doubt whatsoever but that there is a boy child in there," he announced.

"A son!" Fen Fire cried out.

"A son indeed. He is impatient for he tells me that he is eager to be out into the world for he has heard so much about his mother—and his father—that he cannot wait to meet them. And I have counseled him to wait—the world will endure a while longer."

The king's happiness was complete. He showered the priest with questions about the son who was soon to come into the world.

"He has hair the color of his mother's, and likewise his eyes are hers. But his brow is high and proud, and he is handsome like his father," Cunodunum responded with a wry look in his eye.

"What of his strength. Will he be . . . ?"

But the druid took his hand away from the woman and stood up. ‘‘It is not wise to try and find out everything at once. For every living thing becomes itself at the right time, and not before. Our only weapon against time is patience. We must wait, and endure. For the longest length of time will pass as surely as the shortest. And one thing is certain: that at the end of it we will either get what we want, or we will not.’’ No matter how hard the king pressed the priest, he would say no more about the child.

Fen Fire seemed tired; the Chief Druid ordered everyone from the chamber so that she might rest. When they were alone, he sat down beside her again. His brow wrinkled and he rubbed his beard.

‘‘You have other news?’’ Fen Fire asked. He nodded and sighed.

‘‘Adminius and Verica are in Gaul with the generals of the Romans. Caratacus believes that the armies of Caesar will attack in the spring,’’ the priest told her.

‘‘I would that my son were born and already a man that he might be there to meet them!’’

‘‘There will be battles enough for him to fight, fear not.’’

‘‘Or that I could be there beside Caratacus.’’

Cunodunum smiled. ‘‘No one will regret your absence more than he,’’ said the druid. ‘‘But your role is vital here—Caratacus and his brothers are anxious for the support of the king.’’

A look of melancholy stole over Fen Fire’s face. ‘‘I have already spoken to Prasutagus about it, to no effect. He was opposed to the attack on Calleva, and will hear nothing I have said in its favor. Perhaps it would be better if his son spoke to him,’’ she said. She dreaded the thought of another confrontation with her husband. The last had been so searing and painful that she had pushed it out of mind.

‘‘Subidasto is unwilling to approach his father—he seems reluctant even to agree to visit him, for each time he is asked he always has a more urgent matter at hand. Caratacus has pressed him many a time. But the youth is not himself—and has not been for many months. He says you are the best persuader and the king will do whatever you demand."

"I have no such power over the king—or any man. The king is his own counselor."

Cunodunum looked surprised at her response. "But it is well known he respects your judgment," the priest said.

"He is a stubborn man and to press him only makes him more so," Fen Fire told Cunodunum. She was so definite that the druid decided it was best not to argue otherwise. But as he was about to leave, Fen Fire stopped him. She could not let him go back to Caratacus to say that Fen Fire had failed them. She realized she had been thinking only like a wife. "Tell Caratacus that I will do all I can as a wife, and then, if the king remains heedless, as a warrior." Though puzzled, the priest seemed content with that and departed.

It was a season of gray floods and cold clear winds. Her breasts grew big and full, her belly slowly rounded as life quickened within her. Often, the king would lay his head on her belly, and listen fondly as if he could hear signs of his son stirring. And often, Fen Fire stroked his head and thought of the coming spring that would see their son born into the world. But no longer could she think of it only as the season of new life. As her belly ripened, so grew the monstrous shape of war and death.

Came the feast of Brigit and the first milking of the ewes. Soon, the lambs were leaping in the fields near the palace. When the day was dry, and not too cold, Fen Fire liked nothing better than to watch the lambs suckling their mothers. The owl, silent since the Samhain season, was heard again at night. But the wind still thrashed in the boughs, and hailstones battered the roof in storms that seemed to defy any hope of spring. She tried to withdraw into herself again, and push aside the fears that the priest's visit had brought back. But she could not. She knew that before long they would have to be faced.

Not long after the feast of Brigit, on a cold and windy morning, a messenger from Caratacus roused the household. He carried an urgent appeal to Prasutagus to meet with a delegation from the assembling armies at the Ford of the Eels, which lay to the south on the border between the Catuvellauni and Iceni kingdoms. The king, with a weary sigh, said he would summon his warriors and leave at once.

"And I will go with you," Fen Fire told him.

"The time is not right for you to travel. The weather is foul and inhospitable and you are grown delicate."

"Caratacus asked that Fen Fire accompany you," the messenger interjected.

"I go," she said. The king knew she would not be denied.

The Ford of the Eels lay in a little valley among the heath-covered uplands separating the two kingdoms. The morning of their meeting was gray, but made bright by the crested helmets of the assembled warriors from the respective tribes and the sheen of their arms; the bleak heathlands were transformed from an expanse of dull brown into a sea of color as their capes billowed and flapped in the cold wind.

The king brought his chariot to a halt at the edge of the ford to await the approach of Caratacus' envoy where the cold shallow stream gurgled among the glistening stones. Fen Fire stood next to him, a heavy woolen cloak thrown around her shoulders, and her hair unbound. Down the opposite slope of the little valley came a tall warrior on a chestnut warhorse, a troop of nobles in his wake. His boar-crested helmet of bronze was polished like a mirror; his cape was of speckled gold; and on his taut thigh rested a massive sword in a bronze scabbard inlaid with silver and gold carvings. He held an oblong shield with a boss of bronze to his breast. A surge of pride filled the king's heart at the approach of his son Subidasto. "It is as if I were seeing myself when I was young," he said quietly. For a moment he forgot the purpose of the meeting, and the ill it portended. "So, you have come to speak for the Catuvellauni—a people you once opposed," the king said in greeting.

"I take it as an honor to speak on behalf of men such as

Maglocunos and Togodumnus and Caratacus who have entrusted me with this mission. But I am here to speak for all those who value liberty, including many warriors from the Iceni," he replied in a cold and formal tone, never letting his eyes wander towards Fen Fire though she looked at him steadily. The king noticed that many of those accompanying his son were young Iceni warriors.

"If you speak for all who value liberty then you are my spokesman as well, though not by any appointment of mine," Prasutagus replied. "But speak."

"There is a lesson we must learn from the Gauls," his son continued stiffly. "Some made treaties with Julius Caesar, thinking it would be to their benefit to seek his assistance against their neighbor. He was always glad to give it, to help one overcome the other, until the tribes were exhausted and riven. It was only when they found that their country had been overrun by the Romans that they sought the unity that would have saved them. But it was too late. The blood of mother and child butchered together flowed through the streets of their settlements, the ragged columns of prisoners, once proud warriors, were whipped to the slave markets, and their great leader Vercingetorix died in a rat hole in Rome. The rest were left as beggars in their own land. Now that we are faced with the same threat, are we to dispute this lesson? The unity of our tribes is our only hope of survival: we share so much, hold so much in common that to remain divided seems like willful self-destruction. In Britain, the only true border should be the sea, the others are the false and fickle creations of shortsighted men. Just how shortsighted, the army of the new Caesar that is gathering on the coast of Gaul will soon teach us. His fleet is near readiness. And Britain is their goal."

"Aye, most surely. But when the feast of Brigit follows Samhain are we to be surprised?"

"This is no feast I speak of—or if it is, only the crows, the wolves, the wild pigs and other scavengers will enjoy its fruits."

"But neither is it a surprise, my son, to those of us with some experience of the world. What does surprise me is to hear this plea for unity coming from the mouth of one who not long ago pleaded and cajoled me to fight a war with my neighbors."

"Until I saw the greater danger."

"You have given me a history lesson; now let me give you one. You talk of unity in a land which has known only perpetual rivalry. Bounded or not by the sea, we were left enough room to pursue those rivalries as we liked. And we pursued them, and will pursue them as before. It was that which brought your newly found allies into conflict with the Atrebates. In defense, Verica bound himself by treaty to Rome. Rome is sworn to defend him. Verica is driven out, so what should Caesar do? Beg that you take him back again? Plead that in your beneficence you extend him mercy and permit the poor man to return to his kingdom? You have brought me here on a cold and inhospitable morning to tell me what I already knew—that when a great power is insulted it will strike back—that when you open the door to a hungry wolf, it will enter your house and it will not be content with the scraps from your table."

"There is more I have to tell you though I doubt you will want to hear it," Subidasto replied, his face pale with anger. Finally he glanced at Fen Fire. The wind sifted through her hair making it rise and fall; he saw it as it had been—spread out, red against the mossy green of the floor of the cave, more fine and feathery to the fingers than was the soft mattress of moss itself. "Caesar would have come, whatever befell his ally Verica, who was merely a traitor waiting to betray. Rome cannot rest easy while there is a people still free from her chains and able to proclaim their liberty and defend it in arms."

"I know that there are some—on this island as well as beyond it—who cannot rest easy while there is power to be grabbed, booty to be had, kingdoms to be plundered. Men so hungry for power will never be united." Prasutagus dismounted from the chariot and walked to the edge of the stream. He stepped onto the stones, and looked at the faces of the young Iceni warriors gathered around his son.

"Then you are not prepared to join us?" Subidasto asked.

The king glanced up at him disdainfully.

"Caratacus pleads with you to join him against Rome, as these men have done . . ."

"These youths! You will give your lives uselessly. I am your king, and I command you to return across this ford with me, return to your tribal lands, or never dare set foot on them again!" The young men met his plea with shamefaced looks. He grabbed the bridle of Subidasto's horse. "I will hold you responsible for their deaths!"

"And I will hold you responsible for bringing shame upon the Iceni people!" Subidasto reached down to free the bridle from his father's hold when Prasutagus took him by the wrist with such a powerful grip that he pulled his son from the horse's back.

"And who are you to hold your king and father in contempt?" Prasutagus bent his son's arm back, trying to bring him to his knees. With his other hand, Subsidasto grabbed Prasutagus by the throat and the two swayed back and forth until Fen Fire flung herself between them. She pulled them apart.

"This conflict will destroy us so that Rome will have no need to send an army against us!" she cried out. "If father turns against son, and son against father, what hope have we? A family divided against itself points a dagger at its own heart! I have seen one family divided when son rebelled against father—the evil shadow of that conflict now threatens to engulf us all!"

The wind blew more strongly and swept the cloak back from her shoulders. Subidasto saw that she was with child. She held him by the arm but he drew back from her, and wrenched himself free. His wordless rejection stung her more than any blow or insult. In despair, she let him go.

Fen Fire began to tremble. Her limbs became weak, and the world began to turn like a wheel until it was only a blur. She swayed. The sound of the stream seemed to be far off. Both father and son caught her as she slumped forward. In a swoon and bewildered, she looked from father to son. In a perfect world of which she could but dream they would be one instead of these warring opposites that she could never balance nor resolve.

Chapter 15

"I would speak with Sun Fragment," Fen Fire said, sitting up in the dark chamber. Barrel, who was taking care of Fen Fire in a separate chamber from that of the king, looked at her in puzzlement.

"You must rest," she replied, and putting her hands on Fen Fire's shoulders, gently pushed her down again.

"Subidasto. Is he here?" Fen Fire asked.

"No, he has long gone," came the reply.

"Where?"

"To war."

"No—he cannot have gone yet—not without me. It was but this morning I spoke with him and . . ."

"Rest, princess, and you will regain your strength," Barrel told her. Fen Fire closed her eyes. The boy stirred in her womb. She groaned with pain and fell asleep. . . .

First, there was a forest upon the waves. Wood groaned and strained, creaked and heaved, rose and fell as the ships ploughed through the sea towards the coast to bring forth their torrent of metal-clad men. They bore down under her, beating, pounding across her body. She was convulsed with spasms of pain.

The wind whined through the raised spear shafts. The spears whistled through the wind. The wind threw the waves against the rocks, wailing in lamentation at the loss of so many. The spirits of the air howled their own lament. Black flocks of crows clouded the sky. And the heaps of the dead grew larger . . .

When Barrel found Fen Fire, she was standing at the partition, groping for a way out of the chamber.

"Where are you going at this late hour?" she asked her.

"I must gather the herbs while the dew is still on them, for only then are they beneficial for the healing of wounds," Fen Fire answered, still in a trance.

"It is a black and stormy night," said her companion. Putting her arm around Fen Fire, she guided her back to their bed.

Next morning, Barrel told Prasutagus of what had happened. "In her delirium, she speaks only of war, and of your son," she said.

"She is anxious for the child," the king replied.

"I mean Subidasto." The king looked at her gravely.

"She speaks of nothing else but lost wars and renegades?"

"Yes—sometimes she talks of Sun Fragment, but what or who that is, she does not say." Latis, who was pretending to be busy nearby, paused, made curious by this bit of information.

The king went in to see his young wife. She was lying on her back, her hair spread wildly over the white pillow, her face pale and tear-stained. He sat down next to her and took her hand. He kissed her fingers, and bending down, planted his lips on her round belly.

"The Catuvellaunian host has been overwhelmed by the invader," he told her, looking up.

"I know," she answered. "I saw it."

"It is too late for your tears. You must not think of death when you carry life within you. Banish whatever nightmares torment you and your body will grow strong again."

"I will not rest as long as the invaders tread upon this land, for every step they take wounds me. Where is Caratacus and his brothers . . . and your son?" She looked at him, her eyes sunken and tired.

"Concern yourself with the son your womb holds . . ."

"No woman can say what her womb will bear," she responded.

"It will bear a son, strong and well, able one day to take his place at his father's side."

"What of the son you have? If you care not whether he is well and strong then surely that bodes ill for mine!"

"Woman, you talk nonsense whose only effect is to

exhaust you further with fruitless anxieties." The king stood up abruptly. "Conserve your strength for the life you carry and worry not about the world." Without saying more, he left her.

The storm continued to rage that night, and the wind drove the rain in gusts against the palace. The stout oak doors shook, and the partition swayed. The copper shutters on the windows shuddered as the wind battered against them. It howled as if a thousand dying men had one throat. . . .

She stumbled across the battlefield, stepping over corpse after corpse. Ashen faces, streaked red with caked blood, stared at her. In her hand she held a sword, but it hung limply at her side. Crows with bloodied beaks cawed around her. Wolves were dragging a body into the woods beyond; others fought with wild pigs for the possession of another. A man strode towards her clad from head to foot in metal. She could see only his eyes. He drew his short stabbing sword. She tried to raise hers, but her strength was gone. He laughed and pushed her to the ground. She fell on her back. He tore off her tunic exposing her round, full belly. Gripping the sword with both hands, he thrust it into her womb. She cried out with burning pain.

Fen Fire opened her eyes. She was sitting up clutching her belly. The wind roared around the palace, whipping the thatch on the roof. Half delirious, she staggered to her feet. No one was awake—the sound of the storm had drowned out her own wail of pain. Barrel lay curled up, sleeping peacefully. Through the dark Fen Fire slowly made her way out of the chamber. Groping, in agony, she dragged herself along the dark corridor to the rear of the palace, and opened the door leading out to the stables. The horses stirred in the darkness. There was a sturdy war horse near at hand, fit for battle. Flinging her arms around it, she hauled herself on to its back and urged it out into the rain-lashed night. Her one thought was to fulfill the promise made to her brothers and Subidasto: she would aid them as a warrior since as a wife she had failed to convince her husband that he should do so. She would join the Catuvellaunian host wherever they were, storm or no storm, pain or no pain.

Fen Fire buckled over as if a sword had been stuck into her belly. She cried out in pain—but it was an unearthly cry, as if the child in her womb, voiceless, had found a voice to add to hers in its first and final utterance. She went limp, every limb powerless, and slid from the horse's back. With a thud she hit the ground, and rolled in agony on her back, a knot of pain. The rain beat down upon her, indifferent to her suffering.

The whole palace had been awakened by the eerie cry so piercing that even the storm could not drown it. The king and his other wives were startled from their sleep. They found a trail of blood leading from Fen Fire's chamber. They followed it and found her in the courtyard, just beyond the stables, the horse standing licking her pale, pained face. Her son lay dead between her thighs in a pool of thick dark blood, speckled with pieces of straw. Prasutagus fell upon his knees beside her.

"The order of the world has been reversed. Death has come before birth," he cried, lifting up the corpse of his dead son. "My seed's bright harvest trampled into the earth like dead clay, laid waste before the time of ripening." He picked off the pieces of straw that clung to its small, shrunken form.

Her womb bled like a raw wound. They carried her to her bedchamber, where for several days she tossed and turned, stricken with grief.

"Now I have cause to lament like the women of the Catuvellauni who have lost their loved ones," she said to the other wives who cared for her. "A loss that will never be replaced is a wound that will never heal."

Barrel, Fen Eel, Mournful Mound and Screech Owl did all they could to console her, telling her that she would have many children in the future. But Fen Fire in her grief spoke of the last child as if he had died on the battlefield—a victim of the war which had convulsed her womb as it had shaken the land.

Chapter 16

The great palace of Cunobelinus rose up through the morning mists. Adminius paused for a moment as he entered the meadow in front of the stately edifice with its great circular thatched roof and massive wooden pillars, from which so many years before he had been driven like a dog with Fen Fire's javelin pointing at his neck. Through all the intervening years he had waited for this moment, through every disappointment he clung to this hope. Now it had been fulfilled. He had returned, escorted like the most noble of Romans, to meet with Claudius Caesar, reclaim his inheritance and consummate his revenge. Verica was already reestablishing himself in his old capital of Calleva, with added lands and privileges. Adminius could expect no less from Caesar.

Claudius Caesar had arrived in Britain to personally conduct the final assault on Camulodunum. The warriors were disheartened by the previous defeat of their army and the death of Togodumnus, and Camulodunum's massive anti-chariot fortifications proved to be no match for the siege equipment of the Romans. It fell rapidly to Caesar's advance. The victorious legions had transformed the Catuvellauni capital into a huge Roman camp.

Between the dykes and the palace grounds, Caesar's soldiers swarmed like ants. In appearance, one was indistinguishable from another, except for the officers who wore more colorful capes. As Adminius drew nearer, he realized that they were busy stripping the palace rooms of their treasures. The soldiers staggered out of the palace under the heavy burdens of silver and gold ornaments which filled their arms while Caesar's clerks carefully noted what was being taken. The great front meadow, where years before the feast games used to be celebrated, was now rutted from tracks as the oxen carts laden with the precious plunder creaked their way towards the ships waiting in the nearby estuary to carry them to the treasure chests of Rome. Adminius turned pale at the sight.

"What way is this to treat the property of a friend?" he cried out. The officer in charge of the escort clearly did not understand what the Briton meant, for he answered that it was not the property of a friend that was being plundered but that of an enemy defeated in battle.

"This is my inheritance!" Adminius said. "It is for this I returned!"

"It is Caesar's," the Roman replied, bemused at the barbarian's childish misunderstanding of that basic rule of war. Before he could finish, Adminius galloped off, intending to protest to some higher authority.

Caesar chose the long rectangular feast hall (erected for Fen Fire's wedding banquet) to receive the supplications of his allies and those Britons who had not taken arms against him. Its walls were stripped bare. The long tables where the warriors used to eat were smashed up to make firewood. The seats of dried grass lay stacked in a heap outside ready to be torched.

Adminius was announced and, after being thoroughly searched, made his way through the bustling crowd of clerks, civil servants and senior military officers milling around. Claudius wore the cloak of the triumphant general with evident pleasure. His usual stooping, rather hesitant manner was temporarily banished in favor of a more decisive martial look like that of the soldiers on either side of him who were folding up their maps when Adminius arrived.

"May your journey be always an easy one and the road never too long!" Claudius announced. He had been schooled in a few native phrases which he liked to show off. And because of the catch in his tongue, he spoke in a great rush, which always reminded Adminius of the attempts of a swan as it tries to take flight, looking so clumsy as it runs heavily along the ground yet when on the wing a majestic sight. Claudius, when he succeeded in getting off the ground, was capable of some eloquence. Now, in his role of triumphant Caesar, his speech was as smooth and fluent as his manner was confident.

"Father of Our Country, this is not a happy meeting!" the Briton replied in obvious agitation.

"Then you must know of some grievance or disappointment that has been kept from me."

"I am being plundered before your very eyes," Adminius said, looking up at the bare walls.

"By whom?" Claudius asked, as he paused to inspect a haul of ornaments that was being carted away to the convoy waiting outside which would bring it to Rome.

"By your soldiers—the very army whose victories I have aided."

Caesar smiled when he realized the cause of the Briton's unhappiness. "Oh, we have taken only a few trinkets. Do not fret. Your reward far outweighs the bits and pieces we are sending back from Britain. But take them we must, for one day they will be displayed as part of my triumph. And, as they say at the Circus, the show must go on!" He signaled to Adminius to come nearer. "I have granted you extensive estates south of here—I believe they once comprised the personal holdings of Togodumnus." Adminius smiled. His dead brother's lands were indeed extensive and fertile.

"They will flourish under my ownership," he answered, bowing his head in thanks.

"With these will come a generous income for life, which added to what you will earn from your new estates will, I calculate, make you one of the richest men in Britain. As well, I am granting you citizenship of Rome, and appointing you to the senate of Camulodunum when it is fully constituted as the capital of the province. And if you are as loyal as you have been, this will be but the beginning. Who can tell—the future is an open road. Someday your children's children might reach the chamber of the Roman Senate itself." Adminius fell on his knees and kissed the edge of Claudius' cloak. Claudius paused to allow time for the grateful Briton to absorb this prospect and express his gratitude. Then he waved away his officers and clerks.

"But to other matters. You will be interested to know

that King Prasutagus has just today sent us his envoy to offer an alliance,'' he continued, without taking his eyes off Adminius. ''I am strongly advised to accept, since the king commands considerable authority. His allegiance would secure our northeastern frontier. So we might soon be allies.''

Slowly Adminius rose from his knees.

''Once you spoke to me about the king's youngest, and favorite wife,'' Claudius said.

''Fen Fire!'' Adminius murmured, his eyes narrowing and glowing. Caesar smiled, remembering the occasion in Rome when the Briton had enthralled him as he described her, emphasizing her beauty as well as her ferocity.

''You have not forgotten, I see, much less have I.''

''I will neither forget nor forgive!'' Adminius exclaimed. ''I can still feel her presence in this very place. It is as if she has never left it.'' He blanched white, looking around the dining hall that had been erected years before for Fen Fire's wedding to Prasutagus. ''The witch!''

''The wife of our new ally, that's how we must regard her now,'' Claudius said matter-of-factly. These Britons were like children, he thought, unable sometimes to distinguish what was real from what was unreal—confusing facts with the monstrous creations of their own fantastic suppositions. ''Restrain your fears: she is a woman like any other.''

''You would not say that if you knew her! You must see for yourself.''

''But I intend to—that's what I wanted to tell you,'' said Claudius.

Caesar was silent, enjoying the spectacle of the warring emotions that swept through the Briton's face which was by turns white with fear and flushed with thoughts of revenge. Then he summoned to his side one of his civil servants who was busily writing.

''The Iceni Treaty,'' he said. The scribe handed it to him. Claudius read it over very quickly—it was more or less the standard arrangement; guarantees of protection from any aggressor in return for a number of hostages, a token yearly tribute and concessions to Roman traders permitting them to travel securely and freely within the ally's territory. "Insert a clause," said Caesar, "to the effect that among the hostages will be the king's youngest wife." He turned to Adminius. The Briton's fears vanished as the scribe took note of Caesar's words. It seemed that the very act of writing down Caesar's thoughts was the equivalent of securing their accomplishment, such was the mysterious awe in which the natives of Briton held the power of the written word.

"She will eventually grace our triumph, when Aulus Plautius has finished subduing what few enemies remain. But in the meantime, she can be held in some secure place—here, for example, or London, where a watch can be kept on her until it is time to bring her to Rome."

"I would be glad to supervise those arrangements," Adminius said, his eyes gleaming, his spirit exalted by the now certain prospect of Fen Fire's humiliation.

Chapter 17

For many days after the loss of the child, the king would speak with no one. His wives were banished from the warmth of his bedchamber. He did not seek consolation there, neglecting the sympathy and charm of woman's company which it always had been his custom to enjoy. Though he took care to see that Fen Fire was well cared for and recovering, he spent only a little time in her company. He sought solitude, and his place in the feast hall was empty.

Every morning he was gone from the palace before sunrise. He hunted alone until late in the evening, frequently not returning until the following day. Though he brought back deer and boar in plenty, he left them outside for the scavengers to feed on or, when they were full, to rot, not bothering even to give them to his cooks to conserve. He had no thought for food. He seemed sick of all pleasures and distractions except the hunt. Every day news reached the palace with travelers or merchants of the Britons' defeats. Word of the fall of the Catuvellaunian capital Camulodunum to Claudius Caesar, the final destruction of the kingdom of Cunobelinus, the triumph everywhere of Roman arms and the submission of the chieftains in all of the kingdoms in the south, was grim confirmation of what he had said would happen, years ago, before Caratacus, Togodumnus and Subidasto had set out against Verica, when they tried to convince him to join in that foolhardy enterprise. But he shared these thoughts with no one, for it brought him no satisfaction to be proven right on such a matter. If anyone congratulated his foresight and judgment which had so far kept their kingdom out of the most destructive war Britain had yet seen, he would wave aside the compliments and say, "I cannot claim to be a wiseman just because I once stated what was obvious to anyone not blinded by ambition."

The lethargy that had overcome him after the loss of the child was only dispelled by the representations of his chieftains, who urged that he make some gesture toward Caesar, then in Camulodunum. He agreed to send an envoy stating that the Iceni wanted peace and friendship with Caesar.

Prasutagus was surprised at the rapidity with which Claudius responded to the proffered alliance. "It is only proof of how important he regards your friendship," Latis told him. She was impressed by the display the Roman troops made as they rode into the palace grounds in perfect order, not a horse out of step, all wearing the same sensible yet attractive trim uniforms, with shining breastplates, short, beautifully polished helmets that fitted so neatly over their well-clipped hair, knee-length leather tunics and leg-guards so bright and clear that they were like mirrors. They sat perfectly erect on horseback, looking neither left nor right but always directly in front of them. Latis compared their fine disciplined appearance to the gaudy chaos of the local warriors, some of whom were so drunk when they went to battle that for all their fine plumage and multi-colored cloaks they could barely stay on their horses until they reached the palace gates.

"Caesar sends his greetings to the people of the Iceni," the envoy said, speaking through his interpreter, "whose friendship and regard he is most desirous of winning, having heard of their renown for courage, generosity and loyalty."

"The Iceni are aware of the renown of Caesar. We will treat his envoy as if he were Caesar himself. If he comes in peace, he will not find our hospitality lacking," the king answered.

That night they feasted with the king as his guests. The envoy showered compliments on Prasutagus about the good judgment he had shown in sending the delegate to Caesar. At great length he described the benefits of an alliance with Rome—the exalted status of a king recognized by Caesar, the riches of the vast empire from Egypt to Gaul that would soon flow without restriction through the kingdom. "Including the silks from the distant east?" Latis enquired.

"Of course," she was assured, "whatever the people want to buy, our merchants will be delighted to sell. You can be certain that you will lack nothing that befits a civilized people."

Latis listened avidly. She imagined the palaces of Prasutagus decorated with the work of the best craftsmen in Gaul—work that was much finer than anything done in Britain, she thought—and herself attired in the rare fabrics of far-off lands, and scented with their exotic perfumes. Again, Latis was impressed by the straightforward, practical yet courteous manner in which he conducted the discussions.

Prasutagus said nothing until the envoy had finished. Then he asked for the treaty to be read and translated by the interpreter.

"In return for which friendship, and protection from any aggressor, and the other benefits already noted above," read the envoy's interpreter, "the Iceni will undertake to promise to abstain from warlike acts against Caesar, and from forming alliances with those designated as his enemies, deliver on request by the army a specified number of cattle and quantity of grain (both to be determined by the appropriate authorities), pay him a small yearly tribute as a token of good will, and give into his hands as a hostage a relation of the king or high-ranking member of the king's household, to be kept as a security against infractions of the agreement, during which time the said person will be held in a secure place, and accommodated as befits his or her status, with the understanding that if Caesar so desires it the said person will at some future date be brought to Rome for the ceremonial parade commemorating the victory of Roman arms in Britain and the establishment of peaceful relations among Rome's allies among the Britons." Here the interpreter paused a moment and whispered something to the envoy, as if a little surprised by what he read. The envoy nodded, and asked him to continue. "In terms of this treaty with Prasutagus, king of the Iceni, it is specifically stated that to satisfy the clause pertaining to the hostage, the king must surrender his youngest wife, Fen Fire, into the custody of the proper authorities."

Prasutagus called over the interpreter and asked him to point to the words which referred to Fen Fire. After a moment's hesitation, the man did so. The king flattened the treaty against the mead-stained table, drew his dagger and thrust it through the document, cutting away the clause referring to her.

"Only now will I make the agreement with your master," he said to the envoy, who had turned a little pale.

"Indeed, you are not so poor!" Latis whispered in her husband's ear. "You who have six can give up one, that will leave you five; though whether any of the other four deserve the title wife or not, I do not care to say."

"I will put the name of another there in her place," he said to the interpreter, looking threateningly at Latis, "but with Fen Fire I will not part."

"I am under special instructions to see that this treaty is accepted in all its clauses, but most particularly that concerning Fen Fire," the envoy replied, glancing regretfully at the torn document.

"Then there is no treaty between the Iceni and Rome," the king said. The feasting came to a startled halt. "You are welcome to finish eating, and spend the night here," he told the Roman delegation, "but in the morning at dawn you must leave the kingdom and not set foot across its borders again." The king summoned his spearmen to his side and stood up.

"You give up so much for a woman who cannot even breed—a troublemaker—who has already cost you a son!" said Latis, whose dread at losing so much expected prosperity overcame her fear of the king's wrath and his earlier threatening look.

Prasutagus stared at her contemptuously.

"By refusing this treaty," the envoy said, recovering a little from his surprise, "you cannot be considered an ally of Caesar. And those who are not allies may be treated like enemies."

"So be it," the king told him.

"Perhaps in the morning you will think better of it," the envoy responded.

Without saying more, Prasutagus left the feast hall.

"She must be a rare beauty indeed," the interpreter mused.

"She is a wild animal," Latis exclaimed scornfully, "whose antics will disgrace us all!" She smiled at the envoy apologetically. "I will speak with my husband later—I'm sure he will see reason in the end."

As the envoy sat sipping halfheartedly at what was left of his drink, Prasutagus walked along the passageway towards his bedchamber. But when nearly there he paused. He would go to Fen Fire and tell her of what had happened. She would be exalted by the news that he was being pushed into the arms of the very allies he for so long refused to join. But he would rather that than be dictated to in such terms to give up someone he held so dear. No one had the right to demand that of a man.

A dim light came from her chamber. The partition cast a long shadow across the passageway. When the king reached it, from the deeply shadowed interior of the chamber beyond came the sounds of a hushed but animated argument. This was most puzzling. Still recuperating from her miscarriage, Fen Fire had remained alone most of the time, refusing even the comforting company of Barrel.

"But you belong to me. I claimed you before this fraudulent marriage ever took place . . ."

"I care for the king."

"You desire me!"

"You've come too late to claim your prize . . ."

Prasutagus quietly moved the partition aside. As Fen Fire got up from the bed, Subidasto grabbed her by the waist.

At first disbelief held back the outrage that surged within the king. But it took no more than a moment for that barrier to be swept aside—a moment in which he heard and saw his wife with his son as a mistress with her lover.

"Because of you I have lost one son. Can you have tried to take another from me?" Prasutagus asked.

Subidasto sprang up and freed her. All three stood motionless for a long, terrible moment. Instinctively, Fen Fire reached out towards the man she'd hurt, but the king thrust her aside. He would not listen to her tear-filled explanations. He turned to his son, his eyes ablaze with scorn.

"And you dare accuse me of betrayal!" he said, with cold anger. "Skulking in your father's house like a thief. What honor is there in this? Were I of such character I would hand you over now to Caesar, and be rid of you before you bring disaster on us all."

Subidasto glared at his father arrogantly. "I came to salvage something of the Iceni's honor," he said. "Caratacus still hopes for your support . . ."

In a blind rage the king began to draw his sword.

"Go," she pleaded with Subidasto, fearing that one of them might strike a desperate blow. "It is dangerous for you here. Caesar's envoy is outside. But you must go without me. I have made my choice. Go!"

"You will not rest content."

He was gone in an instant, leaving her alone with Prasutagus. Before she could begin to speak the king rounded on her.

"Your womb having taken the seed of my son rejected the fruit of mine, and cast out our unborn child. It would not tolerate such an unnatural conjunction. We can be grateful for it—who knows what monster it might have hatched."

She raised her hands to her ears to block out the hateful words, and flung herself on her bed.

The envoy was surprised to see the king return to the feast hall. His face was a sullen mask. "She is yours," he said quietly.

The envoy smiled. Latis trembled with the excitement of triumph—her only disappointment being that it could not be attributed to her.

Fen Fire was sleeping in her chamber when Barrel came rushing in breathlessly. It was just before dawn, and still half dark. She groped until she found Fen Fire, and shook her awake.

"You must leave at once," Barrel said in a hurried,

hushed voice. In the dim dawn light Fen Fire could see that her companion was pale and frightened.

"What disturbs you so at such a desolate hour?" Fen Fire asked.

"The king means to surrender you as his hostage to Caesar. I could not believe it when I heard him agree to the monstrous scheme after he had opposed it so forcefully."

Fen Fire sat up.

"Rise, make ready."

The chamber was suddenly flooded with torchlight.

"She gives you good advice, a little late for her purposes but fortunately not for ours," said a familiar but unfriendly voice. Barrel threw herself into Fen Fire's arms. Latis was staring at them over the partition with a look of quiet triumph on her face. "How I am loath to break up this scene of tender wifely companionship," she said to Fen Fire, "but you must gather your things and prepare to leave at once. Caesar will not be kept waiting." When Fen Fire did not move, Latis turned to the guards.

"See to it," she ordered. The guards looked at her and then at each other. "The king did not tell us she was to be handed over to the Romans," one said.

"It is the king's wish. But as ever, he has left me to enforce it." She sighed with exasperation. "Now see to it at once or there are those waiting who will!" The men looked behind them. A unit of Roman soldiers was marching towards them, their hands on the hilts of their short stabbing-swords. They formed even lines arrayed one behind the next. Sullenly, and with great reluctance, the two guards walked over to Fen Fire. She rose, gently separating herself from Barrel, who did not want to let her go.

"There is no need to sully yourselves with so demeaning a task, one more fitting for the hands of slaves," the Catuvellaunian princess said proudly. "I am happy to leave this place, regardless of my destination. I am more of a prisoner here than I would be in Rome itself!"

"Then you should thank me." Latis smiled.

"Do not doubt it, one day you will be thanked," Fen Fire answered her. Prasutagus' first wife turned away, fixing her attention on Barrel.

The rain came down in torrents as they hoisted Fen Fire's chest of valuables onto the back of the Roman carriage. Prasutagus wanted the deed expedited as quickly as possible, before the sun's light revealed his shameful act to the eyes of his people. He was comforted to see that the sun was blotted out and that the morning was dark and joyless. But somehow the word had spread with the swiftness of the wind. And in spite of the grey clouds and the pouring rain, the people came, huddled together, soaked, and grim, to watch. As the gates swung open and the escort thundered down the muddy pathway, they cried out in shock and shame, rushing forward to try to catch a last glimpse of their young queen—for they feared they would never lay eyes on her again. There was terrible confusion. The coach was closed and surrounded by a phalanx of horsemen, who beat back the onlookers. Many stumbled and fell in the mud. The old women, drenched, went down on their knees and cried out sorrowfully, "It is cruel, never to hear your laughter again, our red-haired queen. Do not leave us so! Our hearths will be cold without you." The Romans, indifferent to their sorrow, rode on. Soon the coach disappeared behind the curtain of rain, leaving the people to vent their grief against the unheeding walls of the king's palace.

Prasutagus closed his ears to their cries, and barred his gates against them. The more warlike among the nobles of the Iceni, disturbed by what they saw and heard, clamored for some explanation as to why he so willingly surrendered her up as a hostage, knowing how well the people loved her.

"Take it as a sign of how deeply I still care for Fen Fire that I do not tell you. If I did, you might say that exile is too kind a fate for her."

The protests and lamentations did not cease, but grew worse, and the warriors who had worshipped Fen Fire grew more restless. Desperate for solitude to nurse his bitterness, he fled to the Palace of the Mists, in the remoter vastness of the fens where the autumn shrouded everything in fog. The Samhain season soon closed in, and with it the flood of memories that made his solitude a gnawing reminder of his misery.

Chapter 18

The princess Cartimandua was startled awake. Two arms as thick as shipmasts were flung over her. Impatiently she disentangled herself and sat up, brushing her long black tresses from her bleary eyes. She rubbed the red welts on her wrists and ankles, unravelling the willow thongs that still hung loosely from them. There it was again—the bellowing of a bull, reverberating like rolling thunder around the valley which fell away beneath her fortress. So she had not been dreaming. But her companions heard it not. They lay stretched this way and that, a confusion of arms, legs, bushy beards and heads of matted hair. Some lay slumped, their arms drooping over the edge of her enormous lair of straw and blankets; others sprawled out, arms and legs akimbo; others with their beards sticking up into the air still full of ale drops, mead drops and wine drops, which hung from the hairs like beads of dew on meadow grass in the morning. One lay on his belly, his naked back streaked with the red trails her nails had scratched; another had bloody marks on his neck where her teeth had sunk into his flesh. One fondly stroked the long beard of a nearby companion as he slept, no doubt dreaming of the far different encounters of the long dark night before. Among them, somewhere in the jumble, were her three devoted retainers, her stallions as she referred to them, Ship's Mast, Standing Stone and Palace Pillar. She began groping among the heap in search of them. The bull resounded again above the snoring, farting, gurgling, snorting, sniffing, grunting cacaphony which surrounded her. There was only one beast in the world that could have made that sound, and though Cartimandua had not seen it in a long time, she had no doubt as to what it was. It had taken a convulsion in the world to bring them to her, but Maglocunos and the great bull he herded had finally come.

The princess found Ship's Mast and gave him a vigorous kick. "Open your eyes, you lazy wretch!" she cried. He was a large brute with a black beard and hair dyed in three different colors—red, brown and green. He grunted an unconscious reply. She kicked again, and harder, with the heel of her foot. Slowly, ponderously, he turned, cranking open his heavy, sleep-laden eyelids.

He yawned and rubbed his hairy face. "Princess," he groaned groggily, "I'm weary. Must we . . . ?"

"Don't fret, you fool! I've had enough of you for the moment. Get your great carcass out of my bed. Hurry to the stables and harnass my swiftest ponies to my lightest chariot."

The brute stared at her vacuously for a moment. She gave him a third kick. He struggled on to his knees and fumbled among his snoring companions for some clothes. He was greeted by groans and curses. The bull bellowed another time—it was a call Cartimandua could not resist. She leapt up and shouted for her women servants. She strode across the mass of bodies, tramping on upturned faces, squashing fingers, treading on groins without thought or care in her haste to leave. In her wake came a chorus of grunts and curses. The bull roared out again. From somewhere even farther off a herd of cows mooed their response. "The presence of a bull like that makes us all restless," she sighed. The very thought of its potent presence aroused her.

Cartimandua paced about the room, edgy and impatient, as her women servants flocked around her like nervous, bustling little sparrows, trying to dress her.

"That is the bull which will grace my herds," she said as one of her maids placed the gold-besprinkled green cape with the fringed hood over the princess' shoulders. Cartimandua fastened it with a crescent-shaped brooch of silver and hurried to the stables. Ship's Mast had her lightest, fastest chariot waiting for her. Within minutes she was speeding down the steep path that led to the valley and the meadow where her herds were grazing. The long-awaited reunion was at hand.

The wide meadow stretched before her where the morning mist, milk-white, still clung. At its far edge rose a hillock. Cartimandua reined in her horses. Another hill, black and huge, seemed to have mounted on the first. The great three-horned bull loomed up majestically. It turned its vast head towards her. The bull's huge hunched shoulders looked as if they could easily carry a four-horse chariot. Between the two wickedly sharp, flesh-tearing, man-rending horns rose the third bulbous horn, a thing of power and wonder: He Who Satisfies, He Who Nourishes. Slowly the beast came down the sloping hillock moving with such a heaving, weighty, kingly motion that Cartimandua almost swooned to the chariot floor.

Maglocunos emerged through the morning mists riding a pale yellow horse. His curled brown hair was hung with little drops of moisture gathered from the cold mists. He wore an embroidered woollen cloak, dyed royal red, which was fixed around his hairless white breast by a brooch of red gold. Around his neck was a gold torc in the form of a flicking-tongued serpent—the guardian of Andraste's treasure just as he was the protector of her bull. The gold hilt of his sword gleamed in its finely wrought bronze scabbard, while on his feet he wore sandals of linen with leather soles and clasps of white bronze. On every finger gleamed and sparkled rings of silver or gold.

"So, you have come at last to try my pastures, though it has taken a war to get you to accept my invitation. I have been waiting to put them at your disposal, as I have always promised," she said, greeting him. "You will not be disappointed, no more than will the noble bull that you attend upon. In this fertile, well-watered meadow grows the sweetest, most succulent grass in my kingdom. My bounty tolerates no rival, as you and whatever companions are with you will see if you accept the hospitality of my feast hall. Let the bull graze his fill. You are invited to enjoy my hospitality for as long as you desire."

Maglocunos thanked her for her generosity.

"While it is true that it is because of a war that I am

here, it is also true that only a war or the threat of it could have kept me from accepting your proffered hospitality before now,'' he replied.

The morning wind gently ruffled her silken tunic around her thighs. She smiled. ''Ah, yes—wars and alliances bring us together now, a far different occasion from our last meeting. But we must not let them cloud our enjoyment of this one.''

That night Cartimandua saw to it that Maglocunos would have little cause to think of the events that were shaking the world. She spared no effort to be pleasing. Her finest silken tunic, dyed deep green, was held around her narrow waist by a white enamelled belt. Around her neck she wore a long silver chain from which hung two crescent-moon-shaped silver ornaments, one on each white breast. A short green cape graced her flawless shoulders. Each pale lithe thigh was wrapped about in five-fold crisscross fashion by thongs of willow. Her hair was left to hang loose and dark; her fine eyelashes were teased up into perfect little curves, crescent-like; they were so long that when she half closed her eyes they cast thin web-like shadows over her chalked-white cheeks.

As the feast began, darkness fell. Though it was summer, desolation reigned on the hills around her palace and its settlement, ringed by crudely built walls of earth and rough stones. Apart from that on which Cartimandua's fortress stood, no other hill bore any signs of human habitation.

They feasted late into the night. Every time Maglocunos brought up the topic of an alliance between her tribe and Caratacus, she quietly brushed it aside, saying it was a matter for the bright light of day when politics could be discussed reasonably and clearly. She served him the oldest mead she possessed, the taste of which was like honey lightly roasted. Its effects were to put all thoughts of war and wearisome matters out of mind. The only thought that could flourish with its dark, sweet nourishment was that of desire. But Cartimandua was content only to arouse it. When the feast was finished, Maglocunos watched as she went off with her stallions, Palace Pillar, Ship's Mast and Standing Stone, who had spent the night glaring at him defiantly. Though Maglocunos' journey had been wearying, the night brought him no rest. The whole palace seemed to reverberate with her laughter, and then her cries of pleasure, until near dawn.

Several days passed, spent in feasting and hunting. As with the first, the feasting lasted late into the night, with little time for serious matters to raise their heads. And frequently after it ended, there was no restful release until dawn, until Cartimandua and her companions had exhausted themselves. Maglocunos, rising always later, found his days grew ever shorter, and he saw less and less of the sun. Every night he was in her presence, and every night she appeared differently, affording him a glimpse of another aspect of her beauty, yet denying him access to it, other than casual contact as when she would brush past him with a light, glancing touch. Unaccustomed to this sort of treatment from women, Maglocunos grew restless.

It turned cold. A huge corral of massive logs and stone-pillared gates was built inside the fortress for the bull. Winter was approaching, and the beast would have to be taken from the pasture land below. To make matters worse, there had been no talk of the alliance, except in passing. One day when he awoke it was already evening. The feasting had begun. Cartimandua chastised him for being so lazy.

"You have almost missed the feast! But have no fear, the bull is well cared for," she said. "I went down to him myself, to see everything was to his liking in the meadow. He was grazing contentedly, as if he had been there all his life."

"Forgive me," Maglocunos replied. "We have much to discuss, and I have little time for sleeping for I must leave before long . . ."

"Leave? Why speak of leaving when you have just arrived? Is our hospitality wanting?" Cartimandua pouted, pretending to be offended.

"Do not misunderstand me. No one rivals you in generosity. The bull is clearly as pleased with it as I am myself."

She smiled and poured him a cup of old mead. "Anyway, leave to go where?'' she asked, affecting great puzzlement.

''West, to join Caratacus of course, and bring him word of the decision of your people.''

''West–that is impossible. Caesar's legions have already overwhelmed everything as far as the Severn Valley. King Boduocus of the Dobunni is now their ally and he blocks the way to Caratacus.''

''Boduocus will not block my path!''

''But you must pass through his kingdom if you are to reach your brother, and with the great bull with you, you would have to move slowly. You would be so conspicuous that you would soon find yourself trapped. Winter is fast approaching with its snows and storms. Rest here a while longer. We have time yet to decide on the course we must take. I have sent word out to all parts of the Brigantian confederation, asking the tribal chiefs to gather. It will take time, but until then I cannot make any decision, however much I would like to.'' She put her hand gently on his wrist. Her touch was cool and pleasing, her skin delicate.

''You are right,'' he said, drinking from the cup. ''I must not be so hasty: what is done slowly, is done well.''

''That is true of our plans as well as of our pleasures,'' she replied, as her fingertips caressed the soft hairs on the back of his forearm. The smell of the sweet scented herbs with which she perfumed her body filled his nostrils, making him heady for a moment. Caratacus had told him long ago that looking into her eyes was like seeing into a green wood at twilight.

''There is one pleasure that has been too slow in coming,'' he said.

''Patience,'' she sighed. ''You have grown too used to rapid conquests. The sweetest victories are those which are not yielded easily.''

Chapter 19

After all, his ancestor Julius Caesar had lived quite comfortably in a tent, so it must be possible, thought Claudius, looking around him. But then Caesar had made more of an effort to recreate the comforts of Rome by, among other things, transporting section by section his favorite mosaic for the floor of his tent. In contrast, he found the governor Aulus Plautius quite mean with the provisions of civilization. He did not expect a mosaic to walk on, of course, but he did wish that Plautius had at least put down a bit of paving, rather than rickety wooden planks, which tended to come loose quite easily. Claudius was always expecting one of them to spring up and smack him in the face as in some dreadful Attic farce.

The rain beat down upon the huge expanse of leather which comprised the tent where the governor lived for the time being, and which also served as the site of his administrative headquarters in the center of the camp. The builders were hard at work stripping the Catuvellauni settlement of what wood they required to erect (among much else) the quarters that would house Plautius and his household probably as long as he remained in Britain. As for the stone and marble glories of the architects—they were as yet only plans that seemed extremely far off just then, and as Caesar shivered a little, as remote and unlikely as his ancestor's marble mosaic. The guy ropes strained and the leather stretched as the storm came roaring across the hills. It was impossible to stop the drafts from swishing in under the tent, forcing everyone to wrap up as warmly as if they were standing doing sentry duty on some windy fortress rampart. Claudius recalled that Pomponia Graecina, Plautius' wife, had a reputation back in the city of being very spare with her and her husband's money, tending to the more rustic and austere version of stoicism popular in certain quarters. Britain will be just to her taste then, Claudius concluded, as he watched some rainwater squelch up between two floorboards. However, he carefully avoided commenting even once on the adverse conditions, preferring instead a veneer of military hardihood as might be expected of a weather-beaten veteran of wars in far-flung places.

The chief guests were assembled around the central table, with Verica and Adminius next to each other, and the governor on the other side of Claudius. They had already begun to eat when the herald announced the arrival of those for whom Caesar had been impatiently and rather anxiously waiting. The next day, he was leaving again for Rome, and he had been worried that some mishap would prevent them from reaching Camulodunum before his departure. The heavily armed escort marched into the tent, their helmets glistening from the rain, their capes dripping wet. Fen Fire walked surrounded by them, her lose multi-colored cloak thrown back, her head held erect in a manner that impressed Claudius as having a kind of a primitive majesty which caught his attention at once. They went straight to the central table, and parted ranks. Adminius looked up from his couch. Fen Fire's hand shot out and gripped him by the throat, her fingers sinking through his skin. He choked, his face turning a ghastly grey before the guards could break her fierce grip.

"I am ashamed to be so close to your weasel neck without being able to wring it," she hissed. It required four of the escort guards to drag her back as she struggled to pounce on him again. Adminius, rubbing the raw red welt on his neck, looked at Caesar, who in response merely nodded and smiled.

"Just a little test to see if what you've been saying about her was true," he said. "It certainly does not seem to have been an exaggeration."

"She would make a fine match in the Circus pitched against a she-lion, don't you think?" Plautius suggested. "But a few years under our care will improve her table manners."

"In a way it is a shame to blunt the edge of such a keen native blade," Claudius said.

"Keen enough to cut our throats," Verica added. Claudius ordered she be brought closer, so that he might inspect her more carefully. The guards had her by the arms; she was breathing quickly like a wild animal just trapped. She would blend with some forest scene, crouching on naked feet, ready to strike, Caesar imagined. "I never thought the legend of the Amazons as improbable as all that," he mused. "Did not Pompey the Great, a sober enough individual, claim to have encountered them as he marched towards the Caucasus Mountains between the Black and Caspian Seas? He reported that an Amazon tribe joined forces with an army composed of the wild tribes of those mysterious regions to oppose him. After Pompey's victory his soldiers, going about the battlefield looking for spoils, found women's buskins. But of the fabled women warriors, nothing more."

"Then you, Caesar, have outdone one of the great generals of antiquity and provided more corporeal evidence of your victory over the Amazons of Britain," Plautius told him.

"Indeed I have. Evidence most palpable." He lingered over the long red hair, the full mouth, the eyes wild and defiant, the savage nails; she would prove a stern mistress, and to make love to her would be a pleasure made all the more exquisite because it might well prove the last one would ever enjoy. "You will see to it that she is well taken care of until everything is in place," he said, looking at Adminius. "When the time comes for her to go to Rome, you may accompany her as part of the escort and witness for yourself how we will display her at her best."

Adminius thanked Caesar for this unexpected privilege, which he would savor as the consummation of his revenge.

"I cannot wait for you to begin your reeducation," he sneered as she was being taken away. "You have much to learn of civilization."

"I know what true freedom is though I am held hostage. So your lesson is one I could never learn—for I cannot learn to be a slave."

"Freedom," he scoffed, "what you call freedom is merely lawlessness—the freedom to plunder your neighbors, fight wars over cattle, live in perpetual turmoil and have some sycophantic bard celebrate every petty squabble as an epic struggle; what you boast of as freedom is simply endless chaos."

"Enjoy your crumbs from the master's table," she shot back with withering, scornful eyes. "To talk of freedom to you is the most futile thing in the world. I might as well talk of wings to a worm."

He turned aside from her gaze, pretending to be aloof.

Though Claudius did not understand what she had said to Adminius, he did not need to. "A man has no defense against the scorn of a woman," he mused.

Surrounded by troops, they brought her across what had been the great meadow of Cunobelinus. They had difficulty fending off the curious onlookers, who crowded around trying to catch a glimpse of the woman rumored to be a living Amazon. The people pushed and shoved to get closer. And when they did they gawked at her, like men who found themselves confronting a world they had not known existed. Their vacant, idle curiosity, expressed as it was in their ugly anonymous faces, wide-mouthed and staring through dull eyes that seemed only capable of gaping, repelled her. Being gawked at by such a mob made her unhappy, almost ill with a feeling she did not know, had never experienced before. She tried to avoid it simply by ignoring the swarming faces. But she could not: it was intrinsic to the state in which she found herself, and it was called humiliation.

They brought her to a stockade with a stout gate on either side of which were two towers for the guards. In the center of the enclosure there were several capacious army tents. When the gate shut behind her, she stood in the drenching rain for a moment. The rain had not discouraged the curious from gathering at the gate bars. In the distance, through the gate beyond the gawking rain-soaked faces she could just see the thatched roof of the old palace in which she had been raised. Already, it had been partly demolished, the wood plundered for other buildings under construction. The area between the tent and the stockade which surrounded it was a desolate quagmire. The once great settlement, capital of her foster father, had the appearance of a wasteland, as if it had been overcome by some huge wave which had swept away all that she recognized and left behind only a muddy remnant of the world that was.

She shared her stockade with hostages from the various tribes who had reached agreements with Caesar. She was dismayed to see that so many kings had made their pacts with Rome: waiting there to be transported was a daughter of Boduocus, king of the Dobunni, the son of the most powerful chief of the Coritani, and various relatives from the kings to the south of the Thames, including the sister of Cogidubnus, one of the richest. They were a gloomy and despondent gathering. Though treated well—they were not ordinary "prisoners"—all dreaded the coming journey from Britain, dreaded it like a death sentence. All except for Fen Fire cursed the men who had so consigned them to their fate. She had wounded Prasutagus. He had acted out of rage and grief, not from cunning or scheming self-interest. In a way, that reconciled her to her fate; but she could not rest reconciled to the fate of her people—now forced as they were into a slavish treaty with the power that intended to destroy them. Every day she saw that power increase and spread across the face of the land as more troops came through the bustling camp and in their wake the settlers and the merchants. And every day the obstacles to her freedom grew more and more insufferable. Yet, to the eyes of the Romans or of her fellow hostages, she did not betray her growing desperation to be free. Except on one morning, when she heard the cry of the swan flying south with her young. She looked up at the huge white wings beating through the cold blue sky and remembered the swan she'd freed, kicking in the bars of the cage that held it. She was shaken by a pang of grief she could not contain. As the bird flew by indifferent to her plight, she sank to her knees.

"You must accustom yourself to this," Adminius

gloated, from the far side of the gate. He came often, professing to be anxious to make sure she was being well cared for as Claudius had requested. In reality his purpose was to torment her. He always found a few people there who'd come to stare at her. "The Romans enjoy curiosities," he said.

"Their curiosity is degrading," she replied, stepping up towards the gate. The sight of Adminius had revived her spirits. When she looked at him she remembered she had cause to hate and cause to seek her freedom. "It is a vile thing."

"It must be terrible," he mocked her with undisguised enjoyment, "to be so degraded by the eyes of these poor ignorant men."

"But nothing is so degrading as the pleasure derived from degrading others," she reminded him.

"You will soon know the true meaning of degradation," he sneered, smarting under her contempt, "when you appear in Rome with Caesar's other trophies."

"They will never see me in Rome, that I promise!" she swore, gripping the bars with both hands. "I have too many trophies of my own to collect here in Britain."

He stepped back nervously. The guards in the towers above laughed at him. "Don't fret—we won't let her near you," they shouted down. He hesitated for an instant, then turned and walked off as quickly as he could. He had seen the fury against him in her eyes and feared no set of bars could contain it.

"You have done well," a voice said from behind her. A sad-faced man was there, a slave whom the Romans used to serve the hostages, bringing them their food and drink. He was a Briton, and Fen Fire had not had any cause to notice him until then. He glanced up at the guards. "My name is Vetus," he whispered as they opened the gates to let him out.

When he came the next day, Fen Fire watched him carefully. He was haggard and timid in appearance, going about his work patiently and quietly, little different from any other lowly slave she'd seen. "Vetus," she said softly, "who are you?" He looked into her eyes. She saw in his face a strange passivity, mixed with a grim patience—before the overwhelming power of the aggressor man's soul sought refuge in resignation. It chilled her heart more than anything she'd yet seen, for if it took root among the people, resistance would wither like a blighted branch.

"Ah," he smiled, "you would not remember one of Cunobelinus' shepherds, would you?"

Before she could reply, two guards came across to them.

"Malingering, eh?" one of them shouted at the slave, and raised his javelin shaft. Vetus cringed like a frightened dog. Fen Fire stepped between him and the intended blow. She caught the spear shaft with her hand and gave it such a violent twist that the guard was thrown on to the ground. She had planted her foot on the guard's neck with the point of the spear within an inch of his throat before his companion realized what had happened.

"We are not all so easily broken," she said, as the rest of his unit came running to his rescue. "He served me once," Fen Fire told the officer in charge. "I will not see him beaten."

"We were wondering when you would give us a show," the centurion replied as the guard was helped to his feet.

Nothing more was made of the incident, and Vetus was allowed to go about his business unmolested. They spoke together occasionally; Vetus shared a few memories he had of the old king, of Caratacus, Togodumnus and Maglocunos.

"When I saw them riding out together with you at their side in the spring morning and the great hounds bounding before you! Togodumnus the tree-splitter, Caratacus the straight-steerer, Maglocunos beloved of women, and the king—no poor man would go empty-handed from his door, no one in need was ever refused. They were like gods compared to these. There are too many clerks in the world now. It is a pitiful state we are in. I would do anything to be up there in the summer pastures, listening to the blackbirds!" For a moment the mask of slavery was lifted from his face.

"Caratacus and Maglocunos and Subidasto of the Iceni

are alive yet," she said, "your vision still has flesh and bones."

"Oh, I've heard the stories," he whispered, pretending to busy himself at the same time.

"What stories?"

"There's a constant flux of slaves coming in from the west and the north. I mingle sometimes. They talk of what they saw."

"And?"

"Caratacus is a fox indeed. His men are everywhere—places where Caesar would not think of looking."

"Can they be reached?"

"They could, I suppose. But what would be the point of that—haven't you looked around you? Caesar is too strong here."

A patrol came marching between the tents, checking to see that all was in order. Vetus drifted away. After that, she saw very little of him. But when she did, they spoke of the old times, and something of the man's spirit began to rekindle in his eyes.

Another summer came and went. Still Plautius' conquest seemed as far off as ever. Adminius' predictions that Caratacus would soon arrive in chains went unfulfilled and his enthusiasm for taunting her about Rome's invincibility waned. He came to her less and less frequently.

When the governor's imposing residence was finished, she was given quarters in the buildings complex which was surrounded by a high palisade. Her room opened out on a small colonnaded garden planted and cultivated by Plautius' wife Pomponia shortly after her arrival in Britain. Though she was still under constant guard, the change afforded her more privacy. Fen Fire could walk alone in the little garden, watching it grow, listening to the constant din of construction coming in from beyond the palisade.

A new world was taking shape on all sides of her, and she was helpless to prevent it. The great round buildings of her people were being torn down before her eyes, and in their place came long rectangular structures like that in which she was kept. They were hideous to behold, full of sharp corners, without curves, without the beautiful spiral intricacies along whose lines the eye could run contentedly forever and never feel wearied. Every line her eye followed seemed to end in a point or a corner. At first she could not look at them for even a short while without getting a pain in her head. Their angularity was heightened by the barenness within. No shining chieftain's shields hung from their walls, no bright broadswords or golden birds, no pillar richly carved with scenes from the chase, no simmering cauldron at the heart of the house. Between those walls the harper's notes were never heard, nor the song and story of the bard. A solemn stillness prevailed, broken only by the shuffling of some slave or cringing official who came and went as quickly and unobtrusively as possible. Their colorless world engulfed her. She languished for her own kind, and for word of what was happening in the wide world beyond, about which she was told nothing except when Adminius chose to crow about Roman victories. He still boasted that someday soon Caratacus would join her in chains, and she would have the pleasure of his company on the road to Rome. Though what he said was mostly lies, from it she could glean scraps of information—the most important of which was that the war still went on in the west and that Caratacus and his supporters remained active. Then there were her brief talks with Vetus, which gave her some intriguing grounds for hope.

Fen Fire was in the garden one day when she saw Pomponia watching her. She had not paid much attention to the governor's wife until then, except to notice her rather stern though not unpleasing features, and stiff-backed manner which made her seem older than her years.

"I am sick of being watched," said Fen Fire, suddenly walking up to her and speaking to her in her own tongue, of which she'd learnt a little as time passed.

"I am sorry," the governor's wife replied, "but I have been wondering for some time why you do nothing in this lovely garden except pace around like a caged panther. Would you not like to help me cultivate it? I am trying to get my vines to flourish, but it is difficult in this climate with its long, cold winters."

Fen Fire smiled. "Cultivate the garden?" She looked around it with casual bemusement. "I have no interest in cultivating flowers or vines. My garden was the forest. My pleasure is to hunt, not water flowers."

"Do not the women of the Iceni grow plants, gather herbs, tend to their gardens?"

"Some do, if they so choose. But we are not gardeners by nature."

Pomponia smiled, and the character of her face changed, revealing a more sympathetic disposition.

"Yes, I'm told you fight like a man and do much as you please, being under no man's rule."

"I fight like a warrior. And the only thing a man can command of me is my allegiance—if he deserves it."

"And what kind of man deserves your allegiance?"

"One who is brave, generous and free of jealousy."

"Free of jealousy?"

"Surely. A woman's needs are as changeable, yet as cyclical, as the seasons. A wise man lets a woman's desires run their course; but a man who fears them will never satisfy them."

"Is it as easy as that?"

"It is easier than being a slave, either to a husband or to Caesar."

Pomponia was taken by the young woman's openness, her ease and confidence. "Come," she said, "I will take you on a tour of my garden, and we will talk some more."

Over the following weeks, Pomponia learned much about the women of the Britons, and about Fen Fire. When Fen Fire spoke of Andraste and her worship, the governor's wife listened especially intently. Among the Romans, the goddesses were relegated to the status of good wives or virgin huntresses who suffered endless frustration, or devoted housekeepers who tended fires, or decorous mistresses doomed to disappointment. Fen Fire had never heard of such deities as Pomponia described—nor of good housekeeping. Andraste was not a goddess of purity, nor of love. Her goddess was the nurturer and the harvester of life, ruling birth and the battlefield, a goddess of lust and destructivness, as sensual as she was murderous, as irresistible as she was all-consuming. For Pomponia, Andraste proved a wondrous revelation.

In contrast, Fen Fire was horrified by what Pomponia told her of the life of women in the empire's capital. They could do nothing without their fathers' and then their husbands' permission, and even when widowed, and of mature years, were degradingly placed under the rule of male relatives, not being able even to sell their own property without consent. Their abject status horrified her, and the more she heard about it the more determined it made her that she would never set foot in Rome. She would die first rather than live such a life.

The two women not only talked. Fen Fire showed Pomponia how to break any man's grip with a single blow. It was a singular novelty for the Roman lady to learn various different wrestling holds which the two women practiced in the privacy of Pomponia's bathing house. This was an elaborate structure consisting of four different rooms, in three of which there were sluices of water at different temperatures ranging from hot to cold. In the fourth, there were several long couches on which to lie, where, after the bathing, the women could enjoy a massage with oil and different creams. Before long, their intimacy had reached the point where Fen Fire felt able to ask of Pomponia a favor. She wanted the slave Vetus brought to her to serve her. She explained that years ago he had served in her father's palace. Pomponia agreed at once, and the next day Vetus appeared in the governor's residence, assigned to Fen Fire. She also turned a blind eye when Vetus disappeared for several nights at a time, accepting Fen Fire's explanation that he was visiting his family, and made sure his absence was not noticed.

Pomponia knew how much Fen Fire loathed the idea of being finally sent to Rome, and feared that when the time came for her to go she would kill herself. She could not bear the prospect either of her death or that she should wither away in a city she already hated. But the threat of exile in Rome loomed closer with every passing month with relentless inevitability. Pomponia did not know how one or the other outcome could be avoided. She knew only that she would tell Fen Fire as soon as she herself found out, in the desperate hope that somehow she could reconcile the young woman to her fate, or perhaps help her avoid it. But the latter was only a half-formed thought, so subversive and secret, that Pomponia herself hardly recognized it as her own.

One afternoon after bathing, they were being massaged when Pomponia dismissed her slaves. They were left alone. She came over to Fen Fire's couch and sat down at her side.

"My husband received word today from Caesar," she said, gently continuing the unfinished massage with her own hands. "We must return to Rome before the month is out—and so must you. Caesar has grown impatient for his triumphal celebrations. He has deemed it time." She paused. "I'm sorry . . . I fear you'll do something to harm yourself . . . please do not despair . . ."

"Have no fear for me," Fen Fire replied. "I have not yet reached that point." Pomponia's face smiled with relief and surprise.

"Then you might be reconciled to us after all . . ."

"Never," Fen Fire replied.

"Of course. How could it be otherwise," she said with resignation, realizing the foolishness of that hope. Fen Fire was silent for a while. Then she turned towards her new found friend.

"Vetus will have to be gone again tonight . . ."

"You do not have to ask. I give my word, I will see to it that his absence is not noticed," Pomponia answered. Of Fen Fire she demanded no explanation. Pomponia preferred to let that secret, subversive thought she cherished germinate in the enfolding, comforting darkness, beyond the narrow reach of reason.

Chapter 20

The clamor of the past rang in her ears as the carriage bumped over the stone-paved roadway that now ran across the meadow and through the gates of Camulodunum. Between the ranks of the escort Fen Fire could only catch glimpses of the field where once the feast games had been held. It was hardly recognizable. A huge sprawling complex of buildings had engulfed it. Where once the warriors with their high-crested helmets strove to win glory, and the creaking of the chariot wheels echoed until twilight, and the sweet melancholy whining of the wind through the raised spear shafts delighted her ears, there was now the cacophony of swarming anonymous men—slaves, clerks, merchants, who led lives of drudgery and monotony. For a moment they halted their work and came swarming after the convoy, hoping to get a last glimpse of Fen Fire.

"Behold, the last of the Amazons!" Adminius cried as he rode with the escort. For the first time in many months he had the courage to look her in the eye. But he met the same unwavering contempt as before. Fen Fire ignored his foolish and boastful posturing and rested against the chest of valuables that she was allowed to bring with her into exile. She was happy to be out of the city that once had been her home. Her only regret was poor Pomponia—she had left her in a sad state. Pomponia had told her that someday they might meet in Rome, though she knew Fen Fire would do all she could to make that wish impossible to come true. And Pomponia had helped her as she promised. When Vetus never returned, she covered for his disappearance. In the fuss of arranging for the governor's departure—he was to leave shortly after Fen Fire—no one had paid too much attention to his absence.

Out of Camulodunum the convoy rumbled towards the little port the Romans had constructed in an estuary to the east. Their route took them along a narrow, thickly wooded peninsula, to a small fortress which guarded the way to the port. They would spend the night there before going on to the port, a short distance away, where a squadron of ships awaited them. They were due to set sail the following morning. In the late afternoon, they came within sight of the fortress, situated on a rise above a clearing.

The escorting troops were sluggish and inattentive. There had been no trouble in this part of the country since just after the invasion; in fact, it had become boringly quiet, leaving the legionaries with no opportunity for plunder or the taking of good sturdy natives who would fetch a fine price on the slave market that was now flourishing a few miles to the south in London. But earlier on that morning, at least for the troops in the fortress guarding the port, the routine had been interrupted. A man, badly beaten and wounded, had come to the fortress gates. He said he was the survivor of an ambush. A large band of up to a hundred brigands had set upon his merchant convoy, robbed him, and killed his fellows. He begged for assistance in tracking down the villains. The prospect of rounding up a hundred fugitives who might fetch a fair sum at the slave market was a welcome one. Almost half the garrison went out with the officer in charge to find them. In their haste, they had neglected to send scouts in front of them—peace had made them careless. As it had their fellows in the fortress, who ran out to meet them on their return from their hunting expedition, not noticing until it was too late the un-Roman-like long hair that was only just tucked in under the short helmets.

They reached the fort near twilight. The gates were opened and the convoy filed in, led by Adminius. He rode into the fort like a Roman general marching at the head of his triumphal procession along the Sacred Way in the Forum of Rome.

"I have brought you a treasured prize, destined for Caesar himself! Tell your commander to signal the port garrison. We have arrived safely and will join him before dawn," Adminius announced to the guard who had opened the gate. The guard gave no reply, and there was no sound except that of the gates being slammed shut behind them. The ramparts were lined with soldiers. The soldiers in the escort looked up, trying to recognize a familiar face, but in the gathering twilight they were not recognizable. Adminius rode round to the back of the coach.

"Are you ready to spend your last night in your native land?" he shouted in. "Tommorrow you will say farwell to it forever." Fen Fire did not respond. She sat attentively in the darkness listening to the sounds outside. There was a sudden thud, and a loud groan came from where the coach driver sat. Suddenly, the carriage jolted forward wildly, and began swaying violently as the out of control horses bolted. With a crash, it tipped over on its side, throwing her out, along with her trunk which smashed open, spilling everything on the ground. Among the heap of her possessions lay the Spear That Roars For Blood. She grabbed its shaft and sprang to her feet. The carriage driver lay sprawled on the ground, a javelin still quivering in his chest. Everywhere, warriors were throwing off their disguises and swarming over the panic-stricken escort, dragging them from the horses, and finishing off those already dismounted. When a warrior dressed as a Roman officer ran toward her she instinctively raised her spear. He stopped and pulled off his helmet. It was Subidasto. Vetus had not returned from his last mission for her, and though she had arranged for the rebels to mount an attack on the convoy, she'd no idea who would lead it or when and where it would take place. For a moment both froze. Before either could say anything, the tide of the battle swept between them.

On the nearby steps leading to the almost deserted rampart, with desperate courage Adminius fought off all who tried to reach him. If he could reach the rampart, safety was only a leap into the darkness of the woods beyond the clearing. Fen Fire leapt to her feet and plunged through the confused struggle. Adminius reached the top of the stairway as Fen Fire came behind him, bounding up the steps four at a time. He swung round and thrust at her with his sword. A blow from the spear shaft easily knocked it just beyond his reach. His hand shook, his eyes were wide with terror. He backed up against the rampart walkway, Fen Fire stalking after him, a huntress after her prey. His eyes stared at the head of the spear, with its twisted cruel point. Was it glowing and vibrating, sensing his blood like the trembling rod of a water diviner near a well? Or was his fear creating visions, nightmares? He dropped to his knees. "You have shamed yourself enough. At least die like a man," she hissed.

"You will gain nothing from my death but much if I am spared," he pleaded.

"I would sooner spare the louse that sucks my blood. I have postponed this pleasure too long to forgo it now, worthless carcass!" Adminius suddenly drew his dagger and made a desperate lunge at her throat. Fen Fire side-stepped his blow and buried the spearhead into his guts. Adminius uttered a choking cry of agony that shook the fortress. Then he shuddered and his dagger fell from his hand. With one powerful swing, she hoisted him aloft, still skewered on her spear, like a farmer bailing hay on a pitch-fork. He squirmed and wriggled on the spear-head, his blood and bowels pouring down its shaft. Then, with a shove she flung him over the walkway to the court-yard below, ripping out his insides.

"There are three sounds I like most in the world," she cried out as the warriors gathered below to gaze on the hated traitor, "the love cry of a woman, the babbling of a baby, and the gurgle of death in the throat of my enemy when my spear has twisted his guts into red knots."

When Fen Fire reached Adminius he was still writhing in the dirt, the last dregs of his worthless life gushing out of him. Taking a warrior's broadsword, she knelt down beside him. Gripping Adminius by the hair with one hand, she wrenched his ashen, twisted face towards her and put her mouth to his ear.

"I will not let you go so easily, or let that cowardly

soul your body harbors escape me through the merciful intervention of your death,'' she said. He tried to speak, but nothing came from his mouth except a gurgle of blood. ''A curse on your soul,'' she hissed into his ear, ''may it be carried far away on the hump of the cold northern wind to the black wastes that lie beyond, steeped in perpetual darkness, where the iron frost holds hard on to the earth and nothing grows, where there is never seen the light of a welcoming hearth or heard the sound of a friendly voice. May your spirit go limping to the gate of the Other World like a ragged beggar cringing for bread, and may it be always a stranger to the laughter within and the taste of the mead and the touch of the women where the People of the Mounds rejoice eternally.''

The dying man's eyes rolled, and he shook his head for the words tortured him like hot irons searing into the flesh of a slave. But Fen Fire wouldn't stop.

''May your spirit shiver for all time at the threshold of the Land of the Everlasting Ones like a dog driven from the door into the winter's wind, and may whatever seed trickled forth from your accursed flesh wither up or father only what is stunted and twisted, like the soul of the creature that produced it!''

Adminius tried to cry out, but he choked on his own blood. Fen Fire stood up and raised the broadsword over him, its fine blade above his neck. His eyes glared wide as the sword descended: he who is so cursed sees at the moment of death the awful fate that awaits his spirit as it plunges into the black cold void to wander till the end of time. Many who saw the sword sever Adminius' head glimpsed the stricken spirit go squeaking and moaning from the mangled body, sucked out on a powerful cold blast of wind that suddenly came from nowhere. Brave men that they were, they shivered in dread at the specter.

Fen Fire picked up the head and wrapped it carefully in a cloth. ''This is my gift to Caratacus, wherever he is. It is one I should have given him many years ago when I had the traitor at my mercy. It would have spared us much misery,'' she said.

''It was a fine, fierce warrior-like blow you dealt,'' said Subidasto. In one hand he carried his own trophy—

a Roman head—in the other he held his sword, its blade drenched in blood. "Captivity has not dulled your edge."

"Quite the contrary," answered she, "it was a grindstone that has honed every desire, every appetite, to a new sharpness. And this has helped satisfy one—revenge."

"And it has satisfied one of mine," he told her, "to see you free again, side by side with your warriors."

"And freedom will help satisfy the others," she replied. In that hurried, breathless, blood-stained pause, lasting no more than a moment, she was more beautiful than ever.

At the port the sentries were surprised to see the column with its precious prize coming through the evening gloom. Fen Fire was not expected until the following morning. The commander at the nearby fortress had not signaled any change of plan. "They're becoming very slipshod up there," said the centurion in charge of the detachment guarding the port. He looked at the officer commanding the escort, and then walked round to the back of the coach. "I've heard she's a real beauty—a wild cat." He winked at the officer. "Give us a look then." Subidasto nodded. The centurion lifted up the curtain. The dagger-blade glinted for a moment in the torchlight before Fen Fire buried it in his throat.

The sentries were overwhelmed as the Britons burst through into the port. Some warriors were ordered to attack the barracks nearby, which they did, annihilating the garrison and torching the buildings. Meanwhile the rest, with Subidasto and Fen Fire, made for the quayside.

Three ships were waiting in the harbor, one transport and two escorts, intended to carry Fen Fire and Adminius to Gaul. Two of the ships were still being loaded as many of their crew and marine units lounged on the quayside when the warriors descended. These two were taken at once; the marines were easily overcome and slaughtered, and what crew the warriors could muster were ordered back onto their ships. But the third was already loaded and ready to sail. The captain, when he saw the danger, managed to weigh anchor and pull out from the quayside, heading for the midwaters of the estuary where the warriors could not reach them.

"They are leaving without their passenger," Subidasto shouted to Fen Fire amidst the confusion.

"Because their passenger is intent upon a different journey," she answered.

"Can we convince them to wait?"

"You may be sure of it, my bright one," said she.

Taking careful aim, she hurled the Spear That Roars For Blood at the departing boat. It struck the vessel just below the oarsmen's lower deck, not far above the waterline. Then with a plunge she cleaved through the waters, and Subidasto dove in beside her. A host of warriors followed, each eager to outdo his fellow and reach the fleeing ship before him. Subidasto's stroke was stronger than ever. But Fen Fire had the power of a spring suddenly uncoiled and her heels were soon kicking in his face. She reached the ship first and grabbed hold of the spear as she hauled herself out of the water. The marines that tried to strike at her from the upper decks were swept from them by a cloud of arrows and javelins let loose from the companion ships already under the Britons' control. Soon, two warriors had taken hold of every oar in the water, making it impossible for the crew to row. The captain ordered the sails to be unfolded, but by the time they had begun to flap in the light wind Fen Fire had clambered aboard. Subidasto and his warriors came behind her swarming over every side. The soldiers and any of the crew who offered resistance were cut down. Soon, the decks were slippery with blood, and the third ship was theirs.

The captain, a Greek, was brought trembling before them.

"Where are we to go?" he pleaded through one of the Gallic crewmen who acted as interpreter.

"To the open sea and then north," Subidasto replied.

"The open sea!" he exclaimed, more terrified than before. "But it is growing dark and . . ."

"The sky is clear, and the stars will be bright. Follow the North Star."

"We must wait until dawn . . . the seas are too treacherous."

Subidasto grabbed him by the throat and squeezed. "You mean, wait until the Romans can reach us. We took these ships to ensure our escape, not facilitate our capture!" He squeezed harder. The man's face was as red as the flames of the burning port. "Obey, or I will send you on your final voyage—to the bottom of this estuary." The Greek nodded fervently. When one course leads to certain death, any other, however risky, seems preferable. He would do as he was told. Order was restored to the ship, and the crew went about their business. The other two ships followed in their wake towards the sea.

"We are going north—to the land of the Iceni," Fen Fire said.

"As quickly as the wind can carry us," Subidasto answered. Already it was autumn, not long before Samhain, and the fens would be hushed and white with mist. It was a scene she had thought she might never see again.

"Word that I am free will spread like a fire among dry reeds. That is, if the desire for freedom still burns in the people's breasts. Tell me that it does; I have heard nothing but rumors—rumors and lies meant to denigrate all who resisted Caesar as bandits and criminals and quench whatever hope I had that victory was still possible."

"Desire for freedom is a fire that cannot be quenched. The more that freedom is denied to a people the more they desire it," he told her in a voice that was measured and mature, calm and reassuring.

"There are many desires that burn more fiercely the more they are denied," said she. But she hungered for details, not reassurances. She overwhelmed Subidasto and his men with questions. How many warriors were with them? And how many still gave allegiance to Prasutagus? Was he as firmly allied as ever to Rome? And what of Caratacus and Maglocunos about whose fate Adminius used to jest so confidently? Were they within reach? Together were they strong enough to confront the invader?

"We have thousands who are waiting for the signal to rise," Subidasto said.

"I am Saemu, the son of Volisios," said a burly young man coming forward, his thick dark hair and long moustache still dripping wet from his plunge in the estuary waters. After Prasutagus, Volisios was the most powerful of the chieftains among the Iceni. "My brother is with us also—collecting more supporters from the north of the kingdom. My own followers number nine hundred men and his are equal to mine," he said proudly.

"And I can claim six hundred of the bravest who follow me," said another.

"And I the same," a third put in. All of them were powerful figures, worthy companions in any perilous enterprise.

"And we stand not alone in our plans to defeat Rome," said Saemu. "Caratacus and Maglocunos are with us. Even as we speak . . ."

"Where?" she asked, her eyes lit up with fresh eagerness.

"Caratacus is coming from the west, where he has spent these years among the Silures," Subidasto explained. "They have given their allegiance to him as if he was their own chief."

"As have the Ordovices—and the island of Britain knows not warriors who are more fierce than they," one of the others said. The Ordovices dwelt among the highest mountains of the west, guarding the way to the sacred island of Mona, where the druids had their schools of instruction and their holiest groves.

"And Maglocunos?" Fen Fire asked, insatiable for all there was to know.

"He is in the north among the confederation of the Brigantes where he has found support . . ." Saemu recounted.

"From the tribe of princess Cartimandua?"

"Yes, Maglocunos is well-acquainted with her."

"I fear she will prove unreliable," Fen Fire replied, her eyes flashing, "for in her veins the blood of Dark Flame flows, does it not? She never was one to be trusted."

"The last we heard from Maglocunos was that he was attempting to forge a link with the kingdom of Venutius—a leader more to our liking, who has promised Maglocunos his allegiance. But that was a long time ago, and we do not know whether his promises have yet borne fruit," Saemu said.

"She is stalling. We have also heard she is making approaches to Rome, playing one side off against the other," added Subidasto.

"I feel like someone who has been visiting a different world—though I have not left my native island." She sighed, trying to absorb all that she had been told. "In spite of the machinations of that northern witch, what I have heard fills me with hope! But when . . . when will these forces, our forces, be brought together to strike the blow? You spoke of a signal . . ."

"Yes, it could come now, or in a month—we do not know," Subidasto said. "Except we know it must be soon, otherwise they would not have planned to send you to Rome."

"Then your signal is the departure of the governor, Aulus Plautius," she said.

"You guessed correctly," Subidasto replied. "Winter is fast approaching and the weather is deteriorating rapidly. If he does not depart soon, he risks being stranded in Britain—a thing not to be thought of, since Caesar is preparing to celebrate his triumph over Britain. The people of Rome are eager to see for themselves these wild men and their warrior women about whom they have heard so much."

"And will hear more; but why does he delay?"

"Unexpected snows have blocked the mountain passes and held up his replacement in Italy, so we have heard," said one of the other warriors.

"Which means," Subidasto added, "that Plautius will be forced to leave the province while his replacement is still far away."

"Then we will strike!" she affirmed.

Still breathless and bloodstained from the battle, and exhausted with sharing the warriors' excitement as they spoke of their plans and preparations, she rested against the mast. For the first time in years she felt she could fill her lungs with air—air from the salty breeze that was blowing down the darkening estuary and making the great sails full above her. Never had the world seemed so wild and fine a place as at that moment. Her eyes met those of the man she had just outswum. He sat opposite her, his fine legs folded under him, as cool as you please. Her eyes were kindled by his reckless soul. Subidasto had filled out, losing something of that youthful angularity in exchange for bulk that had gathered around his shoulders and thighs where true power resides. He wore a long, well-trimmed brown moustache, and his brown hair had grown thicker and darker; it was laced with vivid streaks of bright yellow and with other bands of blue from bracken and birch die. The carelessness of life's abundance was in his every easy gesture and challenging glance; it had made a dancer of his spirit, as if spring were the only season. It made her cherish him even more, as it would any woman. She would have taken him in her arms there and then and pulled him down to the blood-splashed deck. Now she was the victor in an old contest, yet who knows what might stand between her and the prize? The king had not been spoken of, except in passing, as if he were no more than an inconvenience that would be swept aside. Yet, even if that were true, would it leave the barrier to her happiness still standing? The warriors loved Subidasto, and would follow him to the death, as they would her. But what if she laid claim to her husband's son? For he was that as much as she was Prasutagus' wife. Would they spurn her in horror of incest? When she was delivered into the hands of Rome, the Iceni wept for her with true, scalding tears, regardless of the accusations and the rumors Latis spread against her. In their hearts, the people knew then that tenderness was no crime. But would they remember that old tolerance born of their love if she were now to take Subidasto in her arms and make her claim—to be at his side as his wife as well as his fellow warrior in whatever trials lay before them?

For a while it was her turn to satisfy the warriors' curiosity. She recounted what she'd seen—the new settlements spreading into the countryside, bursting at the seams with merchants from every corner of the world;

the stone-paved roads that ran from one side of the land to the other which no obstacle could block; the soldiers, clad from head to foot in metal; and the slave markets, crammed full with their human merchandise, herded together like cattle, destined never to see their land again. A silence followed, broken only by the sighing of the wind in the sails and the creaking of the ship. Each man among them pictured the scene in his own mind, imagined his own horror.

"Rather death than such a fate," said Saemu.

"We will have vengeance soon," Subidasto affirmed.

"Pleasure and revenge have this in common: the longer they are delayed the greater is the satisfaction they can give," she said.

But he would not be provoked by her taunting. "It has been delayed too long already," he replied dispassionately, apparently heedless to her subtlety.

"Yes," she answered, "we have waited a long time—it seems an age ago since we were masters of ourselves." She paused. "What of the king—my husband?" she asked, risking a little irony. Subidasto did not smile.

"Prasutagus is as stubborn as ever," Saemu said. "He stands by his treaty because he has given his word. But who knows how he might change when he learns that you are with us."

"My father will not change," said Subidasto curtly. He looked at her. Her skin was as white as the feathers of the swan contrasted against the blue when that great bird softly breasts the cold waters of a mountain lake. She lay naked on the green moss, her hair spread out on the cave floor each strand a fine thread of flame, while beyond the waterfall the river went on its way, as ever, winding through the woods. How many turns of the wheel of time since then? How many summers had ripened and faded, with their flowers and fruits? How many petals had fallen from the poppies' frail bloom? Yet an enchantment had been placed upon that memory that with every passing year it should grow more vivid in his mind, not less, compared to which the events even of yesterday were dim ghosts, barely recollected. It seemed at times like a kind of doom, to carry a memory that burned like an ever more intense flame, while everything else so quickly turned to ashes.

And foul like the taste of ash in the mouth was the thought that his father had taken her from him. It made him forget for a moment that it was he who had now taken her.

"Why do you ask of the king, your husband?" he responded, throwing off the final word as if it were a mere useless husk.

"Because his actions will bear upon ours," she replied, realizing that even a gentle irony was too sharp a prod for so sensitive a subject.

"Whatever the king's actions, it is of no consequence now," Subidasto continued, getting up.

"Subidasto is right," said one of his companions. "The people will flock to us in greater numbers than ever now that you are with us."

"Rome will find it has made a treaty with a king who does not possess a kingdom," Saemu claimed confidently, and continued enumerating the list of chieftains and their warriors who were with them. And as he spoke, Subidasto lingered quietly, looking at Fen Fire. Prasutagus had forfeited more than just his kingdom. Compared to her whom he had abandoned, that was the lesser of his losses. But could the father's loss be the son's gain? If he claimed her, his enemies would say his rebellion was an act inspired not by desire for liberty but by lust, his rescue of her would be portrayed not as an act of defiance against an empire but as an act of brigandage by a renegade son. And yet, if he did not, all other victories would seem hollow, however glorious.

Subidasto said nothing, and began to busy himself about the vessel, checking with the captain that all was in place.

They had sailed down the estuary towards the open sea, and looking back Fen Fire could see the port only as a red glare on the horizon. The ship that was to bring her into bondage was the vessel of her deliverance. Had it been only the size of a fisherman's coracle it would have been all the world to her; as she walked about the deck talking to the warriors, it seemed infinitely large because she occupied its bounded space as a free woman. And the joys of freedom are boundless.

The warriors had discovered a few casks of wine on board. They split them open, and soon the mood of celebration and victory was heightened by the pleasures of the free-flowing wine. When the ship reached the open sea it began to pitch and roll, and more wine was spilt than was swallowed. Many of the crew were dark-skinned Egyptians accustomed to the tranquil waters of the Mediterranean. They looked in dread from the boundless seas around them to their captain, hoping for reassurance. Instead, they found him on his knees, his terrified eyes shut, and his arms spread begging his gods to save him from the terrors of the northern deep. The Gauls among the crew, more used to the high seas, did their best to calm them. But only when the wind dropped, and the seas grew more placid, was their courage restored. The Britons were so amused by the captain's behavior that they composed a poem to immortalize it, which Saemu sang with wine-inspired gusto:

"We had a captain until we
Found that he feared the open sea.
When the waves came up
On his knees he'd drop
And he'd pray to the gods that be, that be,
He'd pray to the gods that be."

Subidasto lounged on the small high deck in the stern of the ship listening, occasionally glancing up at the sky where the North Star was their guide. There was a small cabin below the deck which he had told Fen Fire earlier that she should use to get some rest. When it grew late, he saw her rise up from the circle of warriors that had gathered around her. She licked the last beads of wine from her red lips and undid her hair; shaken loose, it tumbled around her shoulders, its strands delicately combed by the gentle wind. Not an eye flickered as the warriors watched her, their mouths gaping open a little in silent wonder at her beauty. Wordlessly, the men paid her the homage that was her due. Then, bidding them goodnight, she went to the cabin above which Subidasto stood, exchanging but a brief glance with him before entering.

That night, she lay in the darkness listening to the wind and the creaking of the ship, as one by one the voices from outside fell silent. Not far from where she lay, her trunk sat, containing, among her other mementos, the head of Adminius. In the heavy seas, the traitor's head had rolled out of its wrapping. Now, every time the ship pitched, it knocked against the side of the trunk. It was by counting the knocks that she fell asleep. Towards dawn she awoke. The deck above her creaked under the tread of someone's footsteps. He paced back and forth, and when he was directly over her he would halt for a moment, as if hesitating.

On another ship, heading for a far different destination, the returning Aulus Plautius, soon to be hailed in Rome as the conqueror of the Britons, turned his face away from the fading coastline and wrapped his general's cloak about him. The taking of Fen Fire had occurred too late for him to do anything about it. Caesar was impatient—the preparations for the celebration were set. His successor would have to cope as best he could. Bandits, that's all they were, mere bandits. He coughed—the island's wretched fogs seemed to have gotten into his very lungs. He cursed the foul weather. And with even greater vehemence, he cursed those who had by their arrogant daring marred the last days of his governorship and cast a shadow over the triumph that he was being recalled to Rome to enjoy.

His wife Pomponia Graecina listened with sympathy and reassured him that it was not an important failure. His reputation did not depend on that red-haired woman, she told him. But she watched Britain slowly vanish from view with far different emotions—emotions a good Roman matron's training in scheming and manipulation would not let her show much less explain. Emotions which conjured up a vision of women no longer in need of such a mask. But for the moment she must wear it, her reputation safe, her soul subversive and concealed.

PART
4

Chapter 21

It was twilight, and a faint autumnal mist had crept over the fenlands. But the lake and the shore of the lake were ablaze with moving, swaying, dancing lights. They lit up the mist so that from a distance it appeared as a cloud radiating light. And from the island in the lake came the sound of sweet music—wafting over the water, the mellow sweet sounds of reed pipes, the steady pulse of the drum beat and the wind-clear winged notes of the harp. The women had gathered by the sacred island of Andraste. Each carried a burning torch, and each waited for the first glimpse of Fen Fire. Some were gathered on the shore, while others waited in the little coracles which bobbed up and down on the lake's gentle waves. From the day she had been made hostage, women had been coming to the shrine to offer up a gift to the goddess and pray for her freedom. But when word spread that Fen Fire was free, they converged on the shrine deep in the fenlands in their hundreds braving the fogs and the cold. They came to thank the goddess. And many nourished a hope that Fen Fire would return there. But for Nemain the High Priestess, it was more than a hope. Every day since learning of Fen Fire's escape, her women had scoured the fringes of the fens, where the sluggish waters merge into those of the great bay which in its turn opens out into the sea. Where else would she seek sanctuary but ahere, in the fenland's reedy maze? Then one morning, half a day's journey from the sacred island, in a swampy inlet the three great vessels emerged from a fog. Subidasto had agreed with Fen Fire: the fenlands provided the protection they needed until they were ready to strike, and when that time came, it would give them access to the very heart of the Iceni kingdom.

They gave two of the three ships back to the captains and their crews, telling them they were free to return to their own lands. Then, guided by the priestesses, the warriors, having fastened ropes around the third ship, hauled it the remaining part of the journey, across the swamp and along a narrow river that brought them to the lake and the lake island.

Fen Fire stood in the prow of the ship as the warriors rowed it slowly into view, her hair undone, flowing freely around her shoulders and over her breasts; in one hand she clasped the Spear That Roars For Blood, and in the other the severed head of Adminius. In the milky mist that clung to the top of the mast, little blue flames danced, demons of the fenlands. The banks of oars rose and fell to a steady beat, and the ship moved with majestic ease into the lake which reflected the torch flames and seemed to be brimming over with fire. With majestic serenity, Fen Fire gazed down upon the upturned joyous faces of her followers in the little boats which swarmed around her. At first they were struck dumb—imagining it was a vision of the goddess herself, descending among them. But looking into her grey eyes they saw they were glistening.

"Your freedom is our first victory," a voice cried out. Fen Fire raised up the severed head, holding it aloft so all could see it clearly.

"And this is our second!" she called out. "Behold the traitor Adminius, whose soul now rides on the back of the north wind beyond the glow of any hearth and the touch of any woman's hand for the length of eternity. No fate more fitting for he who betrays his own!"

At once, with one voice, the women began to chant, "Boudica, boudica, boudica!"—their cry of victory.

"Their cry rings out like a name," said Saemu to Subidasto. Both men were behind her on the ship's prow.

"They have proclaimed her their queen," Subidasto said.

"As they will you their king," his companion replied.

A group of priestesses met the ship to take Fen Fire

with them in their coracle to the island, where she had a gift to lay at the feet of the goddess. Behind, she trailed a wake of fire as the women followed her across the lake.

A necklace of human skulls hung in a great loop, reaching down to the pendulous breasts of the statue of Andraste. She had gathered the flowers and fruits of death which decorated her: men's bones were her bracelets and anklets, men's withered, severed heads a shriveling bouquet of old flowers with which she perfumed her room. The skulls glowed in the dim light. Ages ago, they were men who doubtless found much to laugh at with their fellows. In death, seemingly, they had found something which made them grin perpetually, though what it was no human eye could see. Darkness reigned in Andraste's blank, almond-shaped eyes and between her bent black thighs on which the temple torch flames cast a sheen. She made of her heart a dark well, as dark as it was pitiless. The well of life had become the well of death. Who could say which was the deeper?

Then, between her bent thighs the darkness moved, a shadow within a shadow, as if something had gathered the darkness into itself. Or perhaps it was that the night had become a person. Or that the spirit of Andraste had brought the darkness to life. Nemain, robed in a black cape of crow and raven's feathers, her face masked with black feathers, emerged as if from the very womb-mouth of the goddess. Her long leper-white fingers were covered in half-gloves of eel skin; rings of whorled gold decorated each in the form of coiled serpents; through the cloak could be glimpsed a torc of whorled gold likewise wrought in the form of a serpent twisted around her slender pale neck; it eyes were of precious pearls—distillations of pure light as the woman that wore them was a distillation of all that was dark.

Fen Fire stepped out of the ring of chalk-white priestesses holding the cloth bundle in her outstretched hands. She brought it before the goddess. Nemain parted the folds of cloth and looked into the dead eyes of Adminius that stared at her cold and glassy like those of a dead fish. She lifted the head and held it up to her face.

"What seeds and bleeds, our powers devour . . ." she said.

Gradually, she drew it closer to her until her red lips were almost touching the white lips of the dead man. Playfully, teasingly, she flicked her tongue through the mouth-slit of her mask; mouth parted, she pretended to plant a devouring kiss on his dead mouth, as if she was ravenous for him, then swiftly turning, thrust the head onto a sharpened stake that stood behind her.

"Come, birds of battle, feed on the traitorous breed!" the high priestess said. The women chanted their ecstasy of revenge.

The two huge rooks that nested on either shoulder of Andraste's statue came swooping down. They circled the new offering three times, then both at once sank their claws into its scalp. They drove their heavy spear-like beaks through the flesh and into the glassy eyes, they tore at it ravenously until their claws and beaks ran brown with gore that stained their black glossy wings. Soon it was no longer a recognizably human face.

Fen Fire turned to the priestesses. "Let the vengeance of the goddess on all who betray their own be as swift as the wind and as silent as the web-weaving spider," she said. The fumes from the Cauldron of Inspiration filled the temple. The priestesses drank. They dedicated themselves each to be the vessel of the vengeance of Andraste against all the enemies of the Britons. In the service of Andraste lay perfect freedom. From her they were born. She was their initiation. And they would find in her their consummation. Then they danced, linked arm-in-arm around the head of Adminius, until the temple torches flew by like comets, and joyous exhaustion overcame their limbs. They lay down to rest. Nemain lay next to Fen Fire. Enfolding her dark cape around her she drew her to her breast.

"I have looked into the swirling cauldron," she said. "When we rise and go forth from this place, for many of us it will be the last time. I, for one, will not return. I go into the embrace of the Implacable One. You will replace me."

"I will do as the goddess asks," Fen Fire said, her

white fingers combing through the blue-black locks of the high priestess.

"To know you is to know the goddess herself," Nemain sighed, as her hand glided gently over Fen Fire's taut smooth stomach until it came to rest between her opening thighs like a bird settling in a nest woven of softest down. Fen Fire closed her eyes.

"Let your tongue speak for what the goddess desires," she said, surrendering herself to the high priestess.

When their love-making was finished, for the last time Nemain laid her dark head on Fen Fire's white breast: a raven against the fresh snow.

They did not rest for long. Fen Fire heard the voices that came from across the lake, where the warriors and the other women were waiting, on the shore and the ship. Gently, she left Nemain's side, wrapped a cloak around her and stole from the temple, through the compound and into the grove beyond it. By the water's edge she paused and looked over the lake at where the ship loomed ablaze with lights. On this island, years before, as she made ready for her marriage to Prasutagus, she had thought of the same young man, regretting like many a girl before and since how little she knew of her May Eve woodland lover, in whose arms she had become a woman. That regret was an innocent one, like the tender spirit of summer, which by its own tears nourishes its growth. Now came another regret, blacker, more in keeping with this Samhain season: the knowledge that her lover was the son of her husband created a gulf between them which might prove unbridgeable. It was a regret full of bitter irony—she was denied the man she wanted because of his relationship to the man who had abandoned her! So—was she to lose both? No, she was not so easily denied. By abandoning her had the king not long ago forfeited all right to claim her as his wife? What obligation could she have to Prasutagus now? As for the Iceni, who knew her as his wife, surely they knew that ancient wisdom which holds it is a crime when a good woman goes in want of the man she desires most in the world? Her meditations were interrupted.

From the ship came the sounds of laughter: elusive, and tantalizing. At times she seemed to hear his voice, at times his father's . . .

She returned from the island just after word reached them that Aulus Plautius had departed from Britain. Subidasto had already decided the course he would follow. She thought his strategy a good one.

There was an ancient fortress in the southeast corner of the kingdom, near the border of the ancestral lands of the Catuvellauni, known as the Ring of the Everlasting Ones. It was a perfect circle constructed of stone by the people who inhabited the island of Britain before the coming of Maponos, who forced them to dwell in the mounds and in the hills when he took possession of the upper world. Because it was a fairy place, it was rarely frequented by men and women. But for Subidasto the Ring of the Everlasting Ones had several overriding advantages. It commanded a view of the countryside for many miles, and the hill on which it stood was not only high, but steep sided with one narrow route of access. Most importantly, it would provide Subidasto and his forces with a place of strength from which they could strike west to join up with the armies of Caratacus, who was to attack when he learned of the governor's departure. Then, united, they could encircle the whole Roman province, and strangle the foreign invader in an ever-tightening grip.

As he was discussing this with Fen Fire and his chiefs, the warriors and the women came crowding around them excited by the news. They were joined by Nemain and the island priestesses who crossed the lake to attend the great gathering on the shores. The crowd, impatient and eager for action, proclaimed that together Subidasto and Fen Fire must lead them to create a new kingdom that would not only renounce all subservience to Rome but humble the power of the empire.

"It will be the herald of a new age for the Britons," said Saemu, "when the kingdoms will unite and drive the enemy from the soil and into the sea from whence he came."

"When the land will be purged of the poison of betrayal, of the curse of brother betraying brother," said Nemain.

"Let us mark the beginning of the new kingdom with a new reign," the people cried out. "If the old age is to be ousted, the old forms must be swept aside. They are empty husks!" They turned to Fen Fire.

"You must renounce the old name and take on a new," they told her.

"Proclaim it for me and I will carry it proudly," she answered.

"We have proclaimed it already," they replied, "it is the people's chant of victory: Boudica."

"Your trust, your hope, your devotion has made me what I am. I am Boudica."

"They say that wisdom comes with age—but a new age needs young blood," said Saemu, "and a new reign a new king to rule."

"In the vigor of the king resides the kingdom's strength," added the high priestess.

"And there is none more fitted to rule than you," Saemu announced, his eyes on Subidasto. It was a choice accepted by all.

"Then, our first demand of our new queen is this: you must renounce the old king and take on the young," they called out with one voice. Some of the women tore up reeds and twisted them into a ring. Nemain held it between Subidasto and Boudica. A hush fell over the crowd as they joined hands through the ring.

"Let your reign begin now," the priestess said, "and lead us to victory."

So it was that Boudica, having renounced the old king, took his son.

That night the priestesses prepared a great feast. They ferried food and drink of all kinds from the island, while fires for cooking were built all along the lakeshore. The ship was turned into a huge feast hall, its decks awash with mead and ale. A special throne made of dry reeds matted together was erected on the prow of the ship for Subidasto and Boudica, from where they looked down upon the beginnings of their new kingdom. It was a kingdom born of joy. On the decks and on the shores the people danced to the music of the priestesses. Each warrior took a woman, and each woman a warrior—whomsoever they pleased. Knowing that the morning would bring war and death, that night they knew no restraint. Their new king and queen led them in their revels, dancing among them.

Then, hungrily, she tasted the salt sea on his lips, she felt his hair sticky with the salt sea breezes. Holding him between her thighs she drew the tide of his life towards her and rode on it, buoyed up by its surging power like a boat lifted by the sea with mindless ease.

When the day came, they left the ship. Subidasto ordered heaps of dry reeds to be stacked on the decks, then set fire to them. Within minutes, the whole ship was consumed.

"Let nothing of Rome's survive this reign," he proclaimed, as the flames roared up.

The priestesses gathered around to say farewell, their eyes full of both joy and sadness. Nemain opened her black-feathered cape and drew it around Boudica, enfolding her as with wings.

"O Woman like a flame, remember this," she said softly: "the future is the sacrifice to come." Then Nemain and her priestesses turned their breasts towards their island sanctuary and did not look back until they reached its shores. By that time, Subidasto and Boudica had led their followers into the fens, and the ship was a charred and sinking hulk.

As Samhain approached, and the days darkened earlier, Nemain gathered her women around her before the statue of Andraste.

"The well of death will brim over with blood," she said. She raised up her golden-handled short-bladed sacrificial knife. "We must make good the pact we have made in the name of the goddess: to fatten the crow, the wolf and the wild pig on the flesh of all who have betrayed us; to spare neither them, their women, nor their children, or shed a woman's tear for them."

"By the strength that is in our arms, the devotion that is in our hearts, and the truth that is on our tongues, it will be done," they answered. The pact of death being sealed, each woman was given the name of a victim to find and destroy. And each at her appointed time left the island, having sworn to succeed in her task or never to set eyes on the sacred sanctuary again.

Word of the new queen, Boudica, had spread across the land, a queen who had already defied the power of Rome. From all corners of the kingdom, people streamed to meet them. Subidasto's warriors rode out in columns in all directions to recruit men. They struck at the Roman border to the south, plundering the settlements and destroying the farms. They freed all those the Romans had enslaved and gave them weapons to turn against their former masters. From the north came word that the Coritani were also in revolt, and Coritani warriors were coming to join them. And from the west came the news that Caratacus had already struck. The allies of Rome were said to be in flight from the outlying areas, among them Boduocus king of the Dobunni, who years before had betrayed Caratacus to join with the invader, and Verica, of the Atrebates, of all the traitors the one most hated after Adminius; both were said to be fleeing in terror to the safety of the Roman settlements in Colchester and London. But nowhere proved safe for the Romans or their allies. As the tide of revolt rose, soldiers were struck down even in the streets of London and the capital, Colchester. Soon, every Roman looked on every Briton as a potential assassin.

It was not long before Samhain when the triumphal column led by Subidasto and Boudica came within sight of the Ring of the Everlasting Ones. From a distance, in the cold autumn sunlight, they saw the crystals sparkling in its granite wall. All around the hill on which the fortress stood were smaller hills—mounds constructed by the ancient people before the coming of the Britons. The ascent was along a single narrow pathway; swampy marshes fell steeply away on either side. When they reached the crest they marveled at the nature and size of the blocks of stone used to build the fort. It was a kind of stone not known in that area, one which could only have come from many miles away, and because of the weight of the blocks would have required a prodigious amount of labor to haul any distance.

Though the walls were not high—no more than twenty feet—they were strong and well made. They enclosed a spacious area, ample enough to hold several thousand people. There was a deep well inside the grounds. And at the very center of the fort grew an old, gnarled thorn tree, its branches twisted into every shape. Its small, dark red berries shone on the bare branches like little beads of blood. The circular walls were hollow; a long narrow passageway ran through them along their whole length, with small chambers off it on both sides. Subidasto paused at the entrance to one chamber, which seemed deeper than the others. Two flat stones stood on either side of it.

"Look at this," he said to Boudica, holding the torch close to the flat stones. On each of them was carved a double-spiral. He took her hand and placed her finger on the outermost ring of one of the spirals.

"Follow it with your finger," he said. She did so, running it along the spiral from ring to ring until she reached the very center and the beginning of the next spiral which she followed as she did the first; it led her to the outermost ring. "All things return. It is the way of life and death," he said to her.

"You are familiar with this fort."

"I've known it since I was a boy," he replied. They would make their home there, in the largest of the chambers between the spiral-inscribed stones.

That night Subidasto disappeared earlier than usual from the great fire around which they feasted. All day he had been in a sad, distant mood.

She found him standing in the passageway, in front of their chamber, slowly tracing again the double-spiral course with his finger, following it with fascination from the outer rim, falling inwards towards the dead center then sweeping out again in ever-widening circles. He did not notice she was there until he had completed a cycle.

In the torchlight between the massive stone walls she seemed radiant—as if one of the Everlasting Ones had emerged from their ancient sanctuary. A gold brooch fastened her multicolored cape at her shoulder. A silver-linked belt was clasped around her waist atop a white linen tunic. Her hair was swept back from her face, and held in place by combs and pins of bronze. "What answers do you hope to find in stone?" asked she.

"These stones hold many secrets. Had I all the time in the world it would not be enough to decipher them," he replied. "Our natures are like spirals—they seek to return to that from which they emerged." His finger had halted at the center of the spiral. She put her hand on his.

"Does that give you comfort?"

"Yes—they have trapped echoes that I want to hear again. I will tell you a story about the Ring of the Everlasting Ones. Many, many years ago the fairy people were building this fortress. At the end of each day's hard work, when they had succeeded in putting the blocks of stone in place, a huge red-eyed horse would come out of the swamps beyond and with its great hooves kick the wall down again. Nothing they could do would frighten it away. So, each night they had to watch as their hard day's work was reduced to a heap. Finally, they consulted with their druid. And he came with a hawthorn stick and waited for the horse. As soon as he saw it coming, he fetched it a whack on the rump. The horse let out a terrible cry and galloped off. It never came back. The druid planted the hawthorn stick in the ground and it blossomed into a tree, which has been standing here ever since. And no one dares uproot it—to do so would bring terrible luck."

"It is a sweet tale," she said, "the sort a listless child would enjoy before sleep."

"It is a story that my father told me," said Subidasto. "Often he'd take me hunting in this countryside. Once, after a rain storm, I saw the Ring of the Everlasting Ones shining from far away—you know how the wet rock holds the light. I begged him to take me here—it seemed so fine and lovely. And he did. I saw the hawthorn tree. It was near Beltane, and the tree was ablaze with white blossoms. But he said I must never touch it, however tempted I was by the beautiful flowers or in the autumn by the red berries. I forget how old I was when he told me the tale, but I was still small enough to sit on his knee. Ever since then I never rode past this hill without looking up at the fort. How it would glisten after a shower of rain! And I would think of the red-eyed horse from the bog, or of the old tree or the mysteries of these spirals." He paused. "My father said that in such a place as this, anything that you wish to happen might happen, because of the power of the Everlasting Ones. I believed him then, being a boy who loved his father. But now I know he was wrong."

"What would you wish for?"

"The power that would reconcile my father with me."

"But it could only do so by taking me from your side."

"And that power does not exist here or anywhere in the world," said he.

To hear him say so filled her with joy—and with despair.

"Once, I sought to hurt him through you; but I no longer wish to hurt him. This old fort, these cold stones have driven that delirium from me. To hate something is to seek its destruction, and I cannot hate something which is part of my own nature, for then I would seek to destroy myself. I am his son, and remain so: but I cannot be his subject. Nor can he be mine." He pressed his finger hard against the navel of the spiral as if he would penetrate it.

She took his hand and placed it on her belly.

"Forget the secrets of stone; flesh has its secrets, and they are more yielding to the touch," she said, as he ran his hand over her belly, over her thighs and breasts. "The more it is touched, the more it yields. But only desire can decipher it." He pressed her back against the flat stone. Through her, he would penetrate to the heart of the spiral of being, reaching a point so fine and tender that time would never take the measure of it, though it were a moment only. Life spent spins another into being.

Chapter 22

Latis combed her long yellow hair with a fine-tooth comb of whitest ivory brought all the way from some sunny southern land by a Roman trader and purchased for her by the king. She looked at herself in the bronze mirror, another work of precious craftsmanship as only the Gauls could fashion. Outside the autumn sun was struggling vainly through the clouds, trying to fulfill the promise of the afternoon before, which had been blessed with golden light. Her skin was still pale and smooth as any could wish, except for her mouth; there, from the corners two lines arched downwards, visible even when she was not snarling at someone, which was not often. Prasutagus stood behind her watching her face in the mirror. Those lines had grown more prominent with the years. But on that morning her mouth was not curled disdainfully; rather, it was curled in a smile. "When the new governor arrives," she said, looking at the king's reflection in her mirror, "we must prepare ourselves to spend some time in the south. I expect he will invite us to Camulodunum, for I hear Caesar intends to make it the capital of the new province of Britain."

"He may make of it what he pleases. To us it will always be the fort of Camulos," he shrugged.

"In any case," she continued, ignoring his apparent indifference, "we might go further south. Verica, I am told, has done wonders with Calleva. It used to be no more than a pig pen, but now I hear he has begun a most magnificent villa, building it according to the Roman style, of course. And he is to have a floor built that will be heated to stay warm all winter! They are such magnificent builders, aren't they?"

The king did not say anything. He knew what was coming.

Latis sighed, then shivered a little. "It's a wonderful idea in a climate like ours, is it not?" She cast a mournful eye out of the small copper-shuttered window beyond which the pale sun had given up the struggle, overwhelmed by clouds. Almost on cue, a cold wind whistled through the shutters. Not even Samhain yet, and it was turning as cold as winter.

"Heated floors!" Prasutagus guffawed. "Who needs heated floors when all we have to do is throw down a few good, thick lambskins on the ground?"

"It's not only the floors," she retorted, her voice edged with annoyance. "We live as if nothing has changed. The whole kingdom of the Atrebates has been transformed. New buildings go up every day. Calleva will soon be as fine a city as any in Gaul. Even that coarse and vulgar boor Boduocus is building a fine new marketplace with stone and paving. Meanwhile, we live under thatch like our peasants, so that it appears to the world the only difference between us and them is that we have more of it than they do!"

"Thatch is a fine material for cover and has been as long as anyone can remember," the king replied, rather wearily. "And it is right that we resemble our peasants; since we belong to the same tribe how can we not resemble them? There is no shame in that. Remember, it is their hard work which helps to feed and clothe us. Do you refuse to eat the vegetables from their land that they put on your table?"

Latis stopped her combing. Her husband's devotion to hunting in desolate places and fishing in solitude clearly accounted for this peculiar failure to notice what was happening in the world. "The way you talk! We don't *need* to depend on their produce anymore. We have much more to choose from now—if we have the imagination. There are all kinds of foods from every corner of the empire flooding into the country—fruits and olives from Italy, dates from Africa; indeed, I can't remember the half of them, they are so numerous. We don't have to eat what our peasants bring us." She glared at her husband.

His face had a complacent look which angered her. With him it was oatmeal, boar's meat and ale forever.

"If it won't grow in my own field, then how can I trust it?" he asked. "If it cannot grow here does that not mean that there is something antagonistic between that vegetable or fruit and my soil? And what is antagonistic to a man's soil is not good for his soul!"

"Sometimes I do not understand why you ever entered into a treaty with Rome! Why are you not in the hills with Caratacus and your renegade son?" She flung the ivory comb onto the floor in a fit of temper. "We have gained no advantage from your treaty!"

"Woman," he replied, his voice beginning to waver a little with anger, "we have gained peace from it. That is the only think I wanted from Rome, and I have got it. You continually amaze me. How can a woman who shows such a capacity for intrigue, as well as ruthlessness, both of which are essential requisites if power is to be grasped, at the same time only understand that power in terms of trinkets and baubles, tiled floors, dates and figs? I did not enter into treaty with the greatest power on earth in order that we might walk on warm tiles all winter and tease our appetites with exotic morsels!" Prasutagus rubbed his wrinkled brow. Perhaps it would have been better to have surrendered Latis, not Fen Fire, to Rome; she would have welcomed the change, and he would not have had to endure her constant carping about the lack of it here in his kingdom. "Peace was my object," he reiterated, "peace to enable us to enjoy the prosperity that we possess—there is no one who can equal my generosity in grace and giving in this land. So I am satisfied."

"You are too easily satisfied," she snapped, though she knew full well it wasn't true. What she meant, but could not admit, not even to herself sometimes, was that her husband was lethargic and melancholic, and had been ever since Fen Fire's departure. Sometimes in her fury at this mood of his she had come close to saying to him that he should ask Fen Fire to return and forgive her every transgression. But Latis' pride and her jealousy would not permit her to acknowledge that another woman could still hold sway over her husband's heart, especially a woman who had injured him so deeply. So she would content herself with directing her disdain at his love of old habits, and suffered the consoling delusion that there lay the cause of the inertia which so infuriated her.

Before the king could respond to her attack, Barrel unexpectedly came bursting into the bedroom. Latis flashed her an angry look. "Who told you you could enter here?" she growled before the other woman had a chance to open her mouth. Since Fen Fire's departure, the other wives had been more or less banished from the king's side, and their occasional visits to his bedchamber were supervised by Latis. Prasutagus was content to put himself in her hands this way, simply because he feared that the others, being too sympathetic to Fen Fire, would try to persuade him to take her back. Latis sprang up and went towards the intruder. But Barrel did not back away. "You were supposed to be preparing my bath and not sticking your nose in where it's not wanted."

Barrel gave her a brazen look that surprised Latis, and angered her more. "I have news that will interest the king," she said with a saucy smile. "And yourself if you'll shut up long enough for a person to speak."

"Shut up? Why, you little wretch . . ." She was about to grab Barrel by the hair when the king intervened and pulled her back.

"What is it?" he asked.

"Caratacus has struck the borders of the province," she announced, her eyes aflame, "and—Fen Fire is free!"

As she spoke the other wives came crowding up to the partition and gawked across it, eager to see the effect the news would have on Latis, their hated rival and tormentor.

Though clearly shaken, Latis laughed derisively. "More rumors!" she scoffed. "She is well on her way to Rome by now."

"It were better for you if she were," Barrel answered unflinchingly, "but she is here, in this very kingdom, and thousands flock to see her."

"I don't believe you!" Latis cried.

"Then go into the courtyard—the man is there who spoke with her, and behind him are many others who have seen her as well."

Latis looked at her husband. His face had lost that melancholic, indifferent air, though what had usurped it she could not say, but she could guess. For the king it was as if a burden had suddenly been lifted from his shoulders. He sighed in relief and then smiled, repeating over and over again, "Fen Fire, free?" Though he could have admitted it to no one, as the time approached for her to leave Britain for faraway Rome, he had thought only of her. The worm of grief and guilt was growing fat, gnawing its sinuous way through his heart. Forgotten was his jealousy, his rage at her betrayal with his son; he knew that the deeper wounds were those that he had inflicted upon her. It was some moments before he thought of asking Barrel, "How is it she is free?" At once Barrel's look of triumph wavered a little. She knew that her further news would not be entirely displeasing to Latis; and despite what had happened over the last two years the wives still felt tender towards the king and were reluctant to bring him more misery or unhappiness. Latis saw at once with her sharp eyes Barrel's hesitation. Could she dare hope to gain anything from this disastrous revelation?

"Speak!" ordered the king of Barrel.

She gulped. "Your son has freed her, and together they lead a band of warriors," she replied quickly, and glanced away from Prasutagus.

Now it was Latis' turn to assume a quietly triumphant air. "Well," she said smiling, "it would appear she has fled with Subidasto—no doubt to plot to bring further humiliation and shame and trouble onto your head, to raise a rebellion against you in league with Caratacus. So much for the peace that you have won by your treaty with Rome. You must seize them both at once and hand them over to the proper authorities."

"In this land I am the only authority!" Prasutagus retorted.

"Then you had better exercise it," Latis replied.

"That, woman, is my intention. Now, be about your

business while I attend to mine,'' he said sternly, in a manner she had not witnessed for some time. He left her abruptly and went as the other wives followed behind him to speak directly with those who claimed to have seen his son and wife.

Meanwhile, Latis mulled over these surprising developments with satisfaction. ''This will be the beginning of the end of both my plagues,'' she thought, ''for even if the king fails to deal with his troublesome son and whorish wife, Rome will not endure such an insult to her rule.'' Whatever way it turned out, she could not but gain.

The king found a clamorous crowd in front of his palace. Word had spread rapidly and more people were coming in from the countryside around to see if it were true what they had heard, that Fen Fire was at liberty, having defeated the Romans. It was a fisherman who had first brought word of Fen Fire, and he told the king what he had told Barrel.

''I saw her as clearly as I can see you,'' he said. ''She rode out of the reeds, emerging from a mist, her eyes burning and her horse's flaring nostrils spouting fire, a troop of mighty warriors behind her, Subidasto at her side, and a host of women singing her praises.'' Others, mainly fishermen and peasants, came forward eager to give their own accounts to the king of what they had seen. But they spoke of ''Boudica,'' not Fen Fire. Prasutagus pressed them for details—the color of her hair, her skin, her eyes, thinking that perhaps this Boudica was another woman altogether. Yet, as he listened to their descriptions—the hair a fiery red, the eyes a soft ash grey, and the skin as white as fresh snow—there was no doubt in his mind that Fen Fire had become Boudica: no other woman in the world bore such colors. About his son he asked them only one question: where was he to be found? This they could not answer, except to say that with Boudica and his troop of warriors he seemed to be bound for the southern borders of the kingdom.

As he listened to them it began to snow. Everyone looked up at the sky amazed. It had been a long time since there'd been such an early winter. And this one was unusual also in that it was blowing in from the west. At once the king invited the people in to enjoy his fireplace, and soon they were gathered around the bubbling cauldron. Latis emerged from the bedchamber to find the central hall of the Palace of the Red Yew full of shepherds, herdsmen and fishing folk. Each had a cup of ale or mead in his hand, and each was licking his lips as the spits burdened with roasting pig and boar hissed above the fire. For the first time since the palace lost Fen Fire its great room rang with laughter and animated talk.

"You astonish me," Latis said to her husband. "At a time like this you feast!"

"There is always time to be hospitable," he retorted.

"A time when there is a rebel in your kingdom, and a fugitive."

"I will deal with them both, fear not."

She could not but notice his almost blithe manner, which irritated her, since it did not seem to admit to the gravity of the crisis facing them. But his spirits had risen because they had been unburdened, leaving him free at last to act.

"Well, what do you intend to do?"

"Though it is none of your business, I will tell you. I will find my son. I will scour every wood, bog and hill till I do so. Let him play the rebel; I will prove to be the king. If he wants to fight we will fight, and I will crush him. Let him play the renegade son; I will prove to be the father. Then I will take my wife and bring her to where she belongs, here by my side. Let him play the lover—I will prove to be the husband."

"But she is a hostage. By the terms of your treaty—"

He cut her short. "Before she was a hostage she was my wife, and so remains. The contract still stands; the seven years have not elapsed. I will speak no more. There is too much to be done. And you have guests to take care of." The king nodded towards the peasants clustering around the roaring fire. "See to it that each has a joint of meat in his hand and is well supplied with drink."

Without further loss of time the king called for his finest scouts and trackers. He dispatched them at once to find Subidasto and his band of warriors. Then he sent messengers to summon his chiefs for a tribal council. They arrived through the snow from all parts of the king's wide domains. They assembled in the long hall next to the Palace of the Red Yew: three times thirty men, magnificent in their panoply of bronze and silver and gold. Each wore a torc of twisted gold around his neck, and it would have been hard to judge which was the most splendid, for each strove to outdo his fellows in magnificence. They sat, their woollen capes about their shoulders and their swords on their thighs.

Prasutagus sat in the middle of them, a druid on either side of him and his spearmen behind. That day he wore his yellow hair tied at the back with gold bands. His long beard was finely trimmed, and the yellow circle of the Master Charioteer glowed like a sun on his brow. He gazed down upon the countenances of the men who had for so long given him their allegiance. There were many faces missing. The king asked where they were. Volisios, the most powerful of the chieftains and next in splendor only to the king himself, stood up. "The men you speak of have chosen either to sit back and await the outcome of this convulsion or have gone over to Subidasto already," he reported. He ran off the names of those absent.

"But there are others who should be here and are not."

He paused for a moment as if it were painful for him to continue. "Yesterday," he said, "my three sons, fine, spirited youths worthy of a father's love and praise, proclaimed they were entering the service of Boudica and your son, and left to join them."

Prasutagus knew the youths well. Indeed, years before he had fostered two of them himself in his own house. Volisios looked around him at the other chiefs. "I know I am not alone in my loss." At once another dozen or more voices were raised in confirmation of what he said. They each told the same story—families divided, sons in rebellion swelling the ranks of Subidasto and Boudica. The king's son was also drawing supporters from neighboring tribes, and grew more formidable with every passing day.

The king's scouts had told him that Subidasto and

Boudica were gathering their men in the southwest corner of the kingdom. They had taken over an ancient hill fort as their headquarters. It was known as the Ring of the Everlasting Ones. Being circular in shape and built of stone blocks, it was said to have been constructed by the ancient peoples of Britain before they were forced to live under the earth with the coming of Maponos. It commanded the crest of a steep-sided hill, surrounded by marshy land, from which the countryside could be viewed for many miles around. Prasutagus concluded that their aim was to link up with the forces of Caratacus coming from the west, and so encircle the Roman province.

The chiefs were hotly divided among themselves as to what course of action they should take. Some spoke out for conciliation; they advocated that a messenger be sent to invite Subidasto and Boudica to treat with the king. They argued that at all costs the king had to try and avoid bloodshed between brother and brother, father and son. The king listened to them carefully, respecting their words.

"Indeed, my heart is scalded by the very thought of families torn apart," he said when they had finished. Then he listened to the others who spoke for action, insisting that they should march as soon as they could and confront the rebels with the might of the tribe before they grew more powerful, more numerous, and more arrogant. But even those who spoke in favor of this did so with a heavy heart. And to them the king said:

"You have spoken without bitterness from a desire to preserve rather than destroy. On that we are all agreed, whatever course we advocate."

Throughout the meeting the king had kept his own counsel, and was not seen to prefer one against the other, though he himself had determined what he must do. In order to preserve the unity of the tribe he was careful to see that all sides were listened to with equal respect, and regardless of the outcome each man could leave the council feeling that his contribution was treated with respect and valued. When the time came for the king to speak, the gatekeeper entered the hall and announced that an envoy was at the gates of the palace.

"What manner of man is it?" the king enquired.

"Not of our blood, nor one that I have ever seen in this kingdom before," he was told. "But he comes with an urgent message."

"From whom?"

"From Rome," answered the gatekeeper.

Prasutagus nodded. "We will hear what he has to say."

The gates of the great hall were heaved apart and the envoy, wearing a heavy cloak and a short crested helmet, marched smartly through the parted ranks of the chieftains towards the king. Behind him a troop of Roman soldiers, snow still clinging to their capes, filed into the hall. The envoy was accompanied by a Briton who spoke both tongues; through him he paid his respects to Prasutagus and his assembly. The king returned them and offered the hospitality of his house. The envoy replied that he would gladly accept for one night only, for the urgency of his task meant that he would have to return early the following morning to Camulodunum with the king's reply to his message. Then he unfolded a scroll and read it out. It was from Publius Ostorius Scapula, the new Roman governor of Britain.

"Greetings to Prasutagus, valued ally of Tiberius Claudius Nero Germanicus Caesar, and of the senate and people of Rome, from Scapula, in the name of the above. In this emergency, threatening law and order everywhere, you are asked to cooperate fully. I assume you know your son has kidnapped a valued hostage. While we do not hold you accountable for his violations of all civilized behavior, we do expect you to do either of two things:

"One: If he and the hostage, your wife, are with you, they are to be surrendered at once.

"Two: If they are not in your hands, then you are to inform us at once where he is holding her. This would enormously simplify our task of bringing him to justice for his heinous crime. As I said, we have reached a crisis. Failure or reluctance of any kind to give us necessary assistance under such circumstances will be seen as a grave transgression of our accord. My envoy is instructed to return as soon as possible with one or the other of these requests fulfilled.''

The envoy rolled up the scroll and returned it to the pouch from which it was extracted. His face was impassive, giving no hint of discomfiture at the imperious words his lips had just pronounced. The assembly was silent and sullen. The chieftains' eyes were fixed on the king, scrutinizing him to find a clue as to how he would respond to this peremptory order. They were surprised not only at the new governor's abrupt style and implied discourtesy, but at the fact that he was among them at all. They had not expected him for weeks. The king was not long in replying.

''Tell your master this,'' he said. ''He must learn some lessons before he can deal with us—emergency or no emergency. The first lesson is that no man, whether a pig keeper or a king, is addressed other than with courtesy, especially under his own roof. And the second lesson is this: a family settles its own quarrels. If a son deserves punishment, only a father can administer it. As to your master's 'requests,' I am answering them only out of pity for yourself, since you look like a poor devil who has come a long way on a bad day. Subidasto has not set foot across this threshold for many a long day, nor would he dare to. As to his whereabouts,'' and here the king paused and raised his eyebrows, ''if I knew where he was, wouldn't I be there myself . . . to deal with him the way he needs and deserves to be dealt with?''

The envoy's impassivity crumbled as he listened to the interpreter's words. Lines of agitation swept across his face like ripples over a calm lake. Clearly he was not used to hearing the commands of his master so frankly rejected.

''You must be aware,'' he said, ''that Publius Ostorius Scapula speakes for Caesar himself.''

''Then Caesar does himself a disservice,'' the king replied.

''Perhaps you will think better of this in the morning,'' the envoy suggested.

''And perhaps you will bring me a rat with a blunt

snout,'' said Prasutagus, and ordered his servants to escort the envoy and his detachment to the guest quarters.

The chieftains watched as the Romans, with measured tread, filed out of the hall. When they were gone the king spoke of what was in his heart. ''No royal raiment can conceal so great a grief,'' he said. They listened silently, and gave him their trust—as always.

Later that night when the palace was sleeping, the envoy's interpreter stood by the dying embers of the fire in the guest quarters. Outside the white wind sighed, layering the world with snow. When a man is deep in his own thoughts, the world's convulsions become faint echoes. The worries of his masters, the wars, and threats of war, were far away. So it was that lost in reveries, he was startled by the touch of a hand. A woman stood behind him. In the glow of the fading fires she was handsome and yellow-haired; she wore a heavy woollen cape about her shoulders; only disdain, or some disappointment perhaps (who knows what sorrows women nurse) had left its creases around her mouth, for on her face neither age nor illness nor disease seemed to have made their mark. When he recovered from his surprise he recognized her.

''My dear sir,'' said Latis, ''do not think me rude to approach you at so late an hour.''

''Nor you me, for lingering at so unsociable an hour by your fire when a good guest might be expected to be asleep,'' he answered.

''My house is your house to wander where and when you will. Our hospitality is not circumscribed by the hours.'' She paused, then added, ''Nor is my concern to deter you from your tasks.''

''I fear our tasks still remain to be fulfilled.''

''That is why I am here. In my humble way I think I can advance them.'' She came closer to the fire and glanced around her at the dark spaces in the blackened borders of the great room.

''Nothing but shadows,'' he said to reassure her, for she seemed anxious.

''Your master sleeps?''

''Soundly. His hours are regular. Shall I wake him?''

"No—better to risk no noise other than that which we two are making."

"But the might of Rome stands between you and any risk you take in aiding her."

"I am aware of Rome's position—and power. I know that she rewards her friends, and destroys her foes, one of whom is the king's son."

"He will be destroyed when found, that is certain."

"Yes, and I will tell you where to find him."

The interpreter smiled and moved even closer to her.

"The Ring of the Everlasting Ones—the ancient citadel that our storytellers love to talk of."

"But not your husband, the king. He lied to Caesar's envoy."

"He is a proud man and wants to deal with Subidasto himself. But I fear for him. I fear that when he reaches the Ring he will be persuaded not to punish the renegade but to augment his pernicious efforts with his own, far mightier host that he is gathering. There is nothing more urgent than this! Regardless of this blizzard, you must leave before dawn and inform Ostorius Scapula of what I have told you. Any local tribesman will guide his forces to the place. It is renowned in the area."

"Your loyalty will be weighed in the balance against your husband's treachery," the interpreter said. "And Scapula will take note."

"Now go!" Latis urged in a whisper.

He vanished from her side and into the encircling shadows, leaving her alone to contemplate her action.

"They will call it betrayal," she thought, crouching down by the fire; "but they know no better. I have merely saved my husband from betraying himself. He is a noble but a foolish man—and the red-haired witch was his worst indulgence. She would make him think he was a warrior again, tempt him to compete with his rebellious son in foolish acts of doomed heroics! What a clamor there would have been among his warriors, proclaiming her Boudica—their Queen—or some such presumptuous title. And I fear he could not resist it, and so push us all—his whole kingdom—over the brink of destruction. I would rather risk being called a traitor than risk that. But it has been ever so, since first he set eyes on her, naked, on the wrestling pitch—an earth demon crossed with a woman. As men grow old their self-delusions grow more dangerous—to them and those who depend on them. All I have done is to try and protect him from them. Someday he will thank me. Now I pray to the gods that Rome is swift enough to save him from himself and remove forever that most irresistible and most fatal of attractions, so beloved among the Britons—beauty in rebellion."

Chapter 23

Publius Ostorius Scapula, the new governor, had so far found little to like about Britain. He had sailed into a burnt-out port, a smoking ruin, the very scene of the crime which had inspired the current wave of unrest. Instead of the usual welcoming committee that Caesar's legate might have expected, he had been greeted by a mob of refugees, each vying with the next to assail his ears with a tale of woe and terror. And lost in their midst, the provincial officials and junior army officers left behind by his predecessor, Aulus Plautius, made their excuses for their failure to save the province from the desperate straits to which it had been reduced by invasion from the west and rebellion from within.

It was cold and grey and foggy—sometimes he was able to see no more than a few yards in front of himself. The dampness at that time of year clung to everything. Within a day he was longing for the level plains of Egypt where he had spent so much of his life—there, you could see clearly right to the horizon. But in Britain, the horizon seemed too near—or it disappeared completely.

Even though he had arrived well ahead of schedule, it did little to calm the settlers, merchants and allies, driven to seek shelter in Colchester and London from the attacks of the bandits, assassins and rebels. They were a bitter, frustrated crowd, and when they looked upon the bald-headed legate's tawny-skinned, wrinkled face with its protruding eyes, he realized they were not reassured. He was short, barrel-chested, impatient and tense. And he hated mysteries. But within a few hours of setting foot on the new, much prized province—the jewel in Claudius Caesar's imperial crown—he had heard nothing else, both from the mouths of the refugees and from the provincial officials. The bandits who had snatched a valuable prisoner from right within the province itself had materialized out of a mist, it seemed, and vanished back into one after destroying a fortress, burning the port, beheading a Briton regarded as a useful ally, and stealing three navy vessels. The rebels that had raided across the northern and western borders of the province, according to the refugees who fled before them, were hardly human; depending on to whom you spoke, they were either gifted with invisibility, since they seemed to have emerged from nowhere, or with enormous strength and other attributes of legendary proportions, since they had obviously inspired such terror that no one dared resist them.

However, for Ostorius Scapula the so-called mysteries were either an excuse for sheer incompetence on the part of administration officials or a product of pure superstition that so luxuriated in the minds of the veteran soldiers who mostly comprised the settler population. There was an answer for them both: determined action, swift as it was firm.

Having listened to the various reports, he knew where to begin. A powerful column escorting an envoy had been dispatched to Prasutagus to make the sternest of representations, against the advice of the local officials. Prasutagus was a valued ally, they argued, and under the circumstances it would be dangerous to alienate him. Scapula's reply to this was simple: "The man either has his wife and son with him, in which case he is no longer an ally and will be dealt with as an enemy; or he knows where they can be found, in which case he will cooperate with us in eradicating them—or face the consequences." Since in his view the attack on the convoy taking Fen Fire to the port had sparked off the other troubles, and was perhaps meant as a signal for Caratacus to attack from the west, it was wisest to begin there—at the beginning.

The envoy to the Iceni was due back any day. The Ninth and Twentieth Legions were being dispatched to the west. Units from both were being horsed to give them the mobility necessary to cope with Caratacus' rebel bands who had scored several notable victories there, including the killing of Boduocus, the king of the Dobunni. Boduocus had served Caesar well over the years. His death had spread fear and confusion among the other Britons who had aligned their fate to that of Rome's. Among those who had fled to the provincial capital was Verica, the king of the Atrebates. Caratacus' supporters had raided his kingdom, doing considerable damage over a wide area.

The night before the Twentieth, which was stationed in Camulodunum, was due to leave, Scapula met with Verica in his quarters to discuss how they might coordinate a counterattack. To present as calm and unruffled an appearance as possible, Scapula arranged for the meeting to take place over a quiet dinner. The dining room was a bare, drafty wooden hall, which was still waiting to be replaced by a more permanent and commodious residence. It was almost like dining while on campaign—the structure seemed as flimsy as a tent and trembled as much under the autumn gale that had struck the province that very night.

King Verica had been in a state of distress since his arrival in Camulodunum. He had moped about the place, drinking incessantly and when drunk abusing his companions for having failed him. From the state of anger he then declined with further drinking into a condition of almost childish hopelessness, lamenting the fate of his friend Adminius, with whom he had shared so much in the years gone by, dreading that it presaged his own. To Scapula, it seemed outlandish that a grown man could allow himself to be seen this way in public. Yet, neither Verica nor his companions showed any signs of shame at the display, being quite prepared to bemoan their fate openly and pathetically to anyone who would lend an ear. The new governor was alarmed and expressed his concern to his officers that such a man could hardly be relied upon to take part in a military enterprise requiring steadiness of purpose and judgment against an enemy like Caratacus. But those who had been in Britain some time told him that the Britons were by nature a moody people, given to great and sudden swings of feeling. What they had said was borne out, for when Verica arrived that evening to meet and dine with Scapula, the governor found him in a hearty, even boastful mood.

"We were caught by surprise last time," he said. "But Caratacus' tricks have trapped him. He has advanced too far from his safe areas. We will find him, surround him and annihilate him." The king slapped his ponderous sides with his palms. He was still an impressive man in some ways—being tall, towering above the governor. But the years had witnessed him growing soft and flabby, with a red, blotched face. His chin now rested on several thick cushions of fat.

"He moves quickly," Scapula cautioned.

"To his doom," Verica boasted. "He is striking too far east. I know the route he will take."

"He must realize the danger," Scapula said. "He knows he does not have the strength to confront us."

Verica laughed and drained a full cup of wine in one gulp. He had not lost his taste for his favorite drink, and now boasted the biggest collection of Roman wines in Britain. "Of course he does. That's the beauty of it! He plans otherwise—to link up with the rebels from the Iceni and the Coritani and those who are his supporters within the province itself. Together they would make a formidable force."

"That's why we must move swiftly and squash them separately, one by one while they are still isolated. Three burning blades of grass that would become a forest fire . . ." The governor paused for a moment. The fires had all yet to be found. The king of the Iceni he assumed would help him find and extinguish one. Verica the other. That left the fire within. "How many supporters do you think Caratacus has inside the province?"

Verica grinned. "That is difficult to say, but I know his name is whispered about by many—they have not lost their faith in his power."

Verica grew pensive for a moment, picturing the death of Adminius, slaughtered within a few miles of where he now sat, in the very heart of the province. But within a minute he had shaken off the threatened relapse into despondency.

"And how can one recognize these secret supporters?"

Verica guffawed. "They do not carry marks on their foreheads! I'm certain of that. They are Britons, just like any other Briton."

Scapula mused upon this problem while the slave came in with a serving of oysters. Verica's eyes gleamed at the sight, as he did at the woman that brought them, a handsome dark-haired creature with long legs and fine white arms. He helped himself, slurping one down after another.

"I don't know about finding Caratacus' supporters—but I know where you'll find these oysters," he said, stretching himself out comfortably on the couch and reaching for another from the big stack left on the little table beside it.

"You're a connoisseur, I take it?"

"Of women, wine and oysters, most certainly. Take these for example—I can tell you from their shape and taste that they come from the Colne estuary near Camulodunum," he proclaimed.

"Indeed I am told they do," Scapula confirmed. He was not paying much attention to his guest. Verica's earlier remarks concerning the rebel sympathizers within the province had given him something to ponder. It would be a difficult problem to detect them before they had a chance to strike.

"I hear they are Caesar's favorite," Verica said. "Perhaps that's why he came to Britain in the first place—for the oysters!" He laughed again, as he often did at his own remarks. "And this soft little oyster behind me—now, where does she come from, that's the question." Verica turned round towards the woman who had served him. She was standing behind his couch. She stepped forward out of the shadows.

"From Andraste," said Nemain the High Priestess, swiftly drawing a gold-hilted dagger. With one sharp thrust it went deep into his throat. She gripped his hair and wrenched his head back as the red spout of blood splashed onto the oysters.

"What seeds and bleeds, our powers devour. Traitor!"

she said, pulling out the bloody blade and spitting in his face. When he clutched at his throat she drove the dagger into his groin and then into his chest with such rapidity that she had stabbed him three times before the guards reached her. The first thrust his short sword into Nemain's back. She cried out and fell forward, sinking her nails into the eyes of the dying king. Flailing wildly in his death agonies, he rolled off the couch with the priestess still clinging to him, her teeth now sunk in his wounded throat. Blow after blow rained down on her, until her back and neck were a mess of wounds. But she did not relinquish her grip on Verica until she knew he was dead. By the time the guards succeeded in dragging Nemain off, her fingers were as red as the sacrificial dagger, and the dead king's eyes were merely bloody sockets.

The High Priestess had fulfilled her oath to Andraste. She died with a smile on her face soon after Verica. She did not reveal anything, much to the governor's displeasure. He had hoped to keep her alive long enough to torture her into revealing the identity of the accomplices who had helped her achieve this extraordinary breach of security. The usual procedures were set in motion. The household slaves were tortured, but it appeared she had no accomplices among them. The orderlies were thrashed, but could only reveal that she had been recently sold to the headquarters. The clerk responsible for making such purchases had bought her from a slave trader in Camulodunum whom he admitted he had never seen before and who was not seen again. She had impressed the clerk with her appearance, her knowledge of languages, and her culinary experience: he claimed that she previously had been in the kitchen service of a wealthy merchant who went bankrupt and was forced to sell all his possessions. The merchant proved as elusive as the slave trader. But the murder crystalized an idea that had already proposed itself to Scapula as a solution to the tricky problem of detecting rebel sympathizers.

That very evening, he issued an order forbidding any Briton in the province to carry weapons. Once more the new governor acted against the advice of those officers and civil servants who had been in the province for some time and knew that the right to carry arms was a matter of pride among the people.

All weapons, for whatever purpose, were to be surrendered at once. Special units were dispatched to search every house in every settlement to ensure that the order was complied with. Any weapons found would mean a severe whipping for the owner. It was soon a common sight to see soldiers descending on a village, ransacking houses until what little furniture they had was piled in a heap outside and even the thatch was torn from the roofs. The discovery of a bow and arrow that a peasant might use for hunting meant a beating. Even the finding of a child's wooden sword might give a disgruntled centurion, who perhaps had lost a friend to an assassin, the excuse he needed to take revenge on a Briton whose innocence afforded him no protection. The governor was indifferent to the argument that rebellion suckles at the bitter breast of grievance.

Scapula was examining the golden-hilted dagger, with its entwined serpent, admiring its curious workmanship when the envoy who had been sent to Prasutagus returned.

"We have a friend among the Iceni," the envoy said.

"Then the king cooperates," Scapula said, laying the fatal weapon on the table.

"No—I speak of Latis, his wife," replied the envoy. He explained to the governor what had happened.

"Perhaps our next treaty should be with the king's wife," came his reply. But the task had been accomplished: the source of the trouble had been located. He sent for his best guides, and told his officers that he would personally command the assault on the Ring of the Everlasting Ones.

Chapter 24

The age-old solitude and silence were broken. The Ring of the Everlasting Ones came back to life. Had there been travelers in that remote and desolate countryside, they could have been forgiven for thinking that the Everlasting Ones had returned to repossess what was theirs, and having retaken it were celebrating their victory with all their legendary exuberance. At night the fortress blazed like a fiery ring. The air around it rippled with laughter and the sounds of singing and music. During the day, the activity did not cease, but it was of a different kind and gave a clue as to the causes of the nightly celebrations.

Subidasto and Boudica had made the Ring the center of their rebel kingdom. To the traveler, expecting a scene of fairy festivities, the couple would have seemed no less marvelous for being human; he could not but have shared the wonder and the joy of those who came to pay homage and pledge their allegiance. Boudica and Subidasto received them sitting on either side of the fairy thorn that grew from the heart of the fortress, he in a fine-fringed mantle with a red hood and a white linen tunic, she in a cloak of royal red and under it a tunic speckled with green and clasped around her waist by a belt plated with red gold. Around them stood their spearmen, clasping thick-shafted spears. The fortress was a blaze of bronze; blinding to the eye was the sheen of the sharpened blades and the brilliance of hard-rimmed shields. All who saw them in its midst felt that a new reign had indeed begun, and nowhere was its beauty and nobility more clearly to be seen than in the countenances of the man and woman hailed as king and queen. The Everlasting Ones themselves would not have been ashamed to have acknowledged them as such. But they in their wisdom remained in the Underworld: long ago they had forsaken the vanity of human ambition, and knew too much to be tempted back.

Outside the Ring, on the ground between it and the beginning of the steep descent, a little village sprang up. Huts and shelters made of wood were built against the wall. In these the women and the warriors with their families housed themselves. Trenches were dug in the ground to store grain and other foodstuffs. Boudica made sure that the cauldron which hung over the big fire, always kept aflame in the fortress, was never empty. She trained every woman there to fight as well as the men, and near the beginning of day put them through their exercises with the javelin, the sword and the dagger. Through emulating Boudica, the women were soon as confident and skillful as the men. Bands of warriors radiated out from the Ring like spokes on a wheel, raiding and striking terror into the Roman settlements and the farms of those Britons who had betrayed their own for a plot of land. In the evening, when the warriors returned, laden with plunder, the talk invariably turned to the future: when Caratacus came with his army, how they would drive the invaders into the sea and destroy everything he left behind so that there would remain no trace of their presence. But Caratacus did not come. Nor was there any sign of him.

The berries on the fairy tree grew a darker red as the year died and drew near its close. On Samhain Eve, another light snow fell. The warriors woke to find the tree white except where the berries looked like drops of dark blood that had dripped into the snow. Later that day, as the people gathered the wood to build the Samhain bonfires, a strange horseman appeared on the crest of one of the fairy mounds that lay beyond the foot of the hill. He looked up at the fortress and rode off in an unfriendly haste. Subidasto ordered the people to begin dismantling their huts and shacks outside the walls in preparation for a possible attack. They were doing so when a sound like thunder made them look up at the sky. But after the snowfall, the sky had cleared. It was the thunder of thousands of horses pounding across the plain. Some of their armored and helmeted riders carried small square flags on poles, others carried a standard on which were engravings of the head of Claudius Caesar. Behind the riders, came file after file of marching men, darkening the whole plain.

Refugees had told Boudica and Subidasto that Prasutagus was raising an army to come against them, but they were not expecting the new governor to arrive so swiftly.

"They are as numberless as the snowflakes," said the rebel queen.

"Then let our spears and swords be as beams of sunshine to them, and they will melt before us," Subidasto said.

The army of Ostorius Scapula came to a halt at the fairy mounds. The governor himself, wrapped in a purple-banded cloak, rode with his senior officers around the base of the hill, officiously taking note of all its features as if he were counting the bags of grain going onto one of his merchant ships. When he had completed the inspection, he grumbled that the rebels had chosen the place well. It was a good defensive site, its approaches too narrow for cavalry; and due to his eagerness to squash the rebels as quickly as possible, cavalry was the basis of the force he had brought with him. But it was too late in the day to give battle. While his cavalry formed a protective screen, the infantry made camp for the night.

Clustered on the ramparts, the Britons gazed down at the bustle below them. A picket of pointed stakes sprang out of the ground, behind which row after row of leather tents, neatly laid out in straight lines like the little streets of their cities, was formed into a camp. The work was completed before darkness. Then the camp fell silent.

At sundown, the feast of Samhain began. The great bonfire blazed into flame, melting the snow all around it. On the fairy tree, the melting snow left the berries glistening wet; they shone darkly in the light of the fire. The clamor of feasting spilled over the wall and down the hill to the Roman camp. The Britons looked down from their fortress at the dim and silent camp of the enemy and wondered at how men, when they were so close to dying, could restrain themselves from enjoying to the full what was left of life. Just as the Romans, listening in their darkened tents to the sounds from above, asked themselves what it was doomed men had to celebrate.

Around the bright circle of the campfire, in the shadow of the fairy tree, the traveler might have been forgiven for thinking that he had stumbled upon a vision of the Other World. At its center the young rebel queen, hair undone, breastband unbound, sat with the brown-haired warrior king resting his head upon her lap. All around them, the comforting circle of the warriors and the warrior women, drinking and feasting from the never-exhausted cauldron. They in their turn were encompassed by the stone circle of the ancient fortress which lay under the vaster circle of the black sky. Circles within circles, spirals within spirals, spinning outwards and turning inwards at one and the same time.

When each warrior looked into the Samhain flames he saw his whole life dance before his eyes—the courtships, the battles, the feasts, the journeys, the fights, the raids and the adventures. Occasionally, glancing at the shadows under the walls, they might catch a tantalizing glimpse of a princess of the Other World, in her green glimmering cape with her bright hair and shining eyes looking back at the strong, handsome sons of mortal men. Some pursued these visions along the dark passageway that runs through the wall, from chamber to empty chamber, finding only echoes of a gentle footstep or a peal of laughter or the rustle of a cape. Legend says that some who went into that passageway never came out again (this was the tale that Subidasto told that night); the women of the EverLasting Ones are capricious creatures, on a whim suddenly offering their embrace to a mortal man that once accepted means he is lost to his own kind forever. But that night, as far as we know, no man was lost. At any rate, no woman was left without a man, and those stone walls knew only their sighs as one took comfort in the other.

Only the first cold light of dawn drew them apart. Another mistress beckoned. A fall of fresh snow lay on the ground. In handfuls they scooped it up, threw it around their faces and refreshed themselves.

Subidasto and Boudica led their warriors past the still hot ashes of the Samhain bonfire through the open gates to the hill of slaughter. They loomed above the legions of Caesar, poised and steady as twin hawks, before the plunge into battle. . . .

In the years to come, they would say many things about the battle of the Ring of the Everlasting Ones. But truth is a crooked road that rarely leads men where they had set out to go. Indeed, sometimes it seems to take them around in a circle, so they finish where they started.

According to Ostorius Scapula's own dispatches to Claudius Caesar his master, it was "in truth" one of the greatest victories ever won in the name of Rome—her enemies were vanquished, her honor was restored, with no trace of the rebels left on the face of the earth. Even the fortress was dismantled stone by stone, and the little tree standing at its heart, which the Roman soldiers refused to touch, the governor himself personally cut down, dismissing their superstitious talk about the ill luck attendant upon the deed by a blow of his axe. And Scapula was a modest man. But not a very wise man, as anyone who knows anything about fairy thorns will confirm.

There are too many other versions, accounting for this aspect of it or another to tell them all, including one from Caratacus' bard Bran who claims to have arrived in the middle of the battle with an important message from the chief. But the only truthful one came from the lips of Boudica herself, one night as she lay in the arms of her husband. Her young brown-haired daughter had woken her up a short time before by leaping into their bed and crawling under the piles of sheepskin rugs with which it was covered; the little girl liked nothing better, especially in the Samhain season when the north wind howled and the copper shutters shook on all the windows, and she thought the Everlasting Ones might be on their way to kidnap her. She had been told that the people of the fairy mound loved to plot and scheme to take back with them a beautiful mortal child into the Other World. That was why on that night, which was during the feast of Samhain, when she woke Boudica, her mother called her "my Little Toad" or by some other equally false and hideous name in order to fool the Everlasting Ones who were listening—as they always were at that time of the year—into believing that no such thing as a beautiful child existed in her home.

Boudica couldn't get back to sleep because the child kept pestering her for a story, so she decided that there was no better way of passing the long hours of darkness than by telling her child the story of another Samhain which was to be the last day spent on earth by her father, Subidasto. The girl cuddled against her bosom, while the red cascade of her mother's hair made her think she was sitting under a waterfall, and listened.

"It was a bright cold morning and the snow lay on the slopes of the hill. At the foot of the hill, line after line of iron-clad men, more numerous than the blades of grass in a big meadow, were marching quickly towards us, led by a man with a red-face and no hair who was in a bad temper because he couldn't use his horses. Your father stood next to me. He wore no armor on his body, for he was fearless; he carried his sword with the gold hilt and the broad blade so fine and sharp that he could slice a snowflake with it; on his other arm he carried a shield with a silver rim and a hard iron boss; it was so heavy that it would take three ordinary men to lift it. He had brown hair just like yours, but his was swept back from his forehead to make him look like a lion. And it was dyed red and yellow and green to make him look even fiercer. And the warriors on either side of him were a splendid sight that morning. Each carried a man-length shield on one arm, and a clutch of spears in his fist—two for casting, and one with a broad head for stabbing; and each had on his hip a broadsword, and the polished hilts of the swords sparkled in the cold sunlight—some were fashioned from silver, some from gold, and some had guards of ivory.

"The wind began to blow hard, whining through the raised spear shafts—and that is a mournful sound dear to every warrior's heart. When the battle trumpet sounded

Subidasto bounded forward as powerful and fierce as an advancing boar. The spears whistled over his head, and the air was so thick with them—for the Romans threw theirs, too—that they collided with each other, and thousands were knocked out of the sky. The warriors came behind us roaring and screaming to put fear into the enemy. Your father came on with such speed that he leapt over the first line of Scapula's men as it advanced up the hill, and found himself in the middle of them. And he might as well have been standing with a scythe in a field of corn the way he cut them down, striking such terror into them that they began to fall back towards the fairy mounds. And he went after them, for the battle fury had possessed him—and when that happens a warrior hears only the music of battle and is deaf to everything else—before I had a chance to warn him. For I saw what the danger was. If he advanced too far into their center, he'd be cut off from us. And their chief, Scapula, was no fool—for he saw how he could make use of this; so he ordered his men to fall back even further, drawing more of the warriors after them. In the heat of the battle, thinking that they were winning, they plunged ahead. Subidasto reached one of the fairy mounds before he saw that more and more Romans were closing in on him from every side. He was like a great stag surrounded by whelping hounds, tossing them up in the air this way and that, sending them cringing and howling in every direction. But more of them kept coming from every side. He was struck in the shoulder, in the arm, in the thigh, in the back, and I could see his fair body was covered with wounds. As they closed ranks around him, I called together Saemu, who after your father was the most powerful warrior there, and his bravest men. Together we plunged into the Roman ranks. I had the Spear That Roars For Blood: it was like the prow of a ship driving through the waves the way it opened a path for me to your father's side. But we would have all been surrounded and lost had it not been for the fact of the wind. I think the goddess must have whistled thrice, for the wind began blowing even harder. It whipped up the freshly fallen snow into a terrible blinding blizzard. Scapula's men stumbled around, knocking into each other, tripping and falling, not knowing from which way we were coming. In the confusion we reached Subidasto, just as he had sunk to his knees, exhausted from the slaughter he had given and the many wounds he had taken.

"I gently put my arms around him. In the swirling snow, we carried him back up the slope again to the Ring of the Everlasting Ones. No sooner had we reached the fortress than the wind died down, and the air became clear again. The Romans looked around them at the fearful carnage. But when they went to the mound, where they expected to find Subidasto, there was only a patch of red blood seeping through the snow. And because the wind had blown the snow about the place, this way and that, the Romans were at a loss for a trail—and wondered where he'd gone. So it was that the first of the many stories came about concerning the battle at the Ring of the Everlasting Ones—that your father had gone into the mound to live with the fairy people. But he was with me. We carried him into the Ring and laid him down in the biggest of the chambers that ran off the passageway deep in its walls. Thus arose the second of the accounts of his fate: that he was borne away by the green clad women of the Mound People into the Ring. But it was human hands that brought him there and cared for him. They were my hands that dressed his wounds, and soothed his brow, and held him close to my breast, as I hoped somehow that I could nurse him back to life—there in the chamber where we had lain together full of life, full of desire; for from one springs the other. But he was on the threshold of death; nothing I did could staunch those wounds. Grey cobwebs, fresh herbs aplenty—nothing would help. With every seeping drop of blood his life left him, his heart weakened. I held him more closely and I felt his cheek pressed against mine turn cold. But before he stepped across that threshold he laid his hand on my belly. 'I have sown this fair land,' he sighed. 'I leave it a reluctant farmer who will never see his crop ripen and grow tall under the summer sun. Promise me that our daughter will not be born a slave.'

"I promised, though I barely knew what I was saying.

I was hardly certain myself that I was with child, and did not know at all it would be you, my nut-brown darling. But he had no doubts as he touched me—a last, familiar touch.

"It was with a heavy heart that I made that promise. The noise of battle was booming louder. It echoed down the dark passageway, disturbing the stillness of our chamber. Our warriors were in retreat, being driven up the hill back towards the fortress; and the forces of Scapula were closing in on every side. Defeat seemed certain. And defeat meant slavery or the ignominious death of a criminal. Yet I had promised him you would not be born a slave. Despair seized me. But no sooner had I given my word than Saemu came rushing into the chamber, exhausted, covered in blood, yet with a look of exhilaration in his eyes. 'Scapula has been forced to halt his advance!' he cried. Your father stirred and tried to sit up. 'A vast army has arrived!' Your father's eyes then welled up with of tears of joy.

" 'Caratacus!' he said; it was almost a shout. It was his last breath. Once it was uttered, his head slumped against my bosom, all life drained from him, and he moved no more. He died with the hope of victory rekindled in his heart, and the hope that you, his daughter, would be born untrammeled by the shackles of Rome.

"He is happy then," mused the little girl, "for it has come about. His wish was granted."

"Yes, though it was not Caratacus who had come to our aid. Caratacus had indeed done all he could to reach us—penetrating deep into the Roman province. But he did so only to learn that his brother Maglocunos from whom he was expecting help could not give it—Cartimandua, the Brigantian princess, had seen to it by entrapping him. Instead of giving help, Caratacus was confronted by two fresh legions which threatened to surround him. Had he advanced any further he would have been destroyed, most surely. And with him would have died our hopes for the future. Instead of coming to our rescue he was forced to retreat back across the Severn and leave us to our fate."

Boudica paused for a moment and stroked her daughter's rich brown hair. Near them her husband stirred in his sleep.

"No, it was your other father who saved us on that day," she said quietly.

She had not believed it when Saemu told her it was not Caratacus but Prasutagus who had come.

Boudica, in a kind of trance, reliving that event, did not notice her daughter disentangle herself from her arms and go crawling across the bedding. Boudica's husband shifted towards them as the child planted a kiss on his forehead. Prasutagus opened his eyes. The little girl's smiling face was nestled next to his.

"Will you bring us to the ringfort as you promised?" the child asked the king. He yawned and rubbed his eyes.

"We will set out in the morning, first thing—but only if you allow me to get back to sleep," answered Prasutagus.

"And may I ride next to you as I did last time? Now I'm big enough to hold the reins."

"You may help me hold them then," he promised.

"And may I sleep between you tonight?" she asked with a quick glance back at her mother. Her blue eyes sparkled with expectancy.

"Of course, if your father doesn't mind."

"Come," said the king with a smile, "come, my little cobweb; you can cling to me and keep me warm."

She snuggled up to him like a little bird under its mother's warm feathery breast, and put her small arm across his chest. Soon both were fast asleep. But Boudica could not sleep. The story told to her daughter had stirred the depths of her memory. And from them floated up other images. As she sat, clutching the dead body of Subidasto in her embrace, she listened to the noise of the running feet coming down the dark passageway beyond. All seemed confusion and chaos. A moment later she looked up, bewildered, shocked. Prasutagus stood at the entrance to the chamber, trembling. "My son!" he cried out. With arms outstretched he came toward them. He fell on his knees beside her and threw his arms around Subidasto's body. He kissed the dead, calm face. He ran his fingers through his hair. His tears fell down upon his dead son's pallid cheeks as if, like the rain falling upon the earth, they would cause life to stir again. But death's grip was harder than any winter, however cold its blackest frost.

The king's cries wrung her heart. She was on her knees at his side, her arms encompassing both the dead son and the living, stricken father. Her tears mixed with his, streaming together to mingle with the still wet blood of Subidasto. At last, her love for both men was fused and whole. She cleaved to the king beside the body of his son, and felt she could no more separate herself from him than she could have distinguished her tears from his.

The king placed his son's broadsword on his body and kissed his brow. Boudica laid the Spear That Roars For Blood next to him. It would accompany him on his journey. Then together they rolled the two slabs of flat stone across the chamber entrance. Now came the fulfillment of the promise to Subidasto. The king his father would help her keep it.

They strode through the gateway of the Ring, her hand in his. Scapula and his nervous officers were waiting at the foot of the hill, their weary, bloodied army surrounded by Prasutagus' host. The king walked directly towards them with Boudica at his side, still bloodstained from the battle. The ragged band of survivors watched silently from the rampart wall. From the slope of the hill they could see far—the hills and fields and valleys of three kingdoms were visible on a clear day. All the gathered tribes of Britain seemed at their feet . . .

Boudica pulled the sheepskins over the king, her daughter and herself. The north wind carried with it the season's first frost. Her eyelids grew leaden . . .

The red and flushed face of the governor floated before her eyes; he had small hands, which he clutched together. Though it had been a cold day, he perspired. Boudica and her few remaining warriors would leave with the king in return for peace. Scapula's advisers had huddled together and urged him to accept the conditions at once. Had they not warned him about this very crisis? He would certainly face destruction otherwise. Scapula had no doubt but that they were right. Not only was his army too weakened to meet the army of the king there and then, but he knew that a war with the Iceni would expose the northeast border of the province to a powerful enemy while the trouble in the west remained as yet unresolved. And he could hope for little sympathy from Claudius if the war were to spread and intensify in that fashion. He was forced to concede . . .

Boudica turned to face her companions, man and child. She too had been forced to concede. The long-sought victory had eluded her, but she had won time to bring her child into the world, to reunite the tribe—to bind up all the old wounds at once. The people had proclaimed her queen, and only she could heal the divisions between chief and chief, father and son. So, she became his wife once more. Barrel, Mournful Mound, Fen Eel and Screech Owl, her old companions in this vast bed, were delighted to see her return and replace Latis as the king's chief wife. Under Boudica, their life together would be much happier.

As for Latis, though at first stunned into silence, she had made her usual undignified fuss when the governor agreed to accept her as hostage in exchange for Boudica. At last, she would be able to satisfy her love of all things Roman . . .

Tomorrow they would journey back to the Ring of the Everlasting Ones. It was not as before. Scapula set about destroying the fortress after they had evacuated it. He had demolished part of the walls, but had not discovered the inner passageway; indeed, his destruction had only completed the entombment of Subidasto; and he had uprooted the fairy thorn. Ever since, he was plagued by strange and debilitating illnesses. Cramps and fevers made his life a misery; night brought him no rest, only troubled dreams his doctors could not decipher. He was not a well man. What kept Scapula alive was his pursuit of Caratacus, who with Bran and the chief druid Cunodunum had made the western mountains his own domain. She would not have to wait long, she knew, for word of Scapula's death, though after him would come another.

As Scapula declined, the half-ruined Ring of the Everlasting Ones grew more beautiful with the passing years. Gradually it took on the appearance of one huge grassy mound, a fitting monument to the warrior within it. From all over people came to visit the site; the well in the old fortress became a place for offerings, and Subidasto himself joined the heroes of old, rising beyond the realm of history to that of the fireside storyteller whose skill turns life into legend. The grass and ferns that grew over the ruin were greener and more lush than on any other part of the hill. The Beltane season brought its scarlet poppies and the gold of wild wheat; in the Samhain season, came the red bracken. His daughter loved nothing better than to scramble up the grass-covered stones on limbs that grew stronger with time. Occasionally, she would put her ear to the ground and listen for the Everlasting Ones within.

The king's hand came to rest on Boudica's womb. It was a soft white mound that grew larger with every passing week. Gently he caressed it. She had entered another age of repose before birth, when life fructifies in the moist depths, ripens in the darkness and then is plucked into the light. Of the convulsions still to come, she gave no thought. But when the age of battles dawned again, as she knew it must, it would find her ready.